T0379324

Ibis

Ibis

A Novel

Justin Haynes

THE OVERLOOK PRESS, NEW YORK

Published in 2025 by The Overlook Press, an imprint of ABRAMS.

Library of Congress Control Number: 2024941010

ISBN: 978-1-4197-7277-1
eISBN: 979-8-88707-243-2

Printed and bound in the United States
10 9 8 7 6 5 4 3 2 1

ABRAMS The Art of Books
195 Broadway, New York, NY 10007
abramsbooks.com

For JLH

and

JLR

Ma said that I was her grandmother come back again.

—Merle Hodge, *Crick Crack, Monkey*

ONE

Past Perfect

I

The Scarlet Ibis and the News of the Day

WHEN EVERYONE SAW the scarlet ibis perched atop the once-notorious house of ill repute near the edge of the village, there was a collective shiver, although no one would admit it. At first no one thought anything of the roosting bird. The village was a mile from a tributary that spat river water out into the sea where a mangrove blossomed and where fifty or sixty ibises nested and fed. This ibis had just lost its way, we figured. But the ibis stood on top of the house where Catherine the Great Disemboweler had once ruined the village's reputation through wooing, bulling, then tearing men asunder, and so this ibis unsettled us. It suggested a gravestone marking a glum future.

It tightened anuses.

And so ibis rumors nestled.

"Bacchanal," said Hospedales.

"Commesse," said Miki.

"Maljeau," said the glasses and goateed UWI graduate, aka Royston Burns.

A fourth member of our crew of wet sponges said that the bird had been sent to distract from the news of the day: three village fishermen still missing, held in Venezuela for ransom for a week now. Two newspaper reporters arrived on the third day of the fishermen's disappearance, having caught the story's scent and showing up to poke villagers in the nosehole with their elongated microphones. We said little. But the next day the rest of the island learned all about it,

Extra, extra, the daily gazettes shouted, *another international Venezuelan incident.*

"Gs + Hs," said Hospedales.

Out in the capital, the Minister of National Security shook a finger in the media: *Be careful where you fishermen cast your lines.* But we villagers continued to cast a gimlet eye on the ibis.

"Bad omen," we finally said.

"More like a harbinger," said the glasses and goateed UWI graduate, that fatty bully, fingering his square-cut beard.

We cut-eyed him.

Wind ruffled ibis feathers.

The day before the ibis arrived there was bad news delivered forthwith when the grandmother in Bon Bois, the next village over, met her end when the bus that she was traveling in smashed into a water truck moving in the opposite direction, the truck having hopped the highway median and plowed right into the granny-holding bus. Then there was the rumored burgeoning soucouyant problem as well, and Mark-2, the thirteen-going-on-fourteen-year-old village scamp, said, "That is only a saga boy sucking up everybody necks at night, man."

But the ibis was the worst signal.

Opinions metronomed left then right: the ibis might have been a jumbie bird deployed to bring big bad village luck onto us. We hadn't experienced such sideways luck since the scandal with Catherine the Great Disemboweler courting bad love a year previous with Magnus and Romulus Titus, Miss Titus's two returnee sons, and everyone was anxious to avoid a similar incident. The gazette wouldn't print that kind of news, but the island grapevine was faster anyway, more deliberate, and clearer about this kind of maco-business, all of us burrowing our noses into each other's concerns for cheap entertainment. We knew the reason for all of this—the residual effect of Catherine the Great Disemboweler, or worse, Catherine the Great Disemboweler's spectral mother, Hany.

The morning after the ibis appeared, the gazettes and radios said that the missing fishermen were up a Venezuelan river when they were snatched. We already knew this. The fishing beds in the seas close to our village coastline were almost all fished out, and fishermen were encroaching on Venezuelan waters. Needs must when the devil drives. The Ministry of National Security soon corroborated this up-the-river news and chastised the fishermen in gazetted print. But the ransom that had only been meant for village cell phones and families of the fishermen soon leaked out onto larger social media sites, and soon the entire island knew of the ransom demands: US$200,000 for each of the captured fishermen.

"Them boys dead for sure now," said Hospedales softly, fingering his earring.

Just to make sure that we knew they meant business, the captors delivered onto us an oil-smeared and grease-under-the-nail chopped-off little finger from one of the kidnapped fishermen wrapped in weakened Venezuelan bolívars.

$200,000 each was scribbled on the bill.

"But that looking like Sookdeo finger!" shouted big-mouthed Miki, and Sookdeo's wife, Indira, in her backyard five houses away, heard this declaration and lost consciousness right there among her rows of pigeon pea plants. (Miki was wrong. It was Ramdeen's.)

"But you's a real ass, man," Bunny hissed at Miki later, Bunny being the only fisherwoman in the village, a woman with real clout and arms as big as promises, and who had been visiting Indira when she collapsed and had been the one who carried Indira back into her house from her crash-landed spot among the pigeon peas, fireman-slung over Bunny's shoulder.

We looked to the roof to see if this satisfied the ibis.

It did not.

The reason that we were not completely catspraddled by the ibises was because of our antidote, our countermeasure, our amulet, our little Milagros from Venezuela, who, one could argue, was a harbinger of the ibises, and who we used to justify our actions, us using her as a talisman against evil, a shield against vice, and a cure for the village's low-end venial sins, which had resulted in the specter of Catherine the Great Disemboweler's mother.

The next morning there were two ibises standing on the galvanized roof, the pair of them resembling a recently married couple looking out toward a disheveled future. That the species was the national bird sickened us a little. What good was it when the source and symbol of island pride stood there and encouraged bad luck from a great height? Truthfully, the species itself had been experiencing its own kind of recent bad luck. Two Chinese migrants were held in possession of a juvenile carcass of an ibis a month prior. The Chinese migrants pled guilty in high court, but their attorney mitigated on their behalf, asking that there be no custodial sentence. The lawyer argued that the ibis in this case was literally *brown* and not *scarlet*, so the Chinese migrants were unaware that it was the national bird.

"What you think was their plans for that bird?" asked Mark-2 the scamp.

"Cook and eat," said Hospedales. He spat. He was in his late thirties, and he had recently introduced the earring into his left ear, and we wondered what he was trying to prove. "Or cook and serve. Chinese restaurants popping up everywhere on the island, and grocery beef, dear dear." His dark eyelashes suggested mascara.

Of course everyone turned to Miki when Hospedales hoisted the ibis restaurant suggestion.

"But what the jail is this?" Miki said when we all eyed him. "Is why everybody watching me so?"

He knew.

Miki held a complicated history with the ibis species, one that no one wanted to bring up even in ol talk and fatigue. To break the Miki-accusation tension, thc glasses and goateed UWI graduate said that the scarlet ibis was an environmentally sensitive species, and its protection would entail punitive discipline in accordance with section 70 (2) of the Environmental Management Act, chapter 35:05.

Everyone groaned.

None of us had any use for a UWI graduate who continuously leavened fifty-dollar words before baking them into hundred-dollar sentences.

But we eased up on Miki.

The truth was Miki had been caught and jailed for hunting ibises a year earlier, and when he was released he was bold-faced enough to give an interview to *National Geographic*, whose reporter had shown up on the island to discuss our local status as a prime location for ornithologists, birders, and members of the Audubon Society the world over. It was the glasses and goateed UWI graduate, twenty-four years old, who didn't seem interested in ever getting a job and leaving his seamstress mother's house after all that education, who printed out the article and passed it around the village. By the time the account cycled through the village it was smeared blurry by fingerprints, everyone in the village proud of their desire to keep up with the news of the times.

Miki spoke plainly in the interview about doing a month in jail for those dozen ibises that somehow ended up in his knapsack. When the magistrate sentenced Miki he said that Miki was stealing the country's national treasure. All of this was in the article, right next to a picture of Miki, him gloomy on the printed page with his weird lazy eye, his thinning hair on full display, him talking about how ibis meat does taste sweet sweet and the reporter should take a taste if he ever had a chance.

"But, Miki, how you so dotish?" Hospedales asked, and Miki said the article was over six months old by now, and *how the France the UWI graduate even find it?* There was no love lost between these two, and Bunny now stepped in between them, but no one in the village really expected Miki to tackle the UWI graduate in these constricted times.

There were more important things to consider.

We threw an eye on Milagros playing with the other village girls and foolishly believed ourselves secure.

On the third morning, when four ibises huddled on the roof, we villagers worried about more bad luck and that ibises couldn't count well enough to know that three came before four. The UWI graduate said the ibises were multiplying *exponentially*, and everyone steupsed, bitterly sucking their spit to the backs of their throats. The ibises were mannequin-still in their petrifaction and brilliant red in their plumage. We'd thought to vigil the night before to precisely document new ibis arrivals, but no one wanted to risk seeing something that might wither an arm, or whiten a head, or limpen a piggee permanently. The ibises' crayon-out-of-a-box red feathers startled all of us, and we all knew that they retained that color from eating crabs and other carnivore-diet protein secured from the mangrove swamp close to where the river met the ocean.

The next day the Venezuelans released one of our three fishermen. Ramdeen's family had paid forex $30,000 ransom. Five ibises now sat on the roof. "How the ass they find the money so quick?" the cavalier Mark-2 asked, but no one wanted to venture a theory beyond the selling of a prized Evinrude outboard motor and taking out a second mortgage. On the noon radio broadcast the Minister of National Security said that things were still at a sensitive stage in trying to negotiate the release of the other fishermen. He warned national pundits and radio personalities to be wary in their utterances, that they weren't privy to all the *facts*.

"What pundits? Which part?" Hospedales said. "They were out in Vene waters just like Vene fishermen come in ours. But you see us holding anybody for ransom?" We shook our heads. Hospedales worked on the wharf on the western side of the island. He knew too much and we suspected copious bribe money slipped through his fingers like water. How else could Hospedales afford nice nice clothes from working on the wharf?

"It isn't that simple," Bunny reminded us, plaiting her hair back into two. She knew how this hairstyle caught all the village men's attention, opened our noses, fired our lust, but she did it anyway. "There's *oil* in that water. And we have treaties in place." She lassoed the end of one plait, then the next, with tiny rubber bands. Bunny still held a flame for the currently absent Peter-Called-Peter Cruickshank, them having a five-month affair donkey years ago after a drunken Carnival tryst. She could always be counted on for two things—to mention the underwater oil beds that were the island's primary money-earner, and surreptitiously trying to recapture Peter-Called-Peter's heart.

Peter-Called-Peter Cruickshank, boho village hunk, along with a few of our other ne'er-do-wells, not to mention the three that had been kidnapped, was currently in absentia, gone now for over seventeen days, God knows where, not even to be found in the Clearing working on his wrecked boat that would sink at the sight of water, his pastime of pastimes. We thought at first that maybe he had been kidnapped too but neither he nor the ne'er-do-wells were out on the water for it to make sense. When he was around, Peter-Called-Peter always grew quiet whenever island oil was mentioned, pursing his lips so no one saw his missing front tooth, and happy were we who didn't take a shot of babash, or down an island lager, or sip some puncheon every time Bunny mentioned our regional oil-based Caricom standing for fear of alcohol poisoning. With her constant oil talk she was like her late father, Antonio. "Is only a whole set of misdirection in this place, oui," said Hospedales, which made us wonder what kind of graft he was currently hatching, some new bohbol-passing get-rich-off-Vene-refugees scheme. When the news report, two days later, said that a released and visibly shaken nine-fingered Ramdeen confirmed that the fishermen were in fact on a Venezuelan river when they were held for ransom, we all yawned at the erosion-slow rate of breaking island news, but were overjoyed that one of us had been released.

Be careful of using the word "kidnapped," the Minister of National Security warned in a subsequent radio broadcast, *since we still have tenuous oil and oil refinery contracts with the Venezuelans. Our international stance*, he added, *is one of nonintervention.*

"Gs + Hs," exclaimed Miki.

We all waited for Ramdeen to come lime with us and tell us what went down, wanting to hear his nine-fingered ordeal, but the next morning he relocated to his cousin's house out in the country, the same cousin who had paid his ransom, and two weeks after that he was stabbed to death with an ice pick in front of a rum shop.

The next morning, more ibises.

So, when the from-foreign reporter showed up on the fifth day, the village was in a bad bad place. There were now a dozen ibises roosting on the roof of Catherine's house of ill repute. At first we all thought *here was a little good luck at last*, the reporter with his teeth straighter than 9:15 clock hands, and his clothes brand-new and not secondhand-shipped and sloppy-seconded and delivered in wharf-sent barrels. The reporter said that he was a stringer for a newspaper in D.C., and he seemed disappointed when we said that we'd never heard of the gazette's name. Miki kept the biggest distance from him, his last turn with a foreign reporter having almost ruined him. All the rest of us were initially drawn to the reporter. But in the way that truly good-looking people always carry a whirlwind of sadness twisting in their personalities, we soon recognized the reporter as a harbinger of trouble.

First of all, he didn't come to lime with the rest of us that first day in the gallery in front of Bunny's house on the opposite end of the village from where Catherine the Great Disemboweler did her tawdry business with both Romulus and Magnus Titus, but just installed himself in Miss Titus's house, us thinking at first that he was a long-lost Titus relation or maybe another one of Miss Titus's worthless thug relatives deported from foreign prison instead of just being a lodger. The foreign-born reporter almost had us believe that he was good luck when one less ibis appeared on the roof on the day that he arrived than on the day before, but then we realized that this was just a mistake in accounting, with Mark-2 still having trouble adding correctly on account of his having essentially dropped out of the junior comprehensive to fish full-time with us and make a little money for his fatherless family, Mark-1 having long since abandoned them for a young woman just out of that same secondary school.

When the foreign reporter finally found us drinking our local island lager and liming outside Bunny's house, he stated his bona fides, saying that he was the son of two islanders who had moved to the States and bore him there, and right then he became worse than a tourist in everyone's eyes, worse than a South American pirate, worse than Catherine the Great Disemboweler, and especially worse than the glasses and goateed UWI graduate who burned with a hot envious fever at someone a little more sharply educated than him.

We all knew about these foreign-birthed born-again islanders, who gave their parents shit for the first twenty years of their lives while their parents scrimped and saved and molded them into little princes, all while these heirs made fun of their parents' native accents, and were embarrassed by their parents' low levels of education and their sometimes being in the country illegally and sometimes not being able to speak *properly* to their children's grade- and middle-school teachers during mandatory PTA exchanges as a result of limited educational opportunities in their own pasts. We had TVs. We watched cable. Oh yes, we owned foreign knowledge. We fielded phone calls from distraught village-departed parents about back-chatting children they couldn't deal either a cursory calpet or a blistering backhand because social services would drag them away.

We knew the type.

The foreign reporter's born-again bona fides came later than most—here he was in his thirties and finally seized with nationalist island fever, probably having come down for Carnival the year before, having drunk a little coconut water around the Savannah, eaten a little doubles in the junction, and wined up on a beautiful woman's bumcee behind a big truck, and now he probably wanted to remain forever. He'd unearthed the story on the missing fishermen and wanted to bring international light to it as a way to connect the Caracas troubles to the mass migration of Venezuelans throughout the Caribbean and as far away too as the U.S. border, a microscope we didn't need because it would bring unwanted Ministry of National Security attention and would probably get Barradas and Sookdeo's throats slit, and when no one in New Felicity wanted to say word one to him and his freshwater Yankee accent, he seemed hurt and surprised. Instead we pointed to the Great Disemboweler's horror house at the other end of the village where not-too-holy things had taken place inside, and whose roof now served as a roosting spot for thirteen brightly colored intractable ibises.

He squinted at the ibises toward the outer edge of the village and said, "Birds? So what?"

"But that is the national bird, man," said Mark-2, that scamp, who not only was missing more school than recommended for his age but, we later learned, had a seriously detrimental vitamin D deficiency that bowed his limbs and bucked his teeth and bestowed the curse of rickets. The foreign reporter eyed the birds fixed on that galvanized roof, their feathers slightly ruffling in the wind, and when we didn't say anything else, us also solemnly nailed to the ground as if we owned folded wings, we could feel his frustration silently bustle and bump into us from behind, elbowing its way through our bodies as he returned to his rooming house at Miss Titus's for an early dinner, frustrated at getting no quotes, not word one from us.

When a severed fisherman's arm showed up, rowed over in a pirogue by a solemn-looking Venezuelan Pemón while we all pulled seine onto shore the next morning filled with starfish and small jacks, the arm's blood leaking right through the gazette pages of *El Diario de Caracas* in which it was wrapped like the catch of the day, we lowered our heads, and after trying to determine who might now be a widow, or a mother without a son, or a pregnant common-law girlfriend without a father for her soon-to-be-born child, we called in Corporal Lalchan from the police post in Bon Bois Village, which was only a half-hour walk but was big enough to have a small police outpost, an outpost just big enough to frustrate the locals with any questions or requests the indifferent constables stationed there might have. Corporal Lalchan and his bush mustache took his sweet country bookie time showing up because Mark-2 and his tiny Bon Bois thug friends had once launched scud-missile pebbles from handheld slingshots while remaining hidden far enough away, launching the rocks into the air and letting them fall on a yelling Corporal Lalchan, the makeshift missiles stinging him like hailstones. Corporal Lalchan sighed when he arrived. He'd seen this type of severed-limb nonsense before.

We tried to conduct the Corporal Lalchan interviews as quickly and as quietly as possible so we wouldn't rouse the suspicions of the foreign reporter still asleep in Miss Titus's immaculately laundered bedsheets in her guest room's four-poster bed. Corporal Lalchan set up a 6:00 a.m. office in Bunny's gallery and he interviewed each of us brisk brisk when we'd finished our morning seine pull before finally spiriting away the arm concealed in an old clothes hamper.

We sighed in relief.

We didn't hold any anger toward Miss Titus for boarding the foreign reporter, since her two sons, Romulus and Magnus, those wretches, had abandoned her to seek their fortune in the States, and didn't send back a single Uncle Sam forex dollar to help her buy a little condensed milk or a sack of rice or even some peas. When those wretches were deported back to the island thirteen months ago they'd tried to strong-arm us with their jokey Yankee accents and paroled-Rikers-Island muscles to run things in manners thugly for a while. This was before they fell for Catherine the Great Disemboweler's siren song, her luring first Romulus and then Magnus into her house, both of whom were later found in a worrisome state of dismembered death. The village being what it was, we naturally provided for Miss Titus until she replenished her sanity, and so we were pleased when she was able to wrangle some money from this foreign-born reporter, putting him up in her house and feeding him better than he deserved, us hoping that she charged him an exorbitant nightly rate, and maybe kneading a curse or two into the breakfast johnny-bakes, the rice and peas lunches, and the bake and buljol suppers, *and definitely please, Miss Titus*, we prayed, *lace his peas and rice and bake and buljol with a little local-island senna-pod laxative.*

As the ibises continued to multiply on the roof, the foreign-born reporter continued to show up where we limed in front of Bunny's, him poking his snout around and ferreting story scraps from here and there to line his article's nosy nest. When he latched on to one of us and asked us how we felt about the fishermen from our village being held for ransom and how the Venezuelans threatened to cut up the fishermen limb by limb and repatriate their parts if the ransoms weren't paid, even the glasses and goateed UWI graduate kept his mouth shut.

The reporter was finally able to scam a few words from poor Stacy, who was getting thicker through the waist with each passing year, each pound gained in weight lessening her possibility of marriage, so much so that even our rapscallion Mark-2, Stacy's sixth sibling and only brother, did not tease her. Poor Stacy needed a little company and a little reprieve from having to help her mother take care of the eight other siblings always in some miserable state of undressed disrepair: uncombed hair, missing shoes, torn tunics. The foreign reporter used his good looks and admitted charm on poor Stacy, and we had to plead with her later to please not mention Milagros, who we were trying to keep a secret at Bunny's house. At eleven, Milagros was just achieving puberty and was picking up the local idioms, a scattering of words here and there, but was still clearly washed ashore from Venezuela, a jackpot to the reporter's investigative instincts and newspaper-articled ambition. So we kept her from the foreign-born reporter, not because we thought that he would try something salacious, although Milagros was very dark and very pretty, but because we didn't need any Ministry of National Scrutiny heat in the shape of Corporal Lalchan asking more Corporal Lalchan questions while we still had two kidnapped fishermen out in Venezuela.

When Milagros first arrived, brought to our village in the dead of night by a sheepish and high-smelling Miki, was the one time that we were grateful for the glasses and goateed UWI graduate, him being able to speak a little beat-up Spanish to the girl, and learning that she and her mother had appeared a few months ago in a boat on a night that she'd said was filled with so many fireflies that it seemed like streetlights had guided them to the jetty.

"*This* island?" a bemused Peter-Called-Peter, who was actually present then, had asked skeptically. "*Our* island?"

"¿*Esta* isla?" the bemused glasses and goateed UWI graduate had translated for the young girl, who gave her name as Milagros Alzola. It was here that she cried and asked for her mother, Grecia, and we turned to Miki, who told her that her mother couldn't be with us right now but maybe soon. The glasses and goateed UWI graduate translated, and Milagros wailed louder, and we interpreted her traumatized two-week silence after that as well as we could, us glad that it was bighearted Bunny, who was maybe a little baby-crazy after things went bust with Peter-Called-Peter, who was housing and minding her.

When the foreign reporter came swaggering up to us after his tête-à-tête with Stacy, telling us he knew about the repatriated fisherman arm, and that we might as well tell about everything else since he knew it was Barradas's arm, unmistakable with its cluster of star tattoos, we instead asked him if he knew the story of the mongoose and the ibis. "What mongoose?" he asked. "What ibis?" Whereupon each of us baton-passed the much-handled village story, us saying that it was a scarlet ibis and mongoose who drove Catherine the Great Disembowler out of the village, us watching the reporter's eyes narrow at this little taste of island folklore.

Each of us dolloped a part of the story, Miki first saying that long long ago the mongoose and the ibis had decided to rid the village of a la diablesse, Hospedales saying that to do this the mongoose waited until the la diablesse rested after a night of fornicating before stealing into the la diablesse's room and withdrawing the screws that connected the la diablesse's cow's leg to her hip so that she couldn't walk out to where men drank at rum shops where she winked at them from beneath her broad-brimmed hat, Mark-2 adding that the mongoose then gave the linchpin screws to the ibis who flew them out to the dead drop nadir of the ocean with its oil beds, to the crown of a flowering poui tree, and to a particularly salty dead drop of the mangrove, all the screws forever lost. And then the glasses and goateed UWI graduate added that once the la diablesse was missing a leg and unable to walk around, the villagers took care of her for the good of the village, dismantling the rest of her body and dismissing her forever. The foreign reporter, having imbibed a little of our local lager at last, him finally liming with us, thought we were all mama-guying him, and he laughed with us and sipped his lager, shaking his head and thinking thoughts that we couldn't pry free, all of us knowing just how backward he considered us.

Trouble escalated when the foreign reporter stumbled upon Milagros while she was playing hopscotch with Mark-2's two younger sisters, when we thought he was out in the capital sourcing quotes. Some of us said that it was Milagros's fault for having slipped back into her native Spanish, or for being out in public, or for her being comfortable enough at last to talk in our presence since that night when she first arrived. Others said that it was the foreign reporter's fault for being able to piece two and two together so quickly, him wearing that smile that stated that he had a story he could send on to his Washington newspaper about a brewing international incident between island and continent. Before anyone knew what was going on the foreign reporter was crouching beside Milagros and offering her some foreign sea-salt dark chocolate and firing off a much more upright brand of Spanish than the glasses and goateed UWI graduate had ever mustered, us now realizing that Royston Burns had misled the entire village about his Español dexterity, the reporter asking Milagros all the standard operating reporter questions in rapid-fire fluency, getting her story straight, him scribbling hurriedly in his notebook.

The next morning Miki had to stop that rapscallion Mark-2 from throwing rocks at the squadron of ibises that now occupied the roof, the ibises now owning the entire former roof of Catherine the

Great Disemboweler, more than a baker's dozen of them, and their presence more than just signaling bad luck, their presence just about screaming it out because the journalist's eagle eye meant a story that maybe the U.S. Associated Press news service or the once-British Reuters news service would pick up about our little island village of New Felicity, months after Miki had rescued Milagros, and weeks before the story about the Venezuelan women and girls liberated from a notorious gentleman's club about a mile from here, a club that had confined twenty Venezuelan girls and women aged twelve to thirty-eight to the old converted plantation house that Miki was ashamed to have visited, Miki crying at having rescued Milagros and having to leave her mother, Grecia, behind in that den of iniquity, Miki crying appropriately for once in his life, us having only seen Miki cry uselessly during parang sessions sung outdoors at Christmas, cry at the end of Carnival during Las' Lap, and cry when there were no more lagers in the cooler we'd dragged to the Clearing. We didn't know what would happen to the women who had been liberated from the club, and we didn't know what would happen to Milagros if the foreign-born journalist published a story, but we were still worried about bringing back Sookdeo and Barradas, and we felt that interference in the form of a foreign reporter would bring attention that would get those boys killed.

"What the France," said Hospedales.

"Gs + Hs," said Miki.

"Bacchanal," said Mark-2.

We held a swift village meeting about how to handle the reporter before he disclosed to the world the fact of us housing Milagros. "This is the gotdamn problem with these foreign-born returnees," Hospedales said, still wearing his sharp peach linen shirt, "their lack of situational ethics and knowing when to keep their damn mouth closed." We looked at him funny, thinking he was trying to sound like Peter-Called-Peter, us still not seeing Peter-Called-Peter going on twenty-one days now, him and his missing front tooth in collective absentia.

When an unaccompanied and amputated leg was delivered to us a few days later, it just left on the jetty and necessitating a second call to Corporal Lalchan, everyone remained quiet about the shoo shoo that under the auspices of Miki, Hospedales, the glasses and goateed UWI graduate, and maybe one or two more of us, the reporter was now married to Catherine the Great Disemboweler, *metaphorically* speaking, that he was fertilizing the roots of the mangrove right beside Catherine the Great Disemboweler, that we all had garroted him with the same brand of nylon fishing line that we futilely fished with, had weighed him down with the same beaten and now useless outboard motors that pushed our fishing boats into deeper water, us wielding the same justice as we had with Catherine the Great Disemboweler, the foreign reporter now paired permanently with his forever bride, him and Catherine feeding our ibis problem their new and expanded carnivore diet, bits of flesh floating up and being consumed like the water grubs that rendered the ibises' already-bright feathers a brilliant crimson.

When, ten days later, Corporal Lalchan asked after the foreign reporter, saying that the police force was fielding frantic questions from the foreign reporter's Maryland-based parents, we shrugged our shoulders and said that these were straitened times and that terrible things were happening to local fishermen all the time now in this village with the ocean beds running dry and maybe there not being any fish for Lent, and shouldn't Corporal Lalchan and the Minister of National Security be looking into those things instead? Or were they too weighed down by all the oil and gas treaties that were being signed with our South American neighbor?

Corporal Lalchan pulled a face, and his bush mustache drooped, him knowing that there was no way to get us to spill village secrets once we set our stories straight, us knowing that you needed a human body to build a compelling court case.

The ibises that had once been consigned to the roof of Catherine the Great Disemboweler's house had now flocked down to earth and started to peck around the village grounds, crowding around us and following us like they were trying to pester our consciences into something we had trouble naming.

Before we knew it, both Barradas's and Sookdeo's bodies washed up bloated on our beach, their eyes pecked out or fish-eaten, us not being able to raise the forex $200,000 that their captors had demanded for their safe return or even a Ramdeen-negotiated $30K. Where the hell would we have gotten that kind of money? *If it's not one thing it's another*, we thought, as we spread open that morning's gazette and called Milagros over to practice reading a few words of our nation language back to us.

2

Letters from the Pen of John Cruickshank During Three Years Spent Cultivating Sugar on an Island in West India, 1810–1813 (With a Brief Mention of West Indian Black Vultures)

SEPTEMBER 8, 1810

Dear Bernard,

My arrival on the island was a malodorous one. The scent of something long dead and close to the wharf continued to assault my nostrils long after we made our exit from the port, although luckily it remained hidden from sight. Fish, one hoped, but the odor was more pungent, persistent, and abhorrent. A body probably. Slave, perhaps. Probably a runaway rightly rotting in a ditch. As we docked, a venue of black vultures stretched high above us, their extended bodies scraping the firmament. Waiting for a fortuitous moment, undoubtedly, to address the carcass, maybe a baker's dozen of those d——d markers of doom. It always astounds how they can scent carrion so many miles high. Shand and MacTeer met me at the wharf as required. Shand and his unkempt red beard remembered me from my last visit a dozen years ago. The more recently retained MacTeer, exhibits the low sloping forehead of a miscreant and is in severe need of tonic to modify his carriage, but is otherwise competent. It was he who loaded my trunks and Shand who guided the dray.

Abercromby Hall is as battle-ready as ever. I hadn't known about the jalousies that you added on the eastern side, but they suit, and they do well to encourage cooling winds. Still, the clime of this island is not one that I looked forward to encountering for the next few years of my tenure. Even cool days seem ferried from the darkest circle of hell. The heat was greater as we rode past the market. As we trundled along I witnessed negroes on the block for purchase, and I made note of the day of the week and the time of the day, since I remain cognizant of my remit both to shepherd a profitable harvest to market and to purchase able-bodied Guineas for the next season at a propitious price. There was quite a crowd inspecting the Africans, so I presume every island estate is turning a profit these seasons.

Upon your suggestion I inspected the estate astride the gelding upon my arrival both with and without Shand's accompaniment. The saplings for this growing season, I am pleased to report, are pleasantly hale. The youngest cane, although only currently as high as my knee, also looks very well. Of the forty-odd negroes that you retain, only a few remained in my memory from my previous visit. You did warn me you had had reason to replace some of the troublesome stock, but also it remains difficult for me to distinguish among darkies. Once MacTeer stowed my trunks, and just after the negroes' supper, I gathered them together, had Shand select one of the bigger specimens, and bade Shand to truss him to the post and deliver twenty-five lashes to his back in plain view of the others. The buck who received the punishment understood that I had ordered the display, and he stared lightning at me, sensible to the action but insensible to the thinking behind it. I returned his rude gaze. Then I had Shand cut him down and employ one of the younger negroes to ferry him back to a cabin and salve his skin, and I dismissed the remainder for the rest for the evening.

The kitchen I remembered well. Under Hany's supervision the scullery girls remained focused and deliberate and hummed about like diligent bees. Hany has matured into a fine dark beauty even after a dozen years and two childbirths, and she has wondrously maintained Abercromby Hall's innards, having every wood surface gleam and shine under her reckoning. Not even an ant has the fortitude to cross the transom, and the smell is of something always glorious baking. That evening, I saw her son, James, for the first time. I bade him to dust my jacket, refill my pipe, and black my boots. You are right to say that he bears me a strong resemblance around the nose and eyes. I do not deny that he is most likely my whelp.

Because of the current size of the cane, I believe this year's harvest will exceed the combined hogshead that you reported for last season's. I mean to reach out to Visser in the coming days to see how much he will be able to take to his mill upon June's cultivation. You have stated that the devil himself, disguised as a sharp-nosed Spaniard, serves as Visser's sugar alchemist, and that not even what lies between the queen's legs is sweeter than what he produces.

I will believe it when I taste it.

Your cousin,
John Cruickshank

SEPTEMBER 20, 1810

Dear Bernard,
As I have now settled into routine and responsibility, I wish to express my gratitude once more for your allowing me to run your estate in your absence. My cloathing business suffered far worse from the defeat of the uniformed British than I previously anticipated. I am embarrassed at the debts that I still retain in my failed attempts to make it a profitable enterprise, and it will be two lifetimes before I allow myself, or any of my descendants, to return either to Virginia or Pennsylvania. I am gratified by your generosity, but then we Cruickshanks have always been generous to each other. Our Finlay made several loans

from me back when money was good that I do not expect ever to see returned to my person in this lifetime, brother or not.

Later in the morning I set out on another horseback examination of the estate. During my peregrination I asked Shand to point me in the direction where I would most likely find James. I discovered the boy with other youngsters working the animals, tending the goats and pigs and feeding the chickens. He's a fine-built lad. I will bid Hany bring him to me to examine him and engage in longer conversation, but not yet. I have seen her second child as well, the always-laughing Kate. Although Kate is not as fine or intelligent-looking as James, and certainly duskier, she still exhibits a bit of her mother's handsomeness, and she is a happy bairn. Still, although but one year younger than James, she still acts as if she requires a constant nursemaid, and she ceaselessly busies herself about her mother's coattails in the kitchen.

Your cousin,
John Cruickshank

SEPTEMBER 28, 1810

Dear Bernard,

I set out today to meet with Visser, but both he and his alchemist were nowhere to be found. Other than the windmills he keeps to process the cane, his holdings are not as expansive as yours. I asked someone in his employ—a ruddy-faced Dutchman who gave his name as Anholts, who might have been having a tipple upon my discovering him in a shed sharpening tools—where I could locate his master. I saw my Shand acknowledge him, and I understood that they drank as confederates, Visser's estate being our closest neighbor. He asked if Mr. Visser was expecting me, and I admitted that he was not. "Then you won't find him," he stated sourly, adding that his master was as variable as a windblown kite.

"Tell him Cruickshank paid a visit," I said, but I hold little faith for the message's deliverance. I hope that Visser is not as wretched in demeanor as his servant.

I mean to ask you, dear cousin, about one negro, Polydore, who troubles the house. Because of his slight frame, he is often assigned lighter tasks of keeping the cane's rows clear of clutter and snakes, but he seems to want to fashion himself into my valet. The afternoon that I set out to Visser's he appeared sniveling and bowing, asking if there's anything that needed tending, and Shand dealt him a blow around the ear for his impudence and dismissed him back to his responsibility. Shand added that Polydore often wandered off, drifting to the nearby shore and looking out over the waves, and generally required a clout on the back of his neck to snap him back to sensibility and his labour. When I asked Shand what Polydore required, he replied that Polydore often provided you information, dear cousin, about disgruntled negroes planning mutiny. Is this true? Is his word reliable?

Admittedly, my ears perked upon hearing this. The troubles of 1776 that forced me from my last concern in Virginia are not so far distant in the past, and rebellion still always feels close at hand. "So why, Shand," I said, "did you dismiss him so readily? Would you see my throat slit in the middle of the night?"

"Begging your pardon, Mr. Cruickshank, but I did not want Polydore to take such liberties with you so early upon your arrival. Familiarity breeds," he said, "and there's no worry. None of these niggers has the fortitude to attack you or the house while I maintain patrol." I decided that Shand was right in his course of action, but just as I did not want negroes taking liberties, I similarly did not desire Shand and MacTeer to think themselves above their stations either.

On my return to Abercromby Hall I bade Shand fetch me Polydore from the field so I could separate truth from nonsense directly from the scoundrel. He bowed low and told me of news from the fields, including of three perceived malcontents in the ranks, but could not tell me why they were so. "Give me their names," I said, and his eyes swelled in his head, and he said that he had not yet unearthed their identities.

"Please, Marse Cruickshank," he said, "it take more time."

"Then why do you waste *my* time?" I asked disgustedly and dismissed him back towards his labours. Observing the distaste on my face, Shand offered to loosen the blackguard's tongue. "Do not visit any undue violence upon him, Shand," I said. "For all we know, he is truly ignorant of the mutineers' identities." Also, I did not want him harming, through my own fault, an already weakened stock.

"Aye, sir," he said with a mock bow. If I could dismiss Shand back to Scotland I would, but I doubt MacTeer to be a marked improvement as an estate's man-at-arms.

I retired to the verandah to enjoy my pipe and to wait for the early evening breezes to dismiss cobwebbed thoughts from my mind.

Later, I asked Shand whether it was true that the slave Warburton, who Shand administered stripes to upon my arrival and who is doing poorly, was Hany's "husband" and had sired Kate. Shand said that he was unsure, begging my pardon, but that he did not keep up with the breeding and calving concerns of niggers, and with all required respect, he warranted that I would be wise to limit credibility to any utterings that emanated from Polydore. I told Shand that I would take his suggestion under advisement, but reminded him of his place and scolded him that he should not have selected Warburton for the whipping. "You asked me to choose, sir, and I accommodated," Shand said. "I did not receive a reply when I asked if you required a particular selection." The impudent ass. He is of such slight build, and has title to his own cruicked shanks, that I wonder where he finds the strength to flay the negroes as needed to keep them in line. I wonder whether it is MacTeer who discreetly pulls the levers in the field.

I fear that Warburton may die from Shand's zealous stupidity. What is more, I still have yet to glimpse Visser.

Your cousin,
John Cruickshank

OCTOBER 17, 1810

Dear Bernard,

The harvest remains on track. The cane grows like unwanted weeds, and those in the most promising field already hover just above my waist. I inspected the entire crop myself this morning, and I took Polydore along with me to keep a watch for snakes. Since your corroboration of his integrity, such that it is, I have patiently listened to his whispers. A development: the three miscreants who remain unnamed desire revenge for Warburton's "unfair" whipping. "Names, Polydore," I said. "Without names they remain spectres."

"Soon, Marse Cruickshank," he promised. He made a show of swinging his staff before him and striking it on the ground, better to chase out slumbering serpents that might be woken to strike. These darkies aren't all ox-headed, cousin, and I recognized Polydore's cunning, his aim to drive out serpents both real and bipedal. He still fancies himself my valet, and I often have to dismiss him back to his labours among the cane under threat of thrashing from Shand. Polydore envies James polishing my boots and dusting my coat, and he straggles, and I have to urge him back to his duties. I discern that the other negroes dislike him greatly, even Hany, who usually holds a kind word for all. Once he has provided me the names of the blackguards who whisper about revenge for Warburton, I will have Shand seek them out and display them on the block at the next market. Mutinous thoughts fester and grow gangrenous as limbs and similarly require amputation. But it will not do to first punish them unduly. I have received your advice that to do so only weakens their worth and ability, and I beg your pardon for my impetuousness upon my arrival.

Visser finally deigned to visit me this afternoon, eager to inspect the crop and wondering how much of it would we let him have for his mill. I relayed your recommended amount, and he calculated at once how many hogsheads he could spin into sugar for shipment to England. He seemed satisfied, and only then would he allow me to properly receive him and his alchemist, a Spaniard named Bardales, the wizard that you'd mentioned. Visser wouldn't have any tea, but Bardales did. Visser, who dressed as slovenly as any slave, with a dirty white tunic and trousers that looked like they'd been properly muddied before he pushed his legs through their sleeves, paired with a sweat-stained straw hat, stood gripping the verandah's banister and gazing out toward the cane fields. Visser demonstrated all the crude manners of the Dutch that you'd warned me against: he said that he'd been out hunting when I had first visited, but he did not offer to take me with him on his next excursion. I can only wonder whose auspices allow him to cultivate sugarcane on a British colony.

When Hany brought out the tea, Visser's alchemist Bardales removed a small pouch from his pocket that contained the most recent batch of sugar that he'd overseen at Visser's estate. "Señor Cruickshank," he said, offering to pour some into my tea.

I allowed him.

The sugar, dear cousin, could have been spun in King Solomon's mines. "Is that *only* sugar?" I asked, and Bardales smiled wickedly showing small and even teeth. "We can rule every civilized land beneath God's celestial heavens with this," I exclaimed.

Visser snorted and took more rum, even though it was teatime, and continued to observe the cane and the workers. "We'll be lucky if we can keep the d——d negroes in line for a decade more before they burn down the fields and cut our throats while we lay upon our beds," he said. He was obstinacy itself and owned a clearly contrary nature, and Bardales, embarrassed by his master, did much of the talking from then onward.

"The British empire will maintain its hold tightly on its reigns, sir," I said, and here Visser's snort erupted into a full-throated laugh.

"Your British empire's navy rests upon a receding tide," he said, "and the sun does set. I'm reminded of it every evening when I look out towards the ocean." Although we are not far from the ocean, I doubt Visser actually visits it as he suggests.

As they left, Visser thanked me for my hospitality and said that he must return to conduct repairs on his mill, but would I pay him a visit to engage him in chess? Bardales lifted his eyebrows; clearly this was not an invitation readily given. People are often impossible to figure, dear cousin, inscrutable animals that prandle forth on hind legs.

Your cousin,
John Cruickshank

OCTOBER 27, 1810

Dear Bernard,
Received, yours of October 20. I did not expect that Margaret Robertson would ask of me. I thought that she would have been wedded by now, particularly to that lout whose name is better left unsaid. It gladdens me to think that there might still be a match between us. Of course I remain aware of my commitment of an entire three years to your estate, and though I admit to being lonely, perhaps she will still be available when I return. Perhaps she might be convinced to visit the king's colonies in West India. Perhaps my fortune will recover enough to sway her. For now, I turn to Hany with gratitude. Off in the distance, I hear the estate's cane dogs being fed by Shand and MacTeer,

barking as if baying for blood. I keep my distance from these hounds, wary in the knowledge that they respond only to those two.

* * *

A storm flooded the most prodigious cane field last week and what at first seemed the most promising of yields now hangs in the balance. Young James had warned me in advance of the storm's arrival. I narrowed my eyes. "You believe you can portend a storm's landing?" He shrugged, and he asked me if it would be out of line for him to show me where he liked to fish and observe certain species of birds. I told him I would allow him to accompany me, but that he must be careful because Visser liked to hunt, and he shot anything that stirred in the bushes. He laughed and said Visser could not hit the sky if he aimed directly above him. A clever lad. So, I said, "Show me where there is good fishing, young James," and I clapped him on the shoulder. He pointed out a wide range of birds on our constitutional and astonished me with their names and the mimicry of their calls. He pointed at one particular specimen, red as St. George's Cross with legs as thin as a sugercane's shoot. Later, close to the mangrove, we saw a handful of the d——d vultures feeding on the carrion of something, and all the hairs on my neck stood, the creatures as ugly as the harpies of Jason's voyage.

Later, Hany cut my hair on the verandah. The memory of those d——d vultures still troubled my spirits. She commented that my hair was two finger-lengths too long, and I agreed to sit for her to shorten it. She clipped my nails first, and as she shortened my hair she broached the topic of young James. Kate played quietly at our feet. "What of him?" I asked. The scissors snicked past my ear as she spoke. Was there a possibility that he might be allowed to learn his letters? I was noncommittal. Even the youngest negro in control of his letters can wreak destruction.

She then wondered if there was a possibility that James might be made free. This righted my attention. I held up my hand, and both the scissors and her supplications ceased simultaneously as if tethered to each other. I turned my gaze upon her, and she dropped her head. I asked her where from came this sudden and powerful request? Who had seeded it in her head? Her eyes swelled, fearing punishment. "No one," she said.

"Someone," I replied.

Dear cousin, I now feel as if I must keep my guard up at all times on this island against those who would try to dupe or manipulate me. I remember the conjurer's trick we once witnessed as children whereby the magician bade us follow one hand that held a rose, pulling it close to his nose to smell, whereupon he produced a live sparrow, seemingly from air, with the other. All that spills forth on this island now feels an approximation of such magick, scoundrels having me watch their left hand while their right hand engages in some mischief. I now feel that I can never let down my guard for a moment. Still, I told Hany that I would consider her request. What are your thoughts on this matter? She finished shortening my hair, and I watched Kate and briefly wondered if Hany would next ask about *her* letters and freedom.

That said, Hany is the neatest negress I have ever seen. When I returned, not a strand of my hair, or stray fingernail clipping, littered the verandah. Every snip had been neatly disposed of.

Your cousin,
John Cruickshank

NOVEMBER 5, 1810

Dear Bernard,

I suspect that you have heard from Finlay. Although my brother, he has inherited neither the cleverness nor horse sense of the rest of the family, and from what I gather from our mother he continues to sail close to the wind. His most recent letter mentions his wanting to visit West India for Christmas so that the warm sea breezes and salt air may restore his health and vitality. I wonder who has filled his head with such ambition, perhaps ambition even to take my role here from me. Surely not you, dear cousin? Negroes, overseers, and wastrel brothers who think above their stations really make one consider the direction of the world. Finlay would wilt like a hothouse flower in the winter if he were to visit this climate, and he would be underfoot more than Kate. But I wrote him to say that I would not halt his visit if you gave your blessing.

Admittedly, I would welcome someone who I knew that I could trust and maybe even solicit his opinions about the craftiness that now seemingly closes in on me from all directions. It seems like my effects have been moved slightly in my study, and that when on my constitutional, that the servants are whispering about me.

The harvest does better than worse. Warburton has recovered well enough to return to his labours. Again, my deepest apologies for having him whipped. Your consternation is earned.

Your cousin,
John Cruickshank

NOVEMBER 16, 1810

Dear Bernard,
One afternoon I paid a visit to Visser to play chess to clear my head, as I have done several times recently, but neither he, nor Bardales, was to be found. Hearing a disturbance in his shed I peered in to observe the bare backsides of Shand, MacTeer, and Visser's Anholts, all of them having sport with two young negresses. One was surely no more than a child. The three were so preoccupied with their thrusts that none witnessed me, but I was sure that the child glanced at me. This foal was barely a few years removed from her mother's teat and as similarly aged as Kate, but there she was flattened on her table, her legs thrown apart, and her own bare chest beneath Shand's provocation. I vowed to have strong words with Shand later. I do not write you to query whether I can dismiss him, for I know you trust my decisions implicitly. In the

end, I decided to stay my tongue until a more opportune moment. I would need Shand's assistance with the sale of three bucks per Polydore's warning. I have instead decided to keep a firm eye on Kate. She is but ten, but I put nothing past Shand, who I believe would have his way with chickens and goats and who probably fornicated regularly with highland sheep before he landed here.

All of mankind today seems to be d——d.

Your cousin,
John Cruickshank

NOVEMBER 28, 1810

Dear Bernard,

Finlay has arrived, and he has surprised me in several spheres. His physique, for one, has grown impressive. Once a sickly lad, he has filled out, and whatever he now sups on each day has done him worldly good. He does not take rum, and he limits his tobacco to once every few days. He also delivered to me your letter including the one, most surprisingly, that you passed along from Margaret Robertson. "Is there a potential match to be had there?" Finlay coyly asked.

"No one knows the future, dear brother," I replied as I read and inhaled the perfume with which she had scented the paper. As a gentleman, I will not reveal what she had written, but I will say, dear cousin, that the three years that I promised you seems more and more like a prison sentence imposed upon the British regiment in Pennsylvania.

I introduced Finlay to the estate, and he picked up things quite quickly and impressively. Maybe he has finally come into an understanding of responsibility in his adulthood. I am pleasantly surprised and hope he can keep Shand and the negroes in line.

Your cousin,
John Cruickshank

DECEMBER 8, 1810

Dear Bernard,
The rain brings all kinds of strange creatures to the surface including the half breed with which Cumberbatch used to consort on the other side of the island. Since I know that you disagree with my own comportment with Hany, I am sure that Cumberbatch's behavior scandalised you and that you do not seek an audience with him now that he has returned to Scotland. His concubine was so bold to ask for assistance with her failing crop. This was, of course, unsurprising. Without Cumberbatch's steady hand, the crop was sure to fail. I meant to dismiss her outright, but Finlay said that there may be some benefit to letting her have her word, least of all maybe adding to your holdings. I would not dare to even contemplate such an offer without your consideration.

Your cousin,
John Cruickshank

DECEMBER 12, 1810

Dear Bernard,
Several days ago, Polydore provided me finally with the names of the mutineers: Kitch, Grafton, and Josiah. I dispatched Finlay along with Shand and MacTeer. Polydore had reported that two of the fugitives were located working among the cane, but the three found Grafton by himself. Grafton sprinted off when he spied their approach, which seemed a confession in motion. Shand and MacTeer took hold of him, but even when he had been trussed, he would not admit to his part in a plot. Shand tried to beat it out of him, but Finlay stayed his hand. Brutishness is a tool too often reached for when one would do well to wield an iron fist in a velvet glove. Finlay vowed to have all three of them on the market block soon. The other two were captured, and when neither would speak, all were detained in a cabin reserved for

recalcitrants. This would make us shorthanded at a delicate time, but I aim to secure immediate purchases to replace them.

The following day, Polydore accosted me on my departure to Visser's. He said that he feares for his life, that the other negroes know it was him who provided the names of the mutineers. I told him to return forthwith to his duties. It was the last that I ever saw of him. He has surely run off. I have sent Shand and MacTeer and the dogs on various expeditions to recover him, but thus far they have demonstrated no good fortune.

I look forward to your response on young James's future.

Your cousin,
John Cruickshank

DECEMBER 18, 1810

Dear Bernard,

I have fallen ill in recent days, dear cousin. I did not wish to concern you, but I feare that my condition will have worsened by the time you read this. I have had to deliver the estate's upkeep to Finlay, and it is he who writes this letter from my dictation. Hany ably nurses me, and as I lie here I think of the vultures that I had previously encountered. They trouble my dreams. Chills and fever wrack my body without cease.

Pain shoots down my arms and legs.

Goodly taste has retired from my mouth.

Finlay reports to me nightly, and in addition to taking my dictation, he reads to me.

Dreams hobble me, dear cousin, even beyond those b——d vultures, and I am unsure what is real and what I have imagined. For instance, I recollect that Hany visited me one night in great distress, and upon asking her what was wrong, she reported to me that Shand had issued James five stripes for misshoeing a horse. I told her to send Rebekkah to care for me, and that she was to look after young James until he grew well. But the next morning, there was Hany at my side, wiping my forehead and cooling it with a damp rag. "What of James?" I asked, and she only frowned in confusion.

I asked Finlay if there had been a recovery of Polydore, and he admitted that there had not. This disconcerts me since my trust of Polydore was limited, and his absence suggested too many possible outcomes. Maybe the servants had not been whispering about me but whispering about him. Maybe they have done away with him. Maybe he has run off. If the latter I will task Shand and his hounds to do a thorough search. We need all hands on the proverbial deck to reap the season's harvest.

Your cousin,
John Cruickshank

DECEMBER 28, 1810

Dear Bernard,
My constitution worsens, I feare. I missed Christmas entirely. Finlay told me that James came and read the scriptures to me, but I think this may itself have been a dream as I remember none of it and furthermore have not given James permission to study his letters. I am certain, however, that I dreamt Polydore visited me. Warned me to keep an eye on Hany. "Why Hany?" I asked.

Here his form morphed into Finlay. "Come, dear brother," he said. "Who prepares your meals?" I laughed his spectre out of my room, but aches replaced his vision, shooting pains down both legs.

Finlay returned in another dream, telling me that he didn't want me to worry, but there had been a small shindy on the estate, and that he, Shand, MacTeer, and a few of the estate dogs easily put it down. Sleep comes easily, but such dreams continue to trouble me in their authenticity. I am not sure what to believe. Or whom. Sometimes it feels as if I am not dreaming at all. But in accordance with Polydore's caution, Rebekkah now cares for me most ably.

Your cousin,
John Cruickshank

JANUARY 8, 1811

Dear Bernard,
On the day that I feared that I would breathe my last, Finlay told me that a fire had ravaged the estate several weeks ago. "What fire, Finlay? Why is this the first I am hearing of it? How is the crop?" I asked, attempting to rise, but finding chills antagonizing me, I lowered myself back onto the sheets.

"Do not concern yourself, brother," he said. "Continue your rest." He said that it had been part of the shindy, that along with Shand's and MacTeer's assistance, he had managed everything. I laid my trust in him. Two days later my fever miraculously broke, and I found myself rediscovering my appetite.

As soon as my speech was coherent, and I was able to sit upright, Rebekkah visited and tried to lever hot broth into me. "Not now," I said, wincing against the brightness of the room although the shutters were closed and there was just a lone candle burning in the far corner. I asked Finlay why Rebekkah and not Hany? And where was young James? But he only placed a hand on my shoulder and reinforced my need for rest.

Your cousin,
John Cruickshank

JANUARY 18, 1811

Dear Bernard,
My recovery has been slow and arduous. Certain days feel like a thimbleful of improvement followed by a dram of relapse. I slowly reclaimed my footing and am able to walk the rooms of Abercromby Hall. I trod carefully with a cane's aid, but only as far as the verandah where I inspected the fire's destruction. One of the fields was lost entirely. Slowly, I regained my strength. I received news from three sources: the unvarnished reportage from Shand, the goings-on in the house from Rebekkah, and the deboned fish market stories from Finlay, to whom I have grown close in my convalescence.

Visser, I learnt, tried to access the house to accost me after the fire among the cane, anxious to discover what kind of damage that the crop had taken on, but Rebekkah and Finlay told him that I was too ill to receive visitors. I am told he cursed them both, and he was about to strike Rebekkah when Finlay forcibly showed him out. Ha! I wish only that my hallucinations had granted me that vision.

Your cousin,
John Cruickshank

JANUARY 30, 1811

Dear Bernard,
I am slowly back on my feet and making inspections of the estate. It is much worse than I feared. Two entire fields of crops were lost. Finlay also explained that some slaves had to be sold. I am in no condition to argue with him. We will fall maybe one quarter short of the crop promised to Visser, but even he should be able to demonstrate compassion in this situation.

My strength is finally at the level where I can make accompanied trips into the cane fields. Rebekkah is now my permanent nursemaid, and she advises me to remain confined to my bedchamber for a few days more, but my body craves movement. Habit will remind you of your past self, clear its throat, then clear it harder for you to remember. I still depend heavily upon a walking cane. I asked Rebekkah for Hany, who I have not seen in some time, and she said she is taking care of Kate, who has been sick the past few days.

The breeze that blows across this island is a tonic, but I find my energy bids me to limit excursions. This evening Finlay visited me with upsetting conversation. I had been drifting in and out of sleep; Rebekkah had been wiping my brow with a damp cloth and made sure that I had swallowed some water. Then—Finlay's anxious face.

"Have you considered that someone might have poisoned you?" Finlay asked.

"Why, Finlay," I said, "why would anyone poison me?" I considered the potential suspects: Shand wouldn't since it would be too cowardly an act for him. He would prefer direct confrontation. Besides, he is well fed and sexually sated. One of the slaves? Impossible! They would need to access my food. And, when Kate is not ill and Hany is at her station, she keeps too close a watch over its preparation and administration. Was he suggesting that Hany be the perpetrator? Could she have done it due to my earlier hesitation to release James from his bondage? I think her too clever for that. If I died there would be even less of a chance for her request's success. She must know, Bernard, that you own young James, and that any entreaty on my end would be directed finally toward you.

Why, then, would Finlay seed such doubt in my head? I offered my brother a tight smile. "I am beloved, dear brother. No one would want to harm even the shortest of hairs on my head."

He remained unconvinced.

I sank down warmly into my sheets, and Rebekkah arrived to feed me a delicious broth that she had concocted. I surmise she may be an even better cook than Hany.

Your cousin,
John Cruickshank

FEBRUARY 15, 1811

Dear Bernard,
Life, dear cousin! How sweet it feels to return to it upon eluding death's grasping fingers! How sweet to experience the solidity of earth beneath one's feet after experiencing the ebbing of tides beneath one's back, never knowing if one was being rowed to the banks of the Styx.

I wanted to share with everyone my return to the living. It was too late to provide the usual grog and respite to the slaves that usually accompanied Christmas. But my joyfulness as a revenant reclaiming his life demanded I offer a delayed celebration. I ordered Shand to dispense tankards of grog to the slaves, that they will have the days free from the traditional upkeep and maintenance of the crop. Shand was unimpressed.

Your cousin,
John Cruickshank

MARCH 1, 1811

Dear Bernard,
The cane is truly a remarkable weed, dear cousin. It towers above me, seeming as if it will build a ladder capable of dragging the d——d vultures from the skies. Now and then I walk through a few rows and marvel at its strength and resistance. While there was damage during the fire, as heavy as the winds blow, the canes do not seem as if they will ever break. Do not worry; I never pursue this constitution alone.

I always have Finlay in attendance, and he is always armed. The snakes are the biggest fear, but there may be dissatisfied negroes as well who may still ferry ideas of rebellion. There is a hum that works its way through the cane when the wind blows. The negroes swing their machetes with a single arch of their arms. They work well. There is a skill, dear cousin, in the striking of the machete at the cane's base, and to be sure, some are much better at it than others. Although it does not divest itself outwardly, I am sure that they are all singing the same song inwardly.

Visser sometimes showed up to join me and Finlay. I have grown fond of his gruff manner. He is as slovenly as usual with his broad straw hat and his red face. His cloathing always seems close to tatters, but Bardales told me that his master sees no need to invest in fancy cloathing because it doesn't make a scratch in the ledger of the counting house. Finlay tells me that he wants to continue on here on the island, and I think that he might be better than I at supervising all of this.

I have asked Finlay several times about Hany, as no illness of Kate's may be severe enough to keep her this long from her duties. In response, Finlay finally confessed to me that both Hany and Kate as well as James were lost in the skirmish that brought about the fire. The news unsettled me more than I expected, rendered me to the edge of distress and in the following days I found myself standing on the shore and inspecting the waves.

Your cousin,
John Cruickshank

MARCH 20, 1811

Dear Bernard,
My spirits and my health have lifted these past few days. I find that I am able to take myself on longer walks although I remained dependent

on a cane. I find myself admiring the birds of the island, brightly colored through their chests, but usually dark on their hoods and wings. I contemplated the absence of James and how much I missed him and Hany. Even with Rebekkah as company in my bedchamber, I was bereft.

A few days ago I received a letter from Margaret expressing her availability and enthusiasm for marriage. I wrote to her at once that I very much would like to see her, knowing that she would never come to West India.

Your cousin,
John Cruickshank

APRIL 8, 1811

Dear Bernard,
I hope this will not disappoint you, but I have decided to return to Kirktonhill at the end of this harvest, determined to wed Margaret. Although my fortune has not increased so exponentially, I have deliberated with Finlay and he will continue to work in my stead. If you condone it, he will take my place. Ultimately, this wild West Indian heat does not agree with me, and I find that I cannot tolerate it much longer, and that my illness lingers. My flirtation with death has reordered my priorities, and the loss of James continues to disturb me.

Your cousin,
John Cruickshank

3

In Which Pelicans and Seagulls Roam Roam on the Range

ROYSTON BURNS CAUGHT fatigue about his weight and education like so many clouts about his ears, hot like pepper pellets: *Choonkaloonks, You-We, big man, fatty bully, the glasses and goateed UWI graduate*, etc.; the village men renamed him mainly out of irreverence, fatigue, and spite. His weight rendered him an easy figure of fun. But Royston owned bigger problems. He'd fallen in deep smit with Bunny Walcott much later than most, bamboozled by her brown skin and hotcombed hair. All before that moment he'd hated her like he'd hated Mark-2's sister Stacy—both similarly complected and reminding him of his own weight concerns, surely tipping the scales within ten pounds of his own mass. But while Stacy was as formless as a water tank, Bunny, he admitted, was proportioned, and when he fell in love with her it was like his mouth was perpetually filled with scent from a shopping mall's perfume counter that he couldn't gag away. So precarious was this feeling, and how it watered his knees, that he desperately required respite from the village. University, for a time, resolved this problem. He fled, resided on campus, rarely visited home.

When he returned, he was twenty-three years old, still in love, had gained more weight, and was quick to flaunt his education. The village men pounded him with more fatigue. Two didn't: Peter-Called-Peter Cruickshank and Siddiq, Siddiq being Binary Clem's nephew or godson or cousin or maybe not related to him at all, since people on the island always took in unfortunates because where else would they go? Siddiq was tall and thin, owned an Adam's apple, and kept his hair cut low. A good-looking boy. In contrast, Mark-2, who Royston couldn't abide, was an imp and a terror, the worst of the village louts in his estimation, and as the wretch slid noisily into puberty, he drank like a wet sponge. Whenever Mark-2 eyed Royston walking past him, Royston sensed the imp's mind churning, conceiving of new hurtful shrapnel.

Once the residual bacchanal of killing the journalist had subsided, Royston reconsidered life, at first in tamped-down spoonfuls. Mostly, he stayed at home and worked on his village history project. At twenty-four, with his Bunny-love still hamstringing him, he sometimes needed to be outdoors to clear his head of what he'd participated in, the grisliness of the murder of the foreign-born reporter, even if it meant that he might encounter her. Once, at dusk, he wandered to the mangrove, and Nello surprised him there.

Nello was the village griot.

One time, drunk off white rum, and in the company of the village men, Nello conducted an impressive, fulsome, and uninterrupted oratory in the Clearing about the history of the village, expounding upon slave owners and sugar, British sailors and sea battles, the conniving spirit of the woods that would accept a woman's soul in fair trade, and ending on Peter-Called-Peter's grandfather Hubert Cruickshank planting a grove of zaboca trees on either side of the Clearing like two rows of soldiers where that land had once been sugar sugar sugar, Nello mesmerizing Miki, Mark-2, Binary Clem, and Hospedales like one of those svengalis who charmed cobras. Only Peter-Called-Peter had no use for this recounting, him and his Black consciousness not wanting to learn any more about his white slave-owning forbears than he already anyhow knew. Nello had reeled off information that Royston couldn't find in any archive; it was partly what had inspired him to conduct his own research, to get down the village's history, some of it so grisly that he required reading respites. It was Nello who was the repository of the history of Catherine the Great Disemboweler and her mother.

Now, as Royston was just sitting on buttress roots in the mangrove, Nello's unexpected presence startled him. "That's the thing about the mangrove," Nello said. "It amplifies your hurts and flaws. For me, it magnifies my night blindness." He dropped a hand on Royston's shoulder, held him in place. "What's it for you, You-We?" Royston never expected to find anyone at the mangrove, not after what they had done to Catherine the Great Disemboweler, not after the foreign reporter, not with the permanent smell of sulfur clinging to everything. The Clearing was for congregating, the mangrove was for disappearing.

"I good you know, boss," Royston said to Nello. Other than being overweight, lovelorn, and stung with flat feet, physiological trouble rarely tampered with him.

"You might think so, but be quiet for a moment," Nello advised. "Let your body counsel you." It was here that the ringing arrived in Royston's ears, and his eyesight briefly blurred. Nello reached out an arm to steady him. "You alright, You-We?"

"Tinnitis," Royston replied in a daze.

He'd never experienced it before.

"That's the mangrove speaking truth," Nello said. "Listen to what it has to say."

Siddiq played the sitar and wore soft shoes. He deciphered the pitches of people's voices just by hearing them. "Bunny?" Royston ventured one time.

"Just above a G," Siddiq replied. He knew how Royston felt about Bunny before Royston did, but Siddiq mostly kept to himself and read the Qur'ān when he wasn't liming with Mark-2, who was younger than him. Their Mutt and Jeff friendship confounded Royston. Siddiq read the Qur'ān, and Mark-2 had trouble muddling his way through newspaper articles. It was Siddiq who'd explained to Royston about the Ramsar Treaty that protected mangroves. Just before he went off to university, Royston had taken to escaping his house in the middle of the night, removing the window's wood louvers and slipping out so that his mother, Iris, wouldn't hear. The weight of his infatuation with Bunny crushed his chest and tossed him at night and turned him at dawn. On some of those bleak, sleepless nights, he'd go mangrove crabbing with Siddiq, who was a few years younger than him. At first Royston hesitated at the invitation, thinking that Mark-2 would be invited along and dreading the mangrove becoming a site of malice, but it was just him and Siddiq, which somewhat quarantined his dread. No one ever saw them. Liming in a mangrove in the middle of the night? Madness. Who else would do it? Mangroves permanently wore evil's cloak. Think of the treachery of salt water on its own, then consider fresh water's falseheartedness. Mangroves braided the two elements together. Macajuels slunk through tree branches, and manicou snuffled on treacherous ground. But Siddiq wore a cloak of invincibility about his shoulders, and this goodness seemed to envelop those around him.

Mark-2's sister Stacy once spied Royston escaping through his window like a satisfied bandit. It was the same night that Siddiq kissed Royston that one time. Royston had barely seen Stacy as she sat in the darkness of the front porch, her entire house wrapped in darkness, her rocking on a chair and cooling herself with a Spanish fan. Siddiq kissed Royston flush on the mouth in the mangrove that night, tasting of spearmint, and that was all. Maybe, Royston thought later, to get him to stop talking about Bunny. Maybe to impart some of his innate goodness. Who liked to hear the same fairytale over and over? When Royston returned home in the middle of the night, Stacy was still sitting out on her porch in the dark across the street, oscillating back and forth on her rocking chair. *The Christ*, Royston thought even though he was a true believer, and commandment two of course. But he recognized that Stacy represented the shape of fate and, he wondered, in empathy's blush, how all of Stacy and Mark-2 and the rest of that expansive brood fit together into that tiny village house.

Once, a few weeks after Bunny had taken in Milagros, Royston spied her on a solo walk, and he trailed after her. Even Saint Bunny, he figured, needed a break from sudden motherhood. He followed in part because Bunny headed not toward the beach but in the opposite direction, out toward the Clearing, a space that she'd vowed never to visit. *An enigma*, Royston thought. Bunny looked lovely in a pale blue sundress. Royston examined his own state of dress and saw that everything needed to be changed if he wanted to talk to her, including a T-shirt birdshot with eyeholes and his underwear which had been over-laundered to spiderweb consistency. By the time shame redressed him and he sped off to the Clearing, Bunny wasn't alone: she'd rendezvoused with Peter-Called-Peter. *Balls*, Royston thought, since Peter-Called-Peter, sitting with Bunny at one of the Clearing's mystic picnic tables, was holding Bunny, comforting her, stroking her hair as she cried into his chest.

Royston retreated before they recognized him.

Later, the reason for Bunny's tears became clear. One of Peter-Called-Peter's new sweeties, a light brown beauty called Melanie, had arrived to stay at Miss Titus's for a few days. No one could figure out the reason for the charade; she clearly snuck off to Peter-Called-Peter's house late at night and only returned to Miss Titus's in the pre-dawn when the men went fishing. Why so cryptic? They were both grown. Melanie cavorted in the waves as if it were the first time that she'd seen a beach. Beautiful teeth paired with a nose ring, she stuck around for three or four days. *Where*, Royston wanted to know, *did Peter-Called-Peter find them? What sorcery shaped his charisma?*

In the pre-dawn mornings, when the men had gone out to fish, Royston, weighed down with a kind of spooky romance in his heart, as well as guilt for the foreign reporter's homicide, sometimes wandered out to the jetty. The sun was still a hazy rumor, and the morning light was weak. The first time he did this was a few weeks after the incident with the ibises and the foreign reporter. It was then that he'd encountered the first Venezuelan couple. The woman on the jetty had salt water twisted into her hair and was shivering. The man wore a single flip-flop and owned a cauliflower ear. A wet gray blanket that looked like it had been dragged from a defunct airline's cabin bin sopped their shoulders and drew them together in a single bundle. Royston understood what he was meant to do. *Atone, atone.* The words reverberated in his ear. A corporal work of mercy: provide shelter to travelers.

"Sígueme," Royston said. The pair had no other options, having already given up their lives and life savings to the vagaries of the coyote and the ocean. They had made landfall, but now what? They briefly looked across the water toward their homeland, then they followed him.

One of the last times that Royston encountered Siddiq on Binary Clem's porch, Royston asked him if there was any chance for him and Bunny. Siddiq wore an odd smile. "You want the truth?" He played Royston a song on his sitar. "That's 'Pancham Se Gara,'" he said. "What do you think?" What Royston thought was that, at eleven minutes, it was ten minutes too long. "Well that's what I think about you and Bunny," Siddiq said, laying the instrument across his lap.

"1-0-1-0-0-1," Binary Clem shouted from indoors.

"What did he say?" Royston asked.

Siddiq shrugged. "Probably telling me to stop playing music." So Siddiq played once more, and this time, *somewhere within the music,* Royston admitted to himself, *existed a dire beauty that had the power to destroy humanity.*

The second time that Royston wandered pre-dawn to the jetty, he didn't find Venezuelans but instead discovered Bunny sitting by herself.

Before he could talk himself out of it, he called out so he wouldn't startle her and asked if he could join her. She wore a clean scent that lifted his chin. "Where's the little one?" he asked.

"Asleep." Her sartorial sensibility was a mix of decades, a mash-up of styles. Along with her signature sun dress, she wore legwarmers. Her dimples were in recession, and he worked to make them blossom, but his joke about once playing the triangle in a reggae band didn't land.

He changed tack. "And how are you dealing with your new life?" He'd meant how she was dealing with Peter-Called-Peter's most recent betrayal, but he knew she would interpret it to mean life with Milagros.

"Adjusting." She made room for him beside her, shifting over some more and tucking her skirt beneath her. There were rumors that Bunny's family was Venezuelan from two generations back and had similarly been refugees on the island, but ol talk was ol talk and on this island she could just as easily have descended from Spanish Moors. Bags rested beneath her eyes. She was twenty-eight but looked like she was traversing the potholed back roads to forty. Peter-Called-Peter had hurt her previously, and it was clear that she'd sustained deep wounds from Melanie's recent appearance. As far as Royston knew, nothing romantic had happened for years between Bunny and Peter-Called-Peter, but love could hibernate, and its reappearance was as unpredictable as a coiled serpent's strike. "What are *you* up to these days?"

He told her about his history project, his research of the village's origins. That he spent much of his day wading through the university's digitized stacks. She stunned him with her interest. Their conversation unfolded organically. He asked why she'd never gone to university, and she said what Royston already knew: that she had spent a few years as a teenager at school in the UK but after her father Antonio died . . . *You became too bereft*, he concluded her thought in his head. It had been the same for him when his own father had disappeared.

She now read widely, as her interests dictated. "Tell me a little about this village's past," she said. Royston told her about discovering the letters of Peter-Called-Peter's brutal slave-owning ancestor John Cruickshank in the university's digital archives, and how Cruickshank had documented his cruelty as easily as a cookbook outlined how to sauté mushrooms, and how John Cruickshank had been particularly cruel to one enslaved woman, Hany, and her children: her daughter, Catherine, and her son, James, the former of whom died along with her mother in a slave rebellion and the latter of whom was Peter-Called-Peter's ancestor. Here Royston paused, afraid that the mention of Peter-Called-Peter would upset her but, if it did, she buried any response. And when Royston leaned over and kissed Bunny, recalling Siddiq impulsively kissing him, she hesitated, and then she pulled away, and then she said that she needed time.

Peter-Called-Peter visited Royston on Iris Burns's behest; this seamstress had witnessed her son lovestruck and stupid before. She wasn't sure up under whose pooch he'd settled this time, but she had a good idea. "Just talk to him," she pleaded, clutching Peter-Called-Peter's wrists. Peter-Called-Peter took a break from his boat-building in the Clearing and brought a book with him: *Mindfulness and the Monk*. A beatific man with a shaved head sporting oversized eyeglasses and red fabric draped over one shoulder peered out shyly from the cover. Iris stood beside Peter-Called-Peter in the doorway of Royston's bedroom. "Look who's here!"

"What's good, chief?" Peter-Called-Peter asked as he knocked on the open door, then entered. He handed over the book. "Aunty concerned about you, you know. This got me through some difficult times."

Royston smelled a one-man intervention. He glared at Iris, and she backed out the room. "What have you been up to these days, boss?" he asked Peter-Called-Peter. "Besides boat-building?"

"Trying to save an aloe vera plant," Peter-Called-Peter said, explaining that he'd cut away the dying leaves and was drying out the root to revive it. "And staying on top of laundry."

Cleanliness, plants, and Buddhism, thought Royston. *The secrets to his good fortune. But was that a St. Christopher's medallion around Peter-Called-Peter the Buddhist's neck?* And, finally, *how could you walk away from Bunny, you stupid, stupid man?*

Later that evening, Royston phoned Bunny and, surprisingly, she answered. They chatted some more about his history project, that the research had been distressing him, and when she asked what about it exactly, he hesitated. He wanted to sanitize some of the most violent details that he'd learned, that John Cruickshank's brother, Finlay, had slaughtered some of their slaves who'd tried to escape, buried them close to the beach so that their bodies wouldn't affect the cane crop, using other slaves to sink them deeply beneath the soil. Bunny urged him on, but the details unsettled him and, instead, he began to talk about John Cruickshank's love for Margaret back in Scotland. Bunny paused, then said, "Someone needs to magnify the ugly truth of this village's past." She added, "We are made by history." But the village's truth pressed down on Royston. He clumsily asked about her dreams, and they discussed Bunny's desire to visit Japan. She wanted to visit the Ginkgo Castle in Kumamoto, and she promised him a postcard when she did. The next morning, she was again on the jetty without Milagros, and when he kissed her this time, she let him.

The morning after that, intoxicated and bulletproofed with Bunny-amor, Royston returned pre-dawn to the jetty hoping to see her again, hoping that meeting her there would become some new ritual. Instead, a second couple stood there, having been deposited by a motorboat that had long since zipped away. This man was short and round, and the woman owned a long thin face and very long hair that she'd woven into a single braid that dangled down her back.

Royston recalled the ibises that had arrived on Catherine the Great Disemboweler's roof a month earlier and then how he and the fishermen had disposed of the foreign reporter. One day the ibises were everywhere, walking around the village like they'd secured a mortgage, and then the next morning, as if they'd reached critical mass and achieved all their goals, they were gone. "Sígueme," he said again. He led the newcomers past the Clearing to the old Abercromby House, where Peter-Called-Peter's ancestor John Cruickshank had lain with Hany, a house that no one visited because it never fell into disrepair, not even termites, not even a Jack Spaniard nest dripping from an eave, not even a cracked foundation, and there was that odd silence too when you went indoors that sounded like you were sunk deeply in a cave and you could hear your heartbeat thump in your ears. *But these Venezuelans were not tied to that same past*, he reasoned. *They would not be haunted by its jumbies.*

After that, Royston transformed Abercromby House into a way-station for new arrivals, and he ferried over bedsheets, bottled water, pillows and pillow slips, tin cans of food, and a small transistor radio that he tuned to a different station than the one Peter-Called-Peter infuriatingly insisted on listening to while boat-building in the Clearing. Royston instead played a Venezuelan radio station that came through patchy even on cloudless days and that spoke rapidly about emptying store shelves. Venezuelans continued to arrive on the beach. Royston never again saw the refugees he had delivered, but he knew that if trouble had accosted them, that the chatter would have swum back to the mainland and Venezuelans would have stopped arriving on the jetty. He didn't know where they relocated to on the island once they had left the house, but he'd received them in peace. Slowly, the guilt about the foreign reporter, which once draped about his neck like an old tire, had abated, replaced by his corporal good works with the

Venezuelans and the hope that a relationship was blossoming with Bunny.

He ran into Bunny early one morning a few days later, not predawn, but just before lunch. She was with Milagros, and they were returning from the beach. Royston said hola to Milagros, and she shyly hid herself behind Bunny. "How goes your project?" Bunny asked him.

"Not too bad," he said. "Per your suggestion I have really been trying to learn more about Hany."

"I prefer to think of her as Peter-Called-Peter's ancestor, rather than Cruickshank," she said. "She must have been iron-willed and resilient. A woman to admire."

Royston nodded dumbly. He hadn't considered this perspective. He felt uncomfortable conceptualizing Hany this way, as a real person and not just a figment of history.

He asked Milagros in Spanish if she was going swimming, and the girl buried her face into Bunny's upper arm. *Strange for an eleven-year-old to be this shy.* But aloud he said, "She's cautious."

"With some people," Bunny replied. Royston waved as they walked away.

One Sunday morning, after taking his mother to mass by taxi, Royston returned to find Corporal Lalchan in Iris's kitchen, picking his fingernails with a fork's tines. Feet up on the kitchen table, dirt crumbled from his soles onto Iris's good good tablecloth, his bush mustache that morning particularly well curated.

"So, you reach back," Lalchan said. He recrossed his legs, alternating which foot was on top, a demonstration of easy supremacy. He tossed the fork onto the table with a dull clunk. Royston stood awkwardly in the doorway, sensing a second person in the house. Maybe it was all the mumbo-jumbo that Peter-Called-Peter had been trying to teach him through mindfulness, *calm your breathing, feel your spine,* but in this moment Royston swore the air now vibrated differently. No one ever visited him or his mother, and the molecules seemed to have shifted too much for Lalchan to be the sole interloper. He wanted to run into the bedrooms and throw open closets.

"Now," Lalchan said, "tell me about all these Venezuelans you bringing into the country free free." Royston gaped. Lalchan laughed and Royston caught a flash of gold on a back tooth. "The Ministry of National Security tracing people back to this village you know." He finally removed his feet from the table and stood. He unsheathed his baton and pointed it. "For your sake, partner, don't make me come back," he said. He touched the baton to both of Royston's shoulders as if he were knighting him. Once Lalchan left, Royston, still feeling as if someone else was present, searched the house, but there was no one there. Just in case, he sprinkled some of Iris's holy water in all four kitchen corners and in the chair that Lalchan had polluted.

A few days later, while Royston worked on the village history, Mark-2 knocked a shilling against the wood louvers, and when Royston opened them, the imp gleefully informed Royston that Miki had begun to date Bunny. Royston's stomach rippled.

"*What?*" He rubbed his eyes, then put on his glasses, a recently strengthened prescription. "Who say so? When?" The imp at Royston's bedroom window made Royston feel as if he were in jail. Later, Royston texted Bunny, but she didn't respond. He texted Siddiq, and he didn't respond either. He walked over to Binary Clem's and knocked on the door. He knocked and knocked, and finally Binary Clem emerged in a distressed tank top and a pair of dirty plaid shorts. He handed Royston a note that said *Siddiq gone you know.* "1-0-1-0-0," he added. He shut the door on Royston.

Later that morning, Royston read a front-page article, above the fold, with a picture of Venezuelans in front of the island's United

Nations building. They'd tied their hands to the wrought iron with garbage bags:

> The number of Venezuelan refugees camped outside the United Nations (UN) continues to swell and is now estimated to be over 30. They're demanding a meeting with the UN officials to discuss asylum applications. When this reporter asked them why they tied themselves to the wrought iron, one man said, "Because we're prisoners! We sleep on these streets, and no one cares. Rain falls on us, and no one cares. We have nothing to eat, and no one cares." He added that he and his wife, Paula, just wanted a better life. He complained that the island held no laws that catered to asylum seekers. When contacted, the UN said that they planned to meet with the Venezuelans. When asked how they'd entered the country, the man said that there are some good people on the island, and he described a young man in New Felicity Village who demonstrated all that good could be.

Royston groaned. He recognized one of the couples he'd led to Abercromby House in the photo. He understood that continuing to help newcomers would result in negative attention, but he would continue to do it anyway, as penance for his part in putting the foreign reporter in the river beside the mangrove. But when he visited the jetty the next morning he saw neither Venezuelans nor Bunny, and a kind of grief circled its hands around his neck.

A small ember was the shape that Royston's rage initially took upon seeing Bunny, Miki, and Milagros bobbing out on the ocean in Miki's fishing boat the next Saturday morning, returning to the jetty from a bourgeois morning out. Upon seeing Bunny dressed in her yellow sundress, and Miki, dressed as well as Royston had ever seen him in a crisp white oxford shirt and flat-front khakis, Royston's stomach shifted. Miki skillfully navigated the boat to a stop and then roped it to the jetty. Bunny had combed Milagros's hair into two plaits. Miki gently assisted first Bunny, then Milagros, onto the jetty's shaky timbers. Milagros was laughing.

The ember of rejection burst into a one-alarm fire of anger. Royston knew that he should feel happiness for Milagros. This was a stable environment, a found family. For Bunny too. He knew that love was always patient and kind; it was never jealous, and never rude, or selfish, or resentful, but the lava that bubbled in his chest said otherwise. Royston's rage was still percolating when the trio breezed past him and either didn't notice him or chose not to acknowledge him, so completely occupied were they with each other and their conformist Saturday. But the last cruel cut was when Milagros looked back over her shoulder and smiled at him. Royston couldn't qualify the splintering of his heart then, the shards dispersing to all parts of his body, causing this convulsion, a dry heave that brought nothing up.

Humiliated, he turned toward the jetty, the gravity of his grief pulling him out toward Miki's boat, where he would vent his spleen, or expectorate into the boat, or pull out his piggee and urinate upon its motor, to transfer his fury that he could not direct toward Bunny or Miki or Milagros, since they had already entered Bunny's house with an audible click of the sliding glass door shutting him out, to continue crafting their patchwork perfect family. Royston was impotent in that moment and, standing there, looking out toward Venezuela, he felt a presence, and he turned to see Milagros and a sheepish Bunny, both having returned for the sun hat forgotten on the boat. Royston chivalrously retrieved it, handed it to Bunny, and finally saw her dimples.

But Milagros didn't smile this time, and just as they were about to leave, momentarily overwhelmed by the fire's rage, Royston bent down to her and asked very quietly, "¿Por qué no regresas a Venezuela?"

Milagros flinched. Tugged at Bunny's hand. Bunny held the girl's hand tightly and frowned at him. "What did you say?" She looked at the girl then back to him. "What did he say to you?"

No one spoke.

Admonished, Royston walked off. When he looked back both Bunny and the girl still stood there.

My God, he thought, *what's the matter with me?*

That evening, he phoned Bunny, but she didn't answer. He texted, but she didn't respond. Why waste energy walking over to her house? He sank into his seat, switched on his computer, and clicked through John Cruickshank's letters on the university's archive.

The following morning, another couple, this one so similar they seemed like twins. Short. Squat. "Sígueme," said Royston. He felt like he'd be ambushed as he walked with them, that Lalchan would step out of thin air, seize him, and wrap his baton around his windpipe. But Royston shepherded the Venezuelans to Abercromby House without incident, and when he left them the woman gifted him an origami swan. He accepted it silently, later stationing it on his desk beside his monitor. When he returned home he spent a week sequestered in his bedroom, wallowing in a morass of self-pity.

During this time, Royston visited the Clearing just once. Miki was absent, but all the old soaks were there: Mark-2, Hospedales, Nello, Binary Clem, and Peter-Called-Peter working on his boat and listening to that awful transistor on the same soul-numbing three-artist station. By then Peter-Called-Peter had already ended things with his latest sweetie. "Do you know," Royston said glumly to the gathered group, "that goats are stabled with high-strung racehorses to calm them?" Only Nello paid any attention to him, turning the long-necked bottle up to his lips.

"Righto," Nello said and drank his beer down to the foam. Then, "How's your tinnitus, You-We?"

On Sunday morning a week later, when Royston returned from taking Iris to mass, he again found Lalchan's boots on the tablecloth.

Again, Royston felt that someone else was in the house. He studied the bottom of Lalchan's boots, muddy as always. He'd always believed that policemen wore hard boots, like the defense force did, but Lalchan's ersatz footwear, only made to look like boots, was as soft as any sneaker. "People say that you stop going to church, or at least that you don't go as often. Something making you guilty? Word is that you still take your old mother there and pick her up every Sunday morning though. That nice, man." Royston remained quiet. He understood this to be a don't-speak-unless-spoken-to exchange. There was a different tablecloth this time; he'd washed the last one and startled Iris in doing so, reinforcing her decision to summon Peter-Called-Peter.

"I hear you doing research on the village. Black people, I sure. Always Black people. How about douglas like me?" Lalchan removed his feet from the table. As his feet reached the ground, Royston watched Lalchan remove his sidearm and place it on the table, right where his boots had rested. "Sit down nah, man. You must be tired. You getting bigger and bigger each time I see you."

Royston sat across the table from the policeman. He still felt the apprehension of someone else in the house and the dread of not being able to confirm their presence. The village had always treated Lalchan as a buffoon, and Lalchan knew this, but Royston saw now that Lalchan needed only to peel off one villager from the pack to demonstrate the potency that a badge, a gun, and a gray uniform conveyed. To bring them down and to bite into their haunches. "Nobody don't want to write down what happen to the people like me who mix up," Lalchan said, then belched, and Royston understood that the man had been eating from Iris's fridge, probably the pork baos that Royston had been saving for a snack. Here, Lalchan reached beneath the kitchen chair and placed the newspaper with the article about the Venezuelan protestors right beside the gun. He tapped the article twice with his forefinger. The first time pointing at the quotes: "That's them."

The second time pointing out the hero who had helped them: "That's you."

It was here that the second man emerged from Royston's bedroom, wearing black latex gloves to match his shirt and trousers. Instead of the spike of fear that he thought he would feel, Royston felt an unreasonable calm fall upon his shoulders like a cape. "Someday I feel somebody go have to do it you know," Lalchan said. "It have too much different kind of people on this island, and you have to tell everybody story to get the whole thing down." He gazed at Royston. "How about the Venezuelans? You ever thought to write their history on this island?" He turned to his deputy. "Right or wrong, señor Maldonado?"

Lalchan's deputy said nothing, and Lalchan gave the gun, still supine on the table, a gentle kick with his foot to shift it toward Royston. He gazed at Royston with eyes as muddy as his boots. *Pick it up*, his eyes said. *Pick it up nah, man.* Royston looked away. He knew that Lalchan's arm would strike across the table as quick as a sneeze, the baton a spring-loaded extension of his arm. Royston clearly imagined the broken bones in his hand. The man with the black gloves, who owned a shaved head and a scar notched into one eyebrow, advanced on Royston.

This man was trigueño and a glower on two legs. He wasn't there to serve as a handbrake on Lalchan; he was meant to be the whip. Lalchan removed his grimy boots from Iris's kitchen table and clapped twice. "Alright, pallo," he said to Royston. "I busy busy. Say your prayers and pick out a swim trunks. Is so you like Venezuelans, is best you head over there to lime with them." Royston didn't move quickly enough, and the man with the black gloves suddenly popped up beside him and flicked his earlobe so hard that when Royston clutched it a moment after the pain registered, he expected blood to decorate his fingers. Royston's mind flashed back to primary school when pairs of barbarians would play bokey and flick each other's knuckles raw.

"I don't feel like swimming, you know," Royston said to Lalchan.

Lalchan snorted. Looked to his deputy standing behind Royston. "Could you beat that? Like he's a big sawatee. Like he own house and land and could tell people what he want." The man with the black gloves flicked Royston's other ear, harder than the first, and Royston howled and jumped to his feet thinking that the lobe had torn. His mind sprinted. Would they molest Iris if he didn't obey them? She was still at church, and what would she think if he didn't return to pick her up? "Forget the bathing trunks then," Lalchan said. "It go just look like you couldn't take the soca anymore and had to end it all." Lalchan replaced the handgun in his holster. Royston closed his eyes and breathed deeply. He opened his eyes to see Lalchan close and then gently fold the paper in half. He flicked it with his middle finger. "Is the ministry you know," Lalchan said.

He took the newspaper with him as he led Royston out.

The last time Royston saw Siddiq, Siddiq had told him he'd wanted to visit the blue mosque in Istanbul. "You and Bunny both want to leave this place," Royston said. "She to Japan and you to Turkey."

"People want what they want," Siddiq said.

Royston had grinned. He'd still been hopeful about Bunny at that point. Siddiq had told him that he'd hoped to visit Mecca soon too, but he'd only mentioned it that one time. He'd put a hand behind Royston's head. Caressed his earlobe. When he disappeared for good, he didn't even take his sitar with him.

The sprawl of the ocean once more brought up the taste of Royston's breakfast—bake and buljol that Iris had prepared before she'd gone to church. Lalchan and his deputy marched Royston to the jetty in bright daylight, and no one peeked through a louver, not a curtain flicked. Royston wondered if shouting out would help. Sprinting off. No, that would bring a bullet to the head. A shot in the back. Maybe there was a chance for him in the water. He was weightless in water, and this had always delighted him. As they walked he looked out over the ocean. It was a fitted blue sheet all the way to the horizon. No one bobbed on boats; it was too late in the day to fish.

The water close to the shore churned brown with sand.

They made the right turn onto the creaky jetty and strode its length. A walk to the gallows. The boots of both Lalchan and his henchman thudded. The wood felt cool beneath Royston's bare feet. When Lalchan, standing behind him, waved his gun at Royston to dive in, the jetty swayed, and Royston considered whether to plunge in feetfirst or lower himself in. The water seemed too frigid. He had decided to lower himself in when a kick up his backside splashed him into the water. A donkey-bray of laughter rose up behind him.

Royston flailed. The water's coldness startled. The unexpected submergence made him swallow too much water. He bobbed momentarily. Actually tried to jump straight up and out. He realized that he was burning energy, and he calmed himself to the point where he could tread. Lalchan pointed at him. "Venezuela is that way, big man," he said. "And you look like a strong swimmer."

Royston didn't want to turn his back on the pair. He still expected Lalchan to fire at his head. But when Lalchan's deputy unzipped and began to urinate on Royston, Royston ducked beneath the water and swam farther out. He pushed himself as far as he could, hoping to gain enough distance to prove a difficult target when he surfaced.

Hungry for air, his lungs burning, he burst out of the water. His clothes were metal-heavy; he fought them off his body. He had figured at first that Lalchan had meant just to scare him, that if he really wanted him dead he and his deputy would have bundled him into the back of Lalchan's jeep, executed him, and sunk him into the river beside the mangrove with the foreign reporter and the memory of Catherine the Great Disemboweler. But now he realized Lalchan's plan was always to tire him until he drowned. A simple crime. No evidence of foul play. He'd wash up on the beach and Iris would wail.

He paddled out.

When he was five or six years old, Royston's father, Brigand, had taught him to swim, saying it was the first thing an islander should learn, and then a year later Brigand disappeared. So many people vanished from New Felicity. Siddiq. Catherine the Great Disembow-eler. The foreign reporter. Some more easy to locate than others.

Royston swallowed more water.

The undercurrent was strong.

His legs wearied.

The salt terrorized his eyes.

Lalchan and his goon eyed him from the jetty, barracudas on land.

The gull seemed to have been floating on the water long before Royston grew aware of it, but now Royston noticed it at his weariest. His chest hurt, the water as heavy as a dentist's lead vest. He'd been in the water for close to thirty minutes then, and he'd tried to swim out and around the rocky outcrop to the next beach, but the undercurrent kept carrying him out. "How's it going, fatty bully?" the gull asked, and he recog-nized the gull's voice, knew that it was Mark-2's sister Stacy.

"Hello, Stacy-seagull," Royston said, accidentally gulping water. His legs grew tired of treading.

"Not a seagull," she said. "*Pelican*. A smart fella like you should know the difference." She momentarily ducked her head to her chest. "How's tricks?"

"I'm tired," Royston replied.

"Because you're a fatty bully," Stacy the pelican laughed.

"Are you going to help me?" Royston asked. His legs felt like ropes were tied to them and someone beneath the surface was tug-ging him down.

"You go be alright, big man," the pelican said. "You help plenty people but you not a martyr." Then it flew off.

"Onward," thought Royston.

He swallowed more water.

Felt himself going under.

The boat's engine cut off as it puttered over to Royston. Bobbed beside him. At first Royston thought that Peter-Called-Peter and Siddiq had come to rescue him, but it was Miki and a grinning Mark-2.

"You alright, big man?" Miki asked him as he reached over into the water and helped pull him in. "Dammit, You-We, you big as a house." Here was Bunny's new sweetie, red-eyed with thinning hair and his lazy eye. *What did Milagros see in him?* Mark-2 wrapped a blanket around Royston's shoulders. "You alright?" Miki asked again.

Royston only thumbed the corner of his mouth.

While in the water, he'd wanted Siddiq to come to him. Bird, fish, it didn't matter in what form. Tell him where he was. Where he'd been. Say that everything was okay. Tell him how splendid the blue mosque had been. Sometimes people just left. Royston followed a fish that swam beneath the boat. Mark-2 kept grinning at him.

Royston was sorry about what he'd said to Milagros when she was with Bunny. Later, he would write her a letter of apology, and store it on a flash drive since he was sure she would immediately discard a letter on paper. A flash drive seemed more substantial. As if there was something on it worth holding on to. But it wasn't enough. He'd need to do more. The little girl was the same as the cloud cover, the odd rain that fell when the sun still shone. *She* was the village's fate, always moving, always changing. It felt like taking care of her was the penance that the village could serve to redeem themselves, that caring for her meant that there was a possibility for them to be good once more. Return them to firm karmic footing. Saving her life, giving her succor, balancing out what they had done to Catherine the Great Disemboweler. She was the true harbinger and not Hany. Milagros pointed toward a new direction for the village, not a fearful past, but a compassionate future. When they gained the shore, and Royston made his way slowly back home, he looked toward Bunny's house, and he saw no movement at the window, and he wondered who would rescue the Venezuelans from now on.

4

A Blue-Fronted Amazon, a Congo Gray, and a Timneh African Parrot Sing a Song Through Space and Time

A NAME. MILAGROS plans to return to Venezuela based solely on a name. Not a photograph. Not even an age. Didn't know if Ebrahim Fortunato needed a cane and a dog or if he spent all day peacocking on social media sites. She feels like she's holding on to the thinnest of threads that could snap at any moment. She'd sourced the name from Daniela, a Venezuelan childhood friend who'd escaped to Florida two years earlier. Daniela had been following Milagros's articles on *Scofflaw* and had recognized her name in the murkiest recesses of her mind, she said, a bell finally clanging: *I once knew this girl.* For Milagros's part, she recognized Daniela's name once she'd said she was Carmen's daughter: Carmen, the nurse who'd been Milagros's mother's dearest friend in Venezuela. Daniela is thirty-two now, two years older than Milagros, and although Milagros knows they would have been playmates in Venezuela, she retains only a hazy memory of this camaraderie, just like everything else related to the country of her birth.

Daniela's text had arrived at 6:00 a.m., marginally too early for Milagros's synapses. She was still wrapped in her bedsheets while Juanita puttered around, trying quietly to get herself, and her coffee, ready. Blurry-eyed, Milagros squinted at her phone screen. She listened to the coffee machine change gears. In about an hour Juanita would come in with her clippers and shave Milagros's hair down to the scalp, then kiss its crown. It had become a ritual to start the work week. Juanita had asked to cut Milagros's hair on Sunday evenings instead, but Milagros had demanded Monday mornings.

Milagros wondered how torturous her sleep acrobatics had been the night before. Whether she'd whimpered. Whether Juanita had ended up holding her from thrashing about like she was in the throes of an exorcism. Lately, Milagros's dreams of her mother had been suffocating. She would have considered them fever dreams if she'd been ill. In one dream she stood on a beach, and in every direction she turned—toward the ocean's horizon, up toward a cliff, toward a grouping of caves—her mother stood and said, "I am still searching for you," or "I am with you," or "I love you, Mila." She never shared the dreams in the morning. She wasn't ready. So began the continual lies of no longer remembering her dreams. For all her trouble with slumber, Milagros was condemned to it throughout the night, never woke even through her sleep-time malevolence.

Her attention drifts back to the phone in her hand.

Fortunato is the man you want to talk to in Caracas about missing persons.

Talk to about finding missing persons, Milagros wonders, *or talk to about disappearing them?* Lots of folks were trying to escape Venezuela these days, and here is Milagros attempting to sneak in. She'd read a recent account about former members of the U.S. military—now soldiers of fortune—who'd slipped in to unseat the president and had been captured and imprisoned as spies. A couple of years before that, all American diplomats had been expelled. None of this could be a good sign, so she planned to use her Grenadian passport to travel and to keep her U.S. permanent resident card tucked out of sight.

She is afraid she knows what will happen when she gets there: Talk to this man Ebrahim Fortunato, who knows this man, who can put you in touch with this man. And so on. Infinite regression. Fortunatos all the way down. And all in search of Grecia, a mother who Milagros hadn't seen in over fifteen years, and who might not even be in Venezuela—might not, as hard as it was to even think the words, even be alive—but who Daniela thought might be. Hoped. And based on just this, Milagros was willing to fly into a country she hadn't seen in almost two decades.

Hope is the thing with feathers.

Juanita peered into the bedroom. Grinned. "You're up," she said. She lifts the window it as far as it goes—thankfully for Milagros, only a few inches. She doesn't yet want Brooklyn's heat, or smells, or sounds. Still, Flatbush Avenue's jazz music enters: the car horns' trumpets, the subway's percussion, the patter of street conversation.

Juanita turns on the clippers and all the bees in its hive line up. "You'll be great," Juanita says. "Saskia doesn't want to lose you. She'll want to say yes." The bees drone and Milagros's hair falls to the ground. Juanita etches three neat lines into Milagros's temple and kisses the top of her head.

Now, just as Milagros is leaving the apartment, Daniela texts again.

Maldonado's Fortunato's lieutenant. Here's his number. Be careful. And good luck.

In searching for Grecia, Milagros feels like a cliché, some Dickensian waif, a Victorian stereotype. Daniela's unexpected appearance in her life, her texts, hasn't helped. When Daniela had first reached out, she'd said that Grecia had been in touch with her own mother, Carmen, in a recent phone call. Carmen had been showing symptoms of early onset dementia, Daniela said, but inventing interactions wasn't a symptom. Milagros sat on the information for a few weeks. Allowed it to percolate. She'd tried, fruitlessly, to locate her mother before, with each new dead end more sterile than the last. These breadcrumbs renewed Milagros's vigor. She did due diligence on social media sites, called a few people, even rang a Venezuelan politician who'd been interviewed in the *Times.* All dead ends. By now, Milagros has realized that if she wants to uncover any truth, much less find her mother, she needs boots on the ground.

She's already sitting at her desk by the time Daniela follows up with Maldonado's contact info.

Can't Fortunato just take my call himself? Milagros texts.

Good luck with that, Daniela replies. *The man is a fossil.*

And he'll have information about my mother?

He has information about everyone in Caracas. If she's there, he'll know.

And he'll meet with me?

"Milagros?" Saskia says, and Milagros looks up. "You wanted to meet?" Saskia Jones-Hollingsworth is a woman who seems to have based her look upon a template for "editor"—a splash of gray forelock, smarty-pants tortoise glasses, statement necklace—and made it her own with chunky rings paired with a precise Smith education and sometimes a paisley jacket. Now Saskia, who carries a few extra pounds and is always adjusting her diet, has added a vape pipe and an Afghan draped across her shoulders to her repertoire.

Where're the knitting needles? Milagros wonders as she follows Saskia into her office, feeling a bit like she's been sent to see the principal. So many people have helped Milagros to this point, but Saskia is the most recent and the most prominent, and this isn't going to be a small ask. It's Saskia who had hired Milagros as a *Scofflaw* intern and then had sponsored her for a green card, swearing on all the necessary documents that only Milagros Alzola owned the specialized skills necessary to perform her duties. Saskia's husband, Wils, smoothed out the application lumps, paying for an immigration attorney whose tailored outfits cost what Milagros paid in monthly rent. Milagros had been worried about her undocumented status all throughout college, but the lawyer had just sighed and said that any undocumented person could achieve immunity with the right guardian angel.

Scofflaw was originally a vanity project funded by Wils's hedge fund work. "What does Wils care about a few million," Saskia once confided in Milagros, "as long as I'm happy?" The magazine began as a lifestyle publication for hipsters, counseling on everything from beekeeping on your brownstone roof and how to microbrew small batch beer to how to spin sugar for bespoke desserts, but Saskia, who's both editor and publisher, has been expanding, and it's become something of an actual news publication. Even so, when Milagros makes her request, after Saskia's eyebrows come back down, she surprises Milagros with how plugged in she is to Latin American politics. *Going to Venezuela? At a time like this? Does Milagros know who is in charge of the country? Does she know what crime is like in Caracas?* Saskia sounds like a state department bulletin. She quotes crime statistics. Kidnapping numbers. Murder rates. She quotes lyrics from "Reuters," the first track on Wire's *Pink Flag* album, and the hairs on Milagros's arm bend the wrong way at the words about correspondents reporting on food shortages, crime spikes, and rape. This, Milagros knows, is meant to establish Saskia's odd baseline of concern. Still, she remains unfazed.

"I'm trying to find my mother," Milagros says.

A pause. "Oh," Saskia says.

The second volley of queries is more considered. "I've been toying with turning *Scofflaw* toward grittier fare," Saskia admits. "A little more steel in its scoliotic spine. Venezuela wouldn't have been my first choice, but why kick kismet in the shins?"

Milagros wagers this impending pivot is meant to have *Scofflaw*'s articles better reflect the magazine's Atlantic Avenue neighborhood, with its Arabic markets and gentle denizens. She lets Saskia talk, and her proposal—to report on her trip and write first-person from Venezuela—expands on its own: a Wils fellowship, a healthy per diem, a smartphone for guerilla-style filming online content that could be splashed on *Scofflaw*'s website. Milagros suspects Saskia wants newsy travel writing, but inwardly she vows to deliver her unvarnished experience. The ease of it sticks in Milagros's craw. Saskia warns Milagros not to travel directly to Venezuela, partly because Milagros doesn't quite look like a Venezuelan (*what does a Venezuelan look like?*) but instead like what she is—a Black American.

"Not an American," Milagros says. "A legal resident."

Saskia shrugs. A difference without distinction. Milagros cringes. She has another concern she wants to voice, namely trodding on the toes of Elise, a firebrand colleague who visits exotic locales and catalogs her experiences in *Scofflaw*. Elise is recently back from Cabo San Lucas, and rumor is that she's being headhunted by other online media outlets. Rumor further suggests that Elise is on thin ice with *Scofflaw* if she keeps up her flirtation.

Milagros raises the worry carefully. "I'm concerned about it looking like a soft coup," Milagros says. In Milagros's estimation, Elise has never liked her, and the feeling is mutual. But Milagros doesn't want her trip to Venezuela to be an easy log to add to that adversarial fire. Saskia again waves away Milagros's misgivings. Now that she has made up her mind, these are speed bumps barely worth acknowledgment.

"A coup? This is shadow boxing, kiddo," Saskia says, grimacing at her cold coffee. She sets it down. Reaches for her pipe. "Wait till you get to Latin America."

Although skeptical of Saskia's badgering, Milagros doesn't head directly to Venezuela. Instead, she flies first to Brazil, and files *Scofflaw* stories that focus on the favelas, which compete with Venezuela's as the largest on the continent, shantytowns full of young children half-clothed. Emaciated stray dogs existing either as timid singletons or in crafty aggressive packs. Milagros doesn't mind filing these stories about Brazil—the more light that can be cast on dilemmas in South America the better—but doing them about Venezuela unsettles her.

Saskia's pleased with the first salvo and its response from both established subscribers and an uptick of the newly curious, who have sent letters to the editor saying that more U.S.-based news outlets need to have correspondents providing this kind of truth—how the U.S. sanctions are really hurting civilians. She wants Milagros to dig deeper, to uncover more human interest stories. "The grittier," Saskia says, "the better." Saskia sends Milagros more money with a command to *take a taxi to Venezuela, kiddo*, and she feels like the worst kind of spy, one there to sell out her own people for a clutch of silver ingots.

By the time that Milagros hires a taxi willing to drive her to the Venezuelan border for an exorbitant sum, she's been in regular contact with Ricardo Maldonado, Fortunato's lieutenant, whose texts arrive in dot-dot-dash aridity. Milagros tries to call Maldonado a couple of times, but he never picks up the phone. *Busy lieutenant*, she thinks.

She's already in Colombia when Juanita finally connects. She's like this, easily out of touch. Milagros tells her where she is, what she's doing. "Haven't overthrown the palace yet?" Juanita jokes. Or at least Milagros hopes that she's joking. It can be hard to tell with Juanita.

Milagros holds her breath as she hands over her Grenadian passport, but there are no issues crossing into the land of her birth.

At the hotel she collapses on the bed.

The room's view, as high as a hawk's nest, staggers. *Scofflaw*'s footing the bill and, at U.S. $225 a night, it's pricier than Milagros had expected, although she's told that it costs more now than it would have before the country pegged its currency to the U.S. dollar. An email from Saskia tells her that she'd booked the room for a week, but the reservation could be easily extended. Milagros doesn't doubt it.

The hotel's as busy as a mausoleum. Venezuela, in its current state, is no longer a top tier tourist destination. She gazes at the favelas in the distance. Technically, Milagros is home, but she doesn't know how to feel. Or, rather, she's inundated with emotions—wonder, guilt (survivor's and standard transmission), and hope, and she doesn't know how to disentangle them. Her memories of the country are so brief, so telescoped into the past, that they feel like she's borrowed them from someone else. She thought that she would feel something when she entered the country which would tell her whether her mother's here, but no sixth sense tips her off. Milagros accosts the room's minibar, cracks open miniature bottles of whiskey, and returns to the window.

Time moves differently here.

Viz.: Dusk starts as a slow kabuki dance, and then someone flicks a switch and it's night. The lights of Caracas are a wonder. Buoys that bob on the ocean. Strings of light that twinkle on the mountainside. Just as Milagros is about to turn in for the night, her phone chimes. She expects it to be from Juanita, or maybe Saskia, but it's Daniela, responding to a text Milagros had sent days ago on arriving in South America. *Welcome home*, she says. She's also sent a photograph of Fortunato. Fuzzy. An old man with gray hair ringing his bald pate, bushy eyebrows. *Harmless old fart*, Milagros thinks, stifling a yawn. She silences her phone. Saskia is known to send a volley of emails late at night. But it's unnecessary: all that night as Milagros thinks about Grecia and a possible reunion, sleep remains a fugitive.

In the morning, Milagros inspects Saskia's emails while she has a room-service breakfast. *Exciting Times!* is Saskia's most recent subject line. The Brazilian dispatches have gotten more hits than anything else this month. When Milagros replies to the email, Saskia calls. She's already batting around the idea of sending Milagros to world hot spots and making this a regular monthly feature. What does Milagros think? Milagros grimaces. "I think traveling's Elise's beat."

"Elise's beat is body shots, bathrobes, and bikinis," Saskia says. "Consider it, kiddo."

Milagros hops the elevator, walks the streets around the hotel. A feeling of unease dogs her the entire way.

Returning to her room, Milagros taps out the draft of a new article about her initial thoughts about Venezuela from the perspective of someone who's been away for a while. It demonstrates the tone of a mopey memoir, and she deletes all of it. She's refrained from going to the *Scofflaw* site, afraid of how Saskia might have framed and edited her Brazilian experiences. Dodgy headlines spring to mind: OUR WOMAN IN THE SOUTH AMERICA WILDS, NATIVE DAUGHTER RETURNS, THE REAL BRASILIA. Milagros is wary. In this climate Venezuela doesn't look kindly on U.S. or U.S.-adjacent journalists, especially those who weren't welcomed through the front door. Luckily, she has an excuse to ignore all of it: Wi-Fi, even at this fancy hotel, can be a flicker. She's staring out the window when a text from Maldonado rattles her phone.

Meet me at Cemeterio General del sur @ the grave of Sanchez. Around 4 p.m.

Milagros clarifies: *Ishmael Sanchez?*

4 p.m.

Christ, thinks Milagros. *So dramatic.*

She calls Juanita. "Your pillow still smells like you. And I slept in your boxers last night," Juanita confesses.

Desire momentarily claims Milagros, and she is jarred when her phone vibrates again. She quickly reads an email from Saskia. Elise has taken a job at Condé Nast. "The world is your oyster, kiddo."

Milagros remembers visiting the cemetery with her mother decades earlier. It was about two days before they'd fled to the island. Grecia had wanted, in her words, "to pay homage" to the Santos Malandros, to lobby them for maritime protection on their journey. *But why the need for makeup?* Milagros wondered. *The wine-red lipstick? Having her hair done? Had she meant to flirt with the thugs' statues?* Looking back on the trip, grief washes over Milagros followed by unexpected embarrassment, in part because she knows how things turned out: her mother had put her trust in the fairy dust of faith, then things went pear-shaped on the island, and now where was Grecia?

The hotel secures Milagros an unmarked taxi with a friendly driver named Hidalgo. Somewhere in his midtwenties, Hidalgo has startlingly white teeth. He's drinking aguardiente, and he offers Milagros a bottle that she gently declines.

Milagros peers at the city as the taxi whisks her to the cemetery. At highway stoplights, young men, stripped to the waist, their heads swaddled in T-shirts wrapped like turbans, hold aloft bottled water for sale. Others hoist bags of oranges. Milagros has committed an app's route to the cemetery, and the cemetery's layout, to memory, and when Hidalgo breaks off from the path offering the shortest distance, she stiffens. "Where are we going?" she asks.

Hidalgo addresses her in the rearview mirror. "Gasolina, miss." A glance at the gauge corroborates his claim. At the gas station Hidalgo moves quickly—gas tank, gas pump, and a terse interaction with the attendant in a booth. Milagros tenses. He spends a few moments in brisk conversation, but their Spanish exchange is too rapid-fire for Milagros to nail down after so many years away, the accent more slippery than she recalls. As the two men part she watches Hidalgo hand over a few cigarettes. When the car pulls off off she asks Hidalgo about his family who, she presumes, are the brightly smiling people in the photograph pinned to his visor. "Not so good," he says, and shrugs. His three-year-old daughter needs brain surgery.

"Do you think of leaving? To get help for her somewhere else?"

He shakes his head. "I have four brothers in Colombia, so I have somewhere to go, but for now I stay. We'll see if we can get it done here. Maybe someone will help me." Something unsettles Milagros about this ride, about Hidalgo, but she can't pin it down. Nothing sacred or profane swings from the rearview. The seats are clean. The car doesn't smell. She's just jumpy. Reporter instincts gone haywire. Her missing Juanita.

At the gates of the cemetery Hidalgo tells her that they're here, and he apologetically refuses Milagros's offer of more money to drive her inside. Still, when Milagros offers a weighty tip as she exits, he scribbles his phone number on a card and says whenever she calls he'll return within ten minutes.

She's arrived fifteen minutes before the meeting time, both to measure the cemetery's safety and in case Maldonado arrives early. Afraid to retrieve her phone—Hidalgo's warnings of cemetery muggings give her pause—Milagros navigates her way to the shrine using the map in her mind. There aren't many people, and Milagros wonders if this is bad or good. She gets lost, spies a woman cleaning a grave and adding flowers, asks to be pointed in the right direction, and receives instructions that she hopes are legitimate. "Say a prayer to Petroleo Crudo for me," adds the woman, and Milagros wonders if it's a crack about her complexion. Her shaved head. As she makes her way among the grave sites Milagros briefly ponders if her own mother may be buried here. She banishes the thought.

At the shrine there's a small cluster of five or six people. The air is fragrant with tobacco. A woman smokes a cigar, bends over, taps her hands on the aqua tiles beneath her feet, claps her hands, puffs acrid smoke, ignores Milagros. Inside the shrine stand various three-foot-tall plaster figures of the thugs, all of them exhibiting sunglasses, sporting pistols on their belts, and wearing ball caps turned sideways. Their hands remain pocketed. Milagros knows drips and drabs about their mythology and about the people who revere these saints. People with family in prison pray to them. Those seeking revenge as well. Those seeking safe passage.

Ten feet away a boy smokes a cigarette midway, then sticks it between the lips of one of the statues. The woman with the cigar moves toward one of the statues, lights a blue candle, holds it upside down so some of the wax drips and melts beside the figure, and plants the candle in the wet wax at the statue's feet. She talks to Milagros without looking at her. "Someone killed my son," she says. "He was fifteen." She turns her head and spits. "I'm praying that the murderer dies a painful death."

At any religious site the most interesting are the agnostic. There. Milagros observes the man in his late twenties with a buzz cut and a sketchbook, sitting on a stone bench ten feet away from the woman praying for death for her son's killers. He makes quick strokes. The true believers amuse him.

The artist's lap serves as an unsteady easel. He's as thin as a scratch. Milagros snaps a couple of surreptitious pictures of him on her phone, then returns to mentally composing a story about her trip—the tomb-like hotel, Hidalgo, the worshippers. Every now and then she tilts her head, takes in the artist, and after a few moments, the man senses her gaze and swivels toward her. She issues an awkward I-come-in-peace wave and walks away to write down what she's mentally drafted. At ten minutes past four, Milagros texts Maldonado. She receives no reply. She's just about to text Hidalgo to retrieve her when she feels a shadow across her shoulders.

"You're a writer." The artist has shut his sketchbook, tucked it beneath his arm. "I can tell," he says. "It's in how you hold your neck." *Lousy pickup line*, thinks Milagros. He's lean, and a satchel hangs off his shoulders. His eyes are a little too big for his thin face. His cheeks are pocked.

"You look like a writer too," she says.

He shrugs. "A poor poet," he replies. "But a half-decent artist." He taps his sketch pad. Displays his impression of the woman seeking vengeance for her son. A fair likeness. He has captured her rage. He sticks his sketchbook into his satchel. "You're also American." He doesn't seem to mean it as an accusation, although at first it scans as one.

"I'm a reporter," Milagros says.

He joins his hands together and offers a slight bow. "The most important people in Venezuela today," he says. "My name is Velasco." A hearse glides past, a few other vehicles trailing behind it.

Velasco points out a young woman with a pixie haircut praying at the shrine, his partner, Johanna. Also thin, she looks even more of an artist than he does, both of them of the starving variety. Milagros doesn't ask what she's praying for. Just then a passel of motorcycles appears in the wake of the hearse, low-throated, backfiring, ripsnorting. Some of the riders, Milagros notes, are armed. All wear either ball caps tugged low, bandanas stretched across their faces, or full helmets with dark visors deployed. Seeing them, Velasco urgently calls out to Johanna, and she makes her way toward them.

Just as she arrives, the *pak-pak-pak* of automatic gunfire fire from one of the motorcyclists punctures the air. Everyone at the shrine ducks, screams, then scatters. Milagros crouches into an awkward duck-and-cover run, but she's barely taken two steps when she feels Velasco's hand on her arm. "Please," he says. "It's safer to wait." He pulls Milagros toward the statues, and Johanna joins them. They all crouch into a huddle. The shrine's devotees scatter across the cemetery, a flock of startled birds. The motorcycles crawl past, and there's no additional fire; the short bursts are just salutes to announce their presence.

"No license plates," Milagros notes as the motorcycles depart.

"Yes," Velasco says. "But it wouldn't matter if they'd had them." He shakes his head, shrugs. "Who's going to push back? Who's going to hold them accountable?"

"Pero el poder está en la calle," Milagros says.

"A journalist *and* a dreamer." Velasco smiles. It lessens the pockmarks' power, renders him boyish. "But words don't fill stomachs," he says.

Johanna says, "Once, the motorcycle riders were of the community. Now they're cowards times two—they shoot at the helpless, and they wear masks while they do it."

"Johanna," Velasco says. Her close-cropped hair is ink-black. She and Milagros shake hands, then Velasco pulls Johanna's head into a fierce hug against his chest and kisses her forehead. He says that although he doesn't think anything else will happen, that the motorcyclists were just signaling respect for the dead, that they should leave.

Milagros pulls out her phone. Velasco asks her what she's doing. "Calling my taxi. The person I was meeting never showed up." The couple exchange a look.

"Come have dinner with us," Johanna urges. "He can pick you up afterward." The threat, Milagros understands, has not passed, and no taxi will come for her. Hidalgo is in the wind.

Milagros considers the couple and their offer. Her intuition remains quiet. She hopes her journalist instinct has recalibrated. She accepts.

On a small stove grimed with use, Velasco tends a wok containing stir-fried vegetables. He adds meat that snaps and pops in the oil's heat. He expertly tosses the wok's contents, browning everything evenly. The couple lives on the upper floor of a ramshackle duplex with art canvasses scattered throughout. One painting, reminiscent of Francis Bacon's mode of the macabre, displays a grief-stricken man holding his head in his hands. Standing in the small apartment's kitchen, Milagros spies, through a slightly open door, a bedroom with a broken-down futon as a bed. The kitchen itself is as tight as a clenched fist, and only half-painted; someone seems to have abandoned the cheerful yellow in midstroke. Johanna sees her noticing and hugs herself diffidently, but a wellspring of affection surges through Milagros for this couple. "What's Velasco cooking?" Milagros asks, hoping to diffuse Johanna's embarrassment. "It smells amazing."

Johanna matches Milagros's smile, and she seats them at a small table pushed up against a wall. "He cooks for us every night since I returned three years ago."

"She ran off to the States," Velasco says, his forehead sweating from his culinary efforts. "Madwoman."

"For school?"

"An au pair. I wanted to strengthen my English." Johanna's English, Milagros notes, is flawless.

"I missed her every day," Velasco admits. "I would text her, email her, even write her letters."

Johanna scrunches her nose. "But when I lived here, I could barely see him."

"I was working three jobs to buy a flat." Velasco lowers the flame beneath the wok, then goes over and kisses Johanna on the cheek. Milagros's mind reaches for Juanita.

Velasco returns to the stove and shuts off the flame, then pours out the wok's contents into a large mixing bowl.

"What are we eating?" Milagros asks again.

"Have you had sopa de modongo?" Joanna asks.

Milagros recalls the taste of tripe and searches both of their faces to see if they're kidding. They're not. Johanna hands her a spoon and squares of paper towels as napkins. Gracious hosts, they wait for Milagros to venture the first bite. Milagros lowers her spoon. The first bite crackles with heat. She says it's great.

As they eat, Velasco asks Milagros why she was at the shrine. She hesitates but then reveals her meeting with Maldonado and Fortunato. "It's for an article." She watches the couple's postures stiffen at the names. "They're trouble?" she asks.

"Gangsters," Velasco says. Both hosts remain silent and focus on their food.

Milagros waits, and finally, Johanna says, "Maldonado used to run his own gang before he joined Ebrahim Fortunato."

"Him and his little brother, Pedro," Velasco says.

"*Used* to?"

"They were petty thieves and extortionists, mostly," Johanna says. "Bloodthirsty, sometimes. But they stuck to a few neighborhoods."

"A few neighborhoods but were growing wild and getting worse," Velasco says. He rubs his chin. His stubble crackles.

"Directionless," Johanna clarifies.

"For how long?" Milagros asks.

"Two years?" Velasco says. "Three?"

"But then Maldonado quit," says Johanna.

"Just like that?" Milagros asks.

The couple goes momentarily quiet. Velasco leans in. The walls have ears. "Ebrahim wanted to fold these young malandros into his own gang. Especially Ricardo and Pedro. They refused."

"They were brash," Johanna says. "Headstrong."

"Ebrahim wouldn't take no for an answer." Velasco pauses. Milagros waits for him to continue. "They say Ebrahim invited Ricardo over for a meal."

"To discuss power sharing," Johanna adds.

"The meal goes fine, but Ricardo is still not interested in the offer to join forces."

"Ebrahim shrugs. Tells him to think it over. Takes him to the verandah for cigars and brandy and to inspect the potential wealth that a partnership could afford. To see the extent of his empire."

"In a field behind Ebrahim's house, Ricardo watches some of Ebrahim's foot soldiers playing football," Johanna says. She pauses and looks to Velasco. They're measuring Milagros.

"They had killed Pedro. Ricardo didn't know. They were using Pedro's head as the ball," Velasco says. Milagros manages not to flinch, but her skin prickles.

They switch topics, and continue chatting for a bit, mainly about Venezuela's crumbling economy, but the horror of Pedro's decapitation sucks the air from the room and, fifteen minutes later, Milagros, abruptly exhausted, announces that she wants to return to her hotel. Her desire to flee isn't all mental—her stomach just now gurgles. Hopefully not the tripe.

"I'll give you a lift," Velasco says.

She shakes her head. "There's no need." She raises one of her two phones. "I'll call a taxi."

Velasco issues a simple shrug. "Let me drive you back to the hotel," he insists. "No taxi will come tonight."

He's right. Fifteen minutes earlier, Milagros had briefly excused herself to the bathroom and texted Hidalgo. She still hasn't received a response.

Velasco's car is low on gas, so he steps out briefly to borrow his neighbor's. While they wait, Johanna leads Milagros to the small, cluttered living room. There's an acoustic guitar. A sewing machine. They inspect more of Velasco's paintings. "Are they for sale?" Milagros asks.

"Some," Johanna says. "He's very shy about his work and doesn't like to part with it." Then, out of the corner of her eye, opposite the paintings, there's a small shrine, replete with candles and an altar, but instead of the Holy Thugs, the miniature statue is a muscled goddess astride a tapir.

Johanna watches Milagros inspect it. "I didn't tell him the complete truth about living in America," Johanna says suddenly. "My host family treated me very poorly. Longer hours than I should have worked. Didn't pay me on time. Didn't feed me properly. They said that fruit, bread, and milk were too expensive. 'Buy food or something else,' they said." She hugs herself once again.

Milagros doesn't peg Johanna as someone to stretch facts. She notes to pitch a story about au pair abuse to Saskia.

"I reached out to your state department to complain," Johanna continues.

"*My* state department?" Milagros had provided them a quick outline of her life, including having spent her childhood in Venezuela, but clearly they don't view her as a native.

Johanna smiles wryly. Milagros asks her what the child she took care of was like. Johanna brightens. "Lovely," she says. "Absolutely lovely." Milagros asks if she can interview her for an article about her experience, that she'll pay her. Quotes a figure that's too large for the magazine's usual compensation, but she knows Saskia is a soft touch at this point and will greenlight anything. The figure Milagros quotes lights up Johanna's face, and she clutches both of Milagros's hands. *Gas for the car at least*, Milagros thinks. *Gratitude for this meal.* They arrange to meet at the hotel for lunch in two days.

Back at the hotel Milagros assesses an email from Bunny. She hasn't heard from her in months, not since Bunny disappeared down a rabbit hole to Japan. Their relationship had been shaky then, as it had for many years, and Milagros hadn't tried that hard to keep in touch. Bunny had done her best, but both of them knew that at the heart of Milagros's existence was trying to find out what had happened to her mother, trying to reconnect with her. When she'd first started college, Milagros had worked hard to find her. Called the Venezuelan embassy. Reached out to journalists online and on social media sites. Found nothing. She'd fallen mostly out of touch with Bunny around the same time. Now, she feels both guilty and relieved to see the email. The subject line is simple: *Married!* But the email's a tome, and

Milagros is too exhausted to start it. Promises herself she'll read all of it the next day. Crawls into bed. Promises herself she'll call Juanita in the morning too.

That night Milagros dreams of a U.S. citizenship naturalization ceremony that has yet to occur. Everyone has brought family members with them to the courtroom. Grecia stands beside her. It's the clearest that Milagros has seen her mother's face in years of dreams. Everyone rises when the judge enters the courtroom. The judge says that they're going to be led in the Pledge of Allegiance by a little girl whose parents were themselves immigrants. Before the little girl begins, the judge, who Milagros sees now is Venezuelan, asks each naturalization candidate to stand and say which country they're from originally. Various countries are announced: Barbados, Iran, Turkey. When it's her turn, Milagros cannot speak. She doesn't know where she's from. She's forgotten. The judge grows irate. *Where are you from?* she asks. *Where are you from?* Milagros turns to her mother for help, but Grecia morphs first into Saskia, then Juanita, then Bunny as Medusa. Her long snake locs are sinuous and threatening.

As the little girl starts to recite the Pledge of Allegiance, Milagros watches as the child's neck, bit by bit, stretches at the back of her head, before her chin topples forward and her skull completely detaches from her body. The room of soon-to-be Americans scream. Milagros turns to the judge, who herself has transformed: she's now a muscular, topless woman sitting atop a tapir holding a pelvis above her head. The judge, her eyes now burning, asks Milagros, "Where are you *from*?" She's about to launch the pelvis when Milagros wakes up shivering.

Sweat soaked.

She tosses off the covers, shuts off the air conditioner, gulps a glass of water from the bathroom sink, inspects the dark beneath her eyes, then takes in Caracas at night. *What do you expect with an experimental dinner*, she tells herself. She checks her phone. Nothing from Maldonado, but there's four emails from Saskia and one missed text from Juanita: *Thinking of you, mi amor.* Milagros sighs and returns to bed.

In the morning, Milagros inspects the stubble on her head. It has grown in faster than she'd expected, but she doesn't have her clippers with her. Her stomach still sears. She calls to the front desk for a hamburger with fries and a side of aspirin, her go-to cure for an upset stomach, and while she waits she scans Bunny's email. She fell head over heels in love with a guy named Yoshi who she met in Kyoto. He's Caribbean-Japanese. They're moving back to New Felicity. *Good for Bunny*, she thinks, promising herself to reply later. Bunny is trying; she deserves a long response, even if Milagros will have to swallow some discomfort to do it. Then Milagros emails Saskia, who replies right away that the au pair story sounds fantastic. Next, Milagros texts Juanita: *I hope you washed those boxers.* She adds a smiley face. The meal arrives, but Milagros's stomach bucks and she can't eat it. She downs just the aspirin.

Milagros is flicking around midmorning television when her phone chimes. It's Maldonado.

Got held up yesterday.

Busy times in Caracas.

Shrine of the Holy Thugs. 2 p.m.

Milagros thinks to ignore him, thinks to cut her losses, thinks to bask in her new friendship with Johanna and Velasco, thinks whether she should try to see Carmen even though Daniela has said her mind's like a scattering of jacks. Then she swallows and tries to remember Grecia's face from her dream. She'll meet Maldonado. Impulsively, as she leaves, she pockets the knife that came with the meal.

Hildalgo drives her to the cemetery once more. He's just as nervous. He does not make the offer to pick her up as she exits the car. The cemetery is quieter today. As she stands at the shrine Milagros hears motorcycles approach, motorized bees that finally settle into a permanent hum. They're different bikes than yesterday, and these aren't following a funeral procession. There are seven motorcycles in all. Like those from the day before, there are no license plates, no identifiers, but she is somehow certain that this time it's Maldonado.

The lead bike pulls up beside her, and the rider flips up the helmet's visor. "Private security detail," he says. "Here to take you to your meeting."

Milagros hesitates, suddenly developing cold feet.

"Come on, flaca," the man sighs. He removes his helmet. Ricardo Maldonado looks like he hasn't slept in a month. He's older than she would have thought, in his midfifties, and his shaved head, she has to admit, suits him. Even the scar through one eyebrow looks like it was added for a film shoot, and his shadowed eyes recall the tale that Velasco and Johanna told her about his brother. There's something familiar about him. Milagros folds her arms across her chest. "I'm not sure," she says.

Maldonado revs the engine with a turn of a wrist and all the other motorcycles rev in salute. "And I'm not sure about you," he replies. "You're a reporter who can write basura about us and have the police kneel on our necks, but Ebrahim agreed to see you and here I am." He scowls. She remains apprehensive. "Oye, muñeca. Do you want hand signals? Code words? An engraved invitation?"

Milagros bristles. "Yes," she says. "All three."

Maldonado sighs. Raises a hand, and the hum of the swarm of motorcycles behind him lessens. "Milagros Alzola. Please come with me to meet Ebrahim Fortunato to discuss your mother, Grecia." Milagros flinches. Hearing her mother's name said by this man buckles her knees. "Last chance," he says. He hands her a helmet.

Milagros climbs on behind him.

* * *

Included among the items on a reverse bucket list that Milagros has constructed over the years are a vow never to skydive, never to white-water raft, and never to ride on the back of a motorcycle, but lo, here she is. Riding on the back of Maldonado's motorcycle, gripping his hips, is exactly as unsettling as Milagros would expect, the ride introducing her to every diligent pothole on offer. She feels the jolts in her spine. The noise, she imagines, is what it's like to navigate a hurricane's cockpit.

Before they pulled off, Maldonado said they were headed to a mountaintop view of both the ocean and Caracas. It's a ridiculous trip aboard a ridiculous vehicle, but as they climb, Milagros swoons at the view: even better than at the hotel. Soon the temperature drops, and she shivers and clutches Maldonado's waist tighter. After forty-five minutes they arrive at a flat, tiled outdoor space. Weeds populate the edges and cracks of the ceramic squares. From crumbling bits of wall along the borders, Milagros estimates that there was once a cluster of buildings that occupied this space, but they're lost now. All that remains are vestiges of knocked-down walls and this distressed dance floor. The lone building still at the site, mustard yellow and about twenty-five feet away, is by contrast, well maintained.

Maldonado dismounts, helps her off. "Come," he says, and she follows him to the cliff. She stands far enough away from him so that even with a lunge he cannot launch her. The view of Caracas astounds. It's a different perspective to the antiseptic hotel's. The buildings in the distance are lit like Chinese lanterns. A series of gig lamps. He allows her the view for a few moments, not saying anything, seemingly taking a kind of local pride in what his country has to offer beyond the typical outsider's impression of crippling poverty and the roving gangs of which he is a part.

When Milagros finally turns back around, two things catch her eye: one, a fresh grave beside the building, filled in with reddish dirt.

Who? she thinks. The second thing: capybaras. About a dozen. She hadn't seen the knee-high, doglike rodents in years, not since she was on the island, but seeing them now, scattered across the roadway, sends a rubber mallet tapping a xylophone scale down her back. Where did they come from? They're spread out in various locations, grazing on the grass, and their abrupt arrival and silent movement make Milagros think of theater props.

"Come," Maldonado says, crooking an arm toward her, as if she were wearing a shimmering gown and he were about to help her mount tricky steps. "This way." Then, dropping his arm, he walks ahead of her in a pathway cut through overgrown weeds that lead to the building.

As they walk he tells her that the building used to house a park ranger who maintained the grounds, but who is no longer required. *Was it the park ranger in the grave?* They draw closer to the entrance and the smell of cooking greets her. Above the archway someone has hand-painted a line of scripture: SAN JUAN CH. 6 VERSO 35. And above the scripture, a phrase: CASA DE ALIMENTACION. Before they enter the building, Maldonado holds out a palm. When Milagros doesn't respond, he says, "Do you want me to search you?" She hands over the knife, knowing that there's a more dangerous weapon somewhere on him. "Anything else?" She shakes her head.

Inside, they move past a large room with, surprisingly, a dozen children between the ages of maybe seven and ten sitting in a circle and playing a game: slapping each other's hands, the slaps ticking clockwise. They look happy enough. But when Milagros examines them more closely, she pauses. They're all silent. They're not playing a game, but communicating with each other through their hands. She examines the child closest to her, who tilts his head back in silent laughter, and she sees that he has no tongue. Her first thought can't be correct—that these children have been permanently silenced, that all their tongues have been removed. She has read about New Yorkers who dwell in high-rises who have cut their dogs' vocal cords to appease their neighbors' complaints. But surely that can't be the case here.

She moves toward another of the children to ask her to open her mouth, but Maldonado is moving once more, and she follows him to the back of the building. The smell of food heightens, and then they're in a kitchen where two large pots bubble on a stove, a long table beside it. The kitchen is cluttered with food and utensils, and an older woman with muscled arms and gray spiderwebbed through her hair works nimbly, first chopping onions for one pot, then slicing and plating chunks of bread, stirring another pot.

It's here that Milagros notices Fortunato, slightly hunched, scooping soup from one of the pots into multicolored plastic children's bowls laid out on the table. She smirks: Robin Hoodlum, running a soup kitchen for hungry children. "Bienvenidos, Milagros Alzola," he says, his eyes still focused on his task. "Never mind the gossip," he says, "I am only a humble servant of the people." His voice is higher than she expected. Flutelike.

As soon as each bowl is filled, the woman adds bread to it, then shepherds the bowls off on a tray a few at a time to the room that holds the children. Maldonado disappears the way he came. A kettle on the back burner shrieks, and Fortunato shuts off the flame. "Please sit," he says. "I'll make tea."

After all the bowls have been dispatched, Fortunato serves Milagros tea with too much milk. "Here," he says. "Drink."

Milagros receives the teacup but refrains from imbibing. Fortunato wipes his hands on his apron, and finally assesses her. "This way," he says. He leads her to the backyard. No capybaras here. In fact, it's an oasis—almost feels like a different location entirely. Within the high walls there are well-maintained trees, a fountain, a well-kept lawn. Against the wall sit several pots of flowers.

And then, in three different corners of the courtyard, three parrots on stands. No tethers; their wings must be clipped. One of them lifts a leg and scratches his head. Milagros recognizes it as an African Gray. She thinks to ask about the other two, but refrains. Instead, she asks, "Can they talk?"

"Too much," he responds, and feeds one parrot sunflower seeds from a pocket in his apron. The three perches stand about ten feet away from each other, and in the middle of the yard is one large stand on which all three birds could fit. The one perched at the farthest wall flaps its way to the large stand. *If they can fly*, she thinks, *why do they stay?*

"Now," he asks, "how may I help you?" He shifts his focus to a terracotta pot that holds a spray of bright yellow flowers.

"We could have communicated by phone," she says, trying to reconcile what she's learned about this man with the enigmatic figure who stands before her.

His eyes water. There's an odd gleam as well. *Cataracts*, Milagros thinks. "There's no privacy on phones," he says.

Well, fine. Milagros drives directly at the point. "Do you have information about my mother? Her location?"

"What a question," he says. "An arrow straight to the target. Like the policía. Are you policía?" He addresses another bright starburst of flowers cradled in a pot against the second wall. He inspects its leaves. A second parrot flaps across to the large perch.

She tries again. "I'm looking for my mother," she says.

"A quest," he replies. He looks back at her. "Better to look for your father," he says. "He was an interesting character." Milagros shrugs. She never knew her father and she has never been too curious about him, not beyond wondering who he had been to her mother. Then Fortunato says, "No one takes the time to talk anymore." He crouches beside another plant. Pinches off a delinquent leaf. Assesses Milagros with rheumy eyes. *He'll give me nothing*, she thinks, and a fury descends upon her. Heats her palms. She stifles it, breathes deeply, and heads back through the building. An overly dramatic gesture, since she knows she's not going anywhere without the old man's sanction.

Although it was only dusk in the courtyard, out front it's somehow already well into the night, and there's no sign of Maldonado, his minions, or any of the capybaras. Down the mountain, an indifferent Caracas. She returns to the oasis, unnerved, and notices as she walks past the kitchen that the children have gone completely silent. Not even the click of spoons against bowls. They seem to do everything in rhythm, and this unnerves her.

Back outside, Fortunato alights on a stone bench beside the fountain. It is twilight again, and as Milagros looks around suspiciously, she notices how the air vibrates differently around him. The three parrots grip their perches. He points at her. "I knew your grandmother," he says. Milagros grimaces in frustration. The trip feels like a movement through Scheherazade's tales: each time she meets someone else, there's a new chapter on offer.

But Fortunato doesn't offer any information about her grandmother, any wild geese to chase. Instead, he extends a bowl to her. "Stew," he says. She smells it. There's a familiar spice in there that she cannot identify, but she's struck suddenly by the strong feeling that she shouldn't eat or drink anything here. Even though it doesn't make sense, she feels like she'll be trapped forever.

"Let the children have it," she says.

"We have plenty." He shrugs. "It's very good. We herd the capybara ourselves. They are well treated." He sets the bowl beside his feet. On the perch, the three parrots seem to sway in unison from side to side, and somehow it is this that flusters Milagros most of all.

Quietly, she says, "Have Maldonado take me back to my hotel."

And it's here that the old man's body stiffens. He looks at her but she can tell he doesn't see her. Then he begins to speak like he's not there at all. Like he's standing at the cliff's edge. He talks as though he is inspecting Caracas and annotating his surveillance. His eyes unfocus. "I have three things to tell you." Monotone. "Gratis for good souls, gratis for good souls."

Milagros holds her tongue. *Talking aloud*, she thinks, *would be like startling a sleepwalker.*

"Past, present, or future," Ebrahim Fortunato says. Milagros looks around her. No one. Nothing. Just her and the old man. Yet the air feels empty, like a light socket with the bulb removed. "Which order?" he asks. "Which order?"

Milagros looks at the flowers against the wall. Thinks of the cemetery. Wonders again who's in the grave out front.

"Present," Milagros says. She startles when she hears the center parrot speak.

"Be wary of rushing water," the gray parrot advises, "and muddy pathways." The parrot ducks its head and scratches its neck.

The old man's still in a daze, off in cloud cuckoo land.

"Past or future," says Fortunato. "Past or future."

"Past," Milagros says, suppressing what feels like her participation in some Wonderland where children are voiceless but birds are vocal soothsayers. Anything could shoot out these birds' mouths, and she's afraid that they will reveal some intimacy that she wants sunk into the ocean's deepest trench.

Now the first parrot speaks. "The man who brought you here terrorized your mother a long time ago when he worked on the water. He doesn't remember, and neither do you. But he's suffered, and a leash has been clipped to his neck. He's paying his penance." As with the other parrot, this one stops abruptly.

Milagros's heart seizes. *Maldonado? Her mother?* She wants to lean forward and grab Fortunato by the shoulders and shake him for the answer he will not give her, but instead she studies the old man's eyes. He's still far away. "Future," she says.

"You will take a little girl to her mother," the final parrot says.

"What little girl? And what about *my* mother?"

"Take the little girl to her mother in La Parada and find your own way." The parrot fluffs out its bright yellow and blue and green feathers to inflate itself. Then, before Milagros can speak again, the power cut is over and the light sparks back in Maldonado's eyes. He cricks his neck. "Perdóname señorita," he says. "But what were we talking about?"

The backyard is an oasis, but the building's a haunted house, a repository for parents who fear the worst. All the children are gone and the muscled woman as well—so silently and thoroughly that it is as though they were never there at all, but they could all be stashed in a closet, as silent as regret. Past the sighing front door's rusty hinges, night has again battened down the hatches. It's later than it should be. Milagros rethinks the parrots' preachings and what to make of them. A chill wind goosefleshes her arms, even with the jacket, and she hugs herself. The wind bites harder. The wind isn't hungry, it's insatiable. Milagros shivers, wishes for a knit hat. Present, future: she doesn't know what these mean. But past—a bit of forgotten confetti falling from the rafters, and she knows at once that it's the truth: If Fortunato deals in the transportation of people out of Venezuela, then Milagros and her mother had been his clients all those years ago, and maybe he knows where Grecia is now. Maybe he has done something awful to silence her, as with the children, but maybe she's still alive somewhere. And if Maldonado had hurt her mother, he was the one who had betrayed them.

Out front, Hidalgo waits beside his car, parked where the motorcycles had previously posed like gaunt chrome insects. "Where to, miss?" he asks. The air pickles her skin. *More*, the wind demands. *More*.

"How far to La Parada?" she asks, thinking of the parrot's words.

"On the Colombian border," he says. "Very far."

She tightens her folded arms. Enough. There is no little girl to take to her mother here, only herself, an overgrown girl who wants her own mami. "Take me back to my hotel, then."

"Perdóname, miss. I can only take you to La Parada," he says apologetically. "Per the boss."

"But you asked where to."

He only shrugs. "Per the boss."

Thoughts conduct calisthenics and jumping jacks in Milagros's head. Maldonado and Fortunato and Velasco and Johanna and Hidalgo. *More*, demands the wind. *More.* Milagros covers her ears, stoops to cut down on the air current's demands. Frustration chokes her. "Take me away from here," she says softly.

"I cannot take you without the package," Hidalgo apologizes. He tilts his head toward the building. "Please, miss."

Now Milagros wants to cry. Her phone screen is black, the battery exhausted. No Juanita, no Saskia, no Bunny, not even Daniela. She's an orphan atop a hill at the mercy of a gangster's parrots. She's an inverted Alice, up a mountain rather than down a rabbit hole. "The package," Hidalgo repeats gently.

Milagros drinks in the city's lights. Somewhere down there's her hotel. She reenters the house. Where it had just previously been empty, now one child remains. Maybe six years old. A bloated backpack clings to her shoulders. Milagros gingerly relieves the girl's burden without pushback. It's heavier than Milagros would have expected, packed tight. She searches for a way in, but the zippers resist. *There could be anything in there, Pandora*, she warns herself. *But would something dangerous be strapped to a child? Don't answer that.* Milagros can't leave the girl behind. Milagros knows that no one, and nothing, will return to this site, not even a stray capybara. What will happen to a child who lacks the most important ability, to cry out when in danger?

Milagros must deliver the package. “Come, mija,” she says. “Take us to La Parada,” she tells Hidalgo. She holds the girl’s hand tightly as she guides her into the car’s back seat.

“First,” Hidalgo says, holding out an envelope. “Señor Fortunato asked me to give this to you.”

Although she hasn’t seen the scrawl in decades, Milagros recognizes her mother’s handwriting on the front of it. She grabs for the envelope. There’s a knot at the back of her throat, and she feels like she’s in a coffin being buried alive but her short-circuiting voice can’t reach the gravediggers. “In good faith in advance for the delivery of the package,” Hidalgo says. She slits open the seal. A bundle of pages. The first one in Grecia’s scrawl recounts her and Milagros’s journey to the island. Milagros inspects the following pages. All of them are blank.

5

A Handwritten Journal, in Which Fireflies and Frigatebirds Portend Rough Seas

THE BROKER REMINDS me of an animal that I can't quite name. Something slithery. He tells me to meet him here in Güiria. *Here?* I ask. *In the cemetery?* Right here in the cemetery. How can this be a good sign? I pull Milagros tight against me. Her head reaches just above my stomach. We've heard stories. Marisol and her daughters were to sail to Curaçao from Güiria. They were never heard from again after the boat launched. Marisol's mother still texts her daughter's phone number. Pobrecito. To me that's like sticking your head into a bucket of water to hold a conversation. There are worse signs. *Will it be safe?* I ask the broker.

His face is an eel's. *Claro*, he says. But just in case: you know how to swim, right? He sees my face. *A joke*, he says. *Are you in or out?*

In. Without hesitation.

He taps something on his phone's face. *Sending info about two more passengers*, he says. *You and your pretty daughter. Hermosa.*

I hold Milagros tighter against me. *How will we get there?* I ask.

You're all set, he says. *Your reservation is booked.*

How long will the trip take?

He shrugs and slips his phone into his back pocket. *A few hours.*

Where on the island are we going to land? Will we be safe?

You'll sail through the Dragon's Mouth, he says. He raises fingers. *In two days. Meet me here.* That eel smile. And the thought of a dragon's mouth. Bócas del Dragon makes me think of a squirming snake in a big mud puddle. A snake being all an eel really is. I hand over his payment. I tell him I want to see Fortunato before the trip. He lifts his eyebrows. Wants to know how I know this name, but he won't say the name aloud. He says he will see if an audience will be granted.

You hear these stories. Ours isn't that bad, Milagros's and mine. Really, it isn't. The crossing. Getting here. The boat is meant for ten people. It ends up tuna-can tight with twenty or thirty of us. We ride low in the water. The boat smells of gasoline, rotting wood, and mildew. I keep expecting to hear a cracking sound and to see a leak shoot up like in the cartoons. The boat squats, dangerously close to taking on water. I hold Milagros tight. Mostly women and children on the boat. Only women and children on the boat. Other than gasoline, rotting wood, and mildew, there's the smell of bodies. Also Lysol and vomit and reckless hope. No one wears life vests. Except Milagros. *Where are all the men?* I'm ashamed to think it but, if we were to sink, I'm glad that Milagros is with me. We glimpse the island in the distance. Bit by bit, it draws closer and everyone's hope escalates. The beach is beautiful even at night, which makes me uneasy. Fireflies flare above the water. They seem pinned to the air. Unmoving. Hung like ornaments. These living lights mesmerize the children. But they are children. Then birds arrive to eat the fireflies. They swoop down out of the air and the lights just wink out one by one. It's the middle of the night. No one else seems to notice the lights winking out.

I squeeze my sun quartz pendant tightly.

I hug Milagros tighter.

You hear these stories. They're truly bad. Awful. Makes you wonder how people continue to wrap their arms around religion. People like me. Ours isn't so bad. Our story. Of how we came to the island. It really isn't. You hear the boat sinking stories, and the lost souls stories, and your heart splinters and falls apart. But ours is okay. I used to live on this island once. A different time. Long ago I was a different person. Full of firefly light. The boat that Milagros and I board is tighter than an oyster's lips. My brother, Manuel, used to fish. He stank all the time of fish skin, and fish guts, and fish gills. I wonder where he is. If he's still on the island.

The captain of the boat looks jumpy. His eyes won't stop moving. There's a medical condition for it. Nystagmus. My friend Carmen, a nurse, once told me about it. If the broker had an eel's face this one has the face of a frog. Marisol says frogs in Puerto Rico are called coquí. And they talk more than chickens. *The coquí wouldn't shut up the entire time that I was there*, she'd said. Which was back when people could take vacations because they had a little money. Milagros's father wanted me to give birth to Milagros on the island so he could care for her. But then he disappeared, and his big shot son turned his back on me. Who knew I'd regret that Milagros wasn't born on an island? Who knew that I would, in fact, meet with a gangster? He looked me over with his dead eyes and said that he would hold Milagros's letter for me. I didn't know if I believed him. I wanted to be sure. It felt like I was leaving breadcrumbs for her in case I would somehow get separated from her, even though I didn't want to tempt fate because fate always takes things too far, and being separated from her might become never seeing her again.

Venezuela used to be rich. The captain isn't afraid of our coast guard, he's afraid of the island's coast guard. Cold comfort. But it means that he's sure this old tub will make it that far. It's made it before. A confident vessel. Reliable. He's done this before. He's done this in his sleep. Beyond a frog, his face looks like a crumpled love note pulled from a pocket and spread flat. He says half of our fee will be to pay off the coast guard if we're stopped. No one asks if the deposit will be returned if no payoff is necessary.

Where are all the men on this trip?

You hear all these stories, and here's one more. The children finally feel everyone's fear, especially the three- and four-year-olds. They cling to their mothers' waists and legs. Barnacles. I cling to Milagros. The birthright of every child born in our village is asthma. Every other child had been born with it along with crippled hope and faulty futures. You can tell which children on the boat are from our town by the coughs. They own a sound. Hollowness in their chests. The space hope leaves behind when it evaporates. Milagros never developed asthma. And I knew that she wouldn't from the moment she was born. Hence her name. Everyone wanted to know my secret. Did I name her after seeing a mystical sign? Did I feed her liver oil from fishes? I laughed. I grasped my sun quartz. Who could afford oil from a fish's liver? I shrugged. Now none of the other children's parents can find inhalers or medicine on the mainland. Not even a vitamin. Their staying behind is a flip of death's coin—either from poor nutrition or poor pockets. I think about the jobs that I will take on the island. Cooking and cleaning. Tending bars. I used to be a butcher a long time ago on this island. My English is still good. I once loved a man there.

Milagros's father.

You hear stories. You hear stories about some of the women who head to the island. The jobs they end up with. Awful jobs. Massage parlors. Strip clubs. Some accept it without pushback. Do it willingly. They send back the money they make. Send back medication. I'm not sure I have the guts for that. Word is that there's enough women desperate enough for that other kind of work. That the men don't have to pressure women into doing it, that being poor and hungry make them willing participants. That they quickly disavow any pride and accept this new reality, the only difference here is that the money that they earn can purchase medicine, tampons, a new pair of shoes.

We make it safely to the island. But there are some close calls. High waves lifting the boat off the ocean's carpet. Children and women heaving what little is inside their tummies over the side of the boat. The sounds. The smells. We land on the beautiful beach. Well, the jetty. Which makes me uneasy. Landing on rocks, or on ugly sand, or near an oil refinery, would have made it feel like a debt had been paid. An offering to the god of spite. Yesterday I dragged Milagros with me to the cemetery. To ask the thugs for protection. After I visited Fortunato and left a letter for him to hold. Then I left a copy with Carmen. There were fireflies. Lightning bugs. Eaten up. Plunging us back into darkness. All the fireflies have disappeared.

A man in a tight black shirt and shaved head receives us right there on the island's wharf. Him and his armed goons. He has a scar through an eyebrow. He's going bald. They line us up when we depart the boat. Two lines. They confiscate our phones. It's clear what they're up to. The women in one line are beauties or own firm bodies. I watch one of the goons work his way down the line. Like he's separating the ripe produce from the green. The wheat from the chaff. You, over here, he points. You, over there. The women hold their children tightly and do as they're told. Once or twice they separate women from older daughters. Twelve or thirteen years old. None lift their chins. A few weep. I look at the old tug captain's frog face. He's been paid for this as well. His eyes still jump. I am horrified but not surprised. There were no men among us. From the minute that we climbed on this boat it felt like we were all made to sleep only to awaken to find marionettes' strings attached to all our limbs. The goon approaches me and Milagros. *Just not Milagros*, I think. *Please not Milagros*. The man with the shaved head stoops before us. *My, you're pretty*, says the man with the shaved head. He's dropped to his haunches. His face isn't an eel's or a frog's. There's no animal that compares. He's his own breed. I hold Milagros tight. He looks her right in the eyes.

I've been here for two weeks and I'm ready to kill. They keep me in a room. They keep Milagros away from me. I've hidden my pendant, a gift from Milagros's father. The huevón keeps Milagros from me, and this keeps me on a leash. *Don't worry*, the man with the shaved head promises me. *She's too young*, he says. *Her chest is just plums*, he says. Days later, he sits at a chair in the corner of the room. He crosses his legs. He says that he wouldn't lie to me. He says he'll be completely honest. He says that he has a client who likes that kind of thing. *Joven-cita*, he says. He says that he will keep Milagros safe for him until the client decides if she's his type. *She may not be*, he says. *There's a chance.* Turns down his mouth. He says the client's a big shot on the island. A government minister, if I can believe it. High up. Responsible for latching the gate and keeping people like me out. But he can't get away right now. There's always so much to do. I leap for his eyes. One of his goons knocks me down. *Tigre! Tigre!* He laughs. Crosses his legs.

The men come and I kill them all. I kill them all. I kill them all. In my head. Every last one of them. They come at night.

As a collective. Drunk from some fishing village. They smell like my brother. Fish guts, and fish skin, and fish heads. Rotting. All of them. The boy too. They bring him to make him a man. To straighten him out. You can see. He doesn't look well. Some vitamin deficiency. Carmen would know the name. He didn't want to be there. At first. But he became just like them in the end. All of them. Cochinos. Cer-dos. Rough. I kill him quickly. He is just a boy after all. A quick death is a mercy. I think of Manuel. Of Milagros. The dreams we harbor.

* * *

The one with the sharp shirts and spiced cologne I kill the slowest. Poison. He returns the most. Without the others. He is never embarrassed to be here. He wears an earring. Has eyelashes that should be on a woman. Later he comes in hobbling with a cane, and I think, *good. You're in pain too.* He whispers terrible things in my ears, things that he knows will keep me compliant—that Mila is here, locked away in another part of the house, that he's seen her many times, and, if I'm good, if I behave, that I can see her soon. I know that he's lying, but I can't know for sure. They said she was somewhere safe for now, but what if she's in another room with someone doing terrible things to her? With this horrible man doing terrible things to her? If I know for sure that she is in this house, I would have his eyes as ice cubes in the glass of water that I'm allowed every few hours. But if I try to escape and search for her, I know my punishment will be terrible.

In this house the windows are boarded up, but you can smell oranges.

Then the other one shows up. The one with the floating eye. Miki. I remember him from when he was a teenager. When I lived on the island. I remember his father, Sonny. Ask after Sonny's health. Sonny's passed, he says. I offer my sympathies. He does nothing when he visits except talk of freeing me. He sneaks in food. He has a plan. *We all have a plan*, I tell him. He used to work for Milagros's father, him and Sonny. Sonny helped Hubert plant the trees. Miki tells me he can get Milagros out even if he has to sell his house to raise the money. Doesn't tell me how he knows about her. Doesn't tell me the truth about how he'll do it, how he can convince these cerdos to exchange money for my child's life. I'm suspicious. *Take me as well*, I say. He shakes his head. He is sorry. They might sell a child, but they won't sell a woman.

Carmen shows up to see us off. She and Daniela. Our going-away gift is a life jacket. She apologizes. *I could only get one*, she says. I'm grateful. I pull it on Milagros. I tell Daniela to be good. Hug her tight. *Take good care of your mami.* When I see that there are no life jackets for anyone else I feel bad strapping the lone one onto Milagros. But no one minds. Everyone's snapping pictures with their phones. Like we're boarding a plane for a European vacation. Like we're being *invited* to our island destination. They send the pictures to people, fingers flamenco dancing on phone screens. Or maybe they're leaving breadcrumbs. The boat should only hold ten people. Even I can see this. I hold Milagros tight. Touch the sun quartz for luck. We'll never see this place again. Our homeland. I'm sure of it.

6

A Dark-Winged Corbeau and a Loose-Necked Goose Slip Simple Village Traps

ZABOCA CLEARING'S ZABOCAS were always ripe and ready, on season or off. We tried not to think about this as we diced them into our stews and salads, us suspecting a tortured past with the silk cotton tree some twenty yards beyond the tables. Most of us knew better than to mess with that tree. But the oddest thing about Zaboca Clearing, beyond the perma-green grass and the silk cotton tree and whatever might be buried beneath, was the pervading smell of oranges that floated through the Clearing even though there were no oranges planted anywhere near. It confounded us. It raised short hairs on our necks and goosefleshed our forearms. Tingled the edges of our ears and moistened tear ducts.

It itched our collarbones.

Dimpled our asses in fear.

All of us except Binary Clem, who could never smell the oranges because of the beating he'd once received for not paying off gambling debts which wrote off his senses of smell and taste and the ability to speak in anything other than ones and zeroes like a corrupted code breaker, which we suspected was the final straw that chased off his wife Lorraine, her no longer able to understand the sweet nothings whispered into her ears. Binary Clem would watch us cover our noses with our T-shirts, tank tops, and mesh shirts whenever the smell of oranges would overwhelm us and would ask, *1-0-0-1-1-0-0-1-1*?

"Oranges, Clem," said Peter-Called-Peter Cruickshank, him being the only one of us who understood him. "Still oranges." Peter-Called-Peter had returned, and we were glad that he'd been absent during our recent activities. We never knew how he'd respond to our logic: a tutting tongue and a disappointed headshake. Or worse.

Time had slipped its leash since the incident with the journalist. Shaken by Sookdeo's death as a ransomed captive, his wife, Indira, relocated to her mother's house in Union Village. Her departure saddened us, especially Miki, who wept. We spent more time in the Clearing. Peter-Called-Peter owned a special connection with Zaboca Clearing, his ancestral family having lived in the village for donkey years, them being one of the first families that had been bodied in from Africa and tied to the land and the cane. Village lore from Nello's mouth asserted that Peter-Called-Peter's grandfather, Hubert Cruickshank, had emptied the Clearing space and planted the twenty-five zaboca trees on the twenty-fifth anniversary of the island's 1960s independence and maybe because of the guilt he felt for having relocated his family to the capital. Peter-Called-Peter was the first Cruickshank to live here in two generations.

All of us, including Nello and Hospedales and Mark-2 and the glasses and goateed UWI graduate, etc., allowed Peter-Called-Peter his peace as he approached his wrecked boat resting upon casters that he was lovingly building plank by pointless plank. We harvested a few zabocas and opened some coconut water, cracked some island lager, and whispered *Bunny and Miki, Miki and Bunny, Bunny and Miki*, since a week earlier Mark-2, the village scamp and busybody, had witnessed Miki's arrival at Bunny's late one night with a bottle of wine. He'd delivered the news as we ended that morning's fishless pre-dawn seine pull, and a suddenly tortured Peter-Called-Peter decided to head out to the Clearing to clear his head. "Can we come?" we asked.

"Onward," he said.

We zipped out to the Clearing in his battered yellow Isuzu Trooper, which was begging for a coat of paint and a transmission overhaul, a seat replacement and new shocks, updated spark plugs, and definitely a windshield that didn't own a large crack that snaked across it. We waited for the smell of oranges to settle around us in the Clearing, and when the smell glided in, so too did the spooky sense of familiarity that rendered us sorely afraid.

Village women won't visit the Clearing because of the silk cotton tree and the scent of oranges, not Miss Titus, not Bunny, not Stacy, not Lorraine before she left Binary Clem, not the glasses and goateed UWI graduate's seamstress mother, not Indira before her exit, and Bunny forbade us to bring Milagros. Bunny, who once stunned a blue shark with a punch to the nose before dragging it onto the boat and pummeling it to death with her hands when it refused to surrender its ghost, won't even *mention* the Clearing. Which also made it a good place for village men when we wanted to separate from the women.

To think, gotdammit.

To think this all used to be sugarcane.

To think we are murderers.

Now: Peter-Called-Peter's pitch-perfect singing along to the Mighty Penguin's "You Fraid the Devil" briefly held our attention.

And then: Mark-2 grinning at something someone had texted him, and the blurring of his fingers across his phone's face briefly held our attention.

And then: Hospedales, wearing too much cologne to match yet another loud shirt, briefly held our attention.

But finally, the wind bending in the wrong direction and the overwhelming smell of oranges: this clutched our consciousness.

Nello, whose head often inhabited the clouds above us, and was now sitting on the edge of one of the picnic tables swigging from his lager, set it aside. *The Christ*, we thought. Our local village griot, Nello always wanted to float an idea about the orange smell, but we always told him we didn't want to hear his theory, to *keep it in your back pocket, Roman Nelson*, us preferring Peter-Called-Peter's infernal always-tuned-to-the-Mighty-Penguin-Mighty-Shadow-Bob-Marley-24-7 transistor than to listen to Nello's internal radio signal always tuned to some outer-space-UFO-Eric-Gairy-Grenadian-frequency about the spooky past and its connection to our present. It almost made us long for You-We's learned babble. Nello had recently returned as well, back from one of his communes with nature, and we were glad he also hadn't witnessed our misbehavior, our village mischievousness, our murderous impulses.

We were only at Zaboca Clearing for some forty-five minutes when what happened next chased us back to the village. The sun burned so hot that it baked the ever-cool Clearing air, scorching our lungs and worsening the smell of oranges, when Nello rested his long-necked lager beside him on the bench and folded his hands behind his head and asked, "Did anyone else see her?"

We jumped.

Peter-Called-Peter, whose saw was snagging into the boards just then, him singing Marley's "Bad Card" poorly, his voice signaling to the noise, which was surprising after how well he sang "You Fraid the Devil," halted the saw and silenced the radio as well.

"Repeat that, Nello," Peter-Called-Peter said, laying the saw over one shoulder as he approached us, concerned.

Gs + Hs, we thought, hoping we could bracket away and compartmentalize Nello's unsettling griot statement without closer inspection, him and his Nello-predicted future fears and premonitions twisting and braiding with our past, Nello as skinny as a Phillips-head and twice as deadly when he screwed down his predictions. When Nello talked in this way, in his short bursts, beaming in some far-off Nello signal, him seeing things that we didn't, there was something stickier than mango juice in our hot hands that was about to send us slipping, send us catspraddling to the ground, cracking open our skulls, shaking us fully awake, and pushing us face down into our beach's hot sand.

Peter-Called-Peter asked again: "What did you see, Nello?"

We awaited his chilling verdict with bated breath.

Some of us thinking of sharp-fanged macajuels.

Some of us thinking of rabid mongooses.

Some of us thinking of the scarlet ibises that we were now convinced were Catherine the Great Disemboweler's familiars, us convinced that she'd been more than just the sexiest woman to stroll through the village, a different sexy from Bunny, that she'd been a gotdamned la diablesse, that maybe, worst of all, she was returned from the dead, and this still not dampening our lust, all of us still wanting to crawl into her bed and count her toes. We all knew the history of this village, well-handled stories handed down just like the myth of the ibis and the mongoose. All You-We's research only confirmed it. Added a gloss. We knew from Nello of enslaved women who gave up their babies for some kind of power, gave up the life that was within them to keep safe those children already born. We knew that Catherine was one of those children, and we knew that safe didn't mean alive.

But we all, in our deepest of hearts, suspected what Nello would say, us having been warned, after all, by Mami Ursula and her gold eyes and her green headscarf, Mami Ursula being descended from tribes serving as some kind of check on estate owners' evil, serving as a boundary beyond which they were not allowed to cross.

"Woman in all white," Nello said simply, him telling us that the pure white clothing of the woman he had seen contrasted sharply against her dark black skin, her white white blouse, her white white headwrap, her white white tie skirt, Nello saying that he'd been delivered a vision of her sitting at the picnic table just before we arrived and then he blinked and she went poof, her disappearing, and that the woman was surely Hany, Catherine the Great Disemboweler's mother.

"*These* picnic tables?" Mark-2 said, shooting up from where he sat like he'd settled on a child's scattering of jacks.

"Yes, Smallie," confirmed Nello. He sipped from his long-necked lager before sighting the fear in all of us, Nello never quite being able to figure out why the things he saw and said unsettled us like the second before the gallows ground fell away from beneath your firm feet.

"Shit," said Hospedales, that coward, jumping even further away from the picnic table than Mark-2 had, Peter-Called-Peter saying to him, "Big man like you?" this shaming Hospedales and returning him to our orbit, but only slightly. He tugged at his bright orange linen shirt as if a Jack Spaniard had sailed in between his buttons and settled on his chest, threatening to sting.

It was this moment of suspended animation that froze us like amber-trapped prehistoric ants, us thinking about Hany's revenge, when the following events happened:

The smell of oranges falling away.

The stiff wind trailing off.

The cheeky birds muting their singing.

We were looking at each other, realizing the entire air around us was doing that odd gas station air-shimmy, and then a second stretched to a minute, and a minute elongated to two yesterdays ago. And then our second large earthquake arrived, a real ground-trembler, a shaking that we later learned was Richtered at 7.2 and that sent macaws screeching, dogs barking, and had a saddist one village over in Bon Bois removing all his clothes, running into the sea, and trying to swim to the sister island, his body finally found rounding the bay and washing up far away near the rich people's anchorage.

And then there she was for all of us to see.

Hany.

Standing right there in front of us in the space between the silk cotton tree and the wrecked refurbishing project that Peter-Called-Peter called a boat, Hany dressed in blinding white just as Nello had described, us thinking she'd come at last to avenge her daughter, that this was one of our last few moments alive.

10:42 a.m.! one of us called out, us always making note of the time when Hany appeared, since something always slipped sideways in time's accounting when she put in an appearance, like time bounding ahead in seventeen-minute intervals, or rain falling in reverse toward the clouds, or a Tuesday falling on a Wednesday for three consecutive weeks.

If the now-dispatched Catherine the Great Disemboweler had been spiteful and still developing her powers, Hany, we were sure, was in nimbled full control of hers. *No sudden moves,* we thought. *Silence even your minds.* It confounded us that she didn't just wipe us off the face of the earth.

When we dismissed Catherine the Great Disemboweler almost a year earlier, we knew that there would be a soonish reckoning, and maybe this was where we now stood, us having seen Hany in different guises since we'd dispatched her daughter: a heavily pregnant cow, a loose-necked goose, and the most terrifying of all, a dark-winged corbeau, all these sightings spiteful and rage-inducing. And now although she was dressed in white, the only thing that all of us agreed on later was that she appeared slightly *different* to each of us.

We stood there waiting for her to act, to speak, to wave her left hand and flatten the earth from here to the capital.

But she was even more still than we were.

What was she waiting for?

We'd heard hints and whispers of her since we'd sent Catherine the Great Disemboweler to the bottom of the river beside the mangrove. We'd experienced dry fishbeds and bad breath, dry crop fields and bad religion, dry dandruffed scalps and bad mamaguy. A lightning strike that felled six pouis at once in the woods beyond the silk cotton tree. But those were whispers we'd heard in our heads just before we'd drifted off into shuddering sleep, those whispers that crowded our minds and the smell of oranges that settled in our imaginations. These taunts making us regret slaying Catherine the Great Disemboweler for seducing, then killing, the Titus boys, decimating Romulus and Magnus, her on the verge of tearing the village asunder, us thinking it was only a matter of time before Hany came for the rest of us. Now here was Hany in the so-to-speak flesh returned in a clear and recognizable form, her hair plaited into a diadem, her arms as thick as a glimpse into the future and her moving as slowly as erosion.

"Three," she said. Her voice vibrated and warped and amplified in that tug-of-war way that elongated sound when an ambulance siren stretched: tight like a rubber band, then snapping when it popped up curbside, then wobbling into a different shape when it slung past. ("Doppler effect," the glasses and goateed UWI graduate later told us when we later discussed this episode on Bunny's front porch. "Shaddup," Miki told him, Miki being the only one among our group not currently at the Clearing at this time, him currently wrapped up with Bunny, we suspected, in postcoital bedsheets.)

So we weren't sure exactly what she'd said at first. Then Hany again said, "I promise you three," and that was when we knew for sure that we'd heard what we'd heard, her holding up three fingers to underscore her condemnation and her censure, and then she was gone, disappearing in her own unique way to each of us—for Binary Clem there was a bright flash and then the smell of the gentler brand of household disinfectant, him regaining his sense of smell for this brief moment; for Mark-2 the sound of the post-earthquake earth cracking open loudly and then the smell of recently plowed soil scoured his nostrils; and for Peter-Called-Peter, him seeing her levitate into the sky and disappear into the clouds, which made the most logical sense, us remembering her previously as a corbeau. In addition to all of this we'd experienced a slight humming in our ears in Hany's presence, a sustained ringing, a localized tinnitus that finally evaporated with her final vanishing, the sound lingering in each of *our* ears, even Binary

Clem's, just long enough to make us think that maybe we were all going a little crazy.

10:25 a.m.! One of us shouted out, and it was only later that we understood that Hany's arrival and disappearance times did not track temporally, her somehow leaving before the time that she'd arrived.

"What the France does *three* mean?" Peter-Called-Peter asked right after we regained our horse sense but were still slightly trembling from the earthquake.

We all turned to Nello and cringed at his response: "Three separate bouts of get-out-your-shovel-and-dig-a-moat trouble."

What we didn't realize right then was that we were all moving slowly, and talking slowly, and responding slowly, sounding like we'd each had felling cardiac arrests, little strokes, only truly realizing this when the music on Peter-Called-Peter's transistor sounded like the battery was dying, Robert Nesta M. singing about bad cards, when Peter-Called-Peter had changed the batteries just two days before.

"Gs + Hs," we said, thinking that if Catherine the Great Disemboweler's mother was mentally terrorizing us, since whenever she arrived terrible things occurred, setting us up for retribution, then what would be her final retribution for disappearing her daughter?

We tried to crack the code about what terrible thing her appearance now meant and whether this was the terminal penalty.

"What about death?" offered Hospedales. "People always die in threes."

"1-1-1," said Binary Clem.

"Gs + Hs," Peter-Called-Peter said, more agitated than we'd ever seen him, him losing his Gautama Buddha cool, fiddling with the battery compartment of his transistor radio. "All of you make up your blasted mind."

We felt like we now occupied a curious and unsettling world in which staircases ran upside down from the ceiling like in the book of sketches that the glasses and goateed UWI graduate once showed us on Bunny's porch. When Peter-Called-Peter's transistor snapped back to regular speed, as soon as he gave up and stopped doing anything to it, we understood Hany had briefly rinsed our minds and warped our thinking, that she'd mesmerized us, had rooted us to the spot to keep us from where we should be. It was then we realized that we still hadn't recovered our equilibrium, our precise movements, us still moving a tick behind normal, and it was Peter-Called-Peter who finally realized it, him grasping that it was some kind of Catherine the Great Disemboweler's mother's spell to make us bazodie, and he said "Come," and he was already in front of the rest of us, running off the malaise, long-legging it and fumbling the car keys from his pants pocket, shouting back over his shoulder, "Everybody get into the Trooper now now now. Is misdirecting she misdirecting us."

We were in the Trooper racing back to the village, Peter-Called-Peter stripping his gears and mashing the gas.

Faster faster faster!

Hospedales leaned forward from the back seat and asked him, "What's wrong?"

"What's wrong," Peter-Called-Peter said, glancing up into the rearview, "is that we're not moving fast enough."

Toss the cooler!

Toss the back seat lumber meant for the boat's benches!

Toss Mark-2!

Lighten the load!

We tossed the cooler. We tossed the back seat lumber meant for the boat's benches. We kept Mark-2.

We lightened the load.

Faster, Peter-Called-Peter, faster.

"Good to see you again, my friend," the man with the shaved head and a scar notched into his eyebrow said to Hospedales when we screeched to a halt just outside the village, the sudden halt pinging gravel onto the Trooper's underbody, and the vehicle barely brought to a standstill before we tumbled out, falling on top of each other as we flipped down the driver and passenger seats to clamber over them. "I hope you don't mind," he said, "that I brought some of my friends to enjoy some of your generous hospitality." The man was muscled and wrapped tight inside a black T-shirt, maybe in his mid or late thirties.

Hospedales, last one out and finally freed from the tangle of the Trooper's seatbelt, took one look at this man, the man's sidearm goons, and the lorries that we'd swished past on the side of the road in the Trooper, and he lowered his head and Brahman-bull charged. The man with the shaved head immaculately sidestepped Hospedales's head-down dash, and when Hospedales realized he'd overrun him and turned to charge again, the man dealt Hospedales a neat 1-1-2 two-piece-and-a-biscuit combo that we'd seen only in boxing matches, those bleak rum-battered Friday nights when Hospedales would wheel his television with its spaghetti-long extension cord and illegal cable feed into his backyard, and we would gather round clutching long-necked lager bottles and scotch glasses of rum to watch pirated broadcasts of mostly Mexicans beating each other's heads in. The man with the shaved head dealt Hospedales one of those combos, slick and all flashing hands, and it dropped Hospedales onto his buttocks. We rushed over to help Hospedales to his feet, but his legs disagreed, and Peter-Called-Peter retrieved a handkerchief from his trousers and held it against the Hospedales nosebleed blossom, hibiscus-flower red, frowning at this man who Hospedales had apparently Pied-Pipered into our midst.

We understood that this man with the shaved head, who still held his fighting stance after Hospedales's KO and standing eight count, was someone who Hany had somehow vengefully blown into our lives, that his appearance related directly to hers, this being another marker of her setting us up for a final fall. We knew Hospedales had been fleecing Venezuelan refugees at the wharf on the west coast where he worked, and that was how he knew this man with the shaved head, and this current torment was possibly a reckoning for Hospedales's underhanded dealings and double crosses, that this man and his goons were his comeuppance being paid in full. In our hypothetical visions, this man had been shamed, had been made by Hospedales to pay more than had been agreed, that the man with the shaved head had vowed a stringent vengeance that he was now deploying. It was then that the man with the shaved head let out a piercing whistle and the six lorries that we'd just passed, lined up on the side of the road, clattered and hummed, then coughed and sputtered through the village, them rumbling to a stop right on the lip of our beach pointing their backsides toward the water. An acned lorry driver flicked open his door and tossed an automatic weapon to the man with the shaved head who received it into his hands as calmly as a broomstick.

Systematically, the six dump truck lorries backed up to the sand, and finally from them hopped six more men with automatic guns as long as our thighbones. *Why the guns?* we wondered. *What kind of trouble do they think us capable of?* Surely at the wharf they had seen, Hospedales was all bluff and bluster, that he was just a crooked, greased palm extended for payments. When the lorries were in final formation, them still shaking and coughing, a teenager with bad skin hopped out from the passenger seat of one of the lorries and he ran toward the man with the shaved head holding a few waist-tall shovels. After a few back-and-forth trips he delivered more shovels and buckets to the man's feet.

The man with the shaved head clapped thrice. "Thank you for your kind welcome, island friends," he said. *Venezuelan*, we thought. *Venezuelan for sure.* He held his thighbone-length gun diagonally from his hip, pointed toward the sky. "We are so pleased that you have agreed to help with our endeavor this morning."

Hospedales spat on the sand.

The man with the shaved head ignored him.

Miki, who by now had emerged bleary-eyed and shirtless from Bunny's house, said, "Why you here, boss?"

The man ignored him and looked instead toward Peter-Called-Peter and said, "You. Gather all the men who live here."

Peter-Called-Peter said, "We're all here."

We quick-counted heads. Yes, all the men were here, but the women, including Bunny, Miss Titus, the glasses and goateed UWI graduate's seamstress mother Iris, Stacy and her siblings, and little Milagros, were not. We were grateful for the absence of the women, and for Lorraine's and Indira's permanent village exits, us thinking that the guns and spades were to be used by these men to end our lives and for us to dig our own graves just before that. We'd seen Western films. "No difference," the man with the shaved head said with a shrug. "Less of you just means you excavate more slowly. Many hands would have lightened the workload. Right, Mr. Hospedales?" Hospedales still sat on the ground, his knees drawn up to his chest and his arms wrapped around them. He wore one of those weird little smiles that seemed to say *you may have gotten over just now, partner, but give me a chance and we go see*. "Please select a shovel," the man with the shaved head said to all of us. "Even you, Mr. Hospedales, when you can find your feet."

Mark-2, still spooked from what had happened in the Clearing, was now visibly rattled. He was closest to the man with the shaved head, and he picked up a shovel first. Then Miki, then Peter-Called-Peter, Hospedales, Nello, Binary Clem, and the terrified glasses and goateed UWI graduate. While we received spades, Bunny stepped from her house and onto her gallery. She wore a yellow sundress, and her hair was in two large plaits, and she looked very pretty. Miki told her to get back inside the house, but the man with the shaved head and the automatic weapon invited her out. "She's not a man," Miki said.

The man with the shaved head grinned. "No," he said. "But I don't intend for her to work."

Miki again told Bunny to get back in the house. Bunny took one step back, and the man with the shaved head punched three quick gunshots into the air. Bunny startled. Birds squawked from trees. The rest of us crouched into commas. We'd heard automatic fire before, mainly from the modern-day pirates who sailed the horizon deep into the night's ink, but to hear the *pak-pak-pak* of shots intimately in the blazing daylight was like hearing thunder rumble beneath your bed and your mother telling you there's no such thing as jumbies.

We'd seen death.

We'd seen violence.

We'd recently instigated both.

We'd dismembered a foreign reporter.

Dismissed a sure obeah woman's daughter in Catherine the Great Disemboweler.

But now seeing our own end terrified us.

"You will stop talking," the man said to Miki. "In fact," he added, leveling his gun at him, "why aren't you digging already?"

"We don't know what we're digging for," Miki mumbled.

"Sand," the man said. "You're digging for sand." He told us to load the excavated sand into the buckets and to empty the buckets into the backs of the lorries. "¿Entiende? he asked. Then he approached Bunny, her still on her porch, and he took up one of her porch chairs that we sat on when we held our alcohol-fueled ol talks, and he dragged it out so that he sat in front of the grill of the third lorry. The rest of the men, holding their weapons, stood beside their lorries, soldiers on guard. Then the man with the shaved head beckoned Bunny over, and she went to him, and he said something softly to her that the rest of us couldn't hear. Bunny walked off wordlessly and slipped into her house.

We thought she'd return in a flying Bunny fury, brandishing a Chinese chopper held sharply angled above her head, the very same one with which she chased after Peter-Called-Peter when he announced to her that he didn't want to be paired with her anymore, that he'd started seeing someone else, and that he was ending his Bunny relationship. Instead, Bunny returned lugging her big boom box that sometimes played in low tones while we drank white rum, knocked playing cards, and limed on her porch. The man with the shaved head had moved again to Bunny's porch and, retrieving another chair, took it to his place before the lorries on the lip of the sand. He stationed the boom box on the sand before him and tuned it to the local newscast station where the broadcaster announced that the government was stepping up its registration of illegal Venezuelans. He spread his hands out toward the radio as if to say "There."

The man with the shaved head patted the new second seat beside him.

Bunny grimaced at all of us and sat down.

Miki scowled.

The rest of us dug.

And dug.

    And dug.

        And dug.

The sweat pooled in our ears and scorched our eyes as we fell into an excavation rhythm. Two hours in and we'd loaded one third of our bright beach sand into the lorries, the sand that none of us, except Magnus and Romulus and Catherine the Great Disemboweler and Bunny and Lorraine, had ever appreciated as a place to lounge before the water, to brown themselves even browner, the sand that, later, You-We explained to us was for building a beach on a coastal resort that lacked its own tourist-yellow sand. For the rest of us it was just a walkway as we yawned and set off for the falling-down jetty and then off in our boats, or maybe something to trudge through on our way to flop off the falling-down jetty in diving fun, Siddiq and Mark-2, in particular, indulging in that lighthearted folly.

We dug.

Eventually, a significant sinkhole. The sun blazed. Some of us had stripped off our jerseys and wrapped them around our heads against the sun. Our shirtless brown skins darkened. Three hours in and we needed a break. We all had sweat through our trousers. The men who stood on guard in front of the lorries swigged water from plastic bottles without offering us any. Then Peter-Called-Peter, assessing the wilt in our backs, the thirst on our sweat-wet faces, drove his spade into the sand, stood up straight, unkinked his back. "Enough," he said, "is enough."

The man with the shaved head, sitting beside Bunny now on a level above us, lifted his eyebrows behind his sunglasses. His string of gun-wielding goons rested their water bottles on the fenders of their lorries, tightened their grips on their gun necks, and relocated their trigger fingers. But the man with the shaved head laid his gun on the ground beside his chair on the far side from Bunny, then stood up straight and stretched. Yawned. Reminded us of cats that no longer stray-legged through our village for the charity-thrown fish heads we no longer had any of to throw, cats we'd originally suspected of being Catherine the Great Disemboweler's or Hany's familiars.

"Pick up your spade," he said softly to Peter-Called-Peter. By now Hospedales's eye had blackened and had swollen shut from the combo he'd received, and we thought that if the man had done that to him without much effort, it would take even less effort to command his automatic weapon to bark and split Peter-Called-Peter in half. For this reason, some of us kept digging, but most of us slowed down enough to gaze up at the man with the shaved head as he stood above us on the lip of our disappearing beach, him watching down at us in our deepening sand pit.

Quo vadis, pirates?

"You're killing us," Peter-Called-Peter said. "We need water." The man flattened his eyes. He stood twenty feet away on a ledge made by our excavation. He squatted. He looked like he could leap and land beside us in one bound, yoke our necks in his next move, then floor us in the third. We glanced at Hospedales's swollen eye. We looked from this man to Peter-Called-Peter, then we looked at the gun-drawn goons standing above us at the lip where the sand ended, waiting to see if the man would issue an order for them to open fire upon us, to fell all of us with dumdum bullets after we'd harvested our sand, to complete the task that Catherine the Great Disemboweler's mother had surely sent them on. Finally, the man with the shaved head, without turning, said to Bunny, "My dear, would it be too much to ask you to retrieve us a pitcher of water?"

Bunny stiffened then headed to her house.

"Now, gentlemen," the man said to us, and did a kind of flourishing wave as if we were showing off a new car. "Please."

So courteous, we said later. *The most courteous asshole ever.* We picked up our spades, Peter-Called-Peter last of all.

Then the second-most troubling thing occurred. The man with the shaved head tilted his head at one of his goons, and the goon went into Bunny's house, maybe because she was taking too long, maybe because he just had a bad feeling about the look on her face as she'd left, and then he returned with a kicking and screaming Milagros bundled under one arm, and dragging Bunny behind him with the other. "Oh ho," said the man with the shaved head. He crossed his legs where he sat as if he were at a play watching a new actor enter stage right. "Unexpected cargo." He looked at Bunny, who ceased her struggling now that the other lorry drivers tightened their grips on their weapons. "I remember this niña," he said. "I know where I've seen this muñeca before." Milagros continued to kick, and she caught the thigh of the man who carried her, who swore and released her. But the man with the shaved head stood from his chair and bent toward Milagros and whispered in her ear while pointing at Bunny, and Milagros stopped kicking, her standing perfectly still as if he'd waved a wand. The man with the shaved head looked up at his goon. "Where was she?"

The man massaged his thigh. "The little mule was under a bed." He tested a scratched cheek for blood.

The man with the shaved head sat down again and crossed his legs once more. Lifted his eyebrows. He motioned for Bunny to retake her seat, then he placed a thumb against his lower lip and studied Milagros. "Ven acá, flaca," he said to Milagros. "Come join us." When he sat he patted his lap and, looking at Bunny, Milagros moved slowly toward him. He patted his thigh once more, and Milagros finally settled on his lap, a bird testing a shaky nest. The man placed one hand against Milagros's stomach, an action that blistered our bloods. Then he ordered his goon to go inside to fetch the water that Bunny had forgotten.

Here we turned to Miki, watched to see if he would rush the man with a brandished spade, watched to see if he would slip God out of his thoughts and bum rush him as Hospedales had, watched to see if he'd yell *you big fat soca pig!* and kick him two-footed in the chest. But Miki did none of these things. He just watched all of this transpire, his newly formed surrogate family transferred to some stranger who was stronger and more definitive than him. Observed someone with more steel in his spine destabilize that foundation without pushback. We went, one by one, to retrieve a drink of water under goon supervision. All of us kept our eyes down, unable to look at either Bunny, Milagros, or Miki. We considered instead the shovel-born blisters in our palms beside the fishing and seine calluses, and whether any of us men could ever consider each other to be such again.

We toiled into midafternoon. We settled into a rhythm of the crunch of spades. We filled the buckets. Exchanged positions with Mark-2 so that sometimes he dug, sometimes he ferried half-filled sand buckets to the lorries, us trying to limit his exhaustion. We received only two water breaks in six hours. We listened to the ocean washing up beside us as we worked, our beach fading into lorry cargo beds.

Then the third of the three most troubling things happened.

The remains.

Nello found them first, his spade crunching into a skull.

When he realized what he'd found he turned his head and spat.

We all stopped when we came upon thighbones and armbones, skulls with missing teeth. Caved-in heads. A hot dusty wind wrapped around us, sailing down into this sand-dug valley of death, and even in midafternoon heat we shivered. Then the man with the shaved head said, "Why," holding his gun perpendicular to his body, "have you stopped *digging?*"

We resumed our forced labor.

About an hour later the man with the shaved head clapped four or five times. He whistled sharply. We looked up at him out of our beach pit. "Okay, friends," he said. "That is sufficient." He stood and stretched, reminding us once more of the cats who now avoided our village. Bunny remained seated beside him. By now Milagros had been transferred to her care, and Bunny held Milagros in a protective hug. "You've done very well," the man with the shaved head told us. "You've all done excellently."

Our backs were bent.

Our mouths were cotton.

Our entire bodies were twisted kinks.

"You will soon be rid of us," the man said, eyeing his lorry goons still standing before their lorries' grills. "Soon you'll never have to see us again." Here he looked directly at You-We. The men swung themselves into their lorry cabins and switched on their lorry engines, and all the lorries rumbled and hummed like panting dogs. "Just a few more things," the man with the shaved head said.

Here he bent over, and tapped Milagros's nose and clucked his tongue. Then he took Bunny's hand and kissed it, and then he walked to the edge of the pit, adjusted his firearm, and fired a single shot into Hospedales's thigh, dropping him again to the ground, collapsing him into a Hospedales howl. "That was for your poor *Hospe*-tality the last time that we met," he said. Then he climbed into the passenger seat of the first lorry. "Keep the spades, my good friends," he yelled out the window, "as a memento of our time together." He held a three-finger salute against his forehead. "Y buena suerte." Then the lorries shivered and groaned and grumbled out of our lives with all our beach sand in their trailers.

We quickly gathered around Hospedales to see how much longer he'd live and maybe if we could render his last moments alive more comfortable, all of us except Miki, who watched Bunny grab Milagros's hand and stalk off to her house without looking back at us.

TWO

Present Continuous

7

A Flying Fish Flaps Its Wings and a Frigatebird Keeps Close Watch

WE RESIDE IN a collective Carnival fever dream, our own special Carnival away from the big bands of the city, and here's what occurs in that cumulative reverie: recollections, recriminations, and no got-damn restitutions! We're dressed in pantomime gear in the Clearing, how we drunkards have chosen to celebrate mas': in silence. Dressed in all white, disgusted with ourselves since the man with the shaved head incident, we're moving slowly slowly slowly, pointing accusatory fingers at each other, wearing white even down to our boots. Finger points of recrimination is this year's Carnival theme, but with no music from Peter-Called-Peter's transistor. Our sand is burgled and our manhoods are in the balance.

Instead we point silenced fingers at this new twist: Hospedales, weeks after surviving a bullet in his thigh, brokering to buy our houses out from under us for a suspiciously high price, suspicious since the lack of sand on the now-rocky beach, the beach that now looked like a stripped quarry, cratered the houses' worth. Hospedales offering to buy them on behalf of an anonymous bidder startled us, and we pointed fingers at Peter-Called-Peter upon learning that the buyer is his father, us just now learning that Basil D'Souza is *not* the Minister of National Security's full name, but that the right honorable Minister of National Security is Basil D'Souza *Cruickshank*, father of Peter-Called-Peter, son of zaboca-tree planting Hubert Cruickshank, big village sawatee, and shhh shhh shhh, nobody is supposed to know that, and we're not telling Peter-Called-Peter how we found out.

We point fingers at ourselves for most likely having to sell our houses, because we are money-poor and resource-poor, food-poor and patience-poor, clemency-poor and generosity-poor, and Hospedales's no-longer-anonymous buyer's willingness to pay way over the worth of each of our village houses gives us both avaricious hope as well as uneasy pause.

The Clearing party rolls on.

The central conceit of Recrimination Carnival, our slow-motion finger-pointing silence, allows us to expunge our fury and hopefully not bring it up in conversation ever again. Why judge us for this? It is only silence and slow-motion movements, so why not? Only Binary Clem is allowed to verbalize his denunciations because we mostly can't understand him. "1-0-0-1-1-0-0-1-0-0-1-0," he says just before Bunny arrives, him pontificating and punching an index in the air. "1-1-0-0-1-1!" We keep very very still through all of his remonstrations. We think it has to do with us no longer lending him money to go gambling, us not wanting to see him garrote himself with gambling grief after his wife, Lorraine, walked away, but Peter-Called-Peter won't translate.

The problem manifests and spills over to critical mass when Bunny shows up in the Clearing for the second time in her life, while we're now sitting because of too much babash and white rum chasing our heads, us still wearing white white trousers and white white shirts and wearing full-faced white white santimanitay masks, so that Bunny, rounding the turn and coming to the Clearing like a hesitant horse being ridden into battle, and seeing us all standing there and not moving but instead pointing at each other, us already burdened with affliction and adversity, collapses like she's been felled by a sniper's shot, her falling reminding us of Indira fainting among her pigeon pea plants when she'd learned about her kidnapped husband,

Ramdeen. Miki, of course, rushes over to gather Bunny up, maybe holding her a little too closely and a little too tightly, and then laying her on one of the picnic tables, him removing his sanitmanitay mask, and shouting to the rest of us to "Give her room! Give her space! Let her breathe, dammit!"

We give her room. We give her space. We let her breathe. We press pause on our slow-motion dance of denunciation and accusations. We remove our masks, trying to make sense of this curious affliction of Bunny being here with us in the Clearing. We remove our masks knowing that's that for Recrimination Carnival, us not being able to forget what had happened with the man with the shaved head.

When Bunny comes to, and her eyes focus, and the color returns to her cheeks, she says she needs to get Milagros out of her house, and out of the village, because things are happening out of the ordinary and out of her control. "Say more," we urge. She watches us, still in our all-persecutory whites, and an involuntary shiver rattles through her.

"Tell us what happened," says Peter-Called-Peter.

"Tell us what you saw," says Nello.

"Tell us where Milagros is," says Miki, his face the gravest of us, it looking pale even without the mask, his lazy eye now with a dark circle beneath it, and the rest of us thinking, *please put your mask back on, sad-dist.* Bunny eyes Mark-2, who has not removed his mask, her reaching out to touch it, and asking, "What kabuki hell is this?" We extend some coconut water to Bunny to show goodwill and to settle her mask-rattled nerves, and to show that we're serious about her health and recovery, because why else would we use up our good good chaser without drinking rum? We ask Mark-2 to remove his recrimination mask so Bunny won't close her eyes in fear of all that she sees around her and maybe black out again.

In the backs of our minds we know that this is the perfect time for Catherine the Great Disemboweler's mother to thunder-roll in, there never having been a woman in the Clearing for this long before surely sparking Catherine the Great Disemboweler's mother's spectral outrage, but maybe Hany's hatred is satiated from our recent sand episode, and what happens instead is Bunny saying again that she needs Milagros out out out of her house because in the past few days, these abnormal occurrences: unusual sounds, deviant movements, disappearing objects, and highly suspect odors. "What kind of suspect odors?" an intrigued Nello inquires. He wears his white santimanitay mask atop his head, so in effect his fake face faces the sky, and his reality-facing face faces destiny.

Bunny sits atop the picnic table and hugs her shoulders. Miki sits at the far end of the picnic table and doesn't make eye contact, but just swigs from a long-necked lager, him never trusting our concocted babash or puncheon, only beer for him please and thank you. Bunny explains further the oddities in her house, her saying that when she and Milagros returned one afternoon that the kitchen table had rotated ninety degrees, that her full-length mirror no longer reflected the house furniture behind her, and that a lavender perfume gently danced through the bathroom as well, Bunny hiding her face with her hands upon these confessions in the same way that she covered her face in grief at her father's funeral. Worst of all, she said, the constant depressing of bedsprings at night in her bedroom, sounding like children permanently jumping on a hotel bed, making it impossible for her to sleep through the night.

We've never seen her like this, and our hearts glum. We cannot believe what we're hearing from the woman who's punched a shark, the woman who's turned down almost all romantic village advances, the woman who wore white to her father Antonio's funeral in her refusal to let any of us see her grieve in public or to let the western standard of grief influence her mourning.

"Anything else?" Nello asks, and Bunny says that spices have been disappearing from her spice rack, and that she experiences the scent of spices in places where she shouldn't—paprika on the beach, cardamom at the library, and star anise while walking down the non-spice aisle in the grocery.

We turn to Nello, and he says, "This could be disappearing object phenomenon."

"Or this could be a little razzy-tail Venezuelan girl playing the ass," says Hospedales the agnostic. We ignore him and instead focus on Nello biting his thumbnail and saying this bears much thinking, this bears much consideration, this bears much deliberation.

But when Miki, still not looking at Bunny, but concentrating on his lager bottle, asks again, "Where is she? Where is little Milagros?" we realize that we've overlooked an important detail, a crucial element, and Bunny, not looking at Miki, finally says, "She's with Miss Titus," and our hearts return to their normal lub-dub.

And, to this point, just now there's changing temperature in the air, with the barometric pressure dropping, and the real expected thunder clears its throat in a deep roll, and just to be safe, in case it's absolutely Catherine the Great Disemboweler's mother, we get the hell out of there, us hauling ass out of the Clearing, the thunder pushing closer and closer, and us thinking there's no need to take unnecessary risks where Catherine the Great Disemboweler's mother is concerned, her most likely coming to mess with our time, mess with our heads, and mess with our silent recrimination.

Bunny and Milagros spend the night at Miss Titus's. The next day we meet out in the Clearing without Bunny, and we debate the situation of the extraordinary occurrence in Bunny's house. Nello's worry blossoms, him saying that this could be Catherine the Great Disemboweler's mother spreading past her usual parameters of the Clearing and spilling into the village. We think he may have a point, us thinking that maybe this is another one of the *three* that Hany promised. We cross-question Nello, asking him what he thinks is the next best natural step. He pauses for a moment, then he gives us some pourboires gratis, some words of wisdom gratis, some perspicacity gratis while he's trying to think of next steps.

"Never sweep your house after dark," he says. "That way you won't sweep away your lifeluck."

"Yeah-oui," we say.

"Never gift your sweetie a chronometer," he says. "This way time won't be running out on your relationship."

"Yeah-oui," we say.

"Never gift your sweetie a pair of shoes," he says. "This way she won't turn around and kick you up your royal black backside."

"Yeah-oui," we say.

"When a la diablesse is causing commesse, continue to wear your drawers inside out, because you know why." And he's right—we do know why. We've been doing this incessantly since Catherine the Great Disemboweler's mother's last visit, which led to all the beach sand being spirited away by the man with the shaved head, some of us for the first time wearing drawers just so we can flip them and protect ourselves against obeah.

"But what we going to do about Milagros?" Mark-2, digging a horrors, asks him, always the easiest spooked among us.

"Didn't I just tell you a minute ago?" Nello says.

We turn away from Nello and walk toward Peter-Called-Peter and his boat.

"What do we do about all this?" we ask, Peter-Called-Peter ignoring us and whistling along to a Mighty Shadow tune called "No." "Please, Peter-Called-Peter," we say. "Please." He looks up. Lowers the volume on his transistor.

"I can teach you a sitting technique that will allow the ideal answer to manifest itself in your hearts," Peter-Called-Peter says, "but you may not like all that happens on the journey to the answer or the answer itself."

"Come nah, man," says Miki.

"Alright," says Peter-Called-Peter. "Follow me." And here he switches off his transistor and the Mighty Shadow, shucks off his tool belt, and walks away from the boat he's forever building, moving toward the two picnic tables in the Clearing that arrived one day without us knowing where from, him touching our arms and our legs, bending us into uncomfortable sitting positions. "Like so," he says, gently folding us into a pose he calls padmasana, but that we call this-is-real-pressure-boy, all of us falling over a few times, our faces crunching into the earth, before we could finally maintain the position.

We are bent into this uncomfortable sitting shape, us sitting on the earth at the base of the picnic tables, our legs pretzeled painfully, while Peter-Called-Peter sits comfortably atop one of the picnic tables.

"Now close your eyes," says Peter-Called-Peter.

"That's more pressure," says Hospedales, peeking through one eye.

"Shaddup," says Miki.

"The three points of contact with the earth are vital," says Peter-Called-Peter.

"1-0-1-0-0-1," says Binary Clem.

"But this is real pressure," says Mark-2, struggling with the pose.

"A small man like you should be flexible," says Nello, discounting Mark-2's rickets.

"Remember to close your eyes and keep your backs straight," says Peter-Called-Peter.

"That go be hard for Hospedales," says Miki. "The man more crooked than a dog back leg."

"Why you don't hush your ass," says Hospedales, struggling supremely with the pose, even tipping over before righting himself, us suspecting that pain from his bulletted leg was radiating through him.

"This would be hard for You-We too bad," adds Miki. "Good thing he not here."

"Probably eating out his mother fridge," says Mark-2.

"Why you don't hush your ass?" Hospedales repeats.

"Now," says Peter-Called-Peter. "Follow your breath and relax all of your muscles."

"And how the ass we supposed to do that?" Hospedales asks.

"Why you don't hold your ass and stop complaining?" asks Miki.

We struggle, but most of us approximate what Peter-Called-Peter instructs us on, us thinking maybe this isn't so bad, inhaling and holding for a five count, then exhaling for a seven count, us thinking that just as long as we don't smell oranges everything will be irie, but soon we learn the curse of Peter-Called-Peter's mysticism when, fifteen minutes and twenty-seven seconds into his deep-breathing and spine straightening, various members of our cabal start realizing then recognizing things out loud that they should have kept remanded in their dirty minds, the pose causing us to release what becomes airing out dirty-gray laundry in the public square.

First Mark-2, that wretch, admits that he steals nighties from clotheslines, just to try them on, before realizing that doing this would agitate the village women.

Then Miki groans and confesses that he'd bought Bunny an emerald-cut engagement ring and that he's put a deposit down on an A-line wedding dress with a princess neckline for her, then recognizes that this was presumptuous of him and he should have asked her first.

Then Hospedales confesses that he's taking money and looking the other way when Venezuelans sneak illegally into the country at the wharf and that he does a little coke on weekends when he visits brothels, his voice completely cold and detached as if he doesn't recognize anything, and we think that if realizing then recognizing means that we won't do these things again, then Hospedales will keep snorting his way through weekends. These were things that we had already known but that we had kept to ourselves, but now we were coming to recognize bigger and more important things not related to things that we already knew, like when in a sudden lightning strike moment of recognition, Miki recognizes that we need to get Milagros off the island. "We need to get Milagros off the island," he repeats, and we open our eyes, and we feel something like escaping air pressure pop in our ears.

"Well then," says Peter-Called-Peter, unfolding himself. "I think we've made a lot of progress." He bows to us with joined hands. "Namaste." Then he heads back to his boat, leaving us all twisted and astonished.

Things move quickly after that: we learn that Nello's brother, Caleb, is a pastor of one of those small clap-hand churches in Grenada, him married with two nice nice daughters who, when we reach out to him, says he and his wife, Gloria, always have plenty of room for a child in need of God's protection. We tell Bunny about Caleb and whether she would be willing to stay one or two weeks in Grenada with Milagros to help her settle. "Yes, gotdammit," she says, "but I don't want nobody in my blasted house."

Next, we need to secure a boat to get us to Grenada, and here Hospedales, now walking with a cane after having successful surgery to remove the bullet from his leg that he worked damn hard to earn, says that he knows someone down at the yacht club who could lend us a sixty-five-foot Dutch boyer barge. Peter-Called-Peter eyes Hospedales gravely and tells him, "Hospe, we can't have any extracurriculars on the boat," since Peter-Called-Peter, like the rest of us, knows about Hospedales one time moving Santa Marta Colombian gold, shhh shhh shhh, us now knowing about his weekend cocaína habit as well.

"Hold your ass," Hospedales replies. Soon after this everything snaps suspiciously soundly into place, and in five days we set about our plan, constantly on edge with the smell of oranges breezing, every now and again, through the village, and us keeping in mind the conferred secrets we know now about each other.

We leave early, piling into Peter-Called-Peter's Trooper pre-dawn, us knowing that we need to depart under the cover of darkness to mamaguy the coast guard, to keep their hot hot breath off our necks and their grabbalicious hands off our wallets, none of us wanting to pay bohbol for which the coast guard would surely ask if they hold us. We inspect the boat that Hospedales has secured, decide that it won't splinter and fall apart like the boat that Peter-Called-Peter's permanently building, and we board. Here's what happens before things go sideways, before what really troubles us comes down from the top turnbuckle, what happens before what the glasses and goateed UWI graduate would call acidiferous rainfall in the atmosphere from our island's chemical and oil production, before we're even two hundred yards into open water: Bunny and Miki sprawl into a shouting match belowdecks.

The reason is clear without even trying to listen too closely: Bunny has told Miki that she's sold her house to the Minister of National Security via Hospedales, and that she's moving permanently to Grenada with Milagros. *Papa yo*, we think. *Bacchanal.* Things pitch and roil down below, cupboards slamming and glassware smashing, and we see Hospedales having kittens, his face turning pink, then purple, him clearly wanting to descend to stop them destroying borrowed goods that he'll have to reimburse, but him not wanting to leave the wheelhouse on his battered leg, which means Nello negotiates the racket instead, the rest of us staying above deck, expecting things to quiet down, but them only getting louder, and Hospedales's face stormclouding as he ponders intervening, and just then we see Nello emerge, him carrying a distressed Milagros in his arms, the little girl clinging tightly around his waist, her hugging his neck while Bunny and Miki continue to spit lightning and slap thunder at each other.

It's spooky dark, pre-dawn, and somewhat chilly, but things have ceased and settled somewhat between Miki and Bunny. We wrap ourselves with blankets as we sit on the benches bolted to the gunwales. We leave the island behind. For most of us this is the first time that the coastline evaporates, this being for some of us our longest trip off the island, us not having lived in other countries as Peter-Called-Peter had, and wherever Siddiq is now, and not harboring Bunny's distant Nippon dreams, her climbing on the first rung of emigration by sneakily selling her house. For a few moments the engine's low gear drone is the only sound, the soft slosh of the water as it splits and separates.

Our plan is to spend a few days in Grenada, laze around on Grand Anse Beach, then withdraw our presence from Milagros slowly. But with Bunny and Miki feuding, we wonder if we'll make it in one piece, and it's at this moment that things go pear-shaped with Hospedales tapping on the gas gauge and realizing that we're short of petrol.

It's here that we see the single flying fish, lifting itself about fifteen meters into the air, then dropping just low enough to skim the water, this putting the fear of God in us because we know that you're never supposed to see just a single flying fish, that they always swim in a school of ten to fifteen, and we feel that inevitable shiver as we watch the fish disappear back below the surface and we say nothing to each other.

And then, as we sit on tenterhooks wondering if Bunny and Miki will erupt again, Nello starts to complain about an uneasy feeling in his ears. Tinnitus, he says, naming the ringing. He says that the constant movement of the boat is also nauseating him, making it difficult to maintain his balance. We can't believe it. We tell him to stop complaining. We tell him it's just seasickness. We tell him to ride it out. "It's not seasickness!" he says. We know the look that Hospedales shoots him. We throw a life vest at Nello and tell him to pull it on. We tell him to go belowdecks. We tell him to chew gum. He gives us an evil look as he straps on his vest. We silently condemn each other, thinking that we should have known better, that this is the fallout of Recrimination Carnival Las' Lap, us not even having the good sense to have enough gas for this New Felicity Village voyage of the damned.

"Who the hell invited that Jonah?" Hospedales asks as Nello vomits over the side.

Things worsen. Aside from Miki still fuming, aside from the low gas indicator, aside from Nello's seasickness, aside from the single flying fish: another omen—the frigatebird that swoops down and gulps the winged fish just as it skims the water one last time. We read this as a reflection of the Miki and Bunny blow up, and us as well. Bunny and Miki start a second round of shelling. We don't know what to do, now with the extra element of an upset Milagros. We're aghast. Bunny comes above deck to comfort Milagros but Miki follows her, makes his way to Bunny, and sits on her left while Milagros sits to her right, and suddenly tears are mapping Miki's face, him crying and saying that he can't deal with the thought of Bunny out of his life, that she should give him one more chance, that he'll sell his house and move to Grenada to be with her. Bunny side-eyes him and says, "Get a gotdamn grip, man."

Gs + Hs, we think.

We look away, not wanting Miki to see our loss of respect. We're about a dozen nautical miles from shore now, us still motoring out and fearful of coast guard patrols, or else we would have made Hospedales turn us right back around, all of us uncomfortable and wanting to get off the boat and get away, not knowing what to do with Miki when he puts his sensitivity lights on full beam.

We feel shame too bad for him.

Poor Bunny, we think.

Poor Milagros.

Poor state of affairs for all of us, us wishing, for once, for the familiarity of Catherine the Great Disemboweler's mother Hany terrifying us in the Clearing.

It's Milagros who we watch most closely, Milagros who, returning to a boat for the first time since she's arrived on the island, has grown more and more distressed and unsettled, us watching her shrink down almost to the size of a conch shell. By the time Bunny sits beside Milagros to comfort her, Milagros's leg has become a sewing machine, pumping pumping pumping, her forehead perspiration slick, her eyes shuttering. And when Miki won't let their spat go and continues to hiss at Bunny, it's Nello who ends up removing his life vest and pulling it onto Milagros, him being the one who wraps his arms around her shoulders.

It's Nello who touches a handkerchief to her tears, her chest beating like a frog's, the mucus rivering from nose to mouth, and him and his handkerchief wiping it all away. It's something that we'd always be grateful to him for because soon after that, dawn arrives, and that's when we encounter the floating bodies.

It's the dawn's first bright light that startles us, it streaming across the horizon and grabbing and turning bits of water like glass and shining smartly through them like gems. We're mesmerized by this trick of light, which we hadn't seen in all the hundred million times that we'd gone fishing, probably because we'd never set out onto the water on this side of the island and seen the sun rise from this angle. It's this water-light-glass trick that catches our eye when we see the hands of the first body waving through the water-light-glass like it's gesturing us to admire it, like it's pointing out a piece of crystal to a client in an antique store, the hand motion saying, *see how the crystal catches the light, madam? See how lovely it is?* It's the hand on this body that points out the others, the bodies spilled across the water in an arc like the archipelago of islands that make up the Caribbean, spilled across the water like a cemetery that has flooded and has pushed the buried bodies to the surface.

And there are so many Venezuelan bodies.

From his perch on the bow, Peter-Called-Peter comes across the bodies first, him saying softly, "Cut the engine, Hospedales, cut the engine."

Miki, who's still pleading his lovesick case to Bunny beside her on one of the boat's cushioned rail benches, thinks that Hospedales has cut the engine to eavesdrop, and he says in a voice a little too high, "What the *ass*, Hospedales?" But by now Hospedales sees what Peter-Called-Peter is calling his attention to, Peter-Called-Peter chinning toward the bodies on the water, the rest of us following his direction. Then the sunlight brightens, a light switch flipped, the light still stretching its way across the water, pink and orange and peach, colors that we'd never paid much attention to before, the light lighting the water like a stage and almost rendering the bodies serene. It's now that Miki, who'd just been crying, finally witnesses with the rest of us: bodies all around us, recently lost, not yet bloated, while Bunny discreetly guides Milagros below deck. Peter-Called-Peter retrieves a couple of gaffs, and slowly we begin the task of culling the bodies aboard, Nello, Peter-Called-Peter, and Miki gaffing the dead close, pulling the waterlogged corpses toward us, reaching out for a water-logged arm, or a soggy leg.

The first body we retrieve is connected to the hand that showed us the gemstones of light upon water.

The second body we retrieve is a man whose eyes are still open who seems as if he's looking at something just past our heads, looking for some sort of explanation for all of this, looking perhaps for a reprieve to return home. The third body that we retrieve is a young boy, too thin, wearing only a pair of waterlogged drawers that barely cling, wet and soggy, to his backside, us thinking that maybe he'd stripped off his clothes to swim when he saw that he was sinking into the water. But it's the fourth and fifth bodies that stop us and give us prayerful pause, the mother holding the baby tightly to her chest, holding the baby's body so that it could remain above the water and maybe continue to draw breath, but both of them already lost.

We have pulled aboard all eighteen bodies when we finally come across the two survivors, the two Venezuelans clinging to an old oil barrel, them floating along like oil-wetted seabirds condemned by an oil spill, a natural disaster of our oil treaty's making. The couple, who we later learn from the story in the gazette to be the vessel's captain and his wife, are desolate. They're so weak that Miki has to strip down to his drawers and jump into the water and push their bodies from behind while the rest of us pull them onto the deck, us then taking them below to wrap them in blankets so they won't have to see the bodies that once spoke to them, that once expressed bright-eyed dreams to them, that were hesitant about leaving Venezuela behind.

But then, down below, Milagros engages the descending survivors and, smart girl that she is, she immediately puts two and two together. "Where did you come from?" she inquires in sharp Spanish, even though we're sure that she already knows. "Did you sink?" Then she rushes up to the deck, and we try to steer her away from the side on which the lost bodies are laid out, us having to stack them on top of each other so that they all fit, but she won't be led away. "What happened?" she asks, but we couldn't reply, and Nello finally leads her back down below. Later he tells us that Milagros cross-questioned the captain and his wife until Bunny wrapped her arms around Milagros's chest, comforting her, soothing her, until Milagros's question, the same one over and over, finally dissolved into a whisper.

"Call the coast guard," Peter-Called-Peter says softly to Hospedales, and Hospedales, frozen at first, turning over all the consequences of such an action, realizes that there's no other option, us already running low on fuel, so he finally picks up the receiver and squeezes the button, and after the squelch, he signals the coast guard and reads them our location.

Once we wrap the rescued pair in a blanket, and while we wait for the coast guard, we ask the captain how long they'd been in the water, and he says he cannot remember, him and his wife still in deep shock, their pupils reduced to pinpoints. We try to fill them with hot tea from a thermos, but their shaking hands cannot hold anything.

"The water cold as hell," Miki says after we pull him aboard and wrap a blanket around him too. "I don't know what that was. I never feel anything cold cold so."

Milagros pops her head up here and, despite Bunny trying to get her back downstairs, she stays on the deck and watches everything. When the coast guard cutter arrives, relief floods Hospedales's face when he clearly recognizes the three officers who board. "Is what is all this tra la la, Hospedales?" asks the lead officer.

We turn away as Hospedales folds bills into each officer's pockets. We pretend not to see when he folds some more. We study our feet when he folds even more bohbol. The first payoff, we figure, is so that we don't have to answer any questions about where we're heading without official documentation or clearance. The second payoff is to keep us out of any reports that the coast guard files and to forget that they ever saw us. The third payoff is so that the coast guard won't search the boat, find anything incriminating, or plant incriminating contraband to make a little extra bohbol, and also to make them forget the first two payoffs, coast guard officers being known to charge people for bribing them while keeping the first insulting low bohbol bid folded into their pockets. And finally Hospedales pays them an exorbitant price for some petrol to get us back on track.

"Keep up the good work, fellas," Hospedales says a little too loudly to the coast guard when we're transferring the bodies from our deck over to the coast guard's cutter and when they've provided us with a dribble of petrol to set us on our way. By this point Bunny has led Milagros back below deck, the child in just as much shock as the captain and his wife.

When the coast guard takes the captain and his wife aboard, we see Hospedales limp across and stick some money into the captain's pocket. We know he'd be embarrassed if we say anything, so we don't. The coast guard officers don't ask us any more questions as we complete the transfer of the bodies and the captain and his wife over to them, and because they don't ask us to follow them back, we continue our trip to Grenada, saying nothing for the rest of the trip, Bunny tightly hugging Milagros, and Miki holding his head in his hands.

8

In Which Streamertail Hummingbirds and Cane Dogs Determine the Course of Cruickshank Islanders' Destinies

ME SUPPOSED TO run away from the estate an' up into the mountain in five days with Etto an' we children Catherine an' James, but things feeling mix-up mix-up. Is when Marse John return from Scotland that me an' Etto start planning. "Hany," Etto say, "is go we must go"—but is James me worry about. Me only ask Marse John to let James learn to read so 'im ain't go think we planning anything because Marse John know me ain't leaving James behind, especially if 'im start to read. But past few nights me only feel like something wrong-wrong, an' me can't figure it. Tomorrow me supposed to go in the woods by the mangrove to meet Etto an' make we last plan, but the hair on me arm only bending wrong way, an' me dreams the past few nights heavy-heavy.

In truth me don't have time for this; in fifteen minutes Marse John coming in the scullery barking like cane dog an' looking for 'im dinner. Me listen out for the clock chime. Me is the only one who know how clock does work in this house except Marse John, an' me have to hide this good-good from him. Past few days Marse John blowing hot an' cold an' me never sure how 'im going to be from one day to the next.

"Is Rebekkah doing maljeau," Miss Mitilde say, when me go down to the caneslave cabin to ask she is what troubling me. "Rebekkah working left-hand dumpling an' putting thing in Marse John food an' putting bad eye on you." Miss Mitilde is the last one from she tribe, an' she head wrap up in green headscarf an' even Marse John don't bother she. She does move around the estate doing only what she want. She eyes gold an' dangerous.

"Is so?" me say.

Miss Mitilde say, "Is Mama Binti who Rebekkah dealing with," an' me feel the hair behind me neck bend the wrong way an' everything start to make sense. Me give Miss Mitilde the extra bread me steal from Marse John pantry, an' she grunt, an' in the corner of the cabin me see Agnes sick brown eyes as she lie down dying on she pallet, she eyes burning with hard hate for me for getting to live in Abercromby Hall with me children. Miss Mitilde already start to eat the bread by the time me walk back to the scullery.

Me reach back just in time to see Rebekkah looking in Marse John foodpot, an' me tell she, "Eh, watch I don't break pot-spoon on your head," but she only replace the lid easy-easy, like she is queen of Abercromby Hall. Me fraid she put something in the foodpot, just like Miss Mitilde say, some cotton roots to chase Marse John head an' make he do what she want. Is years now Rebekkah vexed with me, vexed since Marse Bernard tell she 'im prefer me in the scullery an' in 'im bedchamber, an' is banish she get banish with she daughter Sadie down by the cabin, an' me get pull up in the house with Catherine an' James. Is what she want me do? Is like she think me like Marse Bernard an' Marse John with them fatty-fatty self? But is so things does change quick-quick on estate, an' is years now me living in Abercromby Hall. It mean me can't see Etto easy-easy because, when Marse John reach back, 'im say 'im don't want no man caneslave near Abercromby Hall. Worse, when Marse Bernard head back Scotland Marse John come to take 'im place, fatter than when me first see 'im twelve years before, an' 'im only want me up in 'im bedchamber. If Marse Bernard did like being up in me cunny, Marse John love it. Both make me sick-sick. But is so they confuse Rebekkah: she skin light-light, an' me dark-dark, an' is so planter lust for kitchen-girl with light skin that she think things go switch. When I tell Etto later about Rebekkah 'im repeat we need to go before 'im kill Marse John.

"Me an' Sadie having dinner in the scullery with you an' James an' Catherine this evening," Rebekkah say.

"Is so?" me ask. "Marse John know about that?" Is the one good thing Marse John does allow, for me to eat with me children alone every evening. Rebekkah an' Sadie have to eat down in cabins when they housework done. Same time me hear Marse John knock over some books in 'im study walking over here, an' Rebekkah move quick-quick through the back door so he ain't see she, an' is so me know she only wanted to look in the pot to see if she silk cotton roots mash up in the food yet. Me have to keep me eye open. Me look in the pot an' me ain't see nothing she put in.

"Is my supper almost ready, Hany?" Marse John ask, an' me tell 'im by the time the sun start to go down 'im could eat, an' 'im gone back to 'im letter writing. 'im don't make joke with 'im dinner with 'im fatty-fatty self. Me gone to get Catherine an' James to eat them dinner.

Me know Marse John don't want to send me back down to the caneslave cabin because Etto down there, an' Marse John don't want 'im around me, so 'im does keep me an' James an' Catherine in Abercromby Hall. Me know 'im vexed-vexed that Etto is Catherine father. But me worrying now about if Rebekkah put something in Marse John food to chase 'im head. If Mitilde say Rebekkah seeing Mama Binti for tricks, then is so. If Rebekkah put something in Marse John food then everything go turn upside down fast-fast. Me don't want nothing with Mama Binti. It have plenty story about how she price steep-steep, an' me don't want to deal with somebody me can't see. The whispering old women say Mama Binti does blow in the air an' does only show up when she know women want to make a deal, when she know they can't take the iron no more, an' is so why she price steep-steep.

When me reach the front of the verandah, me chest almost collapse when me see Deputy Shand sitting on the step an' Catherine sitting on 'im lap, an' Shand jiggling 'im leg up an' down. Is big stone me look for to bust open Shand head, but 'im see me before me could find one. "Catherine," me say. "Come. Is time for dinner." She stop laughing, an' she climb down from Shand lap. Me send she around the side of the house to the back.

"Kitty just wanted to see what it was like to ride a horse," Shand say.

Me say, "She not name no Kitty, she name Catherine," an' me walk off in case me see big stone to buss open 'im head, me thinking how to tell me daughter not to be by sheself with Shand because shoo-shoo is Shand like to hold down little girls in the canefield. Marse John does call me daughter Kate an' now this quenk Shand calling she Kitty, but is *my* daughter, an' she name is Catherine. Me think Shand already up under Rebekkah daughter Sadie pooch, but if Rebekkah ain't find nothing wrong with that, then is not for me to say anything. Me business is Catherine an' James. Always Catherine an' James. Only Catherine an' James. If me catch Shand with Catherine, me cut off 'im balls.

Me have to turn down the fire on Marse John dinner before me eat with me children. But same time a head poke round the doorframe. Is Polydore, holding out 'im bowl. "Is what you want, Poly? Me need to put out Marse John dinner." Marse John don't like no man caneslave around the house, not even Poly.

"Please, Hany," Polydore say, holding up 'im bowl. "Me still hungry. A little more?" Is Rebekkah who does cook for all the caneslaves down in the cabins, but Etto say everything Rebekkah cook does taste like wood bark. But not even Etto brave enough to sneak up to the house because if Marse John catch 'im, is whip 'im go feel on 'im back. Warburton done get whip for no reason when Marse John reach back. "Please," Poly say. Me don't know how Polydore stay so skinny since 'im always eating, even in the middle of the day 'im does find a way to sneak back from first canefield an' beg for food. Is Marse John scraps 'im want, but me tell 'im me can't give 'im scraps since Marse John ain't eat yet. "Then a little from yours?" 'im ask.

Me give 'im two big spoonfuls of peas an' rice. "Now gwan, Poly," me say, an' 'im take off like puss. 'im brave an' stupid to come here for two spoonful of rice an' peas an' pork fat an' stupid people on this estate does feel whip lash.

After me feed Marse John, an' me eat with James an' Catherine in the scullery, me thinking how James asking me to get Marse James to get 'im to learn 'im letters. 'im did overhear me asking Marse John, an' now 'im don't stop asking me. Miss Mitilde tell me if me really want Marse John to do something for me an' James then me need to get some snips of Marse John hair an' some of 'im fingernail clippings.

"Is so," me promise.

Is two o'clock in the afternoon, an' Marse John gone to play chess, an' me heart beating hard-hard as me getting ready to go see Etto in the mangrove. Is more bad dream me had the night before, an' is more pain in me back, an' something ain't feeling right side up. Me dream that me in canefield that on fire, an' me screaming but nobody coming. When me wake up me feel Marse John fatty belly on top of me an' 'im snoring. Me roll 'im off me an' 'im snort an' 'im keep sleeping, but me can't fall back to sleep. So me sneak over in the next room an' sleep next to Catherine an' James because although the man don't do nothing but play chess, write letter, an' watch cane grow, 'im always tired-tired, an' 'im does sleep hard-hard through the night.

When me reach the mangrove me see Etto. 'im sitting down an' wetting 'im foot in the water. That Etto sit there, not saying nothing, just looking out in the water, make 'im favor James. 'im watching the skinny red bird an' them fly off, an' 'im smile when 'im see me, an' then 'im face go long-long when 'im see something wrong. "Is what?" 'im ask, an' me say me just tired-tired, an' 'im hug me up just so. Me reach up an' touch 'im head, 'im hair knotty-knotty, but 'im say 'im not cutting it. 'im rest 'im head in me lap an' follow the red bird them as them fly off.

Etto say always wait fifteen minutes to make sure that Marse John really gone because is tricks them whiteman planter have, an' 'im might be waiting to follow me. 'im say as soon as Marse John reach back on the island an' whip up Warburton back for no reason, is so 'im know Marse John have more poison than cane snake an' is go we have to go. Is always afternoon when me does meet Etto, when Marse John gone by Visser, an' Shand an' MacTeer sleepy-sleepy from lunch an' it hard for them to cover the five canefields when them sluggy-sluggy. Sometimes me reach an' Etto ain't there, an' sometimes 'im come an' me not there, an' is a whole next week we have to wait again. But things easing up with Marse John going to Visser estate to play chess more an' more. Is today that me need Etto bad-bad; me tired of lying down in Marse John bedchamber, an' me tired of the feeling that Rebekkah working skulduggery an' me tired of having to clean 'im house, an' me tired making sure Shand not bothering me girl child.

Up close me look at the scar around Etto neck that 'im don't like to talk about. Same way me don't like how Marse Bernard bring me from Jamaica when me was small, taking me from my own mother. "Everything set up?" me ask.

"Yes," 'im say.

'im say 'im know somebody up in the mountains already. The only person who run off to mountain an' who ain't get drag back by Shand an' MacTeer an' them cane dogs is Henry, an' plenty caneslave feel Henry dead an' not living in no mountain. Etto try to tell me some bacchanal between Shand and Warburton, but me tell 'im hush, an' me just rest me head on 'im chest an' listen to 'im heart ticking like clock. Me touch 'im hair. "Everything still on schedule," 'im say. Me follow one red bird swooping low down by the mangrove. Is James favorite bird. 'im does like to come out by the mangrove to watch them.

"Is who else going?" me ask. *Besides you, me, an' Catherine an' James?*

"Just one or two more," 'im say.

'im don't want to give me them names because even the trees an' all around the estate does listen. "Any women?" me ask. "Any children?"

"One or two," 'im say.

Is so me know that Kitch an' Grafton in 'im group, an' maybe Warburton. Me know 'im thinking to bring 'im mother Agnes, but 'im can't do it because she sick-sick and ain't go make it up no mountain. Me don't tell 'im that one or two more is too much, an' that is a good way to get catch, but me know me being selfish in just wanting 'im an' Catherine an' James. But then me feel we should try to bring the whole estate, to ass was Marse John. Me touch the scar around 'im neck, an' 'im wrap 'im fingers around me hand an' kiss me fingertips.

"Don't go without me," me say.

Is how often me go from Abercromby Hall to the mangrove to meet Etto? Me should know how to move back and forth by heart. But on the way back me get lost, an' me find that me lost because all the trees an' them looking the same, an' the breeze blowing cooler than usual, an' just so me start to smell orange even though it don't have no oranges growing around here. Me look around an' me ain't hearing no bird singing or animal running through the bush either.

An' is so me get scared.

Then me hear a voice me never hear before, saying [I've been waiting for you, Miss Hany] an' me nearly jump up an' hit me head on a low branch.

"Is who that?" me ask.

[You know who we are] say the voice, an' is so me realize in truth that is at least three voices that me hearing, overlapping, them braiding together like hair plait, one voice bouncing off the next one.

"Is what you want?" me ask.

[No] the voice them say. [We're here to serve *you*]

Is run me want to run, but me find like me two foot can't move good, an' it feel like me knee them ready to collapse.

"Me don't want anything," me say.

[That's not true]

"Me just want me two children to be safe."

[That and more]

Is right away me think about last night an' Marse John wrapping 'im hand around me throat when 'im doing 'im business an' 'im say, "I'm dying, Hany! Oh, I'm dying!" an' me think well then dead!

[I can provide you almost anything your heart desires] the voice say. [If you're willing to pay the cost]

But me barely hear what the voice them say because is run me start to run, an' me feel tree branch scratching up me face, an' me find that, instead of reaching the big open space, that the trees start to close in tighter an' tighter, an' it feel like hand on me throat starting to squeeze, an' it feel like tree root wrapping around me two foot, an' me feel like is tie up like crab me tie up. The last thing me hear the voices them say is [Don't forget his hair] an' then me hear laughing *keck-keck-keck* an' next thing me know is through the trees me pass through, an' me see the back of Abercromby Hall, the back of the scullery where me does spend all day, an' me run fast-fast to reach there. Me think is some wake-up dream except, when me reach, the scratch them still burning on me face. *Is Miss Mitilde tie up with Mama Binti,* me wonder, *or is Mama Binti just know everything so?* Is when me nearly reach the scullery that me see Shand sitting on tree stump, feeding the cane dogs them, throwing raw meat in them mouth, an' 'im watching me hard-hard. Next time me see Etto, me tell 'im me scared, an' 'im say 'im feel Polydore know them plans 'an go say something, 'an is so we stay quiet for another month, 'an me heart quiet down.

In the scullery Marse John vexed-vexed an' want to know where me was? Is so me can't tell 'im any good answer. Then Rebekkah say, "Kate was sick earlier, Marse John, an' Hany just went to find some roots to boil she some tea." Me wonder if Shand tell 'im how 'im see me coming through the woods or if 'im go say anything.

Marse John face settle down. "Still," 'im say, "don't just disappear like that, Hany, even if Kate is ill." 'im wipe 'im brow with 'im handkerchief. 'im looking fat an' flimsy on 'im feet. "Anyway," Marse John say, "I just wanted both of you to know that we'll have a special guest over for dinner tomorrow, and I want you to prepare mutton. Not chicken. Not pork. Not goat."

Visser, me think.

"Begging Marse John pardon," Rebekkah say, "but seeing as Hany so concern with Kate, maybe is better for me to cook your dinner tonight an' let she concentrate on tomorrow."

Marse John think, then 'im say, "Yes, Rebekkah, let Hany take care of Kate." 'im wipe 'im brow again, an' 'im move to 'im study, an' this is how me know is cane breeze blowing hard in the wrong direction now in this house. Etto right. Is time to head up in the mountain with Catherine an' James.

But me still need Marse John hair and fingernail clippings first to smooth the path.

That night me dream that Rebekkah riding on top of Marse John with one set of candle burning around the bedchamber making the place bright-bright while me sitting in the corner with me chin brace on me knees an' me can't move an' have to watch them, an' Rebekkah look over she shoulder an' see me sitting there an' she wink at me, an' is so me know me have to do everything to protect Catherine an' James because is storm Rebekkah bringing by putting things in Marse John food to make 'im do what she want. Brief so the idea of Mama Binti come in me head, an' me making deal with she, but then me see Etto shaking 'im head an' telling me "no." Me wake up, an' Marse John on top of me, snoring hard-hard, an' is so me have to roll the big bobboloops off me.

Next morning me sneak off to see Miss Mitilde again. She does dream too, but while me does dream crooked-crooked she does dream straight-straight. She come from tribe who name nobody suppose to say, an' she is the last one of them on the island. Mitilde eyes bright gold an' she hair tie up tight-tight with green scarf. Me still worried about Shand, but as soon as she see me she say, "You need to go by Mama Binti." She say she dream about Mama Binti an' me, an' me explain how me hear voices in the woods the day before. "Everything getting ready to mash up in your life, an' you need to get in front it. Is so Mama Binti know an' offering a way out."

Me feel sweat on the back of me neck. "Is deal me have to make deal with she?"

Miss Mitilde keep she gold eyes on me. "If you want to try to hold on to what you have," she say. "An' even so self you might not keep everything." She see me fraidy-fraidy, an' she take me hands in she own. They warm-warm. "Is best not to worry," she say. "Is not everything you could hold on to. But be careful," Miss Mitilde say. "What you think is good news for everybody is not always so." She say Rebekkah already planning to move back in the big house. "Get me Marse John hairs an' fingernails," Miss Mitilde say. Me give she three hen eggs me steal for she. In the corner Agnes watching me hard-hard then she turn she head an' spit. Me realize Etto must be tell she that 'im running off, an' 'im can't take she.

Other things make me scared to run, not just when the hair an' nails disappear, but when Marse John brother reach two weeks ago. "This," Marse John say to me an' Rebekkah, "is my brother, Finlay, just arrived from Scotland." Is one big oonks 'im showing me on the verandah. Me didn't even know 'im was coming. Me have to lift up me neck to see 'im face. Right away me know Finlay is horrors since Shand an' MacTeer stand behind 'im, an' both of them looking down on the ground like Finlay have rope tie around them neck like cane dog an' tugging down. Me watching Finlay, but 'im don't see me. 'im only eyeing up Rebekkah smiley-smiley face.

That evening, when Marse John call me an' Rebekkah in 'im study, 'im make we wait standing up like bobolee while 'im finish writing letter. "Are you writing to your cousin Bernard?" Rebekkah ask.

Marse John quill stop scratching, an' 'im say, "That's *Master* Bernard to you, and that is none of your concern." An' is so Rebekkah face get red-red, an' is so me know that whatever magic she work on him with the silk cotton roots, whatever obeah prayer an' tricks she pull ain't take 'im completely yet. Is fight 'im fighting it, an' 'im don't even know self. Marse John continue writing, an' me count off five minutes in me head before 'im finish 'im letter an' 'im say 'im decide 'im want Rebekkah to cook the dinner for 'im guest. She face light up bright-bright. Me know is whatever she put in 'im food making 'im act so. Right then me ask Marse John if 'im want me to trim 'im hair so 'im look smart for dinner. 'im smile an' say "What a good idea," an' Rebekkah face turn stormcloud. Me feel is the last time that she silk cotton roots will let me cut 'im hair, an' me hope this will help me be gone long before it need to cut again, an' me never go have to see 'im fatty-fatty face again. Is while me cutting 'im hair 'im say that 'im decide to let James learn 'im letters. "We'll start in a few days," 'im say.

"Yes, Marse John. Thank you, Marse John."

Me sneak out just before dinner an' take Marse John hair an' nail clippings to Miss Mitilde an' some pig-foot souse that me make for she too.

Me expecting dinner guest to be Marse Visser come to meet Finlay, but is Miss Grace Cumberbatch. Grace Cumberbatch is the kitchen girl from estate on the next side of the island that all kitchen girls does talk about because Miss Grace not no kitchen girl no more. Me always have to tell Rebekkah daughter Sadie, an' the little mouse-face Alice who does help me in the scullery, to stop talking about Miss Grace an' do them housework. Shoo-shoo is when Marse Cumberbatch went back England, 'im leave Miss Grace with house, furniture, an' plenty money coming in every year to mind she. Is so every kitchen girl dream they go end up like Grace Cumberbatch. But shoo-shoo say Grace Cumberbatch make deal with Mama Binti to end up how she end up. How she was nothing but a little caneslave midwife helping deliver baby before Marse Cumberbatch pull she in 'im bedchamber.

Rebekkah say is me have to greet Miss Cumberbatch, so when me hear horse carriage pull up, me go to the door with Marse John. "Miss Cumberbatch," 'im say when 'im open the door. "It is a pleasure to receive you." 'im give a little bow. Miss Grace Cumberbatch dress like all them planter wife, heavy clothes like she ain't born in this island hot-hot heat, an' a parasol holding up over she head. "Hany, take Miss Cumberbatch's effects." Me bow, an' she hand me she hat an' parasol. "Unfortunately her cane crop is struggling this season, so she's visiting our humble estate, with hopes that we will provide her with some small details that may aid her own harvest." Marse John forehead sweaty-sweaty.

Miss Grace say, "You're the one who's humble, Mr. Cruickshank. Everyone knows that your estate harvests the island's sweetest sugar." She talking like she whispering, an' is close-close you have to listen to hear what she say.

Marse John blush an' lead she into 'im study. "Let's have some tea before dinner," 'im say. "Rebekkah should be preparing a marvelous mutton meal I think. In fact," 'im say, "I need to have a quick word with her," an' just so 'im gone.

As soon as Marse John leave the study Miss Cumberbatch inspecting the bookshelf. She move like water pour out tin cup. She fingers move like spider as she inspect the spine of two books, an' she pull one from the shelf an' hold it by she side. Then she perch sheself over the letter on the desk that Marse John start writing. Me want to say *Aye! Miss lady! That is none of your business*, but me think the only thing that a past kitchen girl go hate on the estate is present kitchen girl reminding she of what she was.

Me stand by the door an' sneak looks at Miss Cumberbatch, an' me watch she light-light skin that them planters an' deputy love—Etto say is so them like to see themselves in caneslaves—but me know the woman pretty even though she forehead small-small. Me know that she know me watching, but she don't turn to me. Me realize from watching she that if she once was kitchen girl that she ain't do much kitchen work or cooking or cleaning: she hand soft-soft, an' is so me feel bad because me know is up in the bedchamber Marse Cumberbatch had she all the time once he pull she from learning how to midwife. Shoo-shoo is she had to trade she girl-child life to Mama Binti to make Marse Cumberbatch go back England an' to give she house an' send she money. Is how, me wonder, anybody go give away they child? Me thinking about Catherine when me hear me name, an' me realize is talk Miss Grace talking to me. She ask, "Do you know your letters, Hany? Do you ever read your master's words?"

"Beg your par—" me say.

"Don't beg anything from me," she say, an' she snap the book shut. "Your letters and words," she say. "Do you know them?" She face scrunch up in smile, an' she face look like pussycat.

Is trap this is trap, so me say, "No, Miss Cumberbatch."

"You are right to deceive me," she say. She pick up a next book an' flip the pages quick-quick. "And I don't blame you for your prevarication. For all you know I could be a spy for your patron." She voice go low. "But if what Cruickshank says about your cleverness is true, I'm sure you know your letters backwards and forwards, and that's a start. That's a good start." She look at the clock. Me still don't say nothing. She walk over to me an' look me up from tip to tail.

"You're in dire straits," she say.

"Beg your pardon, Miss Cumberbatch."

"Don't beg for anything from me," she say again. She voice drop. "Does he know that you're pregnant?" Me feel me face stretch tight. Plenty things jump up in me head when she say this. First me think is lie she lying. But why she go lie? Then me think who it go look like, Etto or Marse John? Then me think that if we reach up in the mountain is so it go be harder to feed everybody. An' this an' that an' this an' that, an' me head feeling like Etto an' Miss Mitilde an' Marse John shouting at me at the same time, an' me sit down before me fall down. *How 'im go know if me don't know? an' if this midwife know Miss Mitilde must be know too, an' why she ain't say nothing?*

Miss Cumberbatch produces a farthing. "Tell me the time on that clock," she say, "and this is yours." Me don't say nothing. She withdraw the coin. She voice drop lower. She lean in close. Me suck in me breath. She mouth right next to me ear.

"Do you envy me?" Miss Grace ask.

"Miss Grace?"

"Do you think my life a good one?"

"Plenty kitchen girl want to be like you," me say. "Plenty kitchen girl want what you have."

"And what do I have?" She smile. "Your Mr. Cruickshank is not going to help me out of the goodness of his heart," she say. "The word is his brother has come to the island, and when he comes through that door he will return with his brother who will eye me up and down and see if he wants to spend some time with me, and if he does, if he wants to spread apart my legs, then maybe a deal can be worked out."

An' is so right then Marse John come bumbling in with Finlay beside 'im. Miss Grace step away from me as if is dance ending.

Marse John smiling big-big. "This is my brother Finlay," 'im say. Marse Finlay dress up like 'im going to meet king. Rebekkah walking behind both of them carrying tray with teapot an' cups clinking, an' is so me see bright mark on she neck like somebody suck she right there.

"A pleasure," Miss Cumberbatch say, smiling. She offer she hand to Marse Finlay, an' 'im lift it up an' kiss it. Marse John dismiss me an' Rebekkah, an' me feel bad to leave she alone with them two.

But then me realize me didn't even see when Miss Grace return the books to them rightful place, is so she slick-slick.

That night Marse John tell me 'im starting to feel sick, an' 'im tell me to go stay in the room with Catherine an' James. Me happy to sleep on the floor between them an' not under him fatty-fatty self an' me dream Rebekkah give me some tea to drink. An' then me dream me only making one baby after the next, baby only shooting out from between me legs. Each one is a next color, an' me don't know who the father is. First is a big-head white-white baby who look just like Marse John, then a pretty darkskin baby who look like Etto, then a pale baby who look like Marse Bernard, an' then is ugly redhead Shand baby. An' then me hear laughing from between me legs, an' me look down, an' is Rebekkah face me see, Rebekkah is me midwife, an' she hands deep inside me, an' she pull out a baby an' me see that she hand bloody-bloody, an' is laugh she laughing, an' me can't see who the baby look like.

Marse John start to get better, then 'im get worse, an' a week later, when me gone to get water for 'im me see a small rag knot up on the pump handle. Is from Etto. 'im need to see me quickfast. Marse John still sick in 'im bedchamber, an' me don't see either Shand or Marse Finlay. Me slip off into the canefields to find Etto by the mangrove.

"Tonight," 'im say. "We going tonight."

"Is so?" me ask. "So fast?"

"If not tonight, we might not get a next chance." 'im say how Warburton hear how 'im and Kitch an' Grafton going to get sell in the morning an' how they fraid Polydore done say something about running. 'im touch the side of me face. 'im hand cold-cold. This time, when me walking back, me make sure to follow familiar trail, but is so me get lost again. Me don't know what going on unless is Mama Binti doing it to confuffle me head, an' me start to feel the same way as when Miss Grace tell me I having a next baby, an' me want to sit down, but me know is run me should run, an' is so me make me two foot move.

When me reach in the middle of the woods again, me don't hear nothing, an' this frighten me bad-bad: no bird, no agouti, or no mongoose rushing through the woods an' breaking branches an' twigs, an' no crapaud an' no bullfrog croaking. Is only oranges me smelling when it have no orange anywhere. an' after hearing noise all the time in Abercromby Hall—stupid kitchen girl laughing an' skinning she teeth, or Marse John shouting for me to bring 'im stupid pipe, or 'im stupid slipper, or animal bleating in them pen—the sound of silence heavy-heavy.

Me think about what Miss Mitilde say, but me don't want to be here. Me don't want to deal with Mama Binti.

Then the orange smell get heavy-heavy an' me stand still.

Then the smell of orange disappear, an' is just so somebody start talking, an' me hear three voice in me ear again like is shoo-shoo, an' them voice get louder. It sound like them same three voice right up against me ear, an' it sound like more than three voices talking at the same time, an' is run me start to run, an' tree branch scratching up me face, an' me hearing laughing, *keck-keck-keck-keck*. An' then me reach back by the scullery, an' me see Finlay sitting on the step watching me hard-hard, an' is so me realize me ain't see Poly in some days now, an' me wonder what Warburton an' Grafton an' Kitch do him.

Me try to stay up to wait for Etto, but me fall asleep, and then me wake up hot-hot in the middle of the night, an' me watch outside, an' the sky bright-bright. Me hear shouting, an' dog barking, an' then me see a face jump up by the window, an' it dirty-dirty, an' me heart skip, an' me think is Polydore, but is Etto, an' im breathing hard-hard. "Come!" 'im whisper hard. "Come!"

Me scramble, an' me wake up Catherine an' James. "Come," me say. "Come!" Is tie-up they head tie-up with sleep, an' Catherine start to cry, an' James only rubbing 'im eye. "Come," me say, an' 'im fighting up, pulling back. Me drag them through the scullery, an' me see Etto there by the door. 'im lift up Catherine in 'im arms an' is move we start to move. Me watch around the side, an' me see one set of bacchanal, caneslave running everywhere, an' canefield one on fire. Me start to run to the next canefield that lead to the woods. Me look back an' me see caneslave running this way an' that, an' cane dogs chasing them, an' Shand fighting Warburton, an' MacTeer fighting Grafton. Me see little child naked an' crying an' looking like Catherine, an' me want to go grab she, but Etto calling, "Come!" And me know is Grafton, Kitch, Warburton, an' Etto who start fire in the canefield, to make bacchanal to run.

"Come," Etto say again, an' is run me running, the ground hard-hard below me foot, an' me see that Etto cutting through the cane-field to reach the woods, same woods where me run into Mama Binti. An' is reach we almost reach the woods when me feel a big box on the side of me head an' is tumble me tumble, an' James pitch away from me, an' when me look up is Finlay me see standing over me. Me try to get up, but 'im kick me in me side, an' is so me see Etto set down Catherine, an' 'im charge with 'im head low an' ram it into Finlay stomach. Finlay grunt an' catch Etto by 'im waist an' lift 'im up in the air then slam 'im in the ground. Is get up me get up to rush Finlay, but then me see cane dog barking at James an' Catherine, an' is scream them screaming, an' me rush over to them, but then me feel a big clout on the side of me head, an' is dark everything gone dark.

When me wake up, me know one time me in the small-small shed deputy does use to punish caneslave. Is so they do my mother on the next island before they pull me from she an' send me to this island. It hot-hot an' me leg chain up to the wall. Is by meself me by meself, an' me only counting seconds, minutes, an' hours. Is maybe three hours before somebody come, an' is Finlay, an' 'im set a chair by the door an' 'im sit down an' put 'im hand in 'im chin an' is watch 'im watch me.

"Is where Marse John?" me ask. Me know Marse John not go like no Finlay chaining me to no wall.

"Marse John," 'im say. "Marse John sick. You know that. You made him sick. Whatever you poisoned his food with." *Is not me*, me want to say, *is Rebekkah poison his food*, but it feel like bees and Jack Spaniard inside me head 'an me know 'im won't believe me anyway.

"Me want to see 'im," me say.

'im shake 'im head. "There is no Marse John for you anymore," 'im say. "Not ever again. From now on it's chains and cutting cane."

"Is where James?" me ask.

'im shake 'im head. "You will never see your son again."

"Is where Catherine?" me ask.

'im grin. "Kitty the pussy cat is being taken care of by Shand," 'im say, an' is rush me rush 'im, but the chain ain't let me reach close, an' im laugh, an' me spit in 'im face, an' me see 'im face get hard-hard, an' 'im stand up, an' slap his hand against the side of me head, an' me fall down. 'im stand over me, an' im say, "You will never see your son again, you will never see your daughter again, an' when you've littered"—'im put 'im boot on me stomach, an' is so me know Miss Grace sell me out—"you will never see it again." Then 'im ball up 'im two fist and hit me in the side of me head, and this time everything gone dark.

Me wake up brief-brief an' see Rebekkah. She smiley-smiley, an' she put a tin cup of water next to me, an' is gone she gone, an' is sleep me sleep.

Me wake up again, an' the cabin feeling hot-hot, an' is me mother from the next island me see sitting in the corner, only watching me, an' me start to cry, but me head hurting hard, an' me close me eyes, an' is sleep me sleep.

Then me wake up, an' me see Mitilde, an' she wiping me face with a rag. Me feel me lip bus-up, an' when me try to talk, me whole face hurting. "Shhhhh," she say.

"Etto?" me say.

"Shhhh," she say. She take she two hands an' hold me face. Me see through hole in the roof that it dark-dark. "Listen," she say. "You could stand?" She help lift me up, an' although is pain me feeling pain, me stand up. "Listen," she say. "You could walk?" Each time me lift me foot, is pain slicing through me, but me walk slow-slow to the door with she arm around me. Me look an' see that the chains not on me leg no more. Me go to ask she about Catherine an' James, but she shake she head. "Shhhhh." She hold up she finger. "This is your one chance," she say. She eye more gold than me ever see. She scarf more green than me ever see. "Go into the woods."

"Is where Catherine?" me ask.

"In the woods," she say. "I send she there to wait for you."

"Etto," me say. "James."

"I will take care of James," she say. She point to the woods. "Mama Binti," she say.

As me walk toward the woods everything hurt more. Me start to hear things in the air, an' me look up an' me see one set of hummingbird by me head. Me walk slow-slow toward the canefield that burn down, an' then through the canefield that still standing. With each step more hummingbird reach an' circling me head. What was three hummingbird at the start is twelve now. All around me everything look beat-up an' burn down an' so me only keep me eye on the hummingbird them. The caneslave cabins quiet-quiet. Abercromby Hall quiet-quiet. Me walking slow-slow an' through the cane. Is snake me want to come bite me leg, to bite me foot an' kill me dead, but everything quiet-quiet. An' is so me gone in the woods, an' everything get cold-cold just so, an' breeze blowing hard through canestalk, an' is not cane me smelling but orange when it ain't have no orange.

Then me see Catherine standing by a tree, an' she run up an' wrap she arms around me, an' is sob me start sobbing, an' me drop to me knees and hug she tight-tight.

[Welcome, Miss Hany] the voice them say. [You're brave to come so far when you're in such distress] the voice say, the voice sounding like it in me head, but me used to it now, an' me ain't jump. [Must be something troubling you too bad if you're taking a risk like this]

Me voice ragged, but me say, "Is true. Plenty trouble from all direction." Me standing back up, but is so me holding Catherine hand tight-tight still.

[Plenty trouble indeed] say the voice them, but me still can't see nobody, and me head hurting. [Maybe there's something I can do to help]

Me tell meself me only here because of Miss Mitilde, an' me ain't agree to nothing yet. The voice them sound soft-soft like Marse John bedsheet. [Maybe I can give you something an' you can give me something in return] say the three voices, sometimes sounding like plenty more than three.

"Maybe is so," me say. Then me start hearing cane dog bark, an' Catherine cry out, an' she start to pull, but me hold she hand tight-tight.

[What do you have to offer?] Mama Binti says, an' is so me realize what me desperate for, an' that me would offer anything for it, an' that me go deal with Mama Binti without even seeing she face. Me tell she what me want, me want Catherine an' James an' Etto to make it safe up in the mountains. She say she could help, but me asking for plenty-plenty, an' what me could give she so in exchange?

The cane dogs barking closer an' closer, an' Catherine pulling me hand an' crying, an' trying to run.

Me don't want to say it out loud, what me go give in any Mama Binti deal, what everybody say anybody give up in Mama Binti deal, since me hear that is only one thing that any caneslave have that worth anything to trade. Every time anybody talk about deal with Mama Binti, them mention the same thing that she want from you, them say that they want your child, that them want the girl child in your belly that you ain't make yet. An' is because she go be taking the thing that they know you want most is why she want you to say it out loud so that you know that you trading the thing you should want the most for something you think you want more, an' so that it don't have any misunderstanding. An' they say that when you dead that you go find out the true worth an' the true weight of what you give up. [What] the voice them repeat [do you have that I might want? What is worth something? What is worth all?]

"You know," me say, feeling like a hand getting tighter an' tighter around me throat an' me could barely breathe. "You know." Cane dog barking closer an' closer an' them finding me an' Catherine any second now.

[You have to say it, Miss Hany] the voice them say. [It's the only way that we can help. You have to make it known so that the air can hear, so the trees can hear, so that the birds can hear, so that nobody could say that Mama Binti cheated you out of anything that's yours]

"Is so," me say.

[Say it] the voice them say. The words form in me head an' me start to say them. Me have half of the words out of me mouth, an' me heart getting heavier with each word, like a hand getting tighter around me throat again, the world getting darker around me, but then me hear two voice separate from the voice them: is Shand an' MacTeer talking, coming close, an' me quiet down, an' the hand slip off from me throat, an' light rushing back in, an' me hear water flowing, an' hummingbird in front me face, above me head, an' beside me like them lifting me off the ground, an' me hear bullfrog an' crapaud croaking. The two voices is Shand an' MacTeer saying "There!" Then me hear cane dogs barking hard-hard, rushing me close-close an' me know is Shand let go them leash an' is me neck them jumping for, an' is scream Catherine screaming.

Me touch me belly with one hand an' holding Catherine hand with the other. If me lose James an' Etto then is so me need to keep Catherine.

Me know what so me have to trade. "Take it," me say.

[Are you sure?]

Me have me hand on me belly when me say it again. "Take what inside me," me say. "But let me keep Catherine." An' is so fire from Mama Binti explode through the canefield an' the woods an' burn up the cane dogs an' Shand an' MacTeer, burn all of them so that they screaming an' bawling like is hell they reach hell, but all me pain disappear in the smoke, an' me watching as me body turning into air, as Catherine stop crying and turning into air, as the fire clear everything away, how it make a clearing where me know no cane will ever grow again, a big clearing that me hope go remind Marse John an' Marse Bernard an' all of them that they not going to hold all of we forever.

9

The Devil Flaps His Wings and a Venezuelan Troupial Sings a Song of Hope

RICARDO MALDONADO WORSHIPPED at the altar of his itching ankle. Its discomfort was sovereign. He ignored the ankle's rash although its itch kept clearing its throat and requesting attention. A child worrying a loose thread. A loose tooth. Still, it wasn't the physical irritation that provoked Maldonado but the mental one; here on the island he could stroll into a drugstore and pluck the required medicine from a shelf and, three days later, no more itch.

Not so in Venezuela's parched boticas.

On cue, an itch snipped at his ankle. Once more unto the breach: Maldonado slipped the unbothered foot from its desert boot and tended to the discomfort in the cockpit of the other. This was the purpose of desert boots: the ease of slipping feet free from bondage. On a mission Maldonado wouldn't wear desert boots. But this wasn't a mission, it was an *assignment*. Today he served as the brujo's ambassador.

Here was what Ricardo Maldonado understood as he sat down in the restaurant just a femur's length away from the center of the island's capital: that he and the island's Minister of National Security, whose arrival he awaited, carried similar disdain for each other. Minister of National Security Basil D'Souza directed his scorn at Maldonado because D'Souza fumed at having to deal with an underling instead of directly with Ebrahim Fortunato. By sending Maldonado, Fortunato demonstrated that D'Souza was lesser. Still, the minister had agreed to suffer this flunky arrangement. He understood hierarchy. Being a big jefe on an *island* was dissimilar to being a big jefe on the *mainland*, regardless of the current disparity of national fiduciary fortunes. Besides, Fortunato never left Caracas. And with the current state of affairs between the countries, with the Minister of National Security cracking down on Venezuelan refugees, with certain members of the island's population frothing at the mouth at the Venezuelan influx, Basil D'Souza MP couldn't very well travel to Caracas without every island news outlet, and maybe one or two of Venezuela's, providing him a free colonoscopy courtesy of a tape recorder straight up his rectum. Maldonado had spoken to D'Souza just once to set up this meeting—it was D'Souza who had requested it—and it was then that Maldonado deciphered D'Souza's scorn when he learned that Fortunato would not be the one attending the meeting. Maldonado felt the heat through the telephone receiver. A ripe condescension. A full-flavored contempt. A sense that D'Souza understood Maldonado to be dirt that soiled the underside of Fortunato's boots.

This time Maldonado reached down and scratched his ankle with his butterfly knife. That mission complete, he left the blade there. The weapon felt comfortable against his skin. Because Ricardo Maldonado was a soldier, not an ambassador. In his most recent trip to the island two months earlier he'd stolen beach sand but shot a disrespectful man in his thigh. Back in Venezuela, Fortunato deployed a fixer, Andres. Here on the island Maldonado was Fortunato's disrupter. His rumble of thunder.

When Maldonado had first started working for Fortunato, the brujo reached out his short arms, felt Maldonado's shoulders, then nodded. Maldonado felt Pedro's disapproving shadow, but his brother refused to reveal himself. The next morning, Maldonado stood out in the wilderness practicing sniper shots with a gray-whiskered viejo who tended his mustache with strong-smelling wax. Much later, rumors reached Maldonado that the viejo had been trained at a school in Fort Benning, Georgia, in Los Estados Unidos. And not just trained as a sniper, but also in guerilla tactics and other military ploys. But all he taught Maldonado that month was how to shoot straight from a long distance without little more than a small grunt of approval for a job well done. They ate out of cans and slept in tents and shat in the bushes like warthogs.

The viejo explained to Maldonado that to deploy a killing shot from a long distance, Maldonado mustn't look directly at a target, but ironically needed to engage his peripheral vision to center said target in his scope. The viejo would break an empty bottle of beer and lodge the abridged glass neck on a branch, demonstrating remarkable agility first in climbing the tree, then shimmying back down. Then he marched Maldonado half a mile away from the target and instructed him to strike down the smudge of glass with a single shot. The viejo held a flutter of cloth for Maldonado to gauge the wind's drag out of the corner of his eye. "Think of blowing out a birthday candle," the viejo had said. Maldonado drew in a breath, held it, thought back to his younger brother Pedro's sixth birthday party when they both blew out the cake's candles. Maldonado exhaled gently, pinched the trigger. As he exhaled, he felt Pedro's breath on his neck, and the rifle jumped, and its recoil left a spiteful bruise on Maldonado's shoulder. Half a mile away the knuckle of glass exploded. Maldonado was a natural. "Bueno," said the viejo. And Maldonado never heard him speak again.

After a month of snuffing out glass candles, the viejo returned Maldonado to Fortunato. The brujo once more placed his hands on Maldonado's shoulders. "My parrots reveal the future," he said, "but you are the avenging angel of the present." Here Maldonado believed he caught a glimpse of his brother, just moving out of the corner of his eye.

A pretty, smiling Venezuelan waitress recalled Maldonado to the present when she delivered his coffee. He checked the time then eyed the restaurant. It was midafternoon and he was sitting toward the front where he could assess the minister's approach through the window. Not a bad afternoon crowd, maybe ten people drinking too early while craning their necks up toward football matches on lurid flatscreens. Maldonado kept council with his coffee. He'd swept the place when he'd arrived, searched for points of weakness. A back exit. A shifty cook. An easily prised open bathroom window. He discovered nothing. He settled at the front and waited.

And waited.

And waited.

His hotel sat less than one hundred yards from this restaurant. The walk back would be easy. Pleasant in this weather. It was to be the first time that he and the minister would meet in person. Maldonado recalled the brief phone exchange between Fortunato and the minister months earlier when they had established their little whorehouse in the south of the island. The brujo had said nothing after he, then Maldonado, had spoken to the MP, but Maldonado could tell Fortunato considered the minister a buffoon. Now Fortunato sent Maldonado to make sure that the tracks had been correctly laid down. "I've heard how things operate on that island," he'd said. "Those caníbales sink bodies into swamps." *But we leave them for vultures*, Maldonado thought. Maldonado had to get his hands dirty for that business, and he'd resented it. He'd had to perform a collect and confine with Venezuelan women, newly minted on the island, collect and confine them as they unsteadily stepped off exhausted boats in the middle of the night just to be shuttled off to perdition. He had to abide the knowledge that a part of him was responsible for these women, and sometimes girls, lying on their backs on this godforsaken isla, taking the grunting weight of local men. Knowing this tightened the twist of thorns around his heart and, Maldonado knew, carved out a tighter space for him in hell.

* * *

He eyed an approaching man through the glass pane: again not the minister. Maldonado rotated his coffee cup. He appreciated the place's cleanliness. A staircase led to a gleaming silver second story tank where the proprietors fermented fancy beer. Eyes out the window again. A mountain range reminded him of home. Cheap, bright houses were fastened there as well, slums seemingly the same everywhere in the world. He'd spotted a stadium across the highway.

His ankle called again, and he answered again with the knife.

The minister's arrival was still only speculative, and his anger bubbled. Maldonado thought of Andres, who never had to leave Venezuela, who got to handle the smooth while he had to tangle with the rough.

He thought back to his tío Luis, who, when Maldonado was a boy, calmed him in anxious moments by feeding him stories. Little bites of myths and chews of culture. María Lionza astride a tapir. Armando Reverón's dolls. His tío had sported a sparse mustache whose whiskers never met at the no-man's-land beneath his nose but signaled each other from the borders of his mouth. Maldonado recalled the location of each hair. "Luis moves through life," Maldonado's mother had once said, "like a cloud that doesn't know it births thunderstorms." One day, after teaching Maldonado and Pedro to craft yo-yos from bottlecaps and twine, tío Luis sat on a curb with a bottle of Destilo between his legs and explained that the island was once connected to South America—he used interlocking fingers to show it—a little puzzle piece snapped right onto Venezuela's jagged coastline. Maldonado hadn't believed him and still didn't believe him after Luis lubricated him with a swig of his beer.

Sensing the disbelief, Luis rose despite complaining knees, slipped indoors, and returned with a raggedy atlas to reveal to Maldonado the shapes of the coastlines. The way they lined up. Maldonado had turned to Pedro as Luis spoke, about to make a face that spoke to their tío being loco. Pedro was an easy mark, laughing at all of his brother's jokes. But the map enraptured Pedro. Later, Maldonado learned that everything about Venezuela's natural world held Pedro spellbound. So Maldonado reeled in his *can you believe this loco* face. He paid attention to Luis's map. His tío was right: the coastlines had once shook hands. But now, visiting the island, Maldonado deciphered that these two places couldn't be more dissimilar—they didn't speak the same language, they didn't eat the same foods, they didn't share the same values.

Venezolanos now fled to this island out of necessity, not desire. Crawled on their knees onto overcrowded boats, then, once they arrived, crawled on their knees some more. Sold churros on the capital's sidewalk for bright bills stamped with birds. As Fortunato's lieutenant, Maldonado understood his role in all of this as a sherpa who guided both Fortunato's clients and victims to their destinations as well as a disapproving presence if corners were cut. Yes, the government was the greater force. They were the sabotaging weathervane that spun in whatever direction the winds of economic discontent blew them. Their stance toward the americanos meant less food, less medicine, and less money for the oil vacuumed up from beneath the earth. There was no aspirin in Venezuela, no foot cream to conquer Maldonado's rash.

Maldonado sipped his coffee.

Tapped his ankle.

Cleared his throat.

Still no minister.

The front door opened, delivering a pair of braying locals fresh from work dressed in the white shirt/black pants outfit that the island's worker bees favored.

Maldonado swiped away the coffee's foam from his lip. He usually drank it black, but the waitress had talked him into milk and steam. Fortunato had told him that this meeting was to make sure that his little whorehouse was performing as it should, but that there was a new goal as well—oil exploration and possibly extraction. Another rope tugged between the two countries, them growling at each other over invisible borders for water-bound oil deposits and fishing beds. He scratched his ankle once more.

After the meeting, he promised himself, *a farmacia*.

For now, local time taunted. The minister was purposely late. It was a trick that Fortunato deployed as well, the flex of men of means: to command lesser mortals to stand at atención, then return their enthusiastic salutes with limp greetings. The minister's late arrival sought not just a tepid salute, but meant to push Fortunato to his knees, make him crawl through broken glass and basura. Maldonado's hand shook. He lowered the cup and mentally counted backward from twenty. Sought pleasant thoughts that wouldn't come. He fingered his eyebrow's scar, a tell of frustration.

His brother had been headstrong and greedy. He'd warned Pedro to be patient, and Pedro had told him to change his pad. He saw some of his brother in the minister's power grab. The idea of power was the one thing that Maldonado and his brother Pedro, in their midtwenties, had failed to properly grasp as they'd tried to establish their own megabanda. A megabanda that was testing Fortunato's own claims to certain neighborhoods had landed them on his radar. A small but growing threat to Fortunato's sovereignty. No gang but Fortunato's gang, they'd finally learned. No law but Fortunato's law.

He looked up from his coffee and across the table, and there was Pedro, looking at him with cold eyes. He knew that if he expressed sorrow that Pedro would draw his own knife and reach across the table and slice Maldonado's neck. He had betrayed his brother by bowing his knee to Ebrahim Fortunato. By being folded into his megabanda. "I'm biding my time," Maldonado said. "When the time is right, I'll take care of him. Like tío said, keep your friends close and your enemies closer." He said all of this in a low whisper with his eyes on the table, and when he lifted them, Pedro was gone. Out the window, Maldonado saw a troupial hop twice, then fly off. He had never seen one on the island before.

Maldonado pushed away his coffee. He needed to pee. The minister was now thirty-five minutes late.

His ankle itched like the devil.

Forty-seven minutes past the meeting time and still no Minister of National Security. *Message received.* There was only so long that Maldonado would stand at attention. He would tell Fortunato that he'd waited over an hour for the pendejo. Fortunato would appraise him with his dead eyes and tell him that he should have waited two more, but Maldonado'd had enough. He limped off to relieve himself, planning to then go find some salving cream for his ankle and return to the hotel. It was at the restroom's door where he encountered his counterpart, a thin man dressed in a mid-priced suit, the island yin to Maldonado's South American yang. Clearly the minister's own lieutenant. Hands joined at the triangle of his tie's tip, a prayer maybe to the textile gods, the man stood with shoulders squared.

"Minister D'Souza would prefer to conduct this meeting in his car," the man said. Maldonado nodded and followed. Internally, he cursed himself. Daydreaming, he hadn't seen the man enter. Salt in the wound: Maldonado hadn't made the man wait until he'd relieved himself. As they moved past the table Maldonado saw that by some sorcery the man had already deposited local money beneath Maldonado's coffee cup, the money's green, red, and gray epidermis as bright as Fortunato's parrots' plumage.

Maldonado lowered the flame on his fury and added his own generous tip before exiting with the goon.

"Yeah?" the driver asked beside the car. He pointed to the sky. Blue. Cloudless. The afternoon a warm blanket. Maldonado's tight bladder and turncoat ankle dueled for his attention. He ignored both.

Held out his arms in a T, and the man patted him down, ran the back of his hands along Maldonado's front, his back, and between his legs.

"What's your name?" Maldonado asked.

"I'm just a driver," the man said. His hair was neat, shorn low. He invited Maldonado to enter the back seat but didn't open the luxury car's door for him. Inside, already seated, the minister radiated ease, although the climate control was freezing. Maldonado shivered a quick marimba. Momentarily forgot about his ankle's itch. He had once dragged a clutch of dead bodies into a meat locker set at a higher temperature than the car's current setting. How was this comfortable? The minister's soul must have been the size of a dinner mint.

"Do you know, señor Maldonado," the minister asked, leaning into the *señor* while he kept his eyes forward, "that my people are called West Indians? Brought from the African continent and yet called Indians." The minister shook his head as the car pulled into traffic. He didn't look African to Maldonado. "Of all the ways that the Europeans conceived to keep us confused. They taught us the meaning of their words then reconfigured the code." Maldonado folded a stick of gum, a piece of which always floated about in some crevice of his clothing, into his mouth to chase his coffee breath. Scratched at his eyebrow's scar. Passed a hand over his stubbled head. He needed to shave it again. "This island *used* to have Indians," the minister continued. "Native Indians. But the Europeans killed them off, then brought in Africans. Later, they brought in Indians from East India, so I guess calling all of us West Indians works." He kept his eyes out the window. The post-work traffic bloomed on this two-lane artery that led straight into the town's heart. "All of which is to say, *señor*, that this little island holds a multitude of people from all parts of the world. Yes, Venezuelans are sneaking in, but did you know that there's a high percentage of illegal Nigerians here as well? Lots of Chinese too. How do you suppose they got here?"

Maldonado shivered as sweat congealed at his back's base. The man required no response. Sooner or later the minister would stop circling the runway and land. For now he talked more than a chicken. Above the island's flour processing plant, a flock of pigeons flapped by in feathered formation.

Maldonado considered the island. The troupial. The bright currency, all of which seemed to be stamped with different birds. "Did you ever visit the old Abercromby House down south? The little gentleman's club?" the minister asked, settling his hands on his knees. A deep purple tie clutched his neck. His bespoke suit tight like a second skin. "The gentleman's club that señor Fortunato and I established? You're more than welcome to stop by," the minister said. "Quite a few Venezuelan beauties." His voice carried a wink. Maldonado thought of the waitress and how easily she might have been one of the minister's whorehouse pieces of ass, and his hand twitched, and he caught the driver's eyes in the rearview. If the twitch had been livelier, he was sure, then the man would have smoothly extracted his firearm and placed a bullet very cleanly into Maldonado's head without removing his eyes from the rearview or disturbing the minister with a splash of blood. If Maldonado had been trained by someone who'd attended the guerilla school in Fort Benning, then the driver had attended the school himself. It was clear in his economy of motion, his stride to the car as compact as the viejo's.

Behind the steering wheel sat the minister's own angel of death.

A voice slipped into Maldonado's head.

Now who's loco? Luis asked.

"What do you know about oil, señor?" the MP asked. Maldonado remained quiet. Still no response required. The car inched through traffic. Outside, horns bleated. Snatches of dancehall fell from taxi windows. Had the minister simply arrived late due to traffic? If so, he offered neither excuse nor contrition but kept up the robust conversation with himself. He would eventually state his business, then the car would pull over, and Maldonado would exit, find an alley to relieve himself, return to the hotel, and deliver the message to Fortunato. A pointless trip across the water. The minister leaned toward his driver. "What do you know about oil, Paris?"

The driver tilted his eyes into the rearview mirror. "Its formation or how it operates in our economy, sir?"

The minister leaned back. "I ask the man a simple question and I get a philosopher's response. The people on this island too smart you know."

"Sorry, minister," said the driver. "Gas and oil form from sedimentary rocks. Gas in particular is formed when deposited organic matter is pressurized over eras in these sedimentary rocks. Many of the largest gas deposits are from Devonian swamps."

D'Souza cupped an ear. "Say that last part again?"

"Devonian swamps, minister."

D'Souza leaned back and addressed Maldonado. "You hear that? Swamps. Like the man has a degree in oil formation. He bright too bad."

The mention of swamps sounded alarms in Maldonado's head, Fortunato having told him this was how they disappeared bodies. His ankle seared, but he tended the scar at his eyebrow instead.

"Oil and gas formation requires the breakdown of organic matter, like bodies, over eons, minister. The sediments and organic material need to be deeply buried first. That part is very important, sir."

The minister pulled an impressed face. "Are you bucking for an energy minister portfolio, Paris? Where did you learn all that?"

"Secondary school, boss."

"You see how he smart?" he confided in Maldonado, still without looking at him. But the talk of swamps had infected Maldonado like a splinter, and even in the refrigerated back seat a swatch of sweat visited him again. "Do you know, señor, that just a few short years ago this little island"—he tapped the car's window—"was the chief exporter of natural gas to the U.S.? Imagine, such a small place heating such a large country. What do you think of that, Paris?"

"Hard to believe, sir," the driver replied. Maldonado turned his sniper's eye to the driver. *If ever I have the opportunity*, he thought, *I would enjoy the challenge of putting a bullet in your head from half a mile away.* Paris sneered as if he'd heard the threat. As they inched ahead, Maldonado calculated. If there were no true threat in the car, if he were imagining his life to be in peril and he tried to exit the car, word of his cowardice would reach Fortunato. For now he considered the hint of menace to be the minister's tumbleweed style of communication.

Not a true threat yet, he convinced himself.

"What I need you to tell señor Fortunato," the minister said, sotto voce, "is that early tests have suggested a high concentration of gas and oil beneath that little village down south. Not too far from the gentleman's club. Now, nothing is guaranteed. We could sink a well and find nada, but there's likely massive deposits down there. And if we purchase all the land for below market price, then make the private oil concerns aware of the test results, then everyone eats well." Maldonado exhaled in relief. *All of this just to request a loan?* The minister dropped his voice further. Jammed his mouth against Maldonado's ear. It reminded Maldonado of when, as a boy, Pedro would say that he had a secret to tell him, and when Maldonado would lean in close, Pedro would shout boo! His heart briefly expanded beyond its capacity, provided Maldonado some momentary joy. The difference was the minister's voice smelled antiseptic. "He knows that I would appreciate his investment. Guaranteed rate of return. Just like his sound investment in the sand for the hotel's construction. Just like the investment in the gentleman's club. His return on this venture will be just as substantial."

Maldonado nodded. He rejected his itching ankle's siren call.

Then the minister halted. Leaned away. Shook his head. "Just thought of something, Paris. Did they ever find those Titus boys who disappeared in New Felicity?"

"No, sir. A mystery."

"A mystery." The minister scratched his chin. "No proof. Corporal Lalchan said not a trace was found." He kept his eyes front. "But we know exactly who shot Hospedales." The minister drummed his fingers on the door's handrest, made a couple of popping sounds with his mouth, and then leaned toward his driver. "A new idea, Paris."

"Yes, minister?"

"Maybe I'll just give señor Fortunato the message myself. Lock off any gap in communication. What do you think of that, Paris?"

"A very good idea, sir."

"And, Paris, how you think Mr. Fortunato will act if one of his good good men disappear without a trace?"

Maldonado snatched for his door handle to wrench it open, but the lock refused him. The car had halted, was already at the curb, someone opening the door on the minister's side. The minister buttoned his suit jacket as he exited. Then a large man, doused in a reservoir of cheap cologne, took the minister's seat, sprawling in the back seat. Maldonado reached for his door's handle once more, but another, much slimmer man, wearing a similar suit as the fat one, was already entering there. He forced Maldonado to the middle, the blood draining from Maldonado's hands, leaving them cold.

Both men wore suits similar to the driver.

All dressed for a funeral.

Maldonado's ankle screamed, his bladder percolated.

The car threaded through the traffic, blocking out most of the blockages that came with rush hour. Maldonado sized up each man in the car. No telltale holster bulges on either man, but this meant nothing.

"My name is Rodney," the big one said.

"I don't want to give my name," said the man to Maldonado's right.

The scent of Rodney's cologne expanded as he spoke and filled Maldonado like funeral home formaldehyde. He coughed. The one to his right smelled like a swamp. Maldonado coughed again. It was here that Maldonado heard the GPS's disembodied voice, prompted by Paris's fingers tapping on the screen, calmly state that it was fifteen kilometers to the island's centrally located swamp where its sugar-cane estates once sprawled plentifully. "Big man like you don't know how to get to the swamp?" Rodney teased Paris. "Big man whose job it is to *drive* around the island?"

"Ease him up nah, man," said the swamp man. "Give him a bligh. He never drive past the lighthouse in his life."

"You two mind your business," Paris said to the rearview, "and let me worry about mine. I just looking for the fastest route."

Maldonado said nothing. He understood that three local men, and one visitor, were headed to the swamp, but that only the locals would return. *Offer them money*, he thought. *Then issue them a promise of more.*

But Pedro, now seatbelted in the front beside Paris, turned and glared at the idea of such traitorous behavior.

Escape, then. How? Jump over the fat man? Slide across the swamp man and unlock the door? Attempt to smash the window? The door had already failed him. Maldonado calculated. This was still the city, so he might have some time. But it was the island. With this traffic they might clear the city in five minutes or fifteen. Maybe ten. Outside, the traffic coagulated. It was midafternoon. Maldonado smelled someone's sour sweat, maybe Rodney's wilting through his cologne.

The wall of cologne leaned then collapsed upon Maldonado. He coughed.

"How the man looking sad so?" Rodney asked.

"Nice day like this," said the swamp man. "Visitor to our shores. Getting a tour of the capital. Should be happier."

"Why you sad, brethren?" Rodney leaned forward to catch the swamp man's eye across Maldonado. "How you does say 'brother' in Spanish?"

The swamp man leaned forward to meet Rodney's eye across Maldonado. "Hermano, I think."

"I like that," Rodney said. "Why you looking so sad, hermano? Like you suffer a big-time loss. Like a good woman walk out on you."

"Why everything always have to be about food and women with you?" the swamp man snapped.

Just as Rodney said, "Listen, breds," the road ahead opened up and the car broke free from the traffic's grip, and Maldonado recalled the butterfly knife beside his ankle. If he could snap out the blade then he would be able to take one of these mongrels to hell with him, better the gordo to his left whose blood would gush and stain, like oil from a well, the blood varnishing the upholstery until the car could no longer be used, putting the minister at least into the predicament and expense of securing a new vehicle.

"It making cold in here or is just me?" asked Rodney. He held on to the strap above his head meant for dry cleaning.

Make a left in one mile, the GPS advised.

"Wait nuh," said the swamp man on the right, "you still don't know where you going?"

"The man real kicksy," said Rodney.

"Hush your mouth and let me drive in peace."

"How much time now you make this drive, Paris?" Rodney asked.

"Give him a bligh," the swamp man insisted.

"You shouldn't worry about me," Paris said. "What you *should* be worried about," he continued, eyeing Maldonado through the rearview, "is why he quiet quiet like he find something in the car to attack both of you."

Everyone in the back seat stopped cold. Every man-jack examined the other, then all of them simultaneously reached down to Maldonado's boots. Heads collided. Rodney dealt a backhand to the side of Maldonado's face. The swamp man delivered a rabbit punch to Maldonado's right ear. Maldonado pushed a thumb into Rodney's eye with one hand and reached for his booted knife with the other. "He trying to dig out my eye!" Rodney cried out.

"Hold his ass!" the swamp man yelled.

Paris observed the skirmish calmly in the rearview, both hands on the wheel.

Turn left in one hundred feet, said the global positioning system.

It was over quickly.

Despite his size, Rodney was nimble in securing the knife while the swamp man jammed a forearm across Maldonado's neck to subdue him. Rodney held the knife up against the window. Sunlight twinkled off the blade. "This son of a bitch nearly dig out my eye," he said in wonder. Maldonado lunged for the knife, but the swamp man tightened the arm around his neck and jerked him back, and Rodney calmly elbowed him in his nose. Maldonado's mind scattered.

"But look at my crosses," said Rodney. He elbowed Maldonado in the nose again.

Puzzle pieces, Maldonado thought.

Destilo.

Warm sand, he thought.

Tío Luis.

Hot piss, he thought.

Pedro.

When Paris's phone rang, Maldonado was almost unconscious in the swamp man's grip. "You going to love this, fellas," Paris said as he smoothly took the corner and eyed the mirror. "The big man say to let him go."

"Don't make smoke," said Rodney.

"You sure sure?" asked the swamp man.

"That's what the man said." Paris shrugged, slipped the phone into his breast pocket and slowed the car.

"You see why this island jokey?" the swamp man complained, not removing his arm from Maldonado's neck. Maldonado coughed again. The swamp man kept a hold of Maldonado's neck for a moment longer, just in case the command was rescinded, but Paris pulled over then stopped the car completely. Rodney opened the door and placed a hand on the car's roof to lift himself out. The swamp man dealt a calpet to the back of Maldonado's head as he released him. Put a foot up his ass for good measure.

Rodney reclaimed his seat.

Then the car pulled off.

Out of the car and into the world, light inflated Maldonado. Oxygen buoyed him. Rendered him weightless. The world was mysterious, tremendous, and fascinating. His ankle had stopped itching. His bladder was empty. He felt like the island's breezes lifted him a few inches, then he looked down to discover both of his feet separated two inches from the ground. He took a couple of steps just to be sure and the gap held true.

Then the smell of ammonia clobbered him.

He'd pissed himself.

He laughed at the wet map on his crotch. They'd kicked him out three miles from his hotel. He would return to his room, shower, then switch on the football match. Order room service. Maybe sink a beer. But as he strode a new need to urinate accosted him. The feeling alighted upon him without warning, his bladder suddenly tight as he walked the air above the ground. He supposed he could pee himself again and who would care? Shame guaranteed he would toss the trousers.

After several minutes, he drew level with the restaurant. One of the men had kept his knife, but he was alive, so it had done its job. He would use facilities then return to the hotel to the restaurant's shower. Just as he entered the restaurant, his feet reclaimed the earth.

And keep them there, tío Luis ordered.

Entering the restaurant, Maldonado felt a different surge of joy, the exuberance of a regular entering a familiar watering hole. His waitress brushed passed him with a smile, but she was busy; the crowd had metastasized. But Maldonado's seat toward the front was still free, and he sought it even though his need to pee had intensified. The restaurant was filled with a dull murmur. He needed to sit for a moment, let his feet re-acclimatize to the earth. Just as he was about to reclaim his seat, the waitress swooped down on him and circled her arms around his waist. Startled, Maldonado looked down to see that she'd secured an apron around his trousers to conceal his shame. By the time he sat, a coffee refill sat before him, black and free of adulterants. He looked up to thank the waitress, but she was already clearing another table.

10

In Which Harpy Eagles Exert Their Dominion upon Market Cats

MILAGROS TELLS HERSELF that this time she isn't returning to Venezuela to search for her mother. She's learned that lesson. Or maybe it just feels easier to think of it that way. Her last visit was nine months ago. On the face of it she's returning to pen an article for *Scofflaw*. Maybe. Saskia wants indignant fire and righteous brimstone, but Milagros remains hesitant. She has been brooding, thinking about Fortunato and Maldonado, about their roles in separating her from her mother and possibly relocating them. She has considered all forms of frontier justice for them, hanging them high and leaving them for the birds to have at their eyes. Wrapping them in barbed wire and dropping them down living wells. She's considered an article to expose them. But such an action would require names, and naming names could result in a blindfold and a cigarette. More likely she'll just write about the fallout of the Venezuelan government's astringent measures and the lack of food and medicine. The human-interest angle that focuses on the victims. Venezuela has recently pulled itself up from its knees, taken a standing eight count, and fought its way back onto the front pages after the new opposition leader's vision rippled through the world's undisturbed reflecting ponds. This new agitator shouted and beat his chest and the world's democracies sat up and paid notice. His optimism echoed through the worldwide halls of justice.

For a few days the news machine has returned its foreign policy glance to Venezuela.

And Saskia having a woman in Havana, so to speak, makes her salivate.

Scofflaw's website has been doing boffo numbers with Milagros's recent articles: Brazil, Venezuela, Mexico, Haiti, Cuba: *Americas!* The subscribers, and their bottomless maws, crave more. They covet a more global diagnosis, an editorial prognosis, a telescope beyond their hemisphere. *Give us Syria*, they demand. *Give us Yemen. Give us Addis Ababa. Give us the world.*

"Hell no," Milagros told Saskia when Saskia first pled for her to travel further afield. "That and God's face," she tells Saskia, "you'll never see." But she did travel, so maybe Saskia has seen God. Being back in Saskia's bullpen feels odd, the stale air of the office space stifles—Saskia's vape pipe, *Scofflaw*'s wooden floors, the bated breath of interns. Milagros feels the eyes of the site's writers who are tethered to their desks. They've read her articles, seen her head-shorn image paired with her byline. They're all thinking the same thing: Brave. Stupid. Reckless. But mostly stupid. Milagros, for now, remains the face of *Scofflaw*'s pivot. Saskia crows that she knew the green card that she helped Milagros secure was a smart investment.

But Venezuela has come to haunt Milagros even while awake. Saskia and Milagros hash out the details—Saskia has to promise not to check in as often. Promise not to have Milagros hassle government officials for quotes.

Saskia sticks her pipe in her mouth, then extends her hand.

Milagros exhales.

They shake.

A puff of smoke obscures Saskia's face.

The trip's planned.

Most likely Juanita will fume. When she exits *Scofflaw*'s offices, Milagros tries to decide whether to text her. Nine months prior, when

Milagros met with Fortunato, clinging to his lieutenant's hips—the same lieutenant who had kidnapped her and her mother when they first landed on the island—as he motorcycled her to a mountain headquarters, when she ended up ferrying a child across the border, under gunfire, into Colombia to reunite her with her family, Juanita'd had kittens. It was reckless! She'd been worried! Was Milagros finding her mother really worth risking her life? Their lives? How the hell did this help her find her mother anyway?

When Milagros sees Juanita that night and tells her of the new trip, Juanita's response isn't as bad as initially expected. Juanita, in fact, surprises Milagros, shows only face cards of support, tightly holds any hole cards of disappointment in abeyance. Milagros treads carefully. Searches Juanita's language and delivery for snarky boobytraps but comes up empty. Their lovemaking that night is more intense than it has been in months, and the next morning they remain leg over leg in bed longer than usual. It's five days until Milagros's trip. *Let's see*, Milagros thinks, *if the glue holds.*

Everything about that first trip felt sidereal. As if the mountain that she'd scaled on Maldonado's motorcycle was a platform that tried to launch her into the inky sky. Now Milagros still feels disconnected from the ground, forever floating a few inches above the earth. This current feeling of levitation's a grim curse; what Milagros craves is flatness. If Milagros could fill in the Grecia-shaped absence in her life, her feet would reclaim the earth, she's sure of it. And her birthplace is the only site for her to achieve this goal. Just the thought of it pushes her feet closer to the ground. Her interactions with Fortunato and Maldonado seemed to bring her closer to Grecia, but the impression was of being alive and sent into Hades to retrieve someone already dead. Fortunato and Maldonado are underworld brokers, and she shifts between wanting to dispatch and consort with them.

* * *

This time Milagros flies directly into Venezuela. She suspects her previous indirect route is what, in part, destabilized her. *You need to meet the past head on*, she tells herself. *No slinking across borders.* Trepidation briefly ropes her legs at passport control. Juanita shaved Milagros's head before the trip, so she looks a bit unlike her scruffier passport picture, but there's no undue attention from immigration officials beyond the familiar thousand-yard stare. The hovering of the document beside her face. The hard smash of the stamp. She taxis to the hotel without incident. Familiarity from her previous trip and sturdier Spanish under her belt from practicing with Juanita make her feel less tourist, more returning business expat. Saskia's booked her into the same hotel, and déjà vu reflects from the lobby's mirrors. The woman at the front desk's the same, but Milagros's room is different. Something's off. Same dimensions, but it feels tighter. She searches—under the bathroom sink, rifles the desk's drawers. Hoists cushions. Something she can't finger. She peers through the floor-to-ceiling window. Her room's a couple of floors higher than before, but the view's identical. The houses pinned to the mountainside. She calms herself.

Nothing to fear here.

Then a text from Daniela arrives attached with a sparkler of good news: Carmen has been more lucid than she's been in weeks; would Milagros like to meet? Maybe the next morning? "Sure," Milagros replies. And again, she feels like she's levitating.

Daniela arranges to meet her in the hotel lobby. It still confounds Milagros that she cannot remember Daniela from her childhood, which is particularly frustrating because she clearly remembers Carmen. Remembers Carmen taking care of her on days while Grecia was at work. Remembers Carmen cooking pabellón criollo. She's thinking about texting Juanita, but instead jetlag drags Milagros's eyes shut, and she snoozes, then snaps awake when the presence of someone in the hotel room overwhelms her.

She checks the room.

No one's there.

She texts Juanita and receives a fervid chain of love emojis back.

The next morning, Daniela greets Milagros in the lobby, and her childhood friend focuses on her low haircut. The three lines that Juanita has etched into her temples. "I forgot," Daniela says, "how pretty you were." Milagros smiles her thanks. Daniela remains a blind spot in her memory.

On their way to the nursing home, Milagros insists on paying. "For what?" Daniela asks. "The taxi?"

"Everything." Although Milagros's tête-à-tête with Fortunato was more cryptic than she would have liked, it also instilled a curious reassurance in her. That first page of the letter she received from him makes her think the rest of the pages filled with her mother's tight handwriting are out there waiting for her. Since that letter, Grecia invaded her dreams more often. Milagros wonders if Fortunato read Grecia's letter and switched out the pages with blank ones out of spite. The letter's first page talks about their trip to the island, a kind of archive.

At the threshold of the nursing home, Milagros tenses. She doubts that Grecia has actually reached out to Carmen, but suppose she has? Carmen's diagnosis and swift decline mirrors the country's. Medicine and bandages, Daniela explains, are as ephemeral as butterfly wings. Milagros suspects that, as a nurse, Daniela has connections that have assuaged Carmen's decline, securing her a room that she otherwise would not receive. A window owning a view of a tree-filled park and not the harsh flatland of the parking lot. Access to whatever limited medicine remains.

Although Daniela has prepared her—*mami isn't in great shape*—Carmen's still worse than Milagros expects. Her body's in severe decline. The vinegary smell of old age blankets her. She's two lifetimes older when she should be one. Milagros searches the woman's gaunt face for familiarity, but Carmen's thin hair offers no quarter. A single needle, clamped to a clear plastic tube, drives into the back of one gnarled hand. Carmen's other arm graffities with thin veins. *Soon*, Milagros thinks. *Soon the familiar dirge.*

"Mami," Daniela says, "someone to see you." Carmen's eyes defibrillate, focuses, finds Milagros. *There's no light in there*, Milagros notes, and her heart gutters. Another candlelight of hope snuffed out. But then Carmen's eyes focus on Milagros. "You," she says. With her free hand she reaches up to her neck, searches around her throat, then plucks a pendant free, snaps off a chain bound to her. "From Grecia," she says. Her trembling hand finds Milagros's and makes the deposit: at the end of the chain is a smooth piece of quartz. Milagros turns to Daniela's narrowed eyes. The pendant feels warm. "She wants to talk to you," Carmen says. Then her face animates, a pinball lighting up a table.

"Tía," Milagros says, but Daniela is already working to restrain her mother. Pinning her shoulders.

"It's okay, mami, don't get excited," she says. Briefly the room is a rodeo. Carmen raises her free hand toward Milagros again, her mouth murmuring; she's a fortune teller with a warning, she brings news from the underworld: *listen, listen*, but her words break up upon entry into the land of the living. The bed shifts and metal pings with her effort. Embarrassed at being the cause of this, Milagros, clutching the quartz pendant, excuses herself. In the hallway, she slips to the floor. Runs a hand across her bald head. She shouldn't have come. She thinks to check in with Juanita but holds off. Doesn't want to hear any B-sides off her usual "I told you so" album. She examines the pendant: a divot of undistinguished stone. Another blind spot in her memory.

Ten minutes later, Daniela emerges. Her upper lip perspires. Milagros apologizes. "Not your fault," Daniela says, swabbing her forehead with a tissue. "Rest will right her." Daniela's almost as thin as her mother—hips jut, cheekbones angle. An eating disorder maybe. More likely a lack of food and the strain of elder care. Milagros immediately offers the pendant. Daniela shakes her head. "That's yours," she says. "Grecia gave it to Carmen to keep for you."

"But *when*?"

"Not sure." Daniela pauses.

"What?" Milagros asks.

Daniela shakes her head. "I haven't ever seen her like that before. Once she calmed down she said that she has a package for you from your mother. A couple of letters too. Maybe the pendant was in there."

Milagros's heart leaps. She tempers her excitement. "Is that possible?" If she cannot speak to her mother, reading her words is a welcome substitute. She thinks of the lonely first page of the letter that Fortunato issued her in her mother's scrawl.

"I have a few of mami's things boxed at my place," Daniela says. "I can check, but I wouldn't hold out much hope."

If Grecia did visit Carmen, Milagros doesn't believe that it was recently. Any letter would be over fifteen years old. But that viejo Fortunato held on to her mother's letter for just as long. Why shouldn't she fan an ember of hope?

Humidity accosts them upon exiting. Milagros asks Daniela what it's like to be back. Until a couple of months ago, Daniela worked as a nurse off the books in the U.S., a caregiver for the older parents of surly children who severely underpaid her. Daniela shrugs. "It feels like a house in need of updates." They walk in silence. Milagros asks Daniela if she knows people willing to go on record for a story she's thinking about writing about Fortunato smuggling people, about him smuggling women. She hasn't mentioned it to Juanita, hasn't mentioned it to Saskia, but in her angrier moments, it feels right. Daniela sighs. "Milagros," she says. "Why poke that nest?" But Milagros keeps after her, and Daniela finally smiles and shakes her head. "I'll give you a contact, but will you answer something? I read your story," Daniela says as they wait for the traffic light. "About taking the young girl to Colombia." The article remains one of *Scofflaw*'s most viewed features. "Is there anything else that happened? Anything that you left out?"

True-crime curiosity, Milagros wonders, *or a fascination with gore?* A couple of excised incidents from that night jump to mind, but she says, "Everything's in the story."

"You must have left out a detail or two," Daniela insists. "Sanitized it."

Milagros hesitates. Those experiences are buried for a reason. "It's mostly there," she says.

Daniela takes the hint, leaves it alone. Pigeons lift off just ahead of them. "Do you remember that loco Francisco who used to race pigeons in El Tigre?" Daniela asks. "Well one day he moved to Caracas, released all of them, and this is where they ended up."

"So many," Milagros observes.

"They're here forever," Daniela says. "He's a major reason for the city's pigeon population."

"I don't remember much about back then," Milagros admits. Heavy pigeons quick-marched along the ground rather than flying off.

"A luxury," Daniela says.

Daniela excuses herself to take a phone call, and Milagros finds herself back at the Colombian border.

It's around midnight, and Milagros's mind has been tumbled in a dryer's drum. She's soon to traverse a makeshift bridge, as narrow as a balance beam, across a low flowing river from Venezuela into Colombia. She knows about these trochas, knows about the inherent dangers, but everything feels ethereal just now. There are no other people crossing, just her and the child, and this in itself is improbable. The pedestrian flow from Venezuela into Colombia is a spigot that never shuts off. Earlier in the night prophesying parrots edged her to a mental abyss, but her mother's letter proved to be loose soil that destabilized her footing.

And now a dark forest.

Abandon all hope ye who falter here.

She has folded the letter carefully into her hip pocket. Wants to read it again. Run her fingertips across the lettering. Smell the faded ink. Even if this is all she has gained from the trip, just experiencing her mother's note is a net gain. Not proof of life, but proof of a kind of loose providence that she's happy to momentarily entertain. Her mother's scratches have pitched her into the past like a favorite scent; those unsteady *S*'s and regressive *R*'s returned her to a small room with Grecia nudging Milagros's own hand as a child learning cursive.

The comfort of those memories has been supplanted by dread. Hidalgo's face when he left them suggested that he would murmur a psalm on their behalf. Read a scripture for their safe passage. An unknown night bird calls out and Milagros contemplates all perilous outcomes in the night's ink—that Heftzi will be taken, that Milagros will be assaulted, killed, her body's remains left naked in the dark for the buzzards' buffet. Or that she will get lost in the murk and never make it out. All markers of la frontera's indifference.

"Ready?" she asks Heftzi. The child remains silent, and the bird calls out again, sounding more threatening than it had previously. Milagros grasps the little girl's hand as they set out in the dark.

Their passage immediately grows rocky; there is a riverbed with little to no water. She expects a wolf's howl, a coyote's wail. Before them: Emptiness. Darkness. Heftzi's hand is wax paper; it is only Milagros's that are dampened with anxiety.

They walk the bridge single file. Effectively enter Colombia. Walk a weathered path between crowded bushes. Cigarette butts and crushed soda cans. A scratch of fabric that she is sure is women's underwear. No trouble for her and Heftzi twenty feet in. No trouble fifty feet in. No trouble seventy-five feet in. Around half a mile in, though, a concern. A glimmer of diffuse moonlight on an ankle-high wire, with either end disappearing into the dark. A tripwire. She considers the possibilities—an animal trap meant to send its prey sprawling, the wire clipped to a bell that rings to awake awaiting brigands, a snare that spits wooden arrows tipped with poison.

She doesn't know what to do.

Heftzi grows impatient. Tugs on Milagros's hand. Milagros decides. Lifts Heftzi—about the weight of a bag of oranges—over the tripwire. Then she steps over it herself and, the weight of Heftzi's backpack on her shoulders, her balance dissipates, and she stumbles.

She has barely scrambled back to her feet when the young men are upon her. Four of them. They are boys in one slash of moonlight and gruff men in another. She grips the backpack's straps. The leader wields a machete. Says her clothes are chévere. Asks her who she's crossing with. Milagros replies that they're alone. "Alone?" he asks, his voice spiking. "A young beauty like you? Alone with her young daughter out here?" He reaches out and touches her T-shirt at its hem, where it hits her hip. She slaps him away. "Chévere," he says again. Then: "What's in the bag, señorita?"

"Nada," Milagros says. "Bottles of water."

He lifts his eyebrows.

The other three remain silent now, glowering deputies, in position if she tries to make a run for it. "Who's helping you across?" he asks again. He wants to ensure that he's not stepping on toes. To make sure she's not under the care of someone's auspices. "ELN?"

"I'm alone."

He exhales. "Well," he says, grasping her elbow, "if you're really alone, then you'll have to pay the tax."

"There's no tax to cross," Milagros says, and she snatches her arm away from him once more.

"Of course there is," he says, "and you will pay, chamita, but don't worry. Each of us will only tax you once."

The deputies close in. Milagros's heart thumps. Her instinct is to wrap herself around Heftzi. He reaches for her T-shirt again, begins to lift it, but then drops to his knees like overripe fruit too heavy for its stem. Collapses onto his face. A beat, then a deputy drops as well, except his head explodes first. By now the other two have scattered, but then the third one falls to his knees, blood erupting from his back.

All of this takes place in silence as sudden as a power cut.

Stunned, Milagros freezes, then she runs, tugs Heftzi behind her. They sprint for a full minute. Her lungs are scorched when she realizes that the men have been shot from distance, that she may be next, but she pushes on, sprints again, foolishly hoping to find the right road where she's to be collected.

When Milagros delivers Heftzi about a mile later, both of them breathing heavily from an adrenaline surge, the woman who receives them, a shrunken grandmother with brilliantly white hair, ushers them into a small, unpainted, concrete house. Milagros's heart is still pounding. It occurs to her, now, that perhaps the shots came from a deputy of Fortunato's. A sniper. Maldonado?

The grandmother thanks Milagros profusely. Unzips the girl's bag effortlessly. She removes more from it than it seems possible for the bag to hold—rolls of toilet paper, bottles of aspirin, two large bottles of cooking oil. Essentials tumble out like clowns from a miniature car, scarves from a magician's sleeve and then, finally, an envelope. "For you," the woman says.

When Milagros opens it, two photos slip out. One of Milagros at three or four years old pressed against Grecia's legs. There is a glimpse of who she thinks must be an out-of-focus Daniela at the end of the couch. In the second photo, Grecia holds a diapered baby Milagros in her arms, Milagros's face furiously in mid-cry about an unseen transgression. Grecia wears the same expression of love that Milagros always saw when she imagined her mother. It is the first time she has seen her mother's face in over two decades.

"Oye," Daniela says when she ends her call. "You okay? You look—"

"I'm fine," Milagros says. She feels like a kid has scattered a handful of jacks in her throat, bounced the ball, and scooped up all but one. She downs a glass of water. Such emotions are unaffordable luxuries.

"So, are you working on anything else besides the crazy idea of writing about Fortunato?" Daniela asks.

"I'm not sure. Last time I was here there was a lot more resistance. The people were frenzied for change. Now everything seems settled."

"Calcified?"

"A little."

"Like we've accepted our fate?"

The *Scofflaw* article that featured Milagros shepherding Heftzi into Colombia had landed Milagros offers to freelance for other magazines. Saskia fought off the jackals, signed Milagros up on a two-year exclusive contract.

"Have you heard anything about either Fortunato or Maldonado?" Milagros asks Daniela. She's been telling herself this isn't why she's here, that writing the expose she wants to pen is too risky, but she feels that if she can confirm her suspicions with a second source that maybe she will go through with naming him. The desire to unveil Maldonado is an itch that will not go away.

Daniela picks up her pace and Milagros matches her. "Who knows what to believe when it comes to those malandros?" Milagros isn't listening. She is turning the potential expose of Maldonado over in her mind, her conviction flashing like a kernel of corn in a frying pan. Potential secondary sources. How she will pitch it to Saskia. She shivers unexpectedly. Hugs herself. From her understanding of the old man, he could have someone watching her right now. She knows she's being silly—this is the fear that gangsters sow, water, and harvest. But the feeling hangs around.

"Can you stop by my hotel room?" Milagros asks as they secure a taxi, her voice pitched slightly higher than usual. After her memories about the crossing, after the uncanniness of the room itself, with this paranoia about Fortunato nagging at her, she does not want to be alone. She remembers adjusting rabbit ears on an ancient television as a girl, fighting the snow to receive the picture, standing in one place for stretches so she could digest cartoons. Her mind now feels as if the TV static of her visit will give way to a clear picture if she adjusts an internal antenna.

Daniela frowns. "Is everything okay?"

Milagros doesn't know what to say without sounding like a kook. "There's a faint smell," she says, "and I'd like your help finding it." It's the best she can do. Daniela doesn't quite buy it, but she agrees to assist.

Once in the taxi, Daniela brings up pigeons again. "Do you know about harpy eagles?" she asks Milagros as Caracas blurs past. "They're big eagles, but not the largest. They're rare birds, and their talons are razors." She talks about how one swooped into the market once where many of Francisco's pigeons ended up.

"Like how some animals can sense an impending earthquake?"

"Right. The eagle showed up one afternoon at the market and hunted the pigeons until dusk. Worse than the cats."

"Sounds gruesome."

"It kept diving and snatching. At first it spooked the market-goers, but then, when they realized it wasn't attacking them, they went about their business. But the eagle kept coming even after it had eaten its fill. Feathers everywhere. The pigeons stayed away from the market for a few days after that."

* * *

"I'll tell you the truth," Milagros confesses as she enters the hotel room. "Since I've been here I've had the odd sense that someone's in this room." At the window she snatches open the curtain as if she'll find someone crouched on the ledge.

She expects Daniela to flinch, but she doesn't. "This is an expensive room. Can't imagine anything going wrong here." She sniffs. "Smells fine to me." Daniela walks the room's perimeter, sometimes running her hand against the wall. She eases open the bathroom door, slinks in, shuts it behind her. Daniela's humoring her, except until now she has seemed entirely humorless. When Daniela exits the bathroom, she holds the hair dryer with both hands. "Daniela the exorcist," she suggests. "Let's have a look around." They search the entire hotel room thoroughly—under the bed, behind the shower curtain, in the closet. Milagros relaxes. She's grateful. When they're done, Daniela asks if she could have a drink from the minibar.

"Just one?" Milagros replies. "I'm about to fire four or five shots."

They're both on to a second drink when Milagros remembers the pigeons. "Were the market-goers pleased?" she asks Daniela.

"What?"

"To have the pigeons chased off?" She's thinking of Maldonado again. She imagines his head replaced by a pigeon's, and snorts.

Daniela doesn't respond. Instead, she says, "I think I have your mother's journal." Milagros feels that snow being swept away from the TV screen.

"Why didn't you say?" she says, feeling, despite the alcohol, a sense of exceptional clarity.

"I didn't want to get your hopes up, but I'm pretty sure it was in the package."

Daniela says that she'll go get it, but as soon as she stands up, wobbling, it's clear that her tank's on empty. Milagros says she can spend the night.

Daniela lifts a hand. "I know this town," she says.

Milagros thinks of what it would be like to see more of her mother's handwriting, to read her words, and she's suddenly fighting off tears as she pours herself another drink, knowing that this kind of reckless hope that she now feels is that unremovable splinter under the skin of her relationship with Juanita.

Daniela leaves, drunkenly promising to look for the package from Milagros's mother and to let her know as soon as she finds it. "It's probably nothing," she says again, but Milagros can't give up hope.

It's just after 2:00 a.m., and Milagros is still chasing sleep, flipping her pillows for cool spots, when the bedside phone rings. She wills it silent, but it won't stop. Whoever's on the other end knows that Milagros is here, awake, or else is determined to wake her. Daniela, she thinks, about the package, and Milagros lifts the receiver, but it just keeps ringing. She slams it down, snatches the cord from the wall. She wraps the cord around one hand, grips the chassis of the phone tightly with the other, and strides over to the window hoping the view of Caracas will settle her. But even with the cord ripped from the wall, the phone won't stop ringing. It continues to jangle impossibly in Milagros's hand. She touches the bite of quartz that now dangles from her neck.

And as soon as she does, she knows who's on the other end of the phone.

"Mila," Grecia says when Milagros puts the receiver to her ear.

"Mami." Milagros's chest tightens. This is some sort of trick that combines with her drunkenness.

"You're home," Grecia says. It both sounds like her and doesn't.

"Yes." Milagros doesn't recognize her own voice. "To see you. Where are you?"

"That's good. You did a good thing for that little girl, Mila, getting her to Colombia." The line coughs with static. It intensifies when

Milagros moves closer to the window, and heals when she retreats toward the bathroom.

Milagros's sinuses chime; tears await. "Where are you?" Milagros asks again.

"I'm here," she says. "I was on the island for a while, but I'm back here now."

"Can I see you?"

"Not right now. But soon." Gravel flecks Grecia's voice, as if she's been drinking along with Milagros, just elsewhere. As if they just missed each other in the hotel's hallway when they went to clunk ice into their buckets. It's a voice that's crawled beneath loops of barbed wire to get to where it is. The crackling noise escalates then, gremlins in the phone line, and Milagros moves further into the bathroom, the static retreating when she steps into the bathub itself. Milagros briefly excavates herself from the tub. Looks out at the lights of Caracas from across the room.

Tightens the phone against her ear. "Where are you?"

Grecia doesn't respond. After a moment she says, "It's good to hear your voice, Mila."

"Mami," Milagros says, clutching the phone tightly. She sets down the quartz pendant for a moment, and when the call disconnects, the image of the static-filled TV screen flashes across her mind. Milagros snatches the pendant back up, but there is still a dial tone.

She keeps the receiver tight to her ear. Tells her mother's absence of the things in her life. Her job. Living in Brooklyn. About Juanita. About how much she misses her. All the while she clutches the quartz so tightly that when she releases it an imprint remains nailed in her palm. There's an ache in her chest as she tells of her hurts and hopes. As she talks she feels that giddy sensation of her feet leaving the ground once more, and she closes her eyes and lets the sensation have its way.

* * *

In the morning, a knock.

"Housekeeping."

"Later," Milagros groans. Sleep had come eventually, but restlessly. She'd almost suffocated under the pillows and had to trick herself to get them off her. The night had been a swirl of nightmares, a cutting and pasting of childhood memories with recollections on the island and callbacks of Colombia. The men at the border being shot. Drowned bodies trying to make it across the ocean from Venezuela to the island.

The knock comes again. Insistent. "Housekeeping. A package for you, miss. It says it's from a Miss Grecia Alzola. A woman dropped it at the desk for you last night."

Still woozy with alcohol, Milagros fumbles for balance. She rises with an unsteady newborn foal's gracelessness, inspects the bedside clock on her way to the door. 6:02 a.m. She's wobbly as she flicks on lights. Dances away the pins and needles in one foot. Catches a glimpse of her mother's pendant in the mirror above the dresser. Looks through the peephole. Sees the top of the housekeeper's head. Too short for her face to appear.

"Show me," she tells the voice. An envelope floats to the peephole. "Slip it under the door, please." Milagros's head pounds. The package tries to make its way under, but it's too thick. "Just leave it," Milagro says. Footsteps recede. Milagros waits a few moments, then cracks the door. Keeps the chain on for a moment, then slips it off, looks to the left and to the right. Retrieves the package. She latches the door behind her and slips to the ground with her back against it. Rips open the retaped package, festooned with faded island stamps. She can almost taste sepia. Sees several sheets of paper folded down into thirds. Her mother's handwriting splashed through the pages. They're split into two separate entities. The first contains the remaining pages of the letter that she'd received from Fortunato. There's a telltale slash of a black line that she's seen often at *Scofflaw*'s offices, someone not paying attention as they held the document on the face of the copy machine. Her mother had made a copy of her letter, or someone had done it for her. Maldonado's act of redaction, his withholding the other pages of the letter, had been worthless. For the briefest moment Milagros believes she smells the scent that Grecia once tapped on the points of her wrists. Her mind skitters, and she steadies herself. She reads the words, reads them again. They tell of her and Grecia's trip to the island. Give a couple of Venezuelan names that Milagros doesn't recognize, but that she immediately thinks might, if she can track them down, be good sources for her expose. Maybe this was why the old bastard had removed the pages—for fear fear of incrimination from others who made the trip with Grecia. The second batch of papers, from what Milagros can tell riffling through, talks about Grecia's life on the island when she was in her early twenties. When she met Milagros's father. She mashes the paper against her nose and, again, there's her mother. But then the scent flits away, and Milagros is alone with a smattering of papers and a cut of quartz.

II

A Sweet Dove and a Congregation of Scarlet Ibises

Mila,

I write this a week before you and I journey to the island and with the hope in my heart that my having lived there before means that I will be able to find my feet quickly to care for us. It saddens me that we are no longer able to live in our patria. Not right now. With each passing day, living with you in Venezuela feels more negligent—a constant repetition of not enough, not enough, not enough—and the weight of my failing grows heavier. The move to the island now, when you are just eleven, is a result of both push and pull factors: Venezuela pushing, and the island pulling. The push is the difficult times that Venezuela has slipped into. I see the children in our little town breathing shallow breaths because there are no asthma inhalers to be found. Your abuela, who has recently become eternal, felt pains in her joints but couldn't find an aspirin. Everywhere delivers much hurt but little relief. I begged her to come with us, but she said she couldn't leave Venezuela at any age.

The pull is the memory of your father. I know I have never told you much about him when you ask, but I've never lied to you. I've never told you that he was dead, or that he was wicked. I just said that he didn't live in Venezuela, which was cryptic but true. Your father's name is Hubert Cruickshank. Just over a decade before you were born I'd lived and worked on the island as a butcher's assistant.

This was when Venezuela was a destination that everyone ran toward. People arrived from Turkey, Syria, and Italy to Caracas to feather their nests. The grocery stores were bursting. Medicine was cheap and plentiful. Oil bubbled out of the earth wherever a spade was struck, and it cost less than a bottle of water to fill an automobile with petrol. The Museum of Modern Art displayed works by Dalí, Picasso, and Chagall. Once, a Matisse was stolen, and it caused an uproar and the dismissal of the museum's director. Those European masters are worthy, but for me the greatest of all were the works of Armando Reverón, a local master who painted, and crafted, astounding muñecas. I hope that you will be able to visit the museum one day to see his work. I hope that all Venezuelans will be able to visit it again one day, but I fear the need to survive curtails the need to appreciate art. But I am drifting from my main goal. I hoped to tell you how I got to the island and then fled from it.

Part of my arrival was down to feeling caged when my brother was free. I wanted to come and go like he did and see the world beyond our village. My older brother—your uncle Manuel—was a fisherman who worked with a small crew, and he partly fueled my desire. His constant coming and going struck me as romantic. In some ways he was a good brother, but he was often surly, and his eczema worsened his outlook. He would disappear for days at a time, and when he would return, he would tell me stories about the island. I would always beg him to take me to see it, but he would growl that he wasn't traveling for a vacation, but to catch and sell fish with his panas, and I would just slow him down. He said this so often that I stopped asking him.

Another reason was that I wanted to see what else the world offered beyond Venezuela. Manuel and I had been cast into modest means. For five years we'd lived with our abuela Isabella in a crumbling apartment. Our father's death in a car accident was the catalyst. Isabella's daughter, our mother, Ana, had died a few months after I was born, and Isabella was doing her best with us. With the money that my father had left I was finishing up at a good school. It had been a sore point to him when Manuel had stopped attending school in order to fish. Our father was intelligent, and he desired bigger things for your uncle and me. "Only problem was that you got all the brains," Manuel once grumbled. I felt that I needed to complete school for both of us, but once I did I'd had enough of classrooms. Isabella sensed my restlessness, and when I kept begging Manuel to take me to the island, I think she must have taken him aside and whispered in his ear. He didn't listen to many people, but he listened to her. I'm not sure if she thought there would be less trouble for me as an adventurer, or if she foresaw Venezuela's troubles on the horizon.

One morning, before dawn, Manuel shook me awake and told me to get dressed. When I asked him where we were going, he remained silent. He ushered me onto the back of his motorcycle, which didn't work almost as much as it did, and which he always tore apart when he was at home, spilling parts from it like intestines from a quartered pig. He was sullen and quiet that morning, the way that he was before he went out to fish with his crew. I remember that it was muggy, and I held on to him tightly and felt the thinness of our lives as we moved because even when there was no reason to, he sped unnecessarily and took corners sharply. When I saw that he was pointing the motorcycle toward the dock I grew excited, and my hands tightened on his hips. He had taken me out on his boat before, but I knew that this would be a longer trip, that he was finally taking me to the island.

A month earlier, when I'd told Carmen how I kept begging Manuel to take me to the island, she'd urged me not to go. She was a few years older and more worldly. *What could that teardrop of land in a massive ocean offer?* But she was in nursing school and was promised a good career. She'd just given birth to Daniela and lived with her boyfriend. She was putting down roots. She lived in a smart apartment building in a nicer part of town. I wasn't jealous, but all signs pointed up for Carmen.

The trip to the island took three hours, longer than I'd expected. But when Manuel and I docked, then walked to the small town of Bon Bois, I saw the reason why he'd spent so much time away—a girl, of course, a beauty, Alima, who was keeping him hot, and who was also the reason that he wasn't bringing home much in the way of sales from catches anymore. We met her early in the morning just before she left for work. She had cat eyes, and her hair troubled her shoulders. She sported tattoos on her thighs, a jaguar on the right, and a large swallow in flight on the left, but none anywhere else—*I can only have them in places that are covered or I'll lose my job*—and she always wore provocative earrings, especially a lacquered wooden pair of dolphins that she later gifted to me. Her only blemishes were the acne that sometimes dusted her cheeks and perhaps smoking too much weed. She was very glamorous. She worked at a clothing store in the city, and the discounts that she received kept her stylish.

It turned out that she was part of the reason that Manuel had brought me to the island. Alima had wanted a roommate, but no one local because she said most of the girls she knew were jealous of her, and she didn't trust them. But she liked me right away and told Manuel so. She only talked to me in English because she had almost no Spanish, and she called me a clever kitten because of how much English I already knew. I didn't know what she saw in my brother. But when he was around her he was, as your father would say, a different breed of cat. The first time I went to a club was because she'd made Manuel take me with them, and when I saw him there, dancing to soca with Alima in a way that I didn't know that he could, and smiling in a way that I had never seen in Venezuela, I truly understood the effect that she'd had on him and why he'd spent so much time away. The second bedroom in Alima's apartment was already furnished, and she lent me a few clothes, and we later bought some of my own, and just like that I was living on the island.

At first, Manuel was meant to pay my half of the rent. I didn't understand why he didn't just pay for himself and move in with Alima, but I learned that she wouldn't live with someone unless she was married to them. Trying to pick apart her contradictions was better left for Mary the untier of knots. While Alima was at work one day, Manuel sat on her bed and strummed her guitar, and told me there was a job that I could have right away. I wasn't comfortable having someone—even my brother—pay my way, so I would do almost anything, and he smirked when he told me the job was as a butcher's assistant. He thought that I would turn up my nose, but I surprised him when I said that I would give it a try. My English was always better than his anyway, and talking with customers daily meant that it would sharpen even more.

Alima was thrilled. She hadn't brought up the job at the butcher's to me directly because, not knowing me, she didn't know if I would look down on it. That Sunday, her one day off work, Alima grasped me by the elbow and guided me toward the butcher's shop. The first thing I noticed was the crowd and how much I liked the people in it. It was its own entity. They bumped and jostled each other—*like you's a never-see-come-see!*—wore slippers, tank tops, and shorts, demanded credit, were rejected for credit, wore cigarettes behind their ears, and made jokes at their own and others' expense. Next, the smell swirled in my head—a mix of brine, blood, and the ocean. The shop stood on the main street of Bon Bois, and it was owned and run by Miss Joyce Lee Fook, who perched on a stool at the cash register, owned a huge mole beside her nose, and saw everything, often before it happened. She caught anything that fell before it hit the ground—a ballpoint pen, a coin, a fleck of animal fat. She ran a brisk business that operated with five employees who mostly interchanged as needed. From the moment the doors opened, there was a crush of customers, which then ebbed and flowed throughout the day.

Alima took me to the cash register where Miss Lee Fook rang up customers. Alima had warned me that Miss Lee Fook was known for being a fastidious businesswoman, never allowing even a one cent piece to disappear beneath the counter. (She later whispered that Miss Lee Fook was a dragon who disdained banks and slept at night on a mattress stuffed with all her money.) But Miss Lee Fook's cuts of beef, chicken, and goat were immaculate, easily as good as those in the groceries and markets in the major towns. She worked with imams too, and Muslims were a loyal part of her clientele. She had recently fired a girl because she'd been caught stealing from the register and, like Alima, Miss Lee Fook was growing averse to local help. She was interested in me *because* I was not from the island. Later, when I asked Alima how she knew Miss Joyce had a job opening, she waved me away saying everyone knew everything that occurred on that part of the island, and she continued to apply a coat of peacock-blue nail polish to one hand.

On the morning of my first day, Miss Joyce looked me up and down like a seamstress registering my dimensions by sight, and she put me to work at once. With customers regularly coming and going, I felt like I'd been thrown into a washing machine. Although I spoke English, the island's regional accent sometimes tripped me up. The shop was small but efficient, and Miss Lee Fook demanded it be kept clean—made sure that the assistants, me and the other girl, Maureen, would step out into the crowd and, begging people's pardon, sweep or mop as needed, pushing out bits of paper or meat that had spilled. We also helped bring in deliveries. I concentrated on the work and soon grew used to the smell. I was thrilled to be working and living in a different country. Aspects of the island, how the people interacted, reminded me of home.

At the end of that first day I felt like my arms and legs weren't really mine, but were boiled noodles that had been pinned on and that could be detached just as easily. I showered that evening as soon as I returned to the apartment and, when I emerged, Alima asked me,

"Where's your pay?" I told her what Miss Joyce had said: that I would be paid at the end of the next week if I made it until then. Alima yipped with laughter and said that I was truly a sweet dove and that I was nothing like my brother, and then she warned me not to tell him that I hadn't been paid. "He would have demanded his money as soon as his shift was done and if he didn't receive it he would have burned the shop down."

That night I fell asleep at once, and I dreamed of Manuel standing outside the butcher shop, a can of gasoline in one hand and a lighter in the other, and as he watched it go up in flames, the fire flickering in his lifeless eyes, Miss Lee Fook, now a dragon, screamed at him, smoke pouring from her mouth, commanding him to put out the fire and to fish out three pounds of blood pudding from the bucket in the corner for the next customer.

I woke up twisted in the bedsheets and soaked with sweat.

Manuel hadn't returned that night, and I was glad that Alima didn't ask me where he was.

When I returned to the shop the next morning, having passed the audition, Miss Lee Fook guided me in my duties—storing deliveries, cleaning up after customers, and helping to take orders, and so I spent another day under her watchful eye. At first I was only a helper who cleaned up and aided the senior butcher, a dark man with a shaved head named Mr. Mark, who never demonstrated an inefficient motion, wore a single corn-gold hoop earring, and didn't indulge in small talk. There was the junior butcher, Odell, a thin, light-skinned young man with a wispy mustache and a sharp haircut sporting three parallel lines razor-bladed into one temple, a chatterbox who more than made up for Mr. Mark's silence with his constant jabbering. The final worker was Maureen, in her early twenties, who did a little of everything including helping Mr. Mark, which she hated, and working the register when Miss Lee Fook needed a rare bathroom break or stepped outside to haggle with a delivery man. Maureen loved the cash register best, and I was surprised that Miss Lee Fook allowed her to ring up sales, because it was clear that Maureen was both intelligent and sly, two qualities that Miss Lee Fook disdained, and she surely suspected that Maureen would spirit money out from the register if given a chance. But Miss Lee Fook must have kept her around because she liked pitting her wits against others, and she was fair, never dismissive.

And so, one week at the job became a month.

One time Odell, who often came in a few minutes late, just enough to make Miss Lee Fook grind her teeth (*he parties too much*, she once grumbled from her cash register perch), and who was getting sloppier in his cuts of meat, and who didn't keep his station as neat as Mr. Mark's, missed two days in a row. On the second day Miss Lee Fook pressed me into service: "You'll cut meats today," she said. My head spun as I tried to follow Mr. Mark's orders and Maureen's guidance, all under Miss Lee Fook's gimlet eye. The next morning Odell arrived late, and he and Miss Lee Fook tumbled into a heated argument. When she dismissed him, he demanded his pay, and she chased him out of the shop with a flat-bladed cleaver, and we never saw him again.

All of us pretended to see nothing and just went back to work.

"Papa yo," said one of the customers at the spectacle.

"Gs + Hs," said another.

"Bacchanal," said a third.

But this was how business operated.

I met your father at Miss Lee Fook's. Was he handsome? I certainly believed so, although at first I didn't notice him. I was so fixated on getting the customers' orders right, in making sure that I cut the slices of beef with just the right amount of marbled fat that kept Miss Lee Fook's reputation high, and her profits higher that, at first, he was just another face in the crowd. "It's like watering the drinks at a nightclub just a little," Maureen explained, holding her thumb and forefinger slightly apart to show me what the end result should look like as she demonstrated how to cube fatty pork with the vertical electric blade. Her breath smelled of spearmint. I concentrated mostly on keeping my fingers. "You'll be fine," she said, patting my shoulder. She worked only on weekdays, and on weekends she tended bar in the city. She was patient with me, showing me how to cut and to weigh the minced meat quickly before running it through the grinder. "Why did you leave Venezuela to work at a butcher shop?" she once asked.

"The glamour," I replied. Her laugh was a rifle bolt, and Miss Lee Fook shot us an awful look. By the end of the day I minced meat without error and made sure to measure the right amount of souse, pig's feet, or oxtail for customers who came and went at such a blur that I barely noticed any one customer's face. Miss Lee Fook seemed pleased.

Your father was very tall, and his shoulders were wide wings that spread out on either side of him. His skin was brown and darkened easily in the sun. He had a bit of a paunch, but his height helped dissolve it. He was in his forties, and gray flecked his temples, and he later confessed that he'd started to come to the shop more often while I was there, and he was disappointed that I didn't notice him at first. It seemed everyone else did. It wasn't until Maureen whispered *your boyfriend's here again* one morning that he finally registered. After that I understood how he was different from the regulars—those who flocked to the store for the cheaper cuts of meat, the salt fish and chicken feet—and that he wore stylish shirts and good cologne. He always ordered our priciest cuts in large quantities, and it was only later that he admitted that he never ate it himself, since he mostly ate only seafood, but that he would donate his purchases to a woman one village over in New Felicity called Miss Titus, who would often cook and feed others there, mostly down-on-their-luck fishermen. He explained that his family was originally from New Felicity Village, and he still kept a house there, and that he would live there all the time if he could, always close to the ocean.

The first time that Hubert Cruickshank talked to me for more than half a minute was to ask for cuts of exotic meat during my fifth week at Miss Lee Fook's. He always strode in when the shop wasn't busy, which I first considered to be an unconscious knack, but then learned was by discreet design. He was an odd duck. He loved people, but he was uncomfortable in crowds. He loved laughter and island fatigue, but he was very soft-spoken. His bulk made him uneasy. Even when he spoke directly to someone, and was clearly invested in what they said, his mind seemed preoccupied and distant. I later learned that other than his family, it was the very land in and around New Felicity Village that preoccupied him. He was an entrepreneur who owned a few businesses including a string of popular ice cream shops, and he was an island personality known for his charity, especially to primary schools in poorer areas on the island. And while he was broad-shouldered and imposing, he owned delicate features including small ears and very long eyelashes. He couldn't grow a beard. He was a man who often had to lower his head through doorways and did so when he came to Miss Lee Fook's, which I learned was called the Pig Shop by the locals. And he would disappear, sometimes for entire days, without telling anyone where he went. He said sometimes he wasn't sure himself. "Everyone knows where they've been," I said to him. "Stop pulling my leg." That was when he reached out and touched my hand as it rested on the counter, and my face went warm.

In a word, Mila, he was a dreamer.

The first time that I really noticed him he had returned to New Felicity Village for a vacation to clear his head. He came into Miss Lee Fook's and watched me chopping up oxtail and pig's feet, sluicing them into a bucket. He said my movements mesmerized him and if I could be graceful quartering meat then I would be even more graceful outside of a butcher's apron. Our first extended interaction was during the midmorning lull, after the morning rush, and before the housewives arrived to purchase meat for their families' dinners. Finally, Miss Lee Fook cleared her throat and I looked up to see him alone at the counter waiting to be served. I didn't know where Maureen was, so I wiped my hands on my apron and took his order. He said that his pregnant daughter-in-law had a craving that she couldn't describe. "Wild meat," he said, unconsciously tapping the counter with a finger.

Miss Lee Fook watched to see what my response would be. The shop carried certain cuts of wild meat as a specialty item that was scratched on the chalkboard daily—usually armadillo and manicou and agouti. Today, she'd trained all of us to trumpet a specific cut of wild meat that she'd taken on as a favor from a local hunter but that wasn't selling very well and would have to be thrown out in a few days because she never gave away her goods.

"We have capybara," I told him.

"Perfect," he said. "Just what she needs." He ordered fifteen pounds. At first I thought that I had misheard him. He spoke so softly, and when either saw was in use, he was almost impossible to hear. Also, no one had ordered capybara that week. But if his smile could light the village, then Miss Lee Fook's elation at his request could power the island. I could feel her eyes on me as I put together his order.

As I wrapped the order in grease paper and tied it with twine, a smiling Miss Lee Fook swooped in, which was so infrequent an occurrence that I thought it would split her face. His order was so large that Miss Lee Fook threw in cuts of armadillo meat as a lagniappe, and she urged me to help him carry the large Styrofoam container to his car. I wiped my hands again on my blood-soaked apron, and just as I placed the container in his trunk I heard him ask, in his quiet way, "What's your name?" When I told him, he asked me if I would visit New Felicity Village with him when I was done with work. I told him that I would need to return home to shower first, and when I had done so, and I was drying myself, I peeked through the bathroom window and saw he was already parked out front.

He was anxious that first time that we were together. He didn't take me to New Felicity Village, but to a space just outside of it that locals called the Clearing. At first I thought that I made him anxious, but I learned that the space itself, once a sugarcane field, was rumored to be a site where jumbies gathered (even though he'd never seen any personally). He said that a village terror used to go there and get drunk on cane liquor, and one time a mosquito bit him on the forehead and he'd died four hours later, and since then everyone avoided the Clearing. "But not you," I said.

On either side of the Clearing were trees laid out in regimented regularity. He waved to the west side of the Clearing. "I had all these zaboca trees planted for my son, Basil." Then he waved to the east side. "I had all these zaboca trees planted for my grandson, Peter-Called-Peter." He said that his son, Basil, in his midthirties, was an attorney who was already an MP, and I heard the pride that threaded through his voice. He said that all of this land, even beyond the Clearing, had once been sugarcane, remarkable for the soil to be so fertile this close to the ocean.

It mattered to him to make this gesture, to clear that land, to plant something *different* there. His family had descended from slaves, and he wanted their legacy to be something other than sugar. He wanted me to know that even though his family's legacy was what it was, like that of so many families on the island, no one should have their enslaved past determine their free future. He'd purchased the land that didn't already belong to his family, and he worked with a villager called Sonny and his son, a skinny fifteen-year-old named Miki, to clear it and to plant the zaboca trees there. He said something about the Clearing resonated within him. He said that when the island became independent from the British in the sixties he believed that some kind of permanent positive gesture was required to exorcise past British missteps. Later, he took me to New Felicity Village and showed me the beach house that his family owned. It was modest and, before it had been renovated, it had once been a slave cabin on the estate. I thought about all of this as he made me dinner, calamari to start, and grilled sesame ahi tuna for the main course.

When I returned to the apartment, Alima was waiting for me like a cat at a mouse hole, and I finally understood that, of course, she and Maureen were panas. "So," she said, her hands joined together in prayer, "what's he like?"

Unknown to me, Manuel had returned that night. He'd grown more distant since I'd moved to the island and his comings and goings had become unreliable. When Alima had asked me why that might be, I'd told her he was taking care of our abuela back in El Tigre which, I hoped, was true, since I also thought about her and was secretly mailing money back to her stuffed in envelopes and sandwiched between two sheets of carbon paper. Somehow I knew that she would not be around much longer, and I wanted to return to see her.

That night, when Alima teased me about my novio, Manuel was listening from the darkness of her bedroom, and he emerged from it like Death itself to confront me. "Who's this pendejo you're seeing?" he asked. I felt the pulse in my wrist as I described Hubert. "He sounds too old," he said, his eyes red, alcohol fumes spiking from his skin. "And he sounds like he has a hairy back."

"You haven't met him," I said. "And I haven't met his back."

"*Anyone's* too old for you," he said. He added that he distrusted island men. He said when he met this Hubert that he'd knock his block off. He was staggering, and Alima and I helped him to bed. He'd been away for ten days before he'd showed up that Friday night, drunk until he was almost blind.

* * *

Mila, was part of the reason that I began to see your father because I missed my own? That's a question for brain doctors and one that I don't want to think about too deeply. Not having known my mother, I had been close to my father. Like Hubert, he was kind, but Hubert was generous to an astonishing level—particularly toward the residents of New Felicity Village. I think he considered all of them as members of his ancestral tribe, and he wanted to aid them as much as he could.

I saw him again that Sunday. He saw my worry at once. I told him about Manuel and how he disapproved of us. "Let him meet me," Hubert said, "then he'll *really* disapprove." I told him to be serious. I told him that I felt like I was losing Manuel and this troubled me. I told him that I missed my abuela too, and that maybe I'd been rash in coming to the island.

He took my hand in his. He asked me to visit New Felicity's mangrove with him. Said that it would help clear my mind, and that whatever I decided afterward he'd be fine with. So I let him take me out on a boat into the mangrove at dusk. The smell at Miss Lee Fook's was nothing compared to the mangrove, which was brine and animals' musk. But the sights, Mila. We watched snakes drift from branches, crabs skitter over exposed roots, small sharks dart beneath the boat. Then he cut the engine and we waited for the ibises to return to their nests.

He remained silent as I took it all in. There was a huge flock of them, their red feathers like silk; they moved with startling grace. He confessed his fear that all of it would be lost in a few years. He was working with the government to set up laws to ensure the mangrove's survival. He pleaded with his son Basil to pay more attention to nature. He was trying to twist his arm, to bend his will, to get him to think about the future of the mangrove. He said Basil responded that nobody cared about rivers if those rivers didn't put food in empty bellies. Hubert breathed deeply. He blamed himself for sending Basil to university in Britain. But I told him to hush, and I pulled his head against my chest, and we watched the ibises return home for the night, a staggering sheet of red stretched across the darkening sky. And right then he gave me my favorite kiss.

Later, he gave me a pendant. A medallion crafted from the sun. Quartz, of course, but it somehow caught the light. He said that it possessed powers granted by a conjure woman from a very old tribe that had come across the water. "What does it do?"

"If ever we're separated," he said, "it will let us communicate with each other." He wrapped his hands around mine. *A sweet child's story*, I thought. He looped it around my neck. We spent more and more time together. He spoiled me but was practical as well. When I told him I had a toothache, he examined my mouth. He exclaimed at how many teeth I had. "It's probably your wisdom teeth," he said. "There might be trouble later if you don't take care of them now." He paid for his dentist to pull my four back teeth. Then he said he didn't want to worry me, but he was a practical person who always planned ahead, and he wanted me to think about my future as well. He presented me with a beautiful purse, and inside was money and a plane ticket and a passport from the island. I examined the purse's craftsmanship, wondered how he got the picture of me for the passport, stamped with a gold ibis and another bird on its cover. He admitted that his son Basil was involved. "It's so you can visit your grandmother," he said. "Although I don't want you to leave."

"And the money?"

"For you to purchase a Venezuelan passport and return to me."

"Beware any man who'll take your teeth," a tipsy Manuel warned me a few nights later as he downed a local lager and gutted a carite on the counter that he'd brought home for Alima to fry. He was shirtless and thinner than ever, and his eczema was acting up. He'd spent most of the weekend sleeping off his Friday hangover, and he was still angry at Hubert, who he still hadn't met. I wondered at the true cause of his ache. "When do I get to meet this pervert?" he asked.

"When you're sober," I snapped.

"Leave her alone," Alima said as she set the table. "Let her find her own way."

But she didn't see what I saw. Didn't know Manuel like I did. Didn't know that the linchpin that held my brother's sanity together had been slipping free of its hold since my arrival on the island and now it seemed to be entirely removed. In the time that I'd been on the island I'd grown afraid of Manuel. He'd been growing frustrated due to limited catches, and his absences made me wonder. But not Alima. "Let's smoke some of this sensi," she suggested after dinner, holding up an impressively full sandwich bag of weed.

Mila, there's nothing that pushes two people together like disapproval from their families. I'll be honest—your father never lied to me. I knew that he was still married, his wife a socialite from a wealthy Creole family. He loved his son, but he doted on his grandson Peter-Called-Peter, a teenager readying for college. Then he told me something awful—that he'd told his son Basil about me when he'd arranged for the passport, and he disapproved of us. "You *told* him about me?" I asked. "About us? How did you think he'd respond?" I pushed him in his chest, which had no effect. Hubert explained that he and his wife had long been estranged and had long contemplated divorce and knew that Basil understood that. "She's still his mother," I said. He'd explained the divorce's eventuality, but Basil had surprised him, had grown furious, and had called him an old fool. "What did you think he'd say?" I shouted.

He pulled me into a hug, smothering me with his cologne. But it turned out this was less of a concern than Manuel.

One night the following week, Manuel returned home delirious and flush with both bolívares and island money. He threw them up in the air and danced a little two-step as the cash floated down. Alima didn't hide her suspicion. Like me, she knew no fish that he caught would yield that kind of return. She confronted him. "Are you smuggling?" He laughed, but he wouldn't meet her eyes. "Manuel," she said. "Look at me." But he wouldn't. He just kept laughing. She slapped him hard across the cheek. He grabbed her shoulders and shook her. "Let me go, asshole!" The temperature in the room plummeted. I called Hubert. Ten minutes later he was there, and I slipped out while Alima and Manuel screamed at each other. I spent my first night with Hubert at his house in New Felicity Village.

It didn't take long to learn how Manuel had earned the money. It was in the local newspaper a few days later. He and his fishing crew were accused of being part of a Venezuelan kidnapping ring and had been arrested for seizing local fishermen. I returned to the apartment and showed Alima the article. She wept, and I hugged her. I didn't recognize Manuel's grainy picture. He'd been beaten until his eyes were the size of potatoes. One cheek was swollen to the size of a planet. A marble clogged my throat. Alima was still shaking when I led her to the couch and gave her a glass of water.

Then I called Hubert, but I couldn't string together a sensible sentence. It was as if Alima's nervous energy had transferred to me. My mind skittered. Hubert urged me to speak slowly and explain what happened. He grew quiet when I finally told him. I asked him to help. He said it wouldn't be easy. He knew the magistrate who would most likely oversee the case, and he was a difficult man. I was speaking softly to spare Alima, didn't want to fill her with false possibilities. She knew who Hubert's son was. When I hung up I told her what Hubert had said. "Then there's hope," she said, too nervous to sit still.

I didn't want to risk going to see Manuel in jail because of my status, passport or not. But Alima went, and they told her that she couldn't see him. Dark circles were already stamped beneath her eyes, and they never left. A few days later the headline on the front of the newspaper read KIDNAPPERS TO BE ARRAIGNED. It was the same grainy picture of my brother and his codefendants, but somehow he looked different. Worse. Hardened. Like his hands had been handcuffed behind him the entire time that he'd been in custody. Like he'd been beaten even worse, although no part of the image had changed.

I tried to work at Miss Lee Fook's, but I was too distracted. I felt as if everyone there knew about Manuel. I almost lost the tip of a finger sectioning some lamb. Late that morning, thinking about Manuel locked away, I ran to the toilet to vomit. Miss Lee Fook squinted at me and told me to go home. I wasn't sure if she meant permanently, but I didn't return, and I never received my pay for that last week's work.

I knew that I should stay with Alima to comfort her, but my head was all over the place, and she was out of her mind with worry. It was becoming too much to be there. I felt nauseated all the time. Hubert convinced me to leave. Said it would be better for both me and Alima to have some space. He took me out of the hot apartment one morning when Alima was at work, and he moved me into the Cruickshank beach house in New Felicity Village. I left Alima a note saying that I would be gone for a couple of days.

Of course I was already pregnant. When I told Hubert, he was overjoyed. He said that he knew that it would be a girl, and that he'd always wanted a daughter and that she would be a ballerina and a poet. There was already a lawyer/politician in the family.

As he settled me in the bedroom Hubert said that the house had been in his family for a long time. "Something feels strange about it," I said, testing the bed.

"Strange how?" He looked into the room from the kitchen where he was unpacking some groceries that he had picked up on the way.

"Odd." I couldn't explain it beyond that. I ran my hand over the bedsheet. I touched the quartz around my neck.

He closed the fridge then came into the bedroom. Sat beside me. Rubbed my back. At first it was lovely. Hubert spent days with me, caring for me. He cooked. Put on a radio station that only played songs by the Mighty Shadow, the Mighty Penguin, and Bob Marley, and he turned it up when "Three Little Birds" played, and he held me in his arms and danced me around the kitchen when "Cry to Me" came on, surprising me with his nimble feet. He opened all the windows, and the wind blew through and brought the salted sea air that surprisingly calmed me. On the porch he hung a hammock, and we lay in it together, and he read the daily newspaper to me. I told him not to spare me any news about Manuel, but there wasn't any.

One morning, feeling queasier than usual, I snapped at him. "What's wrong?" he asked.

"You have me playing house when my brother is locked away in some rat-infested island jail. You can get me an island passport, but you can't free my brother?" He looked like I had slapped him and left a mark. He remined quiet for a moment. Then he said it was clear that I needed some time to myself. He stood up and said he'd give me time to calm down. And he was gone. I closed all the windows and killed the radio. He was right. I wanted to be alone.

Miss Titus came by around lunch and brought me food: fried plantains, peas and rice, oxtail soup. I couldn't eat. She looked nervous, and when I asked why, she asked about the house. If I'd heard any noises? When I said no, she said that I had nothing to worry about. When she came back for the dishes, still untouched, I grasped her by the elbow and asked her to tell me the truth. She said that yes, this used to be the worst of the slave cabins, a space where slaves had been punished. When she said this it felt like ants were tunneling through my veins. All the village houses were closing in tightly around me. In the mornings, I would get up early, after the local fishermen rowed out, and I would stand on the beach and look out toward Venezuela.

Two days later Hubert's son, Basil, Member of Parliament, arrived. He didn't knock on the door; he just used a key and slipped right in. I was picking at the lunch that Miss Titus had brought over half an hour earlier. He wasn't as tall as his father, but he was more imposing. In the last few days I'd kept trying to call Hubert, but he wouldn't answer. My face had grown puffy, and I avoided mirrors. Basil looked around the house as if he didn't want even his feet to touch it. Then he grinned and said, "What a thing is a middle-aged crisis." He finally sat on the couch and crossed his legs, and with a wave of a hand he invited me to sit on the loveseat opposite. He looked at me for a few moments without speaking. If Hubert hadn't shown me a picture of him, I wouldn't know that he was his son. His complexion was lighter. His hair straighter. He probably looked more like his mother. He wore a suit, and even though it was a hot day, there wasn't a lick of sweat on him. "You," he said, then he stopped speaking, and he closed his eyes, and he composed himself. When he opened his eyes, he was calm, and the politician in him emerged. His suit was well tailored. He pinched an imaginary thread from his trousers.

"Where's Hubert?" I asked.

"Hubert," he said, laughing. "You won't see Hubert again."

"Where is he?" My face grew warm.

He sat up straight. "You shouldn't be here," he said. "If you know what's good for you, you'll leave and return to whatever Vene drain-pipe you crawled out of."

I wondered if he knew that I was pregnant. I wondered if I should bring it up. He was Hubert's son, and I wanted to believe that he had his father's dignity, his care for others, but I couldn't be sure. I remained quiet. "Here's what's going to happen," he said. "You're going to leave this house before the sun sets tomorrow." He removed his handkerchief and wiped away imaginary perspiration from around his mouth. "If you're still here after that, I'll have you thrown into the cell next to your brother's." This seemed to amuse him and he gave me an awful smile full of beautifully straight and white teeth. I considered my situation. I was from a different country. I was a butcher's helper. I was his father's mistress. I had no right to anything. He stood. "If you're as clever as he says you are, I know that you will leave quickly." Then, like his father, he was gone. If I hadn't been looking directly at him I would have thought that he'd disappeared.

I called Hubert again, but his phone just rang. I kept calling. I grasped the sun medallion and asked it to ask him for help, the way he'd said, but the pendant's powers didn't work for me. He didn't materialize.

He'd disappeared completely.

I paced. Thought. Worried. I called Alima, but her phone just rang. Around dusk I heard a car's engine, and I raced to the window, and it was Sonny and his son, Miki. I ran to the front door and pulled it open, mentally hurrying them in. "Do you know where Hubert is?" I asked. I stepped aside, and Sonny sat where Basil had sat, but then something seemed to trouble him, and he slid down to the other end of the couch.

"I'm here to help you move," he said.

"Did Basil send you?"

"I've never spoken to Minister D'Souza."

I grew hopeful. "Then it was Hubert?"

"I haven't spoken to Mr. Cruickshank."

"Then how did you know to come help me move?"

"I didn't *know* exactly, miss," he said. "But Miss Titus is worried about you. And I'm at your service if you need me."

"Where will you take me?"

"Wherever you need to go," he said.

His son Miki had already collected my meager things and placed them in the bed of the pick-up truck. I asked him to take me to Alima's. When I got there she wouldn't let me in. I kept knocking. "Please, Alima," I said. "Let me speak to you." Finally, the door briefly opened, and a cloud of sensi, a wave of dancehall music, and a garbage bag with the rest of my clothes sailed out.

When I got back outside, Sonny stood beside his truck. He told me that Mr. Cruickshank had a place for me to stay as a contingency, which means that he must have been in contact with Hubert, but I was too tired to fight him. He drove me back toward New Felicity Village but stopped before we got there. "This house," Sonny started as he pulled up in front of the large estate house. But he didn't complete his thought. I knew it was the Abercromby House. It was where Hubert had told me the estate owner had lived over two hundred years ago. Miki, who sat between us, fidgeted. I remembered Hubert saying that all this land had once been sugar, cultivated first by Africans and then by Indians. Sonny said that Mr. Cruickshank had wanted to help turn the house into a museum, but there were problems, the biggest being that it was so far from the island's capital and no one would come.

"Why did you bring me here?" I asked Sonny. He breathed deeply. Repeated that Hubert had made contingencies for me before he'd left. "Where is he?" I asked again.

"This is for you," he said. It was a large manila envelope stuffed tight with local bird-stamped cash.

Abercromby House now belonged to Hubert's family, and it rattled me as soon as I entered. It held no furniture. I wondered if Basil would find me there. Sonny said not to worry, that no one from Mr. Cruickshank's family came here. I saw why. From the outside the house looked serene, but inside it was airless. Like an X-ray of the past's innards. A frozen picture of grief. I stayed in the front room, close to the door, and used my clothes as a bed. I'm not sure what I was waiting for. News about Manuel. Hubert to return. Sonny to bring me food from Miss Titus. The last one of these, at least, happened. The nights in that house were freezing, and the days broiled.

I had nowhere else to go, and my brother was still in jail.

I tried other rooms, but I couldn't go any deeper into the house. It was as if an invisible force pressed against me and prevented me from doing so. I stayed awake all that night thinking about Hubert and Manuel. The next morning, I knew only this about Hubert as sure as I knew that you, Mila, were inside me: that he had disappeared completely, and that I wouldn't see him again. Vanished like a dream that you struggled to hold on to upon awaking. The marble in my throat swelled. My father, my brother, now Hubert, gone.

I stayed there for just under a week. I kept hoping that Hubert would show up, if not for me, then for you, Mila, his ballerina, his poet. You would pull him back. But in my heart I knew nothing could bring him back. I tried to reach out to Alima again, but she wouldn't see me. I tried to find out about Manuel—I called police stations, the court, the jail—but no one would tell me anything. Although Sonny and Miss Titus brought me food, I couldn't eat. On nights when I could fall asleep, I never dreamed. The house refused it. I saw myself in the mirror one morning as I washed my face, and it was the face of someone who had traveled to a terrible place and had a difficult time returning. I caught a reflection of something hung on the wall behind me—a large dark moth—but when I turned around it was gone, and I knew that if I stayed I would be choosing permanent grief.

So for you, Mila—I chose life, and I chose to return to my abuela. I chose to return to Venezuela and have you there and take our chances.

Sonny drove me to the airport, and the island passport worked without issue, just as I knew it would. It was my first flight, and the entire trip I traced my finger over the gold ibis. When I landed at Simón Bolívar

International I changed the envelope's island money to bolívars. I ran my fingers over the golden ibis one last time, then I threw it in the trash. When I arrived at my abuela's, she pulled me into a tight hug. She held me away from her to look at me, but she didn't say anything. I knew that I looked as thin as a razor blade. When she asked me about Manuel, I broke down, and she pulled me to her again, and she got me into bed just before I collapsed. I stayed there for over a week. She did what she could to learn about Manuel, both of us hoping that he'd be deported, but it didn't happen. One day, when I was stronger, she took me to the graves of the thugs to pray for him. Soon I knew that you would be there to help me recover. Soon I knew that you would be there to fill the emptiness.

Mila, I am not sure why I document all of this for you. Being on the island the first time showed me how tricky this world is, how someone you love can be taken away like your uncle Manuel or how he can run away like your father. My biggest fear is that you are taken away from me, or me from you, or that we are separated. I am taking you back to the island because I truly believe that there is nothing for me in Venezuela right now. I was so mad to leave that I met with an old crazy who talks with parrots but who I was told was the best person in Caracas to get me back there without a passport. And to think that I used to own a passport to this very place. I write this almost as a way of safeguarding against us being split up. That if you consider the worst possible thing then it won't occur. Every so often a dream of us being separated shakes me awake, and I cannot move, and I say your name over and over again until my legs allow me to walk, and I go check on you to make sure that you're safe.

Con amor, Mila.
Tu mami.

12

An Impossible Bird

IN GRENADA THE bonds between Bunny and Milagros pilled, frayed, then split. Free from the village's spotlight, the Clearing's congestion, and the troubling tellings of spirits, there was now a clean emotional slate on which Milagros could scrawl. And Milagros selected a rage-filled quill. So, not even a full day into their new lives in a new place, and Milagros forced Bunny into a defensive crouch. Because Milagros asked for her mother. Insisted upon her. Demanded her. Wasn't this the point of the trip? She'd been promised. Weren't they going to find her mami? *Grecia Grecia Grecia Grecia* became the household's silent monastic chant. The invisible kite that darted around their domestic atmosphere.

At first Bunny fended her off. Asked Milagros to help unpack. Suggested a beach trip. A mall excursion to pick out a new bathing suit. Didn't Milagros need a nap? Bunny had hoped that one of these alternative options would entice. But Milagros couldn't be bought off. A force eight gale of dissatisfaction cranked to force ten. Any three-year-old would be proud. It created weariness that wrapped Bunny like a blanket.

Finally worn out, Milagros fell into sleep's chasm, and Bunny screamed into a pillow. Why had she taken on this impossible task? She pinned the blame on whatever dark spirit that had flipped her coffee table in New Felicity, had perfumed her house with spices. *A djinn inhabited me*, she'd confess to anyone who would listen, *a jumbie blight me.* She rubbed at darkened eyes. *Forced my hand, strong-armed my thoughts.*

She searched for mental equilibrium. A few deep breaths that didn't take.

"Cálmate," she told herself.

When Milagros awoke, she was breathing quickly, and a terrified Bunny brought her a glass of water. Milagros explained that terrible sharp-chinned imps and rotten-toothed witches chased after her in dreams.

Bunny pulled Milagros into her arms. She was already planning a call to Lorraine, Binary Clem's estranged wife who lived in Florida, and who might be a savior. She asked Lorraine to look into the procedures for applying for asylum, then she looked into securing a Grenadian passport for Milagros. She called Caleb, Nello's brother and her only connection here, to ask him about black-market passports. Over the phone, she could practically hear the way he shifted uncomfortably from one foot to the next. "Against your religion?" she asked him. When Bunny told him that it was to save the little girl's life, and that money was not a concern, he hesitated, then said he would see what he could do.

On their second full day in Grenada, Bunny stepped out of the shower and into a new Milagros tantrum. Arms pinwheeling. A rending of garments. A throwing around of the body. A gnashing of teeth. Her chest heaving, Milagros briefly paused, then proceeded to fling things at hand around their rental house, a potentially expensive proposition since Bunny had ladled out a large cash security deposit due to no proof of local employment. First Milagros launched a Gideons New Testament north. A bottle of aromatic bitters east. A Daily Word headed west. A butter dish idled on the tarmac ready for southern flight when Bunny gripped the girl's wrists. Looked her directly in her eyes. "Cálmate," she pleaded. Milagros shrugged off Bunny's hands. Sent the butter bell into orbit. Once it smashed into irreparable pieces—one shard sliding spitefully beneath the refrigerator—Bunny released Milagros, slipped outside, and perched on the top step that led into the house until the crashing abated. Bunny recalled her own mother, a fuzzy blur who'd passed away when Bunny was four years old. Left her to be raised by Antonio. She was surprised when the noise died down and the front door creaked open. Her shoulders jerking, Milagros exited into the still air, sat beside Bunny, and wept against her shoulder.

The cave adjusted the equation. That and the golden-eyed woman Milagros encountered on the black sand beach on that second full day in Grenada. Caleb, small-shouldered and thin-mustached, stopped by that morning. One side of his mouth drooped, and Bunny suspected a recent stroke. But goodness radiated from him: his gait, his clothing, his demeanor. This was someone who'd molded his life into service for others, who, when Bunny answered the door with a pinched face that Saturday morning and saw him, was relieved when he asked, "How about a quiet trip to Black Bay Beach?" Bunny approached Milagros on tenterhooks with the offer expecting smoke and thunder. But Milagros received the suggestion serenely. A truce. Cálmate.

Caleb had brought along a copy of the *Grenada Star* newspaper. On the drive to the beach Milagros consumed bits and pieces of Grenada's news. English words that had become familiar, and short sentences she could easily wrangle.

Black Bay. A beach so quiet that when Bunny settled on the towel beside a hastily packed cooler of sandwiches, potato chips, and soft drinks, the waves' meditations lulled her to sleep and left her in twitchy dreams of Miki and Peter-Called-Peter dueling with pistols at ten paces while the rest of the village residents observed from their galleries.

With Bunny asleep, Milagros wandered off, drawn by the cave's invisible pull. Caleb remained smoking in the car, engaged with the cricket match on the radio, cigarette smoke haloing up past his head. Milagros ambled the empty length of the beach until she encountered a wall of rock jutting into the surf. The water wasn't deep; she circumvented the outcropping and claimed the adjoining beach. Her first sight: the dark-skinned woman roosting on a waist-tall stool on the black sand and gazing at an impressive vessel floating about fifty feet out in the bay. Her golden eyes as bright as a flash of lightning. Thirty feet behind her, the caves. The woman wore a hobble skirt and ankle-high boots. She seemed to be calculating how to access the boat without getting wet. Her head was smartly wrapped in a green scarf. Something shifted within Milagros. The feeling that this woman held answers to unasked questions. A key to an as-yet-unlocated vault. "Hola," she said.

The woman kept her eyes on the horizon. "Yes, hello, child."

"My name is Milagros."

"I'm Imogen." The woman finally pivoted. Took in Milagros. She dipped into her skirt's pocket and retrieved a fortune cookie. "Do you see that bird," Imogen said, chinning toward the specimen on the sand behind Milagros. She tore at the plastic with her teeth. "That's an Euler's flycatcher." It was a specimen with a brown shield stamped upon its chest that faded to yellow toward its feet. Imogen read the fortune, crunched the cookie, and then deposited the spent wrapper in her skirt's pocket.

Milagros eyed the hopping bird. "What's wrong with it?"

"What's wrong with it," Imogen said, tapping her flat hand at an itch residing beneath the headscarf, "is that it's supposed to be extinct. It shouldn't exist." She paused. Read the fortune's ticker tape. Shook her head. Pocketed the fortune. "That bird used to be abundant on this island, but hasn't been recorded since the early 1950s." She turned her golden eyes to Milagros. "That, child, is an impossible bird."

This impossibility trapped Milagros's interest.

And then, suddenly, the cave beckoned, a flashing signal atop a radio tower. A legion of indecipherable voices slipped into Milagros's head, a radio station searching for a clean signal among static. It discomfited her. Her first instinct was to run, scramble back to Bunny, but the woman's gaze held her in place. Milagros addressed her. "Can I ask you something?"

"That's already one something," Imogen said.

"Can spirits cross water?"

Imogen paused. "Spirits can do just about whatever they please," she said. "Why should water stop them?"

Milagros searched the sand for pebbles. A shell. Anything to shift her attention from the static in her head. Lessen the whispers. Limit the cave's gravity. "What do you do?" Milagros finally asked.

"Do you mean how I earn a living?"

"Yes."

"I'm a travel escort," Imogen said. "I help others migrate from danger to safety as securely as possible."

Milagros's mind cast back to her mother settling them on the boat that ferried them to the island. Pulling a life vest over her shoulders.

She recalled Bunny and the New Felicity men boating her to Grenada. She remembered the bodies claimed by the water. Finding neither shell nor rock, Milagros turned to the ocean. "Is that your boat?"

"So many questions!" Imogen's golden eyes blazed.

Just then the cave's voices spiked in Milagros's ear. "I have to go," she said. And then she paused, even though Imogen might not like her asking one more thing. "What's in that cave?"

Imogen retrieved a second fortune cookie. "Mostly guano," she said. "Some resentment." She held the fortune away from her eyes to better read it, then frowned.

"People?"

"Distressed bondswomen." She held out the fortune to Milagros. "Here. I think this one is for you."

Milagros pocketed the scrap of paper without reading it. The caves' murmuring voices still had not found a station, but their volume was rising. She backed away from it, looked over her shoulder toward where she'd left Bunny around the bend. "Will you be here if I come back?"

"I don't know when you'll be back," Imogen said. A sneaky wave crashed into the backs of Milagros's thighs and toppled her. She rose coughing seawater. She'd expected Imogen to disappear when she righted herself and she wiped seafoam from her eyes, but the odd woman remained. "Mind your step, child," Imogen called as Milagros scrambled back across the sand.

Later that evening, Milagros's mood was as bright as Bunny had ever seen it. The beach had surely played a part, but surely not just the dark sand's uniqueness. At dinner, Milagros finally confessed to her new friend. "*Imogen?*" Bunny asked. "Who's this character? I didn't see her on the beach." Bunny eyed Milagros, who she could swear, was slightly levitating. She had called Lorraine again, who had said that all they needed to claim asylum at a U.S. airport were passports.

Bunny considered how to ask for asylum from Venezuela for Milagros if she held a Grenadian passport. *A bridge to be crossed*, she thought, after Caleb said he might know someone who could help secure the vital document.

That night, during a restless joust with sleep, a familiar gremlin surfaced: an all-encompassing cardamom scent accosted Bunny. Snaked its way through the windows and wound its way through the house. It intensified with the dawn. "Jesus Christ," said Bunny, gagging. "Not this again." The scent flicked at her nostrils an hour before sunrise, and sleep evaded her until she rose and flung her pillow to the ground. She brushed her teeth, avoided the bathroom mirror, scraped her tongue. She hunted through the house just in case; maybe a bottle of spice had erupted in a cupboard. A search revealed nothing. When Milagros emerged from her room, she was covering her nose. Then, kismet: Caleb called to ask if they wanted to return to the beach midmorning.

Grateful, Bunny accepted.

The beach was empty once more, and they settled on their familiar spot. Caleb remained in the car with the cricket match, the newspaper, and a paper-bagged bottle of beer. Bunny pretended that drinking during the day didn't bother her, and when she eyed Milagros she was convinced that the child was slightly levitating.

When Milagros returned, Imogen was absent, but the cave's call to Milagros had sharpened. Now she clearly heard what the braided voices said to her: [Welcome]

She set off tentatively up the sand. Shucked her flip-flops at the cave's entrance.

Once she'd found a gap big enough to squeeze through, she hesitated. The cave smelled of guavas ripe to bursting. Its sand was smoother than a tamarind seed. A little overhang of rock required navigation—just ducking one's head—and then there was a small drop to a ledge, then another drop into a wide circle of sand. Milagros moved carefully. The voices continued their reception.

Milagros's eyes adjusted. She slapped at attacking sandflies and mosquitoes. The scamps dive-bombed her calves and arms, and the sound of punished skin peppered the anteroom. She carefully lowered herself to the ledge, then down once more to the underground clearing. As she moved into the circle, the gloom lightened like an approaching dawn, and the sand's smoothness gave way to the crunch of sharp pebbles beneath her feet, or maybe broken chip-chip shells. She stepped gingerly. Chided herself for leaving her flip-flops outside. For not having a torchlight. Not donning insect repellant.

The volume of the voices lifted, startling Milagros. [We are Mama Binti] Milagros ducked into a crouch. [We are several, but we know the one voice that you seek]

"Imogen?" Milagros asked. She awkwardly retreated while crouched.

[We know who you seek] the clutch of voices said. [We know who you pursue]

Milagros stood carefully. The mosquitoes had abandoned her. [Offer us oblation] said the voices [and we will give her to you alone]

Milagros's eyes fully adjusted to the murk. The crunch beneath her feet revealed itself to be not rocks or shells but teeth. Either surrendered or snatched. Some yellow, some bright white. Some small, some multifaceted. Some sharp, some flatter. She covered her mouth. Scrabbled backward, her hands extended behind her reaching for the ledge. She turned, tried to climb, but struggled to find purchase. To breathe. She finally managed to pull herself up to the first ledge, then the second, but stopped when the voices refined to a single thread and she heard her name.

[Mila] said Grecia [Mi corazón]

Silence fell like a velvet cape.

Her heart pulled in various directions, and Milagros's mind recalibrated entirely to Spanish, dismissing every jot of English she'd learned. "Mami?" Although clear, her mother's voice held a hitch. Toward the cave's entrance Milagros heard her mother call once more. Heart racing, she scampered forward and bumped her head against the low-hanging rock, briefly knocking herself into a daze.

Back on her end of the beach, Bunny awoke. She lifted out of slumber as if she'd been boosted by a step made of two hands knotted together to hoist her over a wall. She instinctively looked around for Milagros and was relieved and somehow surprised to see that the girl was right beside her. "Been liming with Imogen?"

"Yes."

Bunny deciphered dejection in Milagros. The slump of her shoulders. The bump on her head. She sat up straighter. "Are you okay?"

"I heard my mother."

So this was where Milagros's tantrums had gone. Bunny signaled Caleb, and ice eventually found its way from his cooler to Milagros's injury. "How did you hurt yourself? What did your mother say to you?"

Bunny asked Caleb to take them home.

Milagros, deep in thought, didn't resist.

Milagros kept begging to return to the beach, but Bunny refused, and the tantrums were reinstated. Milagros shot put items with regularity, a human clay pigeon thrower who slung pitchers and tchotchkes, swore in Spanish—refused to speak English—and tore at her clothes, but Bunny held firm until just before she took the child to have her passport photograph taken. To calm her down, to get her to agree.

She could only elicit discipline with a promise to return to the beach.

Back at the beach, Bunny discreetly followed Milagros into the water as she rounded the rocks. She watched Milagros disappear into the cave. Bunny waited a few minutes before she followed, but before she reached the cave's mouth, Milagros exited, blinking against the bright sun. She seemed startled to see Bunny. "No Imogen?" Bunny asked, and Milagros grew silent and sullen. *No Grecia?* is what she understood Bunny to mean.

Bunny at once enforced the beach ban. This time Milagros didn't throw any tantrums, just kept to herself. The silent act troubled Bunny almost as much as the thunder clap and lightning strike version of the girl.

Five weeks later, when Caleb delivered the black market passport, Bunny asked him to take them to the beach once more. During those five weeks, various spices wandered the house in varying intensity. Eventually Bunny developed ferocious migraines. They only abated when she thought of the water, meditated upon it. When Bunny followed Milagros around the rocks this time, she was surprised to see a tall woman who wore an outdated skirt. Milagros flew to her, speaking rapid Spanish.

Bunny called to Milagros. Milagros ignored her.

Imogen introduced herself. "I hear that you're visiting from the island."

"Yes," Bunny says. "First time here."

"For the girl as well from what I understand."

"Both of us."

Imogen nodded. "It should feel familiar," she said. "Similar history here as on your island. Very similar." Then she said that Milagros was a special girl.

"Well, she seems a bit taken with you," Bunny said.

Imogen shrugged. "She's new to this island. I just helped her to become more comfortable." They chatted for a few more minutes. Finally, Bunny used the opportunity to tell Milagros that they were headed to the U.S. the next day. Milagros's eyes widened, then she backed away, then she ran toward the caves, but Imogen chased and caught her. Dragged her kicking and screaming back to Bunny. "I promise that you will see your mother again," Imogen said, "but only if you do what this woman says."

Upon hearing this, Milagros lost all energy.

Imogen released her.

Then, she stooped to address Milagros. "I'm not sure that we'll see each other again. Okay?" Bunny expected tears, but Milagros remained still. Then she leaned over and whispered to Milagros.

As they walked back to the car, Bunny asked Milagros what the woman had said. "She said don't be afraid of spirits, whether they cross water or not."

* * *

On the drive home, Bunny told Milagros about her friend Lorraine from New Felicity, with whom they would stay in Florida, her friend Lorraine who'd felt the wanderlust long before Bunny did, and who'd acted on it. Who'd put aside some money when she realized that her husband Clem wasn't really for her. But first, she told Milagros, they needed to be granted asylum. First they needed to prove that the island had chased them away. Spirits wouldn't cut it. Bunny needed to devise an acceptable threat to grant them access.

The next morning they boarded the flight to Miami International. Bunny expected a tantrum during the flight, and she remained tense throughout. When they landed and requested asylum, the immigration agent sighed, made a phone call, and two officers came and led them away.

THREE

Future Progressive

13

Ortolan Bunting, G—d, and Falling Birds

TROUBLE GURGLED ON the island with various incidents, the first one by land, serving as the prologue for two by sea, and then three by air. The one by land was a robbery at the docking area of the island's airport. Just before noon four heavily armed crooks slipped out of a pickup and into the airport's restricted area, then audaciously held up an armored vehicle. The money had been destined for cash machines on our sister island. The gazette said that by the time the police responded the crooks were long gone. *No sign of the men or the money*, the gazette relayed. *Five million dollars in local currency up in smoke.*

We sucked in our breaths at the bold-facedness.

A few days later, in the Clearing, we witnessed Hospedales in a new suit of clothes and smelling of a finer grade of fragrance. Miki muttered something under his breath, about old thieves profiting from new money. "What was that?" Hospedales asked.

"You heard me," Miki replied.

They bristled at each other and sat at opposite ends of the picnic tables. We knew this was because Miki blamed Hospedales for bringing the man with the shaved head into our midst to steal our beach sand, which rendered Miki impotent in the eyes of Bunny, and served as a catalyst for wrecking their relationship. At least this was our best conjecture. We bit our tongues as we occupied the seats between them. Out beyond the fray Peter-Called-Peter worked on his boat alongside his transistor.

Like the rest of us, Peter-Called-Peter had refused to sell his house to Hospedales's no-longer-a-mystery buyer, but in his case it had worked itself out, it turning out that the contractual impasse with the purchasing party, namely Peter-Called-Peter's father, Minister Basil D'Souza, was resolved when Peter-Called-Peter's father made some quick calls to the bank to confirm what he already knew, that his son was actually in default of paying his monthly mortgage for some three months now, and we learned that Peter-Called-Peter's income was actually paid out to him from a fund held in trust from his grandfather Hubert's estate, and that Peter-Called-Peter's father was in charge of doling out the payment. So all Basil Cruickshank needed to do, in a manner of speaking, was to shut off the Peter-Called-Peter fiduciary spigot—spite was a mean impulse for any parent to indulge upon his child—and the sale would go through.

We felt badly at Peter-Called-Peter's situation, him losing his house against his will, but we'd always felt a shallow resentment toward him, had suspected that he was just playing at fishing while the rest of us were literally fishing for our lives, us knowing that he was just a carpenter-Buddhist who'd come in and snatched Bunny's affection from us and then discarded it, leaving a cavity as large as the excavation that once held our sand. It turned out that Peter-Called-Peter, for all intents and purposes, was evicted, and had to live for a short period at Miss Titus's house, which turned him into exactly the kind of boarder that some of us had always seen him as when he'd arrived in our village, the kind who, once having his house pulled out from under him, needed to pay Miss Titus not just for a roof but for meals as well as laundering.

The airport robbery was so outrageous that the Minister of National Security had to address the media about it. "Any idea about who perpetrated this brazen robbery?" asked a journalist.

"Along with the chief of police, I'm martialing all resources to get to the bottom of this. The government cannot condone this level of lawlessness." Mark-2 read the Minister of National Security's words to us from the gazette.

"Only other kinds of lawlessness," Miki said, eyeing Hospedales.

"What was that?" Hospedales asked.

"You heard me."

A few days later the Minister of National Security announced the purchase of twenty armored personnel carriers. "Every elite police force has these APCs in their retinue," Mark-2 read. The armored vehicles were announced as best practice in international policing. "If officers of the law have to engage with the criminal element in volatile environments where gang members deploy 5.56 and 7.62 millimeter rounds, we can't protect ourselves in regular SUVs."

"Papa yo," said Nello.

"So a bank gets robbed, and the government spends taxpayers' money to fund the police force," said Miki, sprawled out on the far picnic table and imbibing from a long-necked lager. Hospedales fiddled with a toothpick in the corner of his mouth pretending not to hear. "Is so much power Hospedales have?" Miki asked. "One robbery and is so we have to buy military vehicles?"

Hospedales ignored him. He was a man who leaned on a cane, and we remembered You-We telling us the riddle of what goes on four legs in the morning, two legs at noon, and three legs in the evening.

We talked instead about the birds. Since the ibis incident the number of birds had dramatically lessened. And before that, there had been the curiosity of all the birds that had fallen in advance of Catherine the Great Disemboweler and the Titus boys showing up. But just now we were observing flocks of birds in the Clearing, appearing in full singular breed force one day and disappearing completely the next. Three days before we saw two dozen synchronized streamertail hummingbirds moving between the zaboca trees, a blur of beating green wings and red feathers and purple throats. The day after that we experienced a dozen sad flycatchers. Then, just that morning, we saw at least eighteen kiskadees at the edge of the Clearing. The entire space was a confluence of yellow breasts and brown wings. Mark-2 fed them bread heels, but the rest of us remained uneasy. With all these bird appearances we suspected another crushing visit from Catherine the Great Disemboweler's mother on the horizon. She'd promised three, and we'd had two so far, and with it always attached some wretched village luck.

We were almost grateful when the glasses and goateed UWI graduate mentioned one of his arcane facts. He said that the sudden appearance of all the birds reminded him of the renewed ortolan bunting–eating craze in Europe, and when no one asked him about ortolan bunting, he went on talking about them anyway, saying that Europeans would drape napkins over their heads to hide their shame from God for what they were about to do, him adding that an ortolan was the size of a sneeze, but that one could cost up to £100, and that to prepare them, first the birds were blinded or kept in the dark so they would eat continuously and double in size. Then they were immersed in a vat of Armagnac to drown and marinade them.

We all remained in anticipatory silence for a moment. Then Miki, who had tasted ibis flesh, asked, "So what they does *taste* like?"

"Heaven, I suppose," shrugged the UWI graduate.

We all steupsed.

Two days later another incident at the airport, but this time with an international asterisk. The Russian-made Ilyushin cargo planes settled in the airport like two large hens and attracted hemispheric attention when a video of their arrival was posted online. The planes, we learned from the gazette, were operated by Volga-Dnepr Cargo Airlines, and there were chirps throughout the island about this being related to Venezuela, that the planes were being brought in for

Venezuelan military support. "So why they wouldn't just land in Venezuela?" Nello asked.

"Ah, Nello, that is the right question," Miki said. They clinked lager necks.

Soon there was also chatter that Iran would send warships to dock between our island and the mainland. The regional chatter increased, and the international news section of the gazette fattened.

The media created a mini-storm in its reporting, and Hospedales said it was all *tempest in teapot, man.* The media interviewed the Russian air crew and reported their names. We learned that they were staying at the fancy hotel downtown. "We're just here from French Guiana to drop off cargo," the pilot Mikhail Sotnikov said. His copilot was Dmitry Erofeev and the rest of his crew included Viacheslav Losenko, Pavel Lvov, and Valery Miniakov. None of them disclosed exactly what their cargo contained.

"That is a lot of crew just to drop off some supplies," said Miki.

This was a few days before Miki and Hospedales reached the boiling point, when Hospedales tapped Mark-2 in the chest with his cane, and Miki threw Hospedales to the earth and began to flash hands, launching us into action to separate them. But before that occurred the third thing happened, this being the sea incident in which the USNS *Comfort*, a navy hospital ship from the U.S., showed up and docked right where, we surmised, the Iranian warship was supposed to dock. But the navy ship said that it was on a peace mission. It was here to provide free eye, nose, and dental assistance to the island. When we asked the ship's officers whether they would help Venezuelans, the chief officer on the ship referred us to the U.S. ambassador, who issued a statement to the press, saying that they would help only those who sought their help.

Suddenly these international players on our island—Russia, the U.S., and possibly Iran—made us uneasy. We put two and two together and didn't like the arithmetic.

"The eagle and the bear," said the glasses and goateed UWI graduate. Then he explained, "During the Cold War—"

"Shaddup," said Miki.

We were suddenly all anxious to sell our houses and give up our fruitless fishing lines and finally begin a phase of prosperity elsewhere.

Then the assassination attempt on the Minister of National Security shook the island. It happened when the minister was leaving a performance at the new theater with his latest dolly bird. The minister took four gunshots to various parts of his torso and back and was now in critical condition in the hospital. We recognized the assailant's picture in the gazette right away. The article identified him as Ricardo Maldonado, but we knew him better as the man with the shaved head who had stolen all our beach sand. It was surely the same character, the picture in the gazette perfectly capturing his thug personality in finger-staining inked print.

"But what bacchanal is this?" Nello asked as we spread the gazette.

"How come he aim point blank at the minister and the man still alive?" Miki asked.

"But, Hospedales," said that scamp Mark-2 as he showed us the picture, "this is not the same man who shoot up your leg?"

"You mean the same one who make you shit your pants?"

This shut Mark-2 up.

But we saw that Hospedales was worried.

Peter-Called-Peter continued tinkering with his boat and didn't come over to discuss his father being shot. It was only later, as he worked on his boat's stern, that he offered his thoughts. "The real trick," he finally said to us, "is to see if the gunman will give up everyone involved in his schemes including the big boss." Then Peter-Called-Peter returned to working on his boat as if none of this concerned him, and we were astonished at how close he was toward completing his boat, maybe a week or two away. He didn't seem particularly upset that his father had been shot. But in the next few days he disappeared for some forty-eight hours, and we assumed that he'd gone to visit the Minister of National Security in a private hospital where, expectedly, there would be a heavy protection detail.

Then, even before his first court date, just as Peter-Called-Peter predicted, Maldonado began to sing sweet somethings to the authorities. We had already figured that if this Maldonado could be tied to other crimes, then he would try to bring the minister down with him. And, as a side note, we wondered if Hospedales's name would be mentioned, and if he would be dragged into this burgeoning bacchanal. He must have wondered the same thing as well because Hospedales grew nasty around this time, but it was always Miki who lit his fuse, Miki saying that he was tired of people only making the Clearing smell like a perfume counter with so much cologne splashed all over his clothes. Hospedales retorted that if he smelled like fish all the damn time, even when there was no fish to catch, then women would probably abandon *him* too.

Papa yo.

It didn't take long after those opening salvos.

One afternoon Miki attacked Hospedales in the Clearing with scant provocation. He'd probably been turning that jab about Bunny over in his head, it rubbing his ego raw, iron sharpening iron, until he was able to wield it in time as a weapon. It was true that Hospedales had grown jumpier and jumpier with each new report in the gazette about Maldonado's dealings. Who knew the depth of Hospedales's corruption?

The second fight, and the one we termed the boiling point, occurred when Mark-2, reading about the unfolding Maldonado saga, said *aye, Hospedales, the police might come for you next*, and Hospedales, having had enough, poked Mark-2 in the shoulder with his cane and told him to shut his razzy ass, and Miki stood up and, in a surprising dazzle given his borracho state, sprinted from where he sat on the picnic table to where Hospedales sat, and tackled him to the earth, instantly griming

Hospedales's new peach linen shirt. Hospedales acquitted himself better than we expected this time, especially after having recently taken a bullet to the thigh, but eventually Miki overwhelmed him, and we shamefully allowed Miki to get in a few good cuffs before we pulled him off. Both Hospedales's eyes swelled shut, and Nello had to lead him back to the Trooper, and then to his house, to apply ice to the swelling.

The next morning the newspaper said that Maldonado was also suspected to be involved in the airport heist, and he gave up one of his lorry thugs whose picture we recognized, it turning out that this thug smuggled people out of Venezuela regularly, him revealing his own cache of information when the police cross-questioned him.

"Papa yo," said Nello. "Next they will accuse him of stealing the Christ off the cross and the nails too."

"I wonder if he'll give up any sweet-smelling accomplices," said Miki, looking meaningfully toward Hospedales. "Or did you pour that entire bottle of cologne on your clothes?"

"Is what you say?" Hospedales asked, lifting his head and trying to echolocate Miki's voice since both his eyes, now the color of ripe melongen, were still mostly swollen shut.

"You heard me," Miki said. "And if you want me to swell up your two eye again, let me know."

But we saw that sightless Hospedales sensed the noose tightening. We wondered if he would run, if he had connections and a bolthole in Venezuela, him properly gassing up his borrowed drug boat this time. There was reason for fear. The special new vice branch of the island's police force, who had captured Maldonado, was now creating a startling domino effect with Maldonado's confessions. "That fella not smart at all," said Hospedales, his eyes still swollen shut. "Naming names and putting all his business in the gazette." But we wondered if this was just a guilty Hospedales whistling past the cemetery.

* * *

Finally, Corporal Lalchan was named by Maldonado. That was when, we figured, Hospedales would lose his mind. He surely felt his name would be next. Lalchan's face didn't show surprise in his gazette picture. He seemed confident, which rang false to us since we knew him to be a bobolee. "That old wretch," said Nello. The headline above Lalchan's picture read VENEZUELA SEX TRAFFICKING RING BUSTED IN CROOKED POLICE PROBE, and we all sucked in our breaths, getting a clearer picture of the Titus boys' gentleman's club and how two razzy-tail poxy boys from New Felicity could open a business with Venezuelan women. "That old low-down wretch," Nello repeated, us seeing now that Lalchan had been a silent partner of the Titus brothers in their opening their gentleman's club, which as far as we knew was in fact still open, but maybe wouldn't be for long, us thinking after Maldonado's capture and confessions that the special police would soon be putting in an appearance and shutting down the club posthaste. We hadn't seen Lalchan since the Barradas, Sookdeo, and Ramdeen kidnapping, not since the disappearance of the foreign reporter.

Mark-2 read that investigations based upon Maldonado's confession led to a Venezuelan trafficker who indicated that, through his connections with elements in the island's police force, he had been assured of protection and advised where and when to come ashore. The man, we saw, had a face like a frog. "The police officers in the alleged sex ring," Mark-2 read, "also provided secure houses for the trafficked women before they were ferried around the island in minivans."

"Gs + Hs," said Nello.

The lorry goon, for his part, sang even more sweetly than Maldonado, saying that he was the smuggler's contact person on the island, the lorry goon showing the investigative reporter that he had Lalchan's phone number in his phone's list of contacts, him then detailing various conversations that they'd had.

"1-0-1-0-0-1?" asked Binary Clem.

"Yes," said Peter-Called-Peter. "The same Lalchan who always waving his nightstick around. I wonder what go happen to him?"

When questioned by the press as to why a sex trafficker would have his telephone number, Lalchan said he didn't know why, but having someone's phone number did not constitute a crime in the island's constitutional and parliamentary law. From the Lalchan accusation, the Minister of National Security, from his hospital bed, promised that he was working to clean up police corruption and root it out of the island permanently.

More birds appeared, ones that we didn't recognize. It took the glasses and goateed UWI graduate a lot of scrolling through his phone, searches on his laptop, and old-fashioned page turning, to learn that they were orange quits, arrowhead warblers, and lizard cuckoos. It was when he pointed out the crested quail-dove, also known as the mountain witch dove, that we grew concerned for ourselves, and waited in troubled anticipation.

Then, one day, when we were in the Clearing, Nello, in a very dramatic gesture, produced a letter that he said had been sent by his brother Caleb about Bunny and Milagros. It was just over a month after they'd departed for Grenada. We thought that Bunny would have called us once or twice, or texted us now and again, but she'd done neither. Not a peep. We knew that she and Milagros had been shaken by the bodies that we'd seen floating in the water on the trip over, but we had not expected her to go this silent.

Bunny and Milagros, Caleb wrote, had made a decision to leave Grenada. Nello paused after reading this, for unnecessary dramatic effect, and we threatened to snatch the letter from him. Then he cleared his throat and continued, reading that Bunny, feeling that the same spiritual blight that pushed her and Milagros off the island was still haunting them in Grenada, had decided to fly to the U.S. That they were fine and that they would reach out to everyone in New Felicity once they were settled. Nello looked at Miki when he'd read this, but Miki offered no reaction. "What else the letter saying?" he asked Nello, and Nello made a show of turning the letter over to show that there was nothing else. Peter-Called-Peter wasn't there, him off visiting his father in hospital, or else we would have turned to him to hear what he had to say, what direction we should take, what should be our course of action.

We felt rudderless without him.

A few days later, a dour Miki showed up with a woman who he installed in Bunny's sold-but-unoccupied house. At first we were confused. Then we realized that the woman that Miki had stowed in Bunny's house could be only one person, could be only someone who could maybe point a finger at us, who could say that maybe we weren't as innocent as we'd pretended in all this gentleman's club business, someone who had just, maybe, been liberated from that gentleman's club, some of us realizing that this could be a problem, the woman looking exactly like Milagros but twenty or so years older, and some of us ashamedly remembered meeting her, so to speak, in the Titus Boys' club and knowing her in the biblical sense.

One or two of us ventured to the house and knocked on the door, but no one came out. Not even a curtain twitched. We were concerned and guilt-ridden, but we were just waiting to close the sale of our houses so we could pack up our shame and relocate and never see this woman again. We'd already moved most of the women out of New Felicity Village—Miss Titus, Stacy and her siblings, the glasses and goateed UWI graduate's seamstress mother, Iris—but it still worried us that the one woman who remained unsettled our souls. Even Peter-Called-Peter, who had moved in with Nello after Miss Titus left, couldn't help us.

14

The Land of the Hummingbird and the Execution of the Kambu

ON ONE OF the coolest mornings that Mitilde had ever experienced on the island she woke with a start just before dawn. Upon waking she recognized the loss of her sense of smell, a harbinger. An acute warning. The entire estate still stank of smoke, and her excised ability to smell reduced her full participation in communal grief. This further hobbled her. All of grief's dimensions needed to be fully embraced if one were to move past it, including the strife of the odor of burned bodies. Those markers of the estate's greed and cruelty. Plus, Mitilde was wary of any dawn heavy with dew. Aches strafed her legs and lingered at her knees.

On the pallet on the other side of the earth floor Agnes remained alive, suppressing moans and death's probing. Difficult to believe that it was still less than a week after the attempted escape that went wrong and briefly sparked into a rebellion, when Kitch, Grafton, and Etto had attempted to burn all that offended, first the sugarcane fields, then the Cruickshank big house, then the deputies who once patrolled them. The house had refused their wrath, and all three were gone—dead or sold to Barbados. Another of the cane laborers, not involved in the escape, had seized the opportunity to enter the Cruickshank house to slaughter all inside, but MacTeer had shot him in the head.

Other bodies were still missing. Hany. Catherine. Mitilde had pointed them toward the mountain. Gave them a chance with Mama Binti. She'd laid out the possibility to Hany. Mitilde knew that Hany would have tried to bargain to save her entire family, but knew too that she only had enough currency to save Catherine, and even that required the tremendous sacrifice of the child within her. Others were missing entirely. The optimistic part of Mitilde hoped that they had escaped into the freedom of the mountains. The snarl of trees. But the realistic part of her had seen attempted escapes and revolts quickly sputter in the sapling stage. Men had been lost; Mitilde had seen their remains. Women. Children. Those in the cabins were reduced in number and emotion. Now baying dogs and men with long guns had been brought in from nearby estates. The extended howls of strange dogs competed with the constant wailing of babies. These new men supervised the burial of the dead about fifty yards from the water. Usually those who suffered among the sugarcane were kept from the ocean because the estate owners feared that upon sighting the vast stretch of water they would walk right into it to return to their families on the other side of the world.

Mitilde avoided the ocean, preferred the skies.

She had always been considered odd.

She'd received a vision the night before, but it had only confirmed what she'd already known—that the estate's deputies, Shand and MacTeer and Marse John's brother, would come for her when the dust settled. To wait was her decision. Even though the scrutiny of those who worked the fields was more rigorous than it had ever been, she could have slipped past the long guns and dogs. Gained the mountains. Two things held her back: she understood and honored her remit to advise, to guide, to serve. Her kind was linked with Mama Binti long before drunken admirals claimed discovery of this side of the world. Yes, Mitilde could claim the mountains, reside there until she became eternal. Other options: she knew words that would convert her to a kambu, wings, feathers, and beak; she knew words that could lift the majority of these people to the skies and return them across the ocean. But the people did not know them, and they would have to say the words themselves. If the words weren't correctly enunciated, the ground would continue to shackle them, and if even a few were left behind, Mitilde preferred not to think of the retribution they would face on account of her escape. She did not like the idea of leaving them behind. Besides, she had one last task she had promised to complete.

Mitilde adjusted her green headscarf.

Rations that week were limited, not because the food supplies were low, but to suppress the cane laborers and to keep them weak and disoriented. Those who ran the estate were taking stock. Rooting out confederates. Reinforcing their own ranks. Among the dead, Mitilde had not heard either Hany's or Catherine's names mentioned, so she hoped they had reached Mama Binti. One of her final accomplishments. But the current concerns were greater. Some of the men had been pulled from cabins, separated from their women and children and never seen again. New men were brought to replace them and to suffer among the cane, and they spoke unfamiliar languages. Some were whipped outside the cabins, so that those inside could hear their suffering.

One way to maintain disorder was to sow chaos.

Another was to show how bodies could be brought low.

They came for her that evening just before dusk.

Three men with long guns. One man snatched the green tie from her head before he marched her from the cabin, threw it to the earth. Two men stood on either side of her; the one who'd snatched off her headscarf wedged the snout of his gun into her back. It had been a scorch-filled day, and the early evening retained the heat, but Mitilde felt the ocean's wind touch her naked scalp and solicit a shiver.

They marched her across the estate. Smoke still decorated the air, but still she could not smell. Destruction everywhere. The bodies were removed but not the blood that had been spilled from them. The soil dark in patches. She didn't turn away. The earth had borne witness. She paused at one spot, said an invocation. The third man jabbed her in the back to speed her up. He wanted his long gun to do more than sniff at her back.

Just before she was hauled into the house in which she'd never stepped, squeezed among whitemen and their long guns, she found consolation: a single winding hummingbird that flew ahead of her, carving a path through the air, the bird flying then pausing, hovering, then flying forth a bit, then pausing once more, at one point looking back. It was only when Mitilde gained the first step of the house that the bird flew off. As if it had completed its duty. As if it had fulfilled its own oath to remind her of just who she was.

Mitilde remembered the first woman that she'd guided. It had been beneath the ocean's surface, down in the ship's hold, where all the women were chained together, stank of unwashed bodies, excreta, and menstrual discharges, the last of which heightened the smell of the metal that bound them all together. The men were kept in a separate pen, chained in a different compartment. Mitilde was able to slip her chains at will, and this disturbed the surrounding women. There was another rumor that disturbed them more: that she'd allowed herself to be captured and chained. That she'd willingly boarded the boat to offer succor to the seized. The ocean was surly, and the whispers bloomed. People said that she was a spirit. Then they said that good spirits could not cross the ocean, only malevolent spirits could defy nature in such a way. Mitilde had not disputed these words. She'd made her way to the woman in labor. Mitilde tore free some of the little fabric that covered her own body, as rough as shards. She touched it to the woman's forehead. "Is the pain too much?" she'd asked the woman—really a girl—in her language. The girl, her forehead wet with sweat, remained stoic, repressed her screams, but when she couldn't answer, Mitilde knew that she didn't have much time.

She had inched close to the girl's ear. Explained her options. Told her what was possible. A kind of survival. The girl's stomach was a swollen gourd, and neither she nor the child inside would otherwise survive. She had another child in the hold with her. Mitilde told her of a trade that could be made. Above, on the deck, the ship pitched. Mitilde worked to keep this young woman calm. Finished explaining, and the girl's expression, upon learning of what few choices she owned, had broken Mitilde's heart. She left her for the brief time that she would remain alive to make her decision. To decide whether she would summon Mama Binti.

Now, the men with long guns sat Mitilde in a room with books and a clock. Mitilde had stolen the ability to read, but nothing in these books interested her. She had stolen the ability to tell time too, but she had no use for that either. The last thing she paid attention to in the room was the man who sat behind the desk, a behemoth who focused solely on her.

"You want to know why you're here," Finlay Cruickshank said, amusedly watching Mitilde take in Abercromby Hall's innards. "Why you've been ignored until now, why you are suddenly receiving attention." He paused until her eyes rested on him. "It's because this estate is a zoo and, until now, you were believed to be innocuous. I am guessing that you don't know this concept, the zoo. It is where a variety of wild animals are kept. If it sounds dangerous that's because it is. There are always more animals in a zoo than people to maintain it. Sometimes the animals run amok. This estate, here in West India, is its own zoo. And the truth is this zoo has been run haphazardly. At a profit, most years, but with animals often running wild when they should have been penned." He leaned forward. "Now, if it were better run, if it were *properly* run, then clumsy tactics like the random punishment of brutes like Warburton, which I pinpoint as the single cause of all the estate's recent disasters, could have been avoided.

But you also play an important role. Namely, if attention had been focused on the linchpin that held the wheel intact"—he pointed at Mitilde—"namely you, then the zoo would have continued to operate on its precarious axis, with the various animals penned off and blissfully unaware of their incarceration, allowed to eat, defecate, and reproduce without reprisal. The problem occurs when one animal is allowed to move around the zoo, to rile up the others that are penned.

"Admittedly, errors were made by those charged to maintain the zoo. My own brother, overcome with unchecked desires, paid scant attention to the same message that kept returning to him. He allowed your jaundiced eyes and green head rag to become renowned. And allowing a legend to fester is far worse than allowing a nigger to learn to read and write."

He sighed and leaned back, and the chair's leather complained. "And how do I know that you have become legend? Because all the zoo's animals bleat about you. And it's a curious legend, I must admit. A midwife for distressed and grieving mothers. One who brokers a path to the world of spirits. Who arranges the exchange of souls."

Mitilde's gold eyes scanned the room calmly.

"I can only surmise your thoughts," Finlay Cruickshank said. "Or at least as close as my understanding can come to the thoughts of beasts. You are wondering who told me about you. And here's the answer: everyone. Agnes told me. Polydore told me. Rebekkah told me. Even Grace Cumberbatch, who does not reside on this estate, told me once I poured enough wine down her gullet, once she was satiated from pawing at me. And they all told me because their desires are simple and malleable. Polydore's desire was hunger. Grace Cumberbatch yearned for a successful sugarcane crop.

"But I know I cannot punish or tempt you based upon desire," he said, "because the only thing that you desire, that I have learned from everyone who speaks of you, is something that cannot be had. Or rather that can be had even though you resist. They say you desire to return to Dahomey. I have seen niggers from Dahomey, and that is clearly not your land of origin. But I do understand wanting to be somewhere far from here. In that way, your desires and mine are similar, although one is the instinctual call of an animal and the other the pull of a man's past. His family. One might argue that our desires, oddly, ride in similar carriages that traverse different routes." He showed teeth stained by tea and tobacco. "The difference is that your interference has converted a once-thriving zoo. Adulterated it. Enervated it." He suddenly slammed a palm against the desk, but Mitilde did not flinch. "Two fields of sugarcane have been lost to fire. Almost twenty slaves, including one not yet born, have been lost. My brother lies ill in his bedchamber. Mutiny. Perpetrated by the zoo's own animals!" He slammed his hand on the desk again, and again Mitilde did not flinch.

He composed himself. "And the result from these ripples is that various people are understandably upset. My cousin Bernard, who owns this estate, is upset at the loss of production and profit. My brother, John, has lost his favorite nighttime companion."

He tapped fingers on the desk. Mitilde would not be unsettled.

"The estate has lost two able-bodied men in Shand and MacTeer as well as three of its best hounds. But all is not lost." He looked out into the hall behind her. The man with the long gun appeared. "All is not lost. One needs to remain rational in the face of the senseless. Hounds may be replaced. Additional labor may be purchased or sold. And legends may be dismantled." He brought his hands together as if in Christian prayer. "And once dismantled, one has to work hard to drive belief in legends from the minds of believers. But it can be done. And it must be done. But first the legends, myths, folklore, must be excised. So what would you, as someone who serves as both broker and midwife, who allegedly plumbs both this world and the ethereal, what would you suggest be done to extinguish such a legend?" An imperceptible nod, and the man with his long gun entered the room. "How does one shake the belief system of animals?" Another imperceptible nod, and the man jabbed the snout once more into Mitilde's shoulder to usher her out. But she'd already achieved what she'd hoped. The first part of her promise. While being brought into this house, she had glimpsed Hany's son James. And more importantly, he'd glimpsed her.

On that first day of Mitilde's slow execution, when the enslaved were brought forth from their cabins to observe, when the deputies bound Mitilde's hands behind her and led her in front of them, Mitilde rolled the words that could send her to the air on her tongue. Words that could convert her to a kambu. But she resisted saying them aloud even though none would understand them.

She didn't resist the physical torture insisted upon her. When Finlay Cruickshank expounded to all the enslaved bodies about what happened to animals that run amok in a zoo, then issued the order for punishment, the scream that Mitilde released when they slit her hamstring needed no translation. Those in the crowd shrank back, some hid their faces. Finlay Cruickshank dismissed everyone back to their cabins, telling them they would reconvene on the morrow.

In the course of a week, and in front of all the others, Finlay Cruickshank ordered the removal of Mitilde one part at a time.

On Sunday her hamstring was cut.

On Monday a thumb was taken.

On Tuesday an ear was excised.

On Wednesday her Achilles was snipped.

On Thursday, she was branded with a soldering iron.

After each indignity she was thrown into her cabin to fester.

Late on the evening of the branding, James came to her. She had known he would. He washed her wounds, attempted bandages. His face grieved. Gone: mother, father, sister. Hany, Etto, Catherine. Soon, if not already, Agnes. "You miss them," Mitilde said. "But you will eventually have your own family to lessen your grief." Tears arrowed down his face to his chin. He listened as he continued to attend to her.

She pressed the gemstone into his hand. "This is from your mother," she said. "It will bring you closer to Hany." When he accepted it, she squeezed his palm tightly. Its rough edges cut into his palms. "She wants you to escape to the mountains," Mitilde whispered. "She wants you to avoid the talons of the men in that house. Even the one who calls himself your father." The pain pulsed at various points of Mitilde's body. She knew that if she were to live until the morrow, the behemoth would remove her heart for display, would remove her head then stake it to the earth. Her life was forfeit. Even though she knew she was taking a risk, she made sure to ask him all that she needed. "Do you think you can fulfill her entreaty?" she asked him. "Do you think that you can resist what the house offers? All the comforts that marse and them promise in there that the rest of us can't have? The promise to teach you things the rest of us cannot access? Even if you know that up in the mountains you will be cold sometimes and won't always be able to build a fire? Or when you won't always find enough food to fill your belly?" He nodded again, closed his eyes. "Good," she said. She told him to wear the gemstone on his body, that it would offer him protection when he absconded. That Hany would protect him. She had no foresight about whether he would succeed in the escape that had been sown in his head. She had no idea if he had sufficient fortitude or guile. Only that the future of his line, and Hany's line, required it. Mitilde had never guided a man before, never issued one the possibility of good fortune. It was a curious sensation. But she'd kept her promise.

On Friday, when the three men with long guns returned for Mitilde, this time to remove her tongue—one last chance to scream—they found the cabin empty. They foolishly searched all corners, as if she could hide in plain sight. But Mitilde was gone. All that was left to discover, and that they bore to an enraged Finlay Cruickshank, were the numerous feathers of variegated colors that littered the cabin. And when the rumors that Mitilde had escaped circulated among the enslaved people in the cabins, shouts erupted at various times: *Mitilde free! Mitilde free!*

15

In Which Yellow-Chested Kiskadees, Gray-Headed Kites, Ruddy Ground Doves, Squirrel Cuckoos, Tropical Screech Owls, and Potoos Make an Appearance

WE KNEW ALMOST at once that things were moving sideways. We knew it before we saw it. We felt it. In the crooks of our elbows. In the spaces where our collarbones left little dimples. In unexpected and unearned knee pain when we hung our legs off the sides of our mattresses on mornings. The first indicator was when the birds stopped chirping. This may not have seemed like a grand sign, but we were used to certain sounds in the village: the birds always calling to each other, waves rolling up onto the beach in regular intervals, frogs and crickets signaling to each other at dusk. We grew accustomed to Mark-2 and Ramdeen emerging from the direction of the woods with songbirds for sale, bright-eyed birds plumping their cages, these two having mixed up some laglee to stick the birds' feet to the ground.

So when the birds stopped singing we grew guarded.

A few days of nonstop bucket-a-drop rain also put us on edge.

Then the fish began to disappear.

We had seen the fish vanish before. Some years earlier, an oil spill had slicked the ocean's surface between the island and South America when a tanker somehow tore open its side. Venezuela pointed at us, and we touched the sides of our noses and pointed at them: *their fault*, each side said. It didn't really matter. The fish had disappeared immediately, and there was nothing to catch and nothing to eat. We didn't bother to head out on the water in those ink-dark days. We spat on the sand then spat again. Raised our middle fingers to Venezuela in the five-mile distance. We survived by the grace of Miss Titus and ate mostly measly meatless meals. *God bless Miss Titus*, we thought, *and her food-falling-off-the-back-of-a-lorry delivery connections*.

A few months later the fish returned, but already dead and inedible, their silver bellies pointed upward on the sea's surface, dull in the rising sunlight. *Gs + Hs*, we thought. *Look at our crosses*. This begat more lean and hungry months. And so on. The gazette reported the oil spill on the first day and never again. Our story was small, and our village was smaller than the sprats that we could no longer regularly catch, much less carite and kingfish, dolphinfish and snapper. Barradas spat. "You want to know how much they would miss us if we dead? Stick your hand in a bucket of water, and the space that it leave behind when you pull it out is how much they go care." He was headstrong and viperous.

We grew short with each other.

Cruel.

Hold your mudder ass was leveled more than a few times. We didn't lime or knock cards as much as before. We kept to ourselves in our own houses. Indira and Sookdeo, in particular, kept to themselves.

Things worsened.

We weren't superstitious, but we knew how to read tea leaves. We didn't need Mami Ursula for that. Around that same time was when Miss Titus's thug sons returned from foreign. First the birds, then the fish, now Magnus and Romulus Titus. How could we not string-tie all of these events together? You-We started to say something about separating causality and correlation and Miki shut him down with a look. We held too much respect for Miss Titus to say anything about her sons casting shadows upon the village with their presence. But we knew it was their fault.

We knew right away.

Even more than Nello, Ramdeen would catch bad feelings. He knew a week in advance that a week of nonstop rain was coming. He'd warned us about the fish. The birds. Unlike Nello, when Ramdeen spoke, we listened. And grew fearful.

Then the smell of oranges in the Clearing grew overbearing, watered our eyes, twisted our tongues like freshly bitten cashews pulled straight off the tree.

What next? we wondered.

Magnus and Romulus unsettled us. They returned to the island with tight muscles in smedium T-shirts and driving a loud backfiring car that was like a third Titus thug. Flame decals blazed along the chrome doors. LEFT-HAND DRIVE was painted on the rear bumper. They scripted the name BARON S. across the top of the tinted windshield that, at first, we thought read BARONS. We learned every recent and classic dancehall hit from the music spilling loudly from their car's speakers. This was all they played. Magnus and Romulus had left the island when they were skinny teenagers, acned and awkward, and we'd thought that since they'd never returned that meant they'd sorted out their papers for foreign. But first one, then, in short order, the other, was shipped back to us. They came back angry.

We knew their type.

They'd never wanted to come back. They didn't mind if they never saw their mother again. Magnus and Romulus were the sort who proclaimed that if foreign burned down that they would live in the ashes. *Good riddance*, we'd thought, remembering the times when the last of the village cats were set on fire and women's drawers would disappear from clotheslines, when someone chopped away at our good good jetty with cutlass hacks until it became rickety and unsafe. We didn't know for sure that it was the sinistered left-handed fault of Magnus and Romulus, but those suspicious signals stopped happening when they took their island leave.

A little online digging by the glasses and goateed UWI graduate unearthed Titus crimes. He displayed their Riker's Island Prison doc arrest records on his laptop. Dates of birth, weight, hair, sex, height. Race, eye color, marks, scars, and tattoos. We shivered at this reduction of penal nightmares into a few tight words. Miki grew upset. *Right there for the whole world to see!* he bellowed. He'd spent his own brief time in jail, but only for a few ibises and nothing on the level of the Titus boys. We weren't sure if it was online. "I ain't fraid of no wannabe cowboys who get send back," Barradas said, then laughed.

But the Titus boys were serious business because Ramdeen grew nervous.

"Go on," Hospedales told the glasses and goateed UWI graduate. "Keep reading." He did.

He read to us about home invasion, aggravated battery with firearm, and armed robbery. He read to us about attempted murder and intent to kill and injure. He read to us about prison sentences of fifty years, zero months, and zero days for both of them to be served consecutively before consideration of parole.

"Gs + Hs," Ramdeen said.

"Starboys," Barradas said.

"And that is only for their caught crimes," Miki reasoned. "Imagine what they didn't get catch for."

"They should be in jail for life," Sookdeo said softly. It was one of the rare occasions that he was with us in the Clearing. He was usually fishing or with his wife.

"1-0-1-1-1-0-0?" Binary Clem asked.

"Eh?" said Hospedales.

"He wants to know the exact crimes that they committed," Peter-Called-Peter said. The glasses and goateed UWI graduate scrolled down but couldn't find specific details.

"Maybe that's for the best," Ramdeen said, and we didn't disagree with him.

We remained quiet for a moment, and then Peter-Called-Peter switched on the transistor and the Mighty-Penguin-Mighty-Shadow-Bob-Marley-24-7 station crackled to life. We felt as if we'd sunk into a warm bath. "But how the ass they get out of jail already with those long long prison sentences?" Barradas wondered, which, we acknowledged, was a good question. Then Peter-Called-Peter began his hammer-and-saw construction concert on his boat, and Robert Nesta crooned about three little birds, and we exhaled somewhat, Robert Nesta knowing how to lift spirits.

But we paused briefly when we felt a breeze blow though the Clearing.

In the backs of our minds we thought about Mami Ursula, fearing that something bigger was coming and that maybe we should get ahead of it. But we were slightly afraid of Mami Ursula, she of the gold eyes and green headwrap and the tribe that no one was ever to mention.

Magnus and Romulus knew that if we weren't afraid of them then we were at least wary. They knew it because Magnus was knock-kneed, and Romulus was bandy-legged, and none of us ever brought these details up in fatigue and picong, not like we did with Miki's floating eye, or Peter-Called-Peter's missing front tooth, or Hospedales's loud shirts and cologne, or Barradas's single pair of sneakers, or Mark-2's expanded rib cage and buck teeth. Magnus and Romulus would disappear toward the city in their hot rod, and we'd realize that we'd been holding our breaths. In the middle of the night they would roar back in with the car's muffler chuddering and their stereo speakers spitting gunman lyrics courtesy of Cutty Ranks or Terry Ganzie, or Burro

Banton—*Badderthanthem! Badderthanthem! Badderthanthem!*—and they would wake us bleary-eyed and coal-encrusted from our hard-fought sleep with the bass thumping through the ground, up through our thin mattresses, and up into our teeth. A week after the Titus boys showed back up in our lives, the birds surprisingly returned, first the sound of them, and then the sight of them, and we foolishly believed that things were taking a turn for the better. A false dawn, we later learned.

We reconsidered when the returned birds began to fall from the sky. We heard them because they thudded on our roofs, which unsettled us more than the chanting of Cutty Ranks threatening to cut us down limb by limb and to silence us by cutting out our tongues. We would be boiling water for tea tea, or stirring Klim powdered milk into a thin gruel to fill our stomachs and keep our hunger at bay, when we'd hear these heavy sounds like breadfruit or châtaigne thumping onto our ceilings. We sent Mark-2 scrambling up a ladder and onto each of our roofs with a yard broom to push the collection of birds onto the ground before they began to rot.

But they continued to drop from the sky.

They fell in flocks.

They fell in bunches.

They fell on their backs with their beaks up and their wings outstretched. They made a village mess.

Mami Ursula? We thought. *No*, we decided.

Not yet.

But her gold eyes shone in our dreams like the headlights on the Titus boys' car.

One morning, arriving at the Clearing in Peter-Called-Peter's Trooper to escape the Titus boys and to look at his pappyshow of a fishing boat, us having seen what Peter-Called-Peter had done with Miss Titus's porch and knowing that any boat he built would collapse at the sight of water, even if the seas were slight to moderate, even if the waves were up to two meters in open waters or less than one meter in sheltered areas, we saw birds spilled everywhere. The Clearing was where we had gathered more than ever because it was the one place where the Titus boys would not venture, us not being sure if it was because they avoided it as children, having heard the stories from Miss Titus about the space and holding a healthy respect for it. We froze when we saw the carpet of birds, us seeing nowhere to step but on bird carcasses, them being collected up to a foot deep in red, brown, and yellow feathered bodies. The fear in Ramdeen's eyes.

We retrieved a hoe and a rake from the Trooper and cleared a pathway to one of the picnic tables, shoveling the birds out of the way, yellow-chested kiskadees, gray-headed kites, and ruddy ground doves, squirrel cuckoos, tropical screech owls and potoos, and even pigeons we pushed to the left and to the right. We all did our part: Nello, Peter-Called-Peter, Miki, Hospedales, Mark-2, Binary Clem, Ramdeen, Sookdeo, Barradas, and the glasses and goateed UWI graduate. Some of us stripped to our waists because the work was arduous. By the time that we made it to one of the picnic tables, the birds had raised two feet deep ridges on either side of the cleared passage. All of us were drenched with sweat. We turned to the glasses and goateed UWI graduate. "What the France," Barradas asked him, "is all this horse's ass?"

"Well, I'm not an ornithologist," the glasses and goateed UWI graduate said, pushing his glasses up his nose, and Hospedales asked then what the hell was he good for? The return of the Titus boys especially troubled Hospedales because their might was apparent and greater than his.

If Hospedales was a paper tiger, then the Titus boys were prowling Bengals, bush masters, jungle warriors.

Then, one day while we were out in the Clearing, when the birds had stopped falling for exactly twelve hours and made us think that the curse on our village was at an end, the older Titus brother, Magnus, came over to say that they were opening a new gentleman's club soon. Magnus's teeth were incarcerated by braces, and with his hair cut low and carefully brushed, this softened him, us thinking that maybe there was something civilized about him.

Club? we asked. *What damn club?* We grew suspicious. Magnus Titus closed off one nostril with a forefinger and shot off a firework of snot from the other. Peter-Called-Peter continued working on his boat, and the sound of his hammering sounded like a continuous judge's gavel, causing Magnus to wait until Peter-Called-Peter took a break. Peter-Called-Peter didn't ramp with the Titus boys, and they similarly avoided him. Something about Peter-Called-Peter held them at bay, perhaps his clear disaffection for criminal behavior, their stance probably not squaring with Peter-Called-Peter's zen pursuit of transcendence.

Magnus pointed north past the silk cotton tree and toward the woods. "We building about a mile so," he said.

We frowned. "But out there is only bush, man," Nello said. "Where the sugarcane used to grow."

"We clearing out some space. We using good good contractors. Well, we renovating a building out there to tell the truth."

Peter-Called-Peter laughed from his boat. "You mean you planning to use the old plantation slave house? You and your brother real kicksy, yes."

Magnus ignored him.

"How long before it ready?" Hospedales asked, him smelling a good good money-making investment opportunity and already hoping to climb into the Titus brothers' good graces.

Magnus shrugged. "A few months? We working quick quick."

Peter-Called-Peter laughed again. Magnus ignored him again. "Jesus. You mean you're going to use that old haunted house?"

Magnus remained quiet. "We get clearance. We adding on."

"You really planning to use Abercromby House?" Ramdeen asked.

"Plenty space," Magnus said.

"Gentleman's club?" asked Barradas, stroking his goatee.

"Classy ladies," Magnus said. "Not no cheap women." He made a slippery sign for money with his thumb and fingers.

"I hope you not planning to use old jamettes, skettels, and horsefaces from the next village," Hospedales said.

"Don't worry, partner," Magnus said. "We already sizing up some pretty women who will want to work there."

Peter-Called-Peter laughed a third time. "Is that what you call that human trafficking scheme from Vene that you and your brother working?" he asked.

Magnus squinted at him. "Listen, saddist," he said, "we saving lives and providing livelihoods."

"I've been to Venezuela," said Peter-Called-Peter.

"Have you been to their empty grocery stores?" Magnus asked. "Have you been to their ghost town drugstores?"

Peter-Called-Peter pointed his hammer at him. "You and your brother go find your ass in jail again." We sucked in our breaths, but Magnus only laughed and returned to his car with a wave. He'd delivered his message. He fired up his car, and Shabba Ranks exploded from its speakers singing about his trailer-load of girls.

Then Magnus Titus backed up and peeled out.

None of us said anything for a few moments. Some of us were curious about the Titus gentleman's club announcement, but Peter-Called-Peter was uninterested. He returned to work, and we smelled the wood shavings as he planed and sawed. Binary Clem remained the quietest and, we knew that, in his head, he was already at the club, inspecting the carpet, smelling the paint, and eyeing the women, Binary Clem's febrile reptile brain forever fomenting and always felling him into the simplest of honey traps.

But it was when we saw Barradas huddling with Sookdeo, bartering quietly with him to take out his boat to make some extra fishing money, that we knew that Magnus had hooked more than a few of us.

* * *

The birds resumed falling.

They fell with loud screeches.

They fell in shag-carpeted silence.

They fell onto our roofs and sounded like out-of-rhythm pan men playing the worst calypso ever scored.

Each day we arrived at the Clearing to discard their bodies before they began to rot. We dug a pit on the far east side of the Clearing and wheel-barrowed them in. We hoped that we wouldn't dig up any human bodies; this part of the island was rife with dead Africans, us growing up hearing rumors of an incident when the British slave owners buried several delinquent slaves close to the ever-eroding shoreline. By the third day of the bird bodies, the glasses and goateed UWI graduate handed us some printed pages. He'd done some more research and had learned that something similar had occurred a few years earlier in the U.S. with starlings, cowbirds, blackbirds, and common grackles, them falling from the sky just as ours now did. "And what the *ass* that have to do with us, You-We?" Miki asked.

"Well," said the glasses and goateed UWI graduate. "The scientists figured out what was happening." We read his printed pages. The birds had died scientifically. They'd died from blunt force trauma. They'd crashed into trees, cars, and buildings. He said we had nothing to worry about. We crumpled the pages and threw them back at him. We knew this was mamaguy. How could *thousands* of birds die from so few man-made things? *You must think we're bobolees, You-We*, we said. *You must think we dotish.* We were skeptical. This was the same glasses and goateed UWI graduate who'd told us about the Birds Aren't Real Movement, about a group trying to stop an avian genocide, claiming that the U.S. government had replaced all living birds with robotic replicas, that the U.S. government had genocided over 12 billion birds from 1959 to 2001, the real birds being replaced with drone replicas meant to surveil the entire populace. He was worried for the earth's birds.

But a few weeks later he returned to sheepishly say that it was all a performance art joke. Barradas snorted.

But Ramdeen grew deeply concerned, the dead birds troubling him more than the rest of us. It was Ramdeen who was the saddest of all of us when Miki had eaten the ibis that time, and now, no one laughed any longer when we saw Ramdeen take his caged kiskadee for daily walks. He seemed truly grief-stricken when he woke up one morning and found his kiskadee dead in its cage, flat on its back, its beak pointing toward the sky.

One morning, after we removed the Clearing's birds, when Mark-2 was reading to us from that morning's gazette, we heard him say oh-ho. He read to us an article about the Titus boys' club under a heading titled "License Issued for Club to Open Down South."

This was when Barradas finally convinced Sookdeo to take out his boat for a little extra fishing at night. Ramdeen went along because he said he wanted to get away from the negative static that was building up in the village.

The next day Catherine the Great Disemboweler showed up in the village.

And Ramdeen, Barradas, and Sookdeo never came back.

Look, we thought, *at our crosses.*

"Is who that?" Nello asked as she arrived in the passenger seat of a pick-up.

"That," Peter-Called-Peter said, "is bacchanal."

She showed up wearing bright red clothing. Her laugh was a crackling fire. She smelled like burnt matches.

Like mangrove swamp sulfur.

Our cockstands saluted in our drawers.

"Is what kind of top she wearing?" Miki whispered. The sleeves were off the shoulder and the neckline showed the top of her bosom.

"Peasant blouse," sneered Bunny. "Which suits her perfectly."

All that she showed up with were the clothes on her back and the key to the house. She acknowledged none of us as she walked up the steps to the porch.

"Bacchanal," Peter-Called-Peter repeated.

"1-0-0-1," Binary Clem said.

"Lust," Nello corrected, shaking his pants leg.

Catherine the Great Disemboweler chased our heads.

Catherine the Great Disemboweler drove us bazodie.

Catherine the Great Disemboweler had us tootoulbay.

Catherine the Great Disemboweler wore skirts mid-thigh, a different sexy from Bunny, and we saw that paying attention to Catherine the Great Disemboweler out of the corner of our eyes wrecked Bunny, us never before seeing that flat-lined expression on Bunny's mouth before Catherine the Great Disemboweler showed up. Bunny said Catherine the Great Disemboweler was made up like a circus horse, her emphasizing the first half of the animal's name. "That blue mascara," she said.

The trouble with the blue mascara, Bunny said, was Catherine the Great Disemboweler's flat and dead shark eyes. Catherine the Great Disemboweler's eyes might have been shark-flat, but her voice was high and inviting. She made us suck in our stomachs and tuck in our shirts. She conned us to search for clean socks and wear them in sanctioned pairs. We finished our sentences when we talked with her. Pulled on clean underwear. Halted our use of green verbs.

She paid us little attention.

Then Magnus and Romulus noticed her, and we expected the entire village to spontaneously combust. For her to ask for heads on platters. But the brothers Titus didn't fight over her as we expected. They fawned over her just like the rest of us. At first we thought that they wanted her for their gentleman's club. Then we saw that they wanted her for themselves. They limed with her on her gallery like the rest of us limed on Bunny's porch. But at the end of the night they both went into her house and closed the door.

Outwardly we didn't judge.

But inwardly our minds sizzled.

Catherine the Great Disemboweler wore the tiniest bikini we'd ever seen when she headed to the beach, her nipples poking through the fabric and stabbing us right in our imaginations. "Papa yo," said Hospedales.

"G's + H's," said Miki.

"Lord have his mercy," said Nello.

"1-0-1-1-1," said Binary Clem.

Romulus and Catherine the Great Disemboweler splashed around on the beach like tourists. As if a fashion photographer were snapping shots. Flipping off the falling-down jetty and into the water like children. We thought we should warn them that the jetty was a splinter waiting to inject into them, that it was a condemned building waiting to collapse, that it was regret made of rotting wood, but they were adults, and we kept our mouths closed. Plus it was the Titus boys who destabilized it for kicks.

The first Venezuelans that came to the village en masse were through Magnus and Romulus, those grim travel agents. Magnus and Romulus had rented Hospedales's fishing boat and disappeared for a few days. They knew that none of the rest of us would have anything to do with them. The boat returned weighed down with panyol women. We saw the boat pull up to our falling-down jetty right at dawn while we were pulling in a sizable catch, one of the last that we'd had. The catch lifted us and we didn't say anything about Magnus and Romulus Titus escorting women ashore at this time of day. Magnus ignored us as they walked past, but Romulus winked at us. The women were pretty but tired. Afterward we wondered if Hospedales had anything to do with it? "Me? No, papa, I don't mess with people smuggling," he said. "That is hard labor and cat-o'-nine-tails." But we wondered how much he'd been paid for the use of his boat and whether the cost of his conscience had been thrown in for free.

The birds hadn't fallen on the morning that we found the huge brown shipping container on the beach. In the rising sun its rust spots reminded us of illness.

There it was, a huge container on the beach, locked tight. Not even Hospedales's bolt cutter could snip the lock. *Where did it come from?* we contemplated. *When? Who delivered it?* Of course we held our suspicions. We circled twice and then, at its door, Peter-Called-Peter slapped his palm against it. Immediately, someone inside slapped back. Then several slaps sounded like rain on a galvanized roof. And then the sound built, and it continued to resound, sounding like panmen tuning their instruments. "We need to call Lalchan," Peter-Called-Peter said. Hospedales, who may or may not have already invested in the Titus boys' gentleman's club, argued against it. "Listen," Peter-Called-Peter hissed. "You know what's inside this container. If we move now some of them might make it." We hadn't thought about this obvious concern: that there was a fixed amount of air in a sealed container. That some might be clinging to life at this moment, that some might already be lost. "Not just suffocation," said Peter-Called-Peter, "but dehydration too."

Then we heard something come from the far side of the container. When we circled around we saw a tiny hole that we'd missed, about knee-high from the ground. From it an eye peered out. Then a mouth came to the hole. *Help us*, it said in halting English. *Help us*.

When Lalchan arrived he had a lot of questions that he counted off on his fingertips.

"Which one of you paying me to shut my mouth about all of this?"

"Which one of you paying me to move the container?"

"Which one of you paying me to secure the special tools required to open the container?"

"Which one of you paying me to forget that I transport and open the container?"

"Which one of you paying me to keep all of this quiet and out of the gazettes when the container's contents are released?"

"That's a lot of somebodies," said Hospedales reluctantly. "That's a lot of graft."

"Don't even try to big foot me, Hospedales," said Lalchan. "I am an officer of the law on this island sworn to upkeep its logistics and regulations."

Hospedales took Lalchan aside.

They worked something out.

Later that evening the container disappeared.

We returned to the Clearing the next morning.

Everybody was tired from all that had been happening, and we were sprawled out on the picnic tables, run down from our daily bird removal, when Nello began to talk his talk telling us he'd had a vision the night before.

"You mean a dream?" Mark-2 asked.

"Listen with your ears," said Nello.

Hospedales snickered.

Nello said that he had been out in the woods, and had grown weary, and that the leaves of all the trees around him glowed a strange fluorescent green, and he had to sit down beneath the silk cotton tree to regain his strength. He tried to sit out in the open, but the voice in his head urged him to rest beneath the silk cotton tree in the Clearing. We took a step away from him when he said this, us not wanting anything to do with silk cotton trees, not even in idle conversation. He said that when he sat under the tree a shimmering Taino spirit appeared before him, telling him something in a language Nello didn't recognize, but that he anyway understood.

"So who was the Taino spirit?" Miki asked.

Nello lifted his head. "That's not important," he said. "What's important was what was said. It said that a deeply melancholy ancestor is bringing destruction."

"Krick krack!" said Mark-2, that clown, but no one laughed.

"I want you to listen," said Nello, "because terrible things already start up, and they going to go from bad to worse." We remained quiet for a moment.

"Worse when?" asked the glasses and goateed UWI graduate. "Worse how?"

Nello shook his head. "I can't say for sure."

"Will the terrible thing happen to us, or will we do the terrible thing?" asked Hospedales.

Nello shook his head again.

Hospedales tchhed. "What kind of halfway business is this?" he said.

"How to stop it?" the glasses and goateed UWI graduate asked Nello. "How could we stop the terrible thing?"

"You might not like it," Nello said. "It might be too much to ask."

"Spit it out, saddist," Hospedales said.

"We need to go away," Nello said. "For a while. We all need to go away. Let the negative static that build up in the village clear out."

"Hold your mudder ass," said Hospedales right away. "I not going a damn place."

"You see how people is on this island?" said Nello.

"We really have to go away?" asked the glasses and goateed UWI graduate.

"To be sure," said Nello.

"This have anything to do with Catherine?" Miki asked softly.

"I don't know," Nello admitted. "But don't eat any zabocas from any of these trees for a week."

"And light a candle and walk around your bed six times before you go to sleep," Hospedales joked.

Nello shrugged. Briefly, we thought again about reaching out to Mami Ursula, thinking of her as both a spiritual diagnostician as well as a repository of tribal memory, but these very reasons, along with her golden eyes, gave us pause.

The next morning, some of us were gone. Peter-Called-Peter, Nello, and the glasses and goateed UWI graduate had vacated the village. There were those of us who didn't want to deal with the darkness that now always seemed to hover around the village's edges, that seemed to be closing its pincers around it, and that now had seemed to calcify.

And then there was Catherine the Great Disemboweler. We didn't want to discuss the hold that she had on us. She blew through all of our minds like the dust storms that infiltrated the island's airspace every now and again all the way from the Sahara. We couldn't understand what she saw in the Titus boys. But then things grew taut between her and those badjohns.

It started with the container. We knew at once that the container had belonged to the Titus boys. We knew that there might be repercussions for removing it. It happened when the Titus boys and Catherine returned late one night, a few nights after the container had been removed. Catherine the Great Disemboweler was drunker than we'd ever seen, her blue mascara was faded and her lipstick smeared. The Titus boys were drunk too. They woke us up when they pulled into the village and parked in front of Miss Titus's house and kept revving their engine. We all came out of our houses. We gathered close to their car and asked them to be considerate and to lower their stereo. We told them we fished pre-dawn. They emerged from the car like gunslingers. "Where the *fock* is our container?" Magnus asked.

Catherine the Great Disemboweler exited the car too, and she began to laugh. “Container!” she said. Mirth bent her in half.

“Where the ass it is?” Magnus asked us. “Where the gotdamn container that was delivered here?” We said we didn’t know. We saw that his fuse was lit, and the detonation was close.

We’d heard that there had been a dust-up in the city with a man ending up in the hospital. Romulus and Magnus matched a description of the assailants. It was true that there were two of them, and many more of us, but these men were psychopaths. Jailbirds. Returned foreign used. We might have to kill them, because if we left them alive they would burn down the village. But we knew that we couldn’t do that to Miss Titus. These were her sons. These were her heirs, and as much as we despised them, they were part of us.

“Eh,” said Romulus. “Watch. If you don’t tell us what happened to the container—”

“I move it,” said Catherine the Great Disemboweler.

Magnus’s face darkened. “You?” He squinted. “Why?”

“Me,” said Catherine, suddenly sober. “Me, me, me, me, me. I take your container and all the wajangs you had inside. Set all of them free.” Magnus looked at her, trying to figure out if she was lying. He knew that she was a live wire that sputtered and sparked. He knew that she was an unstepped-on mortar, an undetonated claymore. He knew what she was capable of. But why would she do something like that? It didn’t matter. The die had been cast.

Quick as a sneeze, Magnus grabbed her by her hair and yanked her down to the ground. Romulus grabbed her by a wrist. When she screamed, Romulus slapped her across the face. Then the Titus boys dragged her kicking back to her house and slammed the door behind them. Miki rushed to the door and knocked. Banged. “Fellas!” he shouted. “Fellas, it was us. It was us who moved the container.”

But no one came back out.

* * *

The next morning there were cardboard boxes in front of all of our houses. We were tentative. We felt our gonads in our throats. We circled the boxes, watched them from different angles. Lifted them but didn't shake them. There were no markings, no labels. They were each about three feet by three feet by three feet. Finally, Hospedales pulled out a box cutter and he carefully slit the tape atop his box. We held our collective breaths and stepped back. When he flung open the flaps we shut our eyes.

"What the *ass*," he said.

He reached into the box and pulled out a carburetor. We exhaled. Then we opened all our boxes. We found car parts as well. Windshield wipers and tappets. Spark plugs and mufflers. Mark-2 was presented with an intake manifold. Miki received pistons. It was car Christmas. We knew at once that they were from the Titus boys' hot rod. *What kind of assness was this?* We held our breaths and waited for Romulus and Magnus to exit Catherine the Great Disemboweler's house in another rage, but they didn't, and neither did she. We went about our business, but kept one eye on the house, which was quieter than it had ever been.

And then the body parts began to arrive.

Over the next ten blood-soaked days parts of Romulus and Magnus appeared like boxed meals on each of our doorsteps. An ear. A finger. Three shoulder-length locs of hair. The boxes matched the size of the body parts. A matchbox held ten fingernails. An eyeball arrived in a tiny Tupperware container. Most everything else arrived in plain brown boxes. Everyone awoke predawn each day so that they could ferry their box away so that Miss Titus wouldn't see them. So that Mark-2's sister Stacy wouldn't uncover them. So that You-We's mother wouldn't encounter them. We stored the body parts in a refrigerator on the back porch of Peter-Called-Peter's house. He was away and none the wiser.

We held a somber meeting in the Clearing.

We feared that we would soon start receiving internal organs.

We needed to act.

We tried to figure out why this was happening. The closest that we could decipher was because of the women in the container. The birds continued to fall from the sky.

Enough, we said. This was more than we could handle. We needed an expert. We reached out to Mami Ursula with a heaviness we anticipated, us knowing that along with her presence in the village there would return traces of a grief-filled village memory, like the smell of sulfur after the match had been struck or a burning scent after a candle had been snuffed out. Miss Titus said that the last time that Mami Ursula visited the village thirty-odd years earlier, to help plug the hole in a similar widespread mistreatment-of-women problem, that she and You-We's mother had experienced terrifying dreams for two months. Mami Ursula was the one who doled out important balancing-on-the-edge-of-a-cliff village advice. Angels dancing on the head of a pin recommendations. But there were two concerns about Mami Ursula: she didn't like to travel, and she was costly.

"Get her," said Hospedales.

She returned the same as we remembered her. Same upright carriage. Same gold eyes. Same green headscarf. The only thing that was different was that now she moved with a walking stick. Still, she was sprightly. She tested the boards on Miss Titus's porch with her stick. We asked her if she wanted to inspect Catherine the Great Disemboweler's porch, and she said that she would prefer not to although she squinted at it from afar.

We needed some questions answered. *Where did this Catherine the Great Disemboweler person come from?* we asked.

Mami Ursula smiled. "She's been here a long time," she said. "Her mother made a difficult choice a long time ago." Had we heard of Mama Binti? We told her we hadn't. She told us that someone who had become Catherine the Great Disemboweler had been taken in by Mama Binti. That because of this she would return to the village at certain historical pressure points. That she would appear wherever she wanted and looking however she wanted, be it young child or old crone. Were we sure we hadn't heard of Mama Binti? We said that we'd heard folklore stories of jumbies that could appear at whatever age they chose, but didn't know that this was Mama Binti business.

We asked who was her mother?

Mami Ursula tapped her walking stick. "A woman called Hany," she said, "who you will know in time."

We asked how do we get rid of this Catherine the Great Disemboweler that kept mentally sitting all of New Felicity at the edge of a precipice.

She bade us come closer to her, to form a tight circle around her. "Tighter," she said. "Even tighter. So that what I'm telling you doesn't get out." She smelled of chives and chadon beni. Ginger and garlic. Then she said the way out of our troubles lay in an extra-large sack of rice and blue bottles. She said we needed to plant blue bottles on tree branches and to scatter rice around Catherine the Great Disemboweler's doorstep. "The bottles and rice will get rid of your troubles," she said. Then she stood around and waited to be paid.

That was all? We gritted our teeth. What were we to make of this mush?

Hospedales paid her. She folded her money away into her bosom, and she and her gold eyes and her green headscarf and her walking stick ambled out of our lives.

Somehow we knew we wouldn't see her again.

* * *

We decided that we needed to call Lalchan about the body parts. But he beat us to the punch arriving that evening before we signaled to him.

"Bad news, boss," he said, his face long, his bush mustache drooping. "Bad bad news."

"What happen, chief?" Hospedales asked.

"One set of bodies when we opened the shipping container," he said, his face long long. "One set of *deceased* bodies." He said that they found fifteen dead women in there, and about a dozen more clinging to life. "That was a hell of a thing to do to people, I don't care where they from. I going to have to question the lot of you," he said. "Some of you feel you's big jefes." He eyed Mark-2, who shrank under his gaze.

Hospedales sighed and pulled him aside.

We finally told Miss Titus. Sat her on her porch. Told her about her boys. She received the news stoically. Not a tear scratched down her face. At least not then. We confessed our plans to her. "Please, Miss Titus," we said, "let us make this up to you. Let us make this right." She was very upstanding. Very proper. Didn't respond at once. Kept her back straight. Said she didn't want any part of it. Said she knew her boys had been trouble and that they'd dug themselves this hole. She was a woman who believed that her redeemer sent trials and tribulations to the righteous to test their faith.

We told her we'd had Mami Ursula come inspect the situation, and we told her the recommended course of action. Her eyes flattened. She was a Seventh-Day Adventist and wanted nothing to do with any Mami Ursula business even though she'd lost both of her sons. This was her way. We begged her. Cajoled. Said she wouldn't have to do anything other than provide the supplies, which she had to provide to make everything work right, and besides, we didn't have anywhere else to get them. She refused. "I don't want to know anything else about it," she said. "Because what you are planning to do is an eye for an eye."

Later that night we stole into her house and secured what we needed, her not wanting to hand us the items and us not wanting her to see us collect them.

The next day gathered all that we had of the Titus boys and remanded them to Miss Titus for burial. Then we solidified a plan.

At first we heeded Miss Titus's words and did nothing. We kept the bottles and the rice and held hope in our hearts that we wouldn't have to implement Mami Ursula's tactics.

But things crumpled.

Namely Mark-2 starting to vomit off and on all day, namely Stacy tearing her clothes off one Wednesday morning and walking through the village naked, namely the mangrove starting to bubble and boil one Thursday, namely Barradas, Sookdeo, and Ramdeen having been absent now for two weeks, namely Bunny opening her fridge one evening and twenty-six black moths fluttering out, namely three of Mark-2 and Stacy's sisters starting to speak a language none of us had ever heard before, namely Indira's eyes rolling back into her head so that we saw only the whites, namely all the perishables in Miss Titus's house developing mold only a few hours after bringing them in off delivery lorries, namely a Sacred Heart of Jesus portrait in You-We's house shedding a single tear of what his mother believed to be blood, namely a dark cloud of batimamselles buzzing for two days and flying into the village and ending up in everything—our folded-away clothes, floating in our toilet water and water tanks, flying out of newly open bags of bread—so that it was only then that we took action, us realizing that whatever had triggered Catherine the Great Disemboweler had gotten out of hand, was no longer to be contained even after she'd taken apart Magnus, Romulus, and their car.

Late on the night of Miss Titus's food going bad, we scattered the rice around Catherine the Great Disemboweler's house. We stood in the shadows. We waited like sheriffs ready to issue a high noon deadline. We fell asleep. We snapped awake. We whispered to each other whether this was what we really wanted to do. We looked at the moon's glint on the fishing lines that we held in our hands on dry land. This was a full moon night, and we didn't need a torch-light to see. We didn't know what we were waiting for, except Mami Ursula said we would know it when we saw it. And she was right. Here returned Catherine the Great Disembowler to her house, us seeing her for the first time since the Titus boys dragged her away. She was clad in the scantiest scraps of clothes. A two-piece as if she were getting ready to jump up on Carnival Tuesday. We watched her stop and look curiously at the blue bottles stuck on the branches on the tree outside her house. We saw her inspect all the grains of rice scattered outside her front door. We waited until she opened the front door, and stood in the space between porch and house.

And then we moved in.

Quickly.

With purpose.

With fear and hatred in our hearts.

And big hardback men like us began crying as we wrapped fishing line around her neck, as we pinned her arms to her side, grasped her legs together, felt her thrashing underneath our arms, hearing her calling *mummy-mummy-mummy*, all our hearts breaking as we subdued her and led her off to the river beside the mangrove, Hospedales already waiting there with a broken-down outboard motor to garland her neck and extinguish the rest of the life from her.

For a week after that the sky remained overcast. For a week after that there were dead hummingbirds everywhere. For a week after that we felt tiny eruptions in our stomachs that limited our food intake. Sharp pains in our scrota that made it difficult to pee. Things soured after that with Miss Titus briefly losing her mind when the grief of her loss bore its full weight upon her, and Iris, the goateed and glasses UWI graduate's mother, had to go over to feed her and clean her and take care of her in the way that Miss Titus often fed and took care of all of us.

When Peter-Called-Peter and Nello and You-We returned, the birds had stopped falling, Miss Titus was recovering, and we could finally eat a little bit of dried toast and drink a little bit of PG Tips. But the scent of oranges blew through the village strong strong and lingered for a week, and we knew that there would be big fallout from our actions, that Catherine the Great Disemboweler's mother, Hany, as Mami Ursula had prophesied, was on her way. And when the first earthquake shook us, a 6.7 on the Richter, we stood in the thresholds of our houses, and held our breaths, and braced our hands against the doorframe, knowing we deserved whatever happened to us.

16

A Flutter of Doves and a Circling Red-Tailed Hawk

HERE WAS MILAGROS at a student protest in Caracas, acutely feeling the aches and pains of her previous two visits, but perhaps doing the most reckless thing possible: searching for a source rather than minding her surroundings. She was primarily back in Venezuela to hunt down a contact provided to her by Daniela, a woman named Anna Aguilar who had ended up detained in the same house on the island and used for her body just as Grecia had been, who had probably made the trip thinking the same things that Grecia had—that the world would be gentler just a few miles away. Milagros had gone through the standard social media sites searching for Anna Aguilars, and had worked her way through them until landing on two who seemed to fit. She had called Daniela to thank her for the lead, but her number was disconnected. When Milagros was done here, she vowed to track down her childhood friend.

Milagros had visited the first Anna the night before, a small haunted woman who wavered between not wanting to say anything and wanting to have Fortunato jailed. Anna finally revealed some incriminating details to Milagros after admitting that her own daughter had been taken away from her on that boat trip, that she'd never seen her again. She told Milagros about how she'd learned about Fortunato, how much money she'd had to pay. How many women were detained in that house on the island. Made to lie on their backs. How the island police finally rescued them after first being complicit. Milagros had already typed up the woman's account in a frenzy that morning, had drafted an article that she secured in her email's draft folder and had addressed to Saskia. She weighed the risks of hitting send. But after reading her mother's letter, her journal, she felt compelled to reveal what she'd learned. What had happened to those women.

She would think it over during the march.

She wasn't flying completely solo. She was staying with Mauricio, a local journalist who she'd met in Miami a few months earlier. This wasn't a needle-in-a-haystack operation, as Juanita had previously insisted on categorizing her trips to Venezuela; through Mauricio, Milagros had already been in touch with Faisal, a student leader who'd helped organize this protest. Faisal owned an impressive daily blog that called out the government's shortcomings, and he was willing to go on the record about his experiences and his group's goals.

Faisal was also a young father, and the look of joy that Milagros observed in seeing him hold aloft his eight-month-old baby to the camera on social media posts sent a rush of emotions through her. She'd recently learned about her own father, who for all of her life held the consistency of smoke. Hearing his name and that he was from the island became no more than a factoid in her life. But her mother had loved him. And because of that Milagros existed. She grasped the sun quartz pendant that now never left her neck.

She scanned the impressive crowd, but Faisal was nowhere to be seen. The protest was a planned march toward the federal prosecutor's office. Milagros had arrived early to jot a few notes about the crowd's mood, to note what speakers were bellowing through bullhorns. "Get all of it down," Saskia had said when she'd emailed her about this article. Saskia had promised her the site's total attention, a focus on the situation in Venezuela. Milagros knew that the Fortunato article would tantalize Saskia. *Scofflaw* was now leaning heavily into the credibility it had recently built upon the back of Milagros's other stories. It wasn't a complete rebrand, but Saskia was lining up investors to scale up *Scofflaw*'s reimagined, and now burgeoning, international news arm, *Scofflaw Postco*, without troubling Saskia's husband Wils for investment. Saskia had already begun hiring intrepid young journalists who were unafraid to wander onto the front lines of countries tottering on economic and political scaffolds. To Milagros, she touted a breathtaking draft that she'd read from Scott Leung in Hong Kong. "All of your work in South America," Saskia said, "has led to this."

The crowd swelled. With at least five hundred people by conservative estimate, and more arriving each moment, the growing crowd was spilling over the plaza's container. Milagros saw now that she should have arranged to meet Faisal at an easily locatable landmark. She'd still received no response from an earlier text. Her only hope now was that Faisal would take to the stage at some point to remonstrate through a bullhorn. Raise a rallying fist. Urge everyone on. The police and the military remained a troubling potential hurdle. At any point their appearance could result in cracking skulls and detention of protestors. Thankfully, security forces were not yet present in high numbers. But that could change in a blink. Even the sky seemed suspect: gray and clearing its throat of thunder rumbles in anticipation of possible rain in the midmorning distance.

Counterbalancing her fears was Mauricio. With him she'd felt safe. When she'd met him a few months earlier at the journalism conference in Miami, he'd been the one to approach her. Had known her work from *Scofflaw*, knew that she was originally Venezuelan. She'd been surprised that she was able to keep up with his rapid-fire Spanish, and even more surprised when he said she was an important international journalistic voice for Venezuela. One of their own. "Well, not exactly," she'd demurred.

He'd grasped her elbow. "Tu eres venezolana," he'd said.

Unexpectedly, her throat had hitched and the tears came. He'd invited her to return to Caracas to pen articles to help rally the international community with more exposure. She'd expressed reservations.

Things were growing tenuous with Juanita, who was frustrated that she was so often away. As avaricious as Saskia was, she was also growing concerned. "I would have to shut down everything if anything were to happen to you, kiddo," she'd said. "My heart wouldn't be able to take it. You're more important to me than whatever the site produces." Plus, each time Milagros returned to Venezuela, she felt as if more and more emotional shrapnel lodged beneath her skin.

"Isn't there anything you want to write? I can help you find the sources," Mauricio had urged. She weighed whether to tell him about the article that she was working on about Fortunato, fearful that he would tell her that she was insane and that the repercussions would be extreme. "Think it over. Por que, tu eres venezolana," he'd repeated.

That old Pied Piper's melody.

The sky was an aged gray T-shirt peppered with birdshot. The office buildings leaned over, peering down upon the crowd, curious at why they'd all gathered. As more people arrived, different speakers took to the stage: a young woman with thick eyebrows stirred up the crowd, a young man with muttonchops eulogized the students who'd been disappeared or jailed, a child got up and shakily spoke about her missing father. Students banged on drums, buckets, and garbage cans. Young women in the crowd sealed their mouths with masking tape with scrawled "Venezuela" across them with red lipstick. A small drone whirred overhead, recording for someone's vlog. Mauricio drifted through the crowd. Sourced quotes. Lifted a hand in recognition at panas, people who he had drunk with and dreamed about a future Venezuela. He was sweating when he reappeared beside Milagros. Interpreted her concern. "You're worried," he said.

"About Faisal," she said. "I hope he's okay."

"He's okay," Mauricio promised. "But don't be disappointed if he doesn't show up. His appearance after organizing something like this would make him an easy target."

Milagros agreed, although she'd wanted badly to shake Faisal's hand. Instead, she snapped a few pictures. Looked for someone else to interview. Kept a watch on the skies. She noted a lone red-tailed hawk riding a high thermal, flapping its wings once or twice to gain altitude. She rubbed the back of her neck. Her previous experience with parrots still resonated.

Then, a moment of anxiety: she lost sight of Mauricio for almost ten minutes before spotting him off to her right, still working the crowd, meeting with other associates. She berated herself. She was clinging to him like a life raft. The unfounded optimism of a breadcrumb trail that might lead to her mother. Milagros was also comforted in the knowledge that somewhere in this crowd Mauricio had backup. He promised her that his friend Andres, a former member of the national guard disillusioned at the government's direction, was there to watch over them. But, as with Faisal, he was nowhere to be seen.

"So he's a bodyguard?" Milagros had joked upon hearing about Andres at Mauricio's apartment. "In a crowd as wide as the ocean and with sharks in the guise of the police sure to arrive?"

Mauricio had offered his lopsided grin. "Think of him as more of a guardian angel." He didn't say much more, but in his brief description he'd made Andres sound like a Swiss army knife. A detergent one spreads over an oil spill. A blanket to wrap around one's shoulders when surprised by a grease fire that threatened the house. When she'd asked Mauricio for a picture of Andres, Mauricio had replied, "Don't worry. It's more important that he knows what *you* look like." Andres, he said, was chévere. But Milagros couldn't help but think of a sniper stooped in a faraway tree, his scope sighting down on her, the rifle coughing quietly when the trigger was pulled, which reminded her of Maldonado and that night crossing into Columbia. Who does the guardian angel protect? Her stomach shifted.

The last speaker wrapped up, and the march lurched forward like someone had released an emergency brake. The crowd took to the blacktop, filled the streets, made it impossible for cars. Chants, raised fists, banners. Horns honked in consternation and support. Call and response on a megaphone. The protest found its rhythm. The streets were theirs. A young woman shouted toward sidewalk onlookers to join them in taking down the piece of shit government. Young men in the crowd clad in tank tops and tugged-low ball caps watched with darting eyes. Backpacks were slung across their shoulders which contained, Milagros suspected, the raw ingredients for Molotov cocktails—bottles brimming with kerosene, shreds of rags, lighters. She understood the young men's twitchiness. She'd be nervous too if a bomb were strapped to her back. Milagros felt she was slowly shuffling onto a high wire without a net.

Juanita had disliked Mauricio as soon as Milagros had mentioned him upon her return from the conference. The very idea of him. Milagros had known that she and Juanita were on swampy ground, but she hadn't suspected how swampy until her previous return from Venezuela. What was Milagros's depression after another failed attempt to locate Grecia, Juanita read as post-trip moodiness, and was furious about Milagros's reluctance to discuss any of the trip's details. Milagros had mentioned nothing of the astonishing exchange with Grecia through the sun quartz pendant, which she'd explained away as a flea market purchase. Her reinvigorated belief that her mother was alive somewhere in Venezuela.

Milagros and Juanita had dodged discussions of the safety issues that Milagros might face before that last Venezuelan trip. Juanita had shown the face cards of support beforehand, but it had been a different story upon Milagros's return. Juanita, Milagros knew, nurtured a fear of the potential dangers that Milagros might experience each time she returned to Venezuela, ideas sourced from *The Nation* and *The Atlantic*, journalists in Iran and Russia imprisoned on trumped-up espionage charges.

So when Juanita grew angry the night before Milagros left for this trip, Milagros had been expecting it, although not the shape that Juanita's anger took, the bubbling lava of anger toward Mauricio. She and Juanita were having dinner when, apropos of nothing, Juanita intimated that there had been hanky-panky between Mauricio and Milagros.

"*What?*" Milagros asked, a forkful of pesto-covered pasta paused at her mouth. She'd observed flashes of jealousy from Juanita before, but not this full-throated roar.

"Is Mauricio *seeing* anyone?" Juanita asked.

"Are you kidding me?"

"How big is his apartment?"

"Jeezus," said Milagros, lowering her fork with a clink. "I don't know. But his dick is huge."

"Does he have a couch?"

"We'll be sharing his bed. I've already asked him to be a sperm donor." She stuck the index finger of one hand into the hole made with the index finger and thumb with the other. "Set up a meeting with an ob-gyn for when I get back?"

Juanita smashed a plate.

"You're embarrassing yourself," Milagros sing-songed before pulling on noise-canceling headphones and relocating to their bedroom to finish packing. She'd been stung, but also too frustrated to care. She felt like her mother was pulling her toward some kind of fated coda. The phone call on her previous trip seemed a promissory note. Milagros texted Juanita when she landed in Venezuela but heard nothing back; all was radio silence up to and including today. *Let her be pissed then*, Milagros thought as Mauricio showed her to his guest bedroom and she grasped the pendant around her neck.

Milagros had kissed each of Mauricio's moonfaced cheeks when he'd met her at the airport. Huge shadows undergirded his eyes. He'd been paunchy in Miami, but he was bulky now. At least thirty pounds heavier. Stress weight from stress eating even though there still wasn't much on Caracas store shelves.

"Just the one bag?" he'd asked, taking it from her.

"Traveling light," she said.

"Smart." She'd begged him to tell her what she might bring for him, staples that might be unavailable, any medicine that he might need. He had eventually asked for a bottle of aspirin, so she'd brought five. They fell into the easy conversation that they'd begun when they'd first met at the conference, when she'd confessed all the details she'd been suppressing until her mother's words had torn it all back out of her, told him everything about her past in a way that she hadn't yet told Juanita: How she and her mother Grecia had escaped to the island from Güiria when she was a girl, how they'd been kept in a filthy brothel when they'd arrived on the island, and how she'd somehow, like her name suggested, miraculously gone untouched through all of it. How she'd been rescued by fishermen and cared for by Bunny. Her escape to Grenada. Her escape *from* Grenada. Maldonado. Fortunato. The furious desire to write about all of it. Something in Mauricio just brought it all out of her in a torrent. Milagros was shaking when she'd stopped talking, and when she broke down, Mauricio held her while her tears soaked his shirt. "Lo siento," he said stroking her head. "Pero tu eres venezolana."

Milagros's pulse quickened upon seeing a woman beside her holding a length of corrugated sheet metal as a shield. Along with the men with backpacks, this woman was expecting a battle. And it was becoming clear that it wouldn't take much to spark one. Milagros kept close to Mauricio. She suddenly understood that there was no Andres, that Mauricio had conjured this commando security blanket whole cloth. Sensing her anxiety, he'd invented a superhero. The crowd inched toward an overpass. Cars perched there honked. The heat. BO. Slogans. Bottled water. Chants. Clapping hands. Mauricio asked if she was okay. She marched on. People held aloft cardboard signs stamped with invectives against the government.

Skyward, still that lone red-tailed hawk.

On the overpass someone waved a huge Venezuelan flag in solidarity with the marchers below. A cheer rose from the crowd. The young woman with the shield chinned toward a middle-aged bearded man. "Sacerdote," she told Milagros. All around this priest people held placards with pictures, and beneath them the names and the death dates of the deceased. All the remembrances carried the word "asesinado." They turned a corner and the crowd slowed. They'd arrived at the building of the federal prosecutor. Milagros looked up and searched again for her red-tailed hawk. *There*, she thought. *That dot.*

As the crowd stagnated, Milagros was scanning once more for Faisal when déjà vu jolted her. Off to the left. A face she recognized. Not Faisal. A woman. Who? Where? When? A flash of memory. The pixie-haired Johanna, who she'd met along with Velasco from the cemetery on her first trip. Even thinner than before, her face now all angles. Dressed in black in this heat. She held a poster with Velasco's picture. Milagros didn't want to consider "missing" meaning "dead," but the high possibility of it felt like a sudden cold hand at the back of her neck. Milagros wanted to approach her, place a comforting hand on her shoulder. *Remember me?* She made a move toward her, but Mauricio touched Milagros's wrist with one hand. He frowned at his phone.

"Wait." He bent to her ear. "Faisal has been detained. When the crowd finds out, they're going to lose it. We need to leave." To the front of the crowd, a line of police in riot gear—helmets, shields, nightsticks—guarded the building. They were in the midst of assuming a two-layer position, with the front row setting their shields in an unbroken front line and, behind them, the second row of police arraying their shields to form a sloped roof to protect their helmeted heads. Mauricio tugged on Milagros's arm, but just then the crowd surged forward and a Molotov cocktail somersaulted over their heads and exploded against the line of shields. The police responded at once. Tear gas canisters rocketed from the police ranks and dropped among the crowd who screamed, ducked, and scattered. One of the young men reached into the backpack's pocket and then launched a rock at the police. Milagros searched for Johanna, but she was gone. Mauricio too. Then the crowd surged forward, the police pushed back, people fell, and the trampling began.

The first time that the secret police had taken Mauricio was soon after he'd returned from the conference in Miami. They'd only held him for a few days. Charged him with inciting violence with the articles he'd written for American websites. A judge ordered him not to leave the country. His pasaporte was seized. Then the police took him away. Even though he'd been hooded, he knew that he was being taken to El Helicoide. He felt the incline, heard the car's engine whine. That time they just jailed him. Kept him in a cell for a few days. Ignored him. Barely fed him. Then released him. No interrogation, nothing. The second time the police took him, three months before Milagros arrived, he wasn't so lucky. Torture this time. Milagros had asked him what it had been like in there. He'd joked, said they knew that he liked nipple clamps in the bedroom but they hadn't received the memo about his distaste for electricity. He didn't say anything beyond that, but Milagros caught him, a couple of times, staring at the stamps with an image of El Helicoide he had pinned to his fridge. He'd told her that the secret police was proud of their prison fortress and the best way to demonstrate that pride was to issue national stamps. He had purchased the stamps to convince himself that the incident held no power over him. But the way he looked at them, as though he was looking for the window of the room where he'd been caged, told a different story. She'd watched him move over to his desk, his breath heavy, and concentrate on a framed picture of his son. He'd picked it up and gazed at the boy. His breathing gradually returned to normal. It was like he was poisoning himself with the stamps only to take the antidote of the photograph.

The line of riot gear police maintained their defensive stance and everywhere in the crowd was chaos. Horns honked. Rocks flew. The crowd scattered. Milagros kept low to the ground and briefly caught a glimpse of Mauricio scampering by. All around them people shouted, zigzagged toward the sidewalk, abandoned posters that were immediately trampled. Tear gas canisters arced through the air and thunked to the ground. Hit the blacktop, spun, and spat smoke. A young masked protestor charged the wall of police and scrambled over their roof of shields to be received by a battery of nightsticks. Milagros soaked a bandana with water, then tied it around her nose and mouth. More gas canisters arrived, leaving contrails in the air. Screaming, the crowd further scattered. Milagros moved toward the sidewalk, watched as a young woman darted toward a smoking canister in the street, swiped it up, and boomeranged it back toward its point of origin. Milagros tried to shout for Mauricio, but she'd lost him in the tumult, and the gas tightened her throat. Beside her a fraction of space opened, and she filled it. Pushed toward the sidewalk.

Then she heard the familiar hum, the hum that sometimes seeped into her spikiest dreams. Motorcycles. Colectivos. With the line of police in the front, and the men on motorcycles throwing people aside and firing live ammunition into the crowd, the shouts and yells collapsed into screams. Milagros was crouched into a ball with her hands over her head when a voice hissed in her ear and an icy hand touched her neck. It wasn't Mauricio. "Come!" Before her, another explosion. Screams. People scattering. She tried to shake off the stranger's touch. "It's Andres," the voice hissed. Just as he said his name, a blast erupted.

Milagros was lifted and thrown backward.

A few moments after she landed she felt shrapnel injections in her side. Her ears rang. A muffled version of Andres's voice sounded again. "Can you stand?" He helped her to her feet, looped an arm around her waist, and guided her down a side street and through an alley. The roar of the crowd tapered. Dust covered her face as if she'd emerged from a collapsed building. Andres marched them toward a black Land Rover, installed Milagros in the passenger seat, then slid behind the steering wheel. He reversed quickly. "Mauricio," Milagros said, grimacing. Her side felt torn open, and she checked for blood. There was more than a little.

"When the colectivo arrives," Andres countered, shifting the vehicle into gear. "Mauricio knows what to do."

Behind them, another blast.

She thought of Mauricio being separated from his son and maybe never seeing him again, just as she had been separated from Grecia. Then the pain spiked above her waist, and her mind went blank.

Dust swirled. Black smoke from downtown's chaos billowed upward. Milagros searched for her red-tailed hawk, for its gliding wings, but the sky was occupied by three or four black helicopters now. Her side barked. Red decorated her hand. Ribs surely bruised. Possibly broken. She pressed her damp bandana to her side, then reached for her trouser pocket. She still had her phone and her keys, including one for Mauricio's apartment: She called him and his phone rang without answer.

Milagros didn't know what sorcery Andres had indulged, what spell he'd cast, but they were soon skirting Caracas. The car climbed into the hills. "Where are we going?" She thought about Mauricio in El Helicoide.

"A resort was planned up here," he said. "Buildings were built but not finished. Money for the project disappeared, and so did the builders. So the people moved in." They drove past thin shirtless children who ran after the vehicle, laughing and waving. They parked on a flat landing in front of the abandoned resort.

"Come on," he said, sliding out of his door.

Milagros was skeptical, but she followed him. "Where are we going?"

"Keeping you safe per Mauricio's instructions." He chinned over to his left as they walked. "An Olympic-sized pool was meant to go there." There was a large muddy field instead where kids played fútbol. Johanna and Velasco's anecdote about Maldonado's brother, Pedro, returned. "This way."

She followed him through an archway and into a maze of passages that she wouldn't be able to navigate on her own. Andres moved with quick short steps down a slender cinderblock passageway, the space so tight that two people couldn't walk side by side holding hands. She trotted to keep up. As they passed rooms, music fell out, children peered out, adults stepped out to inspect them: a woman holding a colicky infant, a shirtless man sporting a flat-brimmed baseball cap. Milagros glanced into these open doorways; the rooms were mostly painted aqua. The external walls were rough and unfinished.

"Wait here," Andres said when they arrived at a room as nondescript as all the others, except this one was conspicuously bare, aqua walls yes, but no furniture other than a battered Turkish rug centered on the floor and a door to the outside. Before he disappeared deeper into the apartment, Andres turned to her, and she saw him clearly for the first time. Indio. Medium build. Muscled. Hair cut high and tight. Built to blend into any crowd. She saw how he could have been part of a police force. She wouldn't have been surprised if he'd been marching five feet away from her. Then he left. With her adrenaline now fading, Milagros's injuries came into sharper focus—a bruised wrist, a bump on her forehead, and what felt like a javelin stuck in her side. She swallowed a couple of the aspirin that Mauricio had insisted that she bring with them that morning. The walls on either side of the room seemed to squeeze her in and, momentarily, she was back in the marching crowd. She reached out a hand to steady herself with the wall.

She cleared her mind. Did a few deep breaths. In through her nose for four seconds, held her breath for seven, then whooshed out through her mouth for eight seconds.

As painful as it was, she slowly reentered her body. By the time Andres returned, she was again able to stand on her own. But the image of Mauricio being separated from his son in the same way that she had been separated from Grecia came to her mind, and this time it wouldn't be brushed aside. Andres beckoned her, then pointed to a bedroom adjoining the empty Turkish carpeted living room. He posted himself at the outer door so no one else could enter the domicile, and she entered the bedroom.

Inside, Fortunato fed a parrot on his shoulder.

He was slightly more stooped but still sprightly. No apron this time, no room filled with children. Just him and his birds. A quick scan revealed a second parrot perched in the corner. It fluffed its feathers. Doubled its size. There was no third parrot. "Only two?" she asked.

"Time moves on," he shrugged. "We all become eternal." He continued to feed sunflowers to the gray parrot on his shoulder. "Thank you for returning the little girl to her grandmother. They're all each other has."

"When did you get into the business of reuniting families instead of separating them?" Milagros once more felt like she was observing herself from a distance. Like she was separate from herself. Asking the journalistic questions that she shouldn't. An outburst would not help her add to her article or keep her alive. Nor would panic. She breathed again. More discreetly this time.

"All I've ever done is try to help people." The old man shrugged. "Yes, sometimes for a profit." He approached Milagros, then abruptly reached out and grabbed her sore wrist. She felt lightning and winced. Quicker than she expected, his mouth was by her ear. "You've been writing about me," he said. "Asking questions of old women. Reporter questions. Trying to get them to say terrible things about me. And I don't like that. I want you to think very carefully about what your life is worth to you before publishing anything else. Don't dismiss the courtesy that I am affording you." He released her hand, and pain shot down her arm and down into her feet. He turned his back and returned to where he'd been. "Leave Venezuela. And don't delay looking for something that cannot be found."

"The truth cannot be suppressed," she said.

"You would be surprised," he said. "The truth can be bent and—" He went rigid, and Milagros, suspecting a stroke, expected him to keel over. Instead, he went into a trance that she'd seen before, and she found herself holding her breath.

"Past or present," Fortunato said. "Past or present."

"Tell me about my mother," Milagros said to the parrots. She was more familiar with the routine, but in her head the parrots were transporting her into her worst fears: a world where her mother was already gone, and if this were the case, then Milagros just wanted confirmation. Otherwise the dreams of possibility would dance in and out of her mind for the rest of her life. "Is she still alive?"

"You once sailed on a boat filled with lost souls," the first parrot said.

"My mother," Milagros said, hoping her voice could help keep her out of the mental labyrinth of death, "is named Grecia Alzola. Is she still alive?"

"That was the past. Only the present remains," the parrot said. "Only the present remains."

"My mother," said Milagros again. "Is she in Caracas?"

The second parrot swayed. "Your mother awaits you on the island," it said.

"Grecia Alzola?" Milagros asked. "Grecia Alzola is on the island?" But the parrot went quiet and light returned to Fortunato's eyes. He appraised Milagros. Milagros's throat was dry. "How do they know?" she said. "Do you steal children's voices and give them to your birds? Is that what fuels their sorcery?"

He looked at her sadly. "Listen to yourself," he said. "They're just birds."

"They render prophecies," she said.

"The parrots work on their own time," he said. "All I have for you is advice and a lift to the docks. I've provided the first. Andres will assist you with the second." The parrot on his shoulder shuffled from one foot to the next.

"To take me where?"

Fortunato regarded her calmly. "Let me reinforce this advice. Don't write about me. Don't put my name in print. For you this would be disadvantageous. Don't ruffle my feathers and I won't ruffle yours."

Milagros ignored the threat. "Take me where?"

"To the island, of course." He approached the second perch. Fed the parrot there a few sunflower seeds. "Home."

"I thought you didn't remember."

Fortunato looked blank for a moment, and then his face shifted. "The birds? Did they mention the island? How curious."

"Then why are you sending me there?" Milagros cried. "And what about my friend Mauricio?"

"You are more confounding than the parrots. Who is this Mauricio? Why should I care about him?"

"My friend was taken by the police."

"And this doesn't seem like enough warning for you to leave?"

Just then, Andres stepped into the room. Fortunato turned to him. "Why are you two still here?"

Milagros quickly weighed two options—she could attack the old man, plunge her thumbs into his eyes, but her body was too broken for that. She could also spit in his face, but that also would probably result in even more damage to her body from Andres defending his boss. Instead, she hoped that her final words would trouble him: "I've known the damage that you've caused," she said. "And I read the rest of my mother's letter that you deemed fit to withhold from me. I hope your parrot is right, and she's on the island, because I desperately need to learn how you've treated other women like her."

Milagros switched on the Land Rover's radio for news reports, but nothing was said about the protest. She switched it off in frustration. She told Andres that she didn't care where he was taking her, but they needed to make a detour first. He kept his eyes on the road. "I can't take you to Mauricio's," he said. She insisted. Just for a minute. "He's not there," Andres said. They navigated back streets.

"Then let me out right here."

Andres glanced over at her. Performed a quick mental calculation. Asked her for the address.

"You and that brujo both know where he lives," she said.

Mauricio's place was just as they'd left it that morning, but Milagros knew it wouldn't be this way for long. She wondered whether he was connected to Fortunato through Andres or whether Fortunato simply kept tabs on everyone in the city, but she dismissed the thought. Not now. Andres stood guard at the door. He was probably armed, but what was one gun against a squad of jackboots? She moved quickly.

They would come soon after they secured Mauricio. Would toss his apartment. Seize his computer. Take Milagros, if she were still there. Her U.S. permanent residence card would mean nothing. It would probably do more harm than good. They'd pop the staples from her Grenadian passport and pull out each page slowly like wings from a housefly. Shred it before her eyes. She collected one or two more things. Hid some money on various parts of her person. Slung her bag over her shoulder. Just as she turned to leave, she felt a knot of guilt in her back. A stab in her side. Her injuries flaring.

"We good?" Andres asked.

"No," she said. She retrieved the photo of Mauricio's son. Secreted it into her bag. When he returned she'd send it to him. If. "Now," she said. They hurried out of the building.

Fortunato was right; she needed to go to ground. As Andres drove, Milagros didn't pay attention to anything outside her window. Her mind ping-ponged between her mother and Mauricio and whether the fate that seemed to be settling upon her since she had spoken to her mother on her last trip operated on some kind of karmic barter, that she would get to see her mother again, but that she first needed to lose her friend in trade. *You're relying on a parrot's prophecy*, she told herself, the various pains in her body denying her from thinking too long about any one thing. But the parrots had been right before.

The pain in her side exhaled just then, and Milagros winced. Would she accept the trade of Mauricio's freedom in exchange with another conversation with her mother? In exchange for seeing her? The knot of guilt in her back for considering such thoughts wouldn't be untangled. Mauricio had told her he'd been arrested twice before. Would they release him a final time? She couldn't tell any of this to Juanita, the one person with whom she should be able to relay her thoughts, traitorous or otherwise. Milagros couldn't call her. She would have to explain her injuries, and Juanita would blow up. Their argument would devolve once more into the futility of Milagros trying to find her mother, Juanita accusing her of being unable to release the past and what that intimated, that Milagros was afraid of moving into the future with her partner. But how could she explain to Juanita that none of this was futile? That she felt as if she were being pulled along, now more than ever toward her mother? Her mother was alive and on the island. She knew now that this was correct. The parrot confirmed it.

Milagros's pains settled into consistent throbs, and she was able to compartmentalize her treacherous thoughts about Mauricio and think about her mother more clearly.

Faint memories and impressions of her mother came into relief, like rubbing the side of a pencil's point over a blank sheet of paper after the sheet above it had been torn away. The television in her head was finding the signal, clearing the static. Her mother on the boat, squatting to look Milagros in the eyes and saying that if the island tried to separate them that she didn't know what she would do. Her eyes were wet, and just before she pulled Milagros into a rib-crunching hug, Milagros had glimpsed the quartz pendant around her mother's neck. She had never seen her mother wear it before. Maybe she had worn it to keep them together.

Andres pulled up to a depressed-looking dock. They were in Güiria, the same departure point as when she'd left with her mother as a girl, and all the grief for her mother now mixed with her fear for Mauricio, and the knot in her back swelled and mirrored the pain in her side, and then Milagros found herself pushing tears to the side of her face. She grasped the pendant so tightly that it marked her palm again. She felt guilty about leaving when Mauricio was still missing, but she'd decided that she had to go. It felt like the pendant was pulling her, and she was following it, not Fortunato's orders. She might see her mother again.

She hoped that Mauricio would understand.

* * *

She and Andres didn't stand on ceremony after he helped her down to the boat. He returned her bag. Jumped in behind her and handed a thick envelope to the boat's captain.

When he returned to the dock, Milagros touched his arm. "Find him. Please." She couldn't read his eyes. They shook hands.

"Take care," he said, then turned back to the Land Rover.

This boat, unlike the one she'd boarded as a child, was a diamond. All sleek lines. The captain never left the pilot house. His first mate was a shirtless mongoose of a boy, twelve or thirteen, sun-darkened with a mop of unruly hair. He looked familiar, and at first Milagros couldn't place why—and then, as though pulling the memory from fog, realized that he recalled Mark-2. The boy walked the boat's gunwale, sure-footed, and untied the ropes. Besides these two people, Milagros was the only one on the boat. The boat's remaining space, she knew, was to fill with items from the island that would then be smuggled into Venezuela's black market: powdered laundry detergent, powdered milk, powdered sugar.

If the Venezuelan coast guard stopped them Milagros doubted that she alone had enough currency to buy her freedom. She would have almost preferred to be on a boat weighed down with people. She closed her eyes for much of the trip, anxiety balling in her throat to match the knot in her back which connected to the pain radiating down her side which communicated with her hurt wrist. Her body was a switchboard of ache. The thing that calmed her most was telling herself that she *wasn't* going to make it. That the boat would splinter. That the engine would sputter and die. That pirates would intercept them.

The captain was a pro, however, and whomever he was paying off on the island gave them no trouble as they docked a few hours later in a slip with other boats of similar build. She slipped the boy one hundred dollars as she got off. “Muchos éxitos,” she said.

She was here, now, with no idea where to go.

Her mother, on the island. She tried to think where to start, but the pain in her side was building to a crescendo, superseding the aspirin’s effects.

When she looked down she saw her side was bleeding through the towel that Andres had given her. Her wound should probably get stitched up, but this would have to wait. While in the taxi she thought about who to call. When her phone found a signal, she saw Faisal’s and Mauricio’s names were scattered across various social media sites. *#dóndeestáFaisal* and *#dóndeestáMauricio* everywhere, along with the names of dozens of other leaders. Various posts accused SEBIN, Venezuela’s intelligence service, of the violence toward the protestors.

She rubbed her eyes. It was all becoming too much. It was as if her life had folded onto itself and become a paradox, that she was caught in a whirlwind that kept throwing her backward rather than moving her forward. She rummaged in the bag she’d grabbed from Mauricio’s and pressed one of her clean shirts against her wound. She opened her email. Scanned the draft of her article on Fortunato and human trafficking. Added a few more lines. She knew she had enough to publish. She sent it to Saskia.

17

When a Cocrico Flaps Its Wings

WE WERE CLINGING to life on Peter-Called-Peter's boat, which he didn't have time to paint, much less name, all of us still stunned at being chased onto it by a giant tsunami wave that sent us sprinting for the Trooper, then stripping the Trooper's gears as we sped to the Clearing where the boat was almost finished. We clambered aboard and were now clinging to whatever we could upon it as the tsunami wave waters arrived, us mostly holding tight to the gunwale, praying that the water that was now swarming around us and lifting us wouldn't flip us over or spill us. It was the third earthquake in two weeks, we knew, that set it off, this one an 8.2 on the Richter, sucking the water out to the horizon—all of us at first wincing with our hands like visors atop our brows after we ran out of our shaking houses and watched the water disappear—and then shooting it back toward our sand-stolen beach less than five Clearing-scrambling minutes later.

This was the morning that we'd all planned to move, all of us having sold our homes to the Minister of National Security through Hospedales, us deciding to scatter to different parts of the island, except for Binary Clem, who had already left the day before, him having long sold his furniture in his house since Lorraine and Siddiq had already left him and he had no love left to tether him to the structure.

Another thing unsettled us, namely the special guest that Peter-Called-Peter had brought along, the thin woman who Miki had installed in Bunny's house, the one we all knew to be Milagros's mother even though she never came outside or even gazed out the windows, who he'd pulled from Bunny's house when all of us, anxiously waiting in Peter-Called-Peter's Trooper for him *to move it, dammit, Cruickshank*, and looking back over our shoulders at the water that had pulled away from the beach, but was soon to slingshot back toward us in a fury, us wondering why Peter-Called-Peter wasn't already behind the wheel and mashing his foot on the gas and speeding us away.

Instead, Peter-Called-Peter slipped out from the driver's seat, walked toward Bunny's house as if he were taking a gotdamn windy walk on a lover's stroll on the beach, or had forgotten the Trooper's keys on Bunny's bedside table, and when he returned he was holding the hand of Milagros's mother, maybe twenty years older and frail enough that we could see that it looked like she might be with child. "This," Peter-Called-Peter said by way of introduction, "as some of you know, is Grecia Alzola."

We had already known this, of course. What we didn't know was what she had told Peter-Called-Peter about us. Most of us gawped. Some looked away.

Then Peter-Called-Peter said, "Rise up from the front seat, Nello," and Nello sheepishly scrambled to the back of the Trooper with the rest of us.

Grecia lifted her head and ran her eyes over us. "I'm happy to already know some of you," she said as she eyed Miki. "I'm pleased to meet others," she said to Nello. "And some of you I wish I could forget." Here she glared at Hospedales. We looked around at each other and we wondered what it was that Hospedales had done more than the rest of us that made her flatten her eyes at him. She said something softly under her breath in Spanish as she snapped on her seatbelt. And just in time. Behind us we could see the water, done holding its breath in the distance, suddenly exhaling, releasing like an arrow slung toward a bullseye.

Peter-Called-Peter slipped from first gear to second as we raced from the village, us remembering from reports we'd read in the gazette years earlier about the ravaging destruction of the Boxing Day tsunami in Indonesia that Bunny had once told us about, that when the water fully returned in a few minutes it would do so with a hydrogen bomb's furied force, that the seawater would wash away the village and anything that had remained in it, that it would tear apart all of our empty houses like sneeze-filled tissue paper.

We were out on the water, as disoriented as a child getting ready to pin the tail on the donkey, or pressed into piñata service, Peter-Called-Peter's boat rotating through various tsunami-wave revolutions so that we didn't know which way we were pointing when we finally settled. When our stomachs recalibrated, we saw that there was water water everywhere, that there were no landmarks left to orient ourselves since the water was all around us, even covering treetops, and we wondered which direction we should go. "Is a good thing we have a compass," said Nello, and for the first time that we remembered, we saw Peter-Called-Peter look sheepish. "We have a compass right, Cruickshank?" Nello repeated, him always nervy on water, and again Peter-Called-Peter looked away. "But what the jail is this," Nello said. "You mean we don't have a compass?"

"The boat barely finish," said Peter-Called-Peter.

"But we have the sun, man," said Mark-2 the obtuse, us not having the heart to tell him that you couldn't guide a boat by the sun, only by the stars, and although nightfall was still some six or seven hours away, it was overcast, and the only thing that was clear was the trouble we were in.

We waited. Those of us who were meeting Grecia for the first time looked around at those of us who clearly had met her before, since those jokers gave themselves away either by looking off to the sky, or studying the horizoned distance, everywhere but at this newcomer and especially everywhere but at her stomach. And so it was we eventually learned bits of the story of Miki rescuing Milagros, that he'd done so because he had met her about a decade earlier, along with his father Sonny, and his father had taught him to offer help if ever asked. Miki had been able to negotiate purchasing Milagros's freedom from the gentleman's club by taking out a second mortgage on his house, but he could not afford Grecia as well but, luckily, just some weeks later, the special tactics force of the police raided the gentleman's club and rescued all the women including Grecia, and Miki went to pick her up after the police processed and released her.

And it wasn't just Hospedales who'd gone to the Titus boys' gentleman's club, but that it was a few of them who had taken Mark-2 there, as a birthday present, telling him, "If you don't use your piggee on a woman by the time you're a teenager, it will fall off." It was easy now to see who had gone on that man-making adventure, easy to see that Hospedales, Binary Clem, and Mark-2, of course, were all involved, that they had gone to parry, and all of them had clearly gone to Milagros's mother, had lined up at her door, even though they were told by the madam installed at the front door that there were other Spanish on the premises. But something about Grecia's face when she had lined up along with the other women and girls had beguiled the whole troop of them, all of them lagered up and ready, not one of us yet having met Milagros. Now we could see the shame staining the faces of the guilty, who wouldn't even make eye contact with Grecia, except Hospedales, who smirked at her until she jumped across the boat to claw out his eyes, and it took all of Peter-Called-Peter's and Miki's strength to lift her off him, Grecia getting three good-length scratches down one side of Hospedales's face.

"Still a fighter, I see," said Hospedales, and Grecia spat in his face, saying if he had really touched her daughter as he'd kept professing while she was a prisoner, as he'd said whenever he'd visited her with his cheap cologne, that she'd kill him.

Here Miki turned toward Hospedales. "You did *what*? You told her that you'd slept with her daughter?" And then we were pulling Miki off Hospedales, but not before he had gotten in a right cross that opened up Hospedales's lip.

In the late afternoon, we saw them.

The birds.

At first we weren't sure. Half of us had been drinking, so the birds could have been a mirage. We had kept from each other's throats after Miki and Hospedales because we'd had the good sense to pull the cooler from the back of Peter-Called-Peter's Trooper as we abandoned it for his boat, and in there were a large number of long-necked lukewarm lagers, two bottles of coconut water, some rum, puncheon, and babash, and even a couple of bottles of gratefully misplaced water. We reserved the coconut water for Mark-2 and the water for Grecia. "Don't get *too* drunk," Peter-Called-Peter warned the rest of us.

"Shaddup," said Hospedales.

It was Mark-2 who'd seen the birds first and, feeling the most shame-faced of all of us for having done whatever he'd done with Milagros's mother, he pointed them out flying low across the water.

"Is what kind of birds is that?" he asked.

Miki squinted. "Cocricos," he said.

"Jumbie birds," Hospedales said. "Steer away from them, Cruickshank."

"Cocricos aren't seabirds," Miki said. "They'll head for land soon. Steer toward them, Cruickshank."

"But where they heading?" Nello asked.

"Venezuela," said Grecia, the first thing that she'd said for a while, her surprising us with the gravel in her voice. And although she'd spoken just above a whisper, all of us heard her clearly. Peter-Called-Peter pointed the boat toward the birds. Land was land. We could figure things out later.

By now the water had somewhat settled. When the waves had first accosted us, they'd roiled, and Peter-Called-Peter at the tiller was holding a heated nautical disagreement with the waves. He surprised us with his skill. At one point a rogue wave had rebuked Peter-Called-Peter in a watery riposte, a wet retort, and it was only his savvy as a captain, which we didn't know that he had, which we hadn't seen before when we were fishing, that kept us from capsizing. Still, the wave had lifted us some twenty feet in the air, and when we'd smashed back down on the surface of the water, we'd all felt that the boat would crack in half, us still getting drenched and wishing we knew the words to whatever prayer it was that the glasses and goateed UWI graduate was feverishly intoning in his corner of the boat. So when the waters calmed, and we saw that pair of brown fowl flapping low over the ocean, their feet skimming the water, we were much more settled.

We hoped that they were pushing toward land.

We crossed our fingers.

Three hours in and Grecia had calmed down somewhat, but we placed her as far from Hospedales as we could. She wasn't too pleased with other passengers, but it was Hospedales in particular for whom she clearly held the most venom. After a few hours, we grew languid in the heat, our beer-battered brains simmering, all of us grateful for the sunset and mentally cursing Peter-Called-Peter for not building some shade on his blasted boat. All that we heard now was the sound of the boat's engine, us trying not to think of what would happen when we ran out of gas, Peter-Called-Peter only just having filled it up the first time from the now empty jerry cans. The birds still flew ahead of us, them not having once rested, and it unsettled us that they meant to sail us off the end of the earth, recalling ibises and Catherine the Great Disemboweler.

Mark-2, who had lowered his head atop the cooler, finally straightened his back and asked, "Where we going?" He was afraid, and he blinked rapidly, maybe from the sea spray, but probably so that he had an excuse for his eyes watering. He was right. South America should have appeared by now, and none of us wanted to utter the truth—that we were directionless on open waters and were drifting without compass or consequence.

"Curaçao," said Hospedales.

"Aruba," said Miki.

"Venezuela," said Grecia. We still hoped that we hadn't been on the water too long for any of those to be destinations we'd shot past. We waited for Peter-Called-Peter to throw in his two navigational cents from the tiller.

"We're running low on gas," he said instead, and at the same moment another rogue wave lifted us in a swell, then crashed us back down to the water's surface, all of us gripping the sides of the boat, concentrating on not being thrown overboard. Deluded, we denied that we owned only a fistful of zabocas to eat, a dribble of gasoline to power us, but all the beer that we could handle, to render us in a dreamy morphined haze.

We kept our eyes on the birds, still flying low ahead of us, this other bird sent to countermand the ibis.

The next birds we all recognized on our own: a kettle of corbeaux circling above us. We didn't mention them to each other, already knowing what they represented. As evening approached, Hospedales tapped his cane and said, "I think we really heading in the wrong direction you know," and Nello laughed.

Some of us braved a look at Grecia, her body limp, her head pressed against Peter-Called-Peter's legs. She didn't seem particularly bothered, her knees drawn up to her chin hiding that child belly that guilted us, her body present but her mind breaking biche. When she spoke next and asked where Milagros was, all of us avoided her eyes, whether or not we had tortured this woman with our past actions, except for Hospedales, who had tortured her worst of all by saying he'd slept with her daughter, which we hoped was a lie. "You," she said, kicking Miki's foot. "When you rescued Mila you promised me that you would keep her safe for me. That when I saw you again, you said that you would take me to her. Just like your father took care of me long ago." She kicked his foot once more, harder this time. He shifted his foot. "But here I am, seeing you, but I'm not seeing her. Where's Milagros? Where's my daughter?"

Then Grecia buried her head in her hands and wept, and we cowards looked off into the ocean, again except Hospedales who instead looked like he was coming up with something terrible in his reptile Hospedales brain, some new kind of taunt, imagined or real, this woman sparking his desire for cruelty. We wondered if he went to different women in that brothel, and whether he used rubbers with them, maybe landing them in even more trouble, offending them even further, with big bellies. Then Grecia started to talk about Milagros, telling us about her as a child, about how it was an act of God that she hadn't been born with asthma when every other child in their town had developed it. She knew Milagros was a lucky child because of this, and even though she knew it was a risk to boat over to our island with no prospects, no papers, and no pasaporte, it was because she knew that Milagros was blessed, that she'd been, in some way, *chosen*, that Grecia had taken the risk to boat over to our island, thinking that her daughter would serve as a talisman of fate, her returning to the land of her father.

"So what went wrong?" Nello asked quietly.

She said things didn't work out exactly as she'd planned.

"Still," she said, and she looked from Miki to Peter-Called-Peter. "There are some good people on this island," she said. "There are people who are kind and decent and know how they should act toward those not as fortunate, those who are not as well-off." We expected her to turn an accusatory eye on Hospedales, but she didn't. She had stopped looking at him at all, like she didn't want to remember that he existed, but those of us who looked closely saw the pulsing vein in her neck. She just kept looking down at the deck and talking about Milagros, saying that she was sure that it was Milagros being on their boat from Venezuela to the island that had kept them from sinking, that there had been worse waves than those that were troubling us now. And she kept asking again, where is Milagros, asking us and not Hospedales, still not looking at him, and for some reason none of us could say anything at all.

Through all of this we snuck glances at Hospedales at the boat's bow, saw that he'd pulled a toothpick from somewhere, held his walking cane between his legs and was now the very picture of louche nonchalance, his straw fedora pulled low, and the toothpick hanging out of one corner of his mouth, and it was here that we wondered whether what he'd said he'd done to Milagros was true, whether he was being cruel for cruelty's sake or whether he had some great design of viciousness toward Venezuelan women.

"Milagros is safe," Miki said then. We were surprised at this tactic, this graying of the truth. Milagros is safe with our friend Bunny in Grenada," Miki said.

Here Grecia lifted her head, and her face brightened. She looked up at Peter-Called-Peter. "Is this true?" she asked, but it was Miki who answered again.

"We sailed them safely over there months ago," Miki said, him looking like something had fluttered free from his heart. And maybe we all wanted to feel that way too, because then we told her about Bunny, about how she'd kept Milagros since she'd arrived in our village, how she'd kept her safe, how she'd kept her protected from malfeasance. How she'd taken Milagros to Grenada to keep her even safer. Here

Grecia swallowed a swig of water, as if this news suddenly revitalized her thirst and her desire to live. And, for the first time, even those of us who had done something evil to Grecia felt slightly redeemed, us telling Grecia how we'd helped Milagros with her English, how we'd protected her from sand pirates, how we'd kept her from seeing dead bodies on our way to Grenada. We said that Grenada was the safest place for her, that the turmoil on our island and our village couldn't travel that far, and that Milagros and Bunny were much safer there than on Venezuela or on our island.

"Oh," said Grecia, crying again. "God bless Bunny. God bless the good ones among you." Then, in a fluid motion, she turned her head and spat once more in Hospedales's face. He didn't flinch. This was a man who had previously been shot. He just calmly retrieved a handkerchief and wiped his face and continued to look like he was considering some kind of plan.

"But your daughter's not safe," Hospedales said softly five minutes later. "These cowards are lying to you." He shifted the toothpick from one corner of his mouth to the next, and we looked at each other, wary of his new burgeoning cruelty. "Nello's brother Caleb sent us a letter weeks ago saying that Bunny and Milagros were lost. That they'd gone down to the beach and that both had disappeared. That the police had conducted a search and hadn't found a trace of them." Hospedales grinned evilly.

We wavered. "That's not true," said Nello. "That's not true. They're in New York."

Hospedales lifted his eyebrows at Grecia. "See? They just told you that they were in Grenada. Is there a Grenada in New York? Like there's a Jamaica in Queens?"

Grecia laughed a bit, then dropped her arms between her knees. "Every time you talk to me it's a new lie," she said. "Every time you would visit me in that filthy room, with your dirty cologne, there was a new lie. More lies than stripes on a tiger." She seemed much calmer. "You stank of lies that your cologne couldn't hide. You can't overpower me anymore. I am free of that cage. I know that I will see my daughter again. I know this because my love for her cannot be weighed down by the anchor of your lies. I know this because I have spoken to her right here." She touched her chest, impervious to Hospedales's words. Then she closed her eyes and smiled softly. For half a minute she seemed to be doing breathing exercises. When she was done, she turned her face to the sky as if the sky had requested it. She said some words softly beneath her breath. And then, before anyone could do anything, a blade appeared in her hand, and it flashed as she leaned across and plunged it right where Hospedales's liver would be.

Later, Nello would claim that Hospedales had seemed to have been expecting it. Because Nello said he'd seen Hospedales turning the lion's head that decorated the top of his walking stick. *Unscrewing* the head. That in the moments before Grecia lunged, he'd pulled a blade free from the cane's guts as if he were retrieving a hatpin from a churchgoer's Easter hat. And Nello swore that Hospedales had stretched out to stab Grecia before she'd reciprocated in kind.

In her wounded state, Grecia refused everything but sips of coconut water. Miki had been the one who wrestled the knife from her hand, but she'd accomplished her goal, and he had a difficult time calming her down because the blood from her wound was coming faster than he knew what to do with it. He'd stripped his T-shirt from his body and held it against her side, but the T-shirt soon turned the color of her blood. So he sat beside her and tried to maintain the pressure. Nello had turned to help Hospedales, to help him with his own wound just above where one lung resided, the blood flowing much more quickly than even the blood from Grecia's wound, the blood gushing from Hospedales, so much of it coming so fast, telling us that there was no way for us to stop it.

Grecia looked out into the distance, and her gaze was so clear-eyed, so focused, that we were sure that she was looking at something specific, even though we knew that her life was leaving her. We followed her eyes until it came into sharper focus for us. Out on the horizon we saw them, saw that she was looking at Catherine the Great Disemboweler and her mother Hany, them standing about fifty feet out on the water, both dressed in blinding white.

"Gs + Hs," we heard Nello say, and we saw him look toward the rest of us, but he didn't have to add anything; we saw them as well. We knew that all of us seeing Catherine the Great Disemboweler and her mother was not a good sign, that it was, along with both Grecia and Hospedales now being stabbed, the worst possible signal for us, worse than the cocricos who'd been guiding us having now disappeared, worse than the corbeaux overhead now growing exponentially in number, them looking like huge bats in the dusk ready to dive-bomb.

We assessed Hospedales, who bled through the blanket that Nello held against his wound. We looked at Grecia, pale and sweaty, Miki pressing his shirt against her deep laceration.

It was here that the glasses and goateed UWI graduate spoke, him saying that he wondered if all of us were already dead, and whether Peter-Called-Peter was the dread boatman Charon meant to ferry us to the underworld. Here the despondent Mark-2 released a loud sob, and Miki gave You-We a big cut-eye. Hospedales was groaning from his wound. Miki was holding Grecia, who was babbling, her looking off toward Catherine the Great Disemboweler and her mother and saying *what would I have to give up? What would*

I have to trade? and Miki trying to calm her down, his arms wrapped around her. You-We continued speaking, saying that we were all paying for each other's transgressions, all of our sins and mistakes, and that we would soon learn what the dire outcome would be, what the wages of sin were. He said that he suspected that we'd crossed the thin membrane between life and afterlife when we'd climbed aboard the boat and the tsunami wave was what had snipped the fragile line that had connected us to life. Grecia continued to look out across the ocean to the figures of Catherine the Great Disemboweler and her mother, talking to them, from what we could tell bargaining for her life, her pupils dilated, as large as shillings, her saying over and over again *I need to see Mila. I need Mila to be safe until I can see her again. I need to see Mila.*

Finally, You-We stopped talking, but the silence that he'd left behind seemed too heavy a burden to bear. It was here that Peter-Called-Peter turned the tiller over to Nello—"Keep us straight, Nello," he said—and he tried to patch up Hospedales as best as he could, tearing strips from his white linen shirt to wrap around Hospedales's stomach. "You're making these injuries a habit now," he joked, but Hospedales sat in silent shock.

Peter-Called-Peter finally sat back beside Hospedales, exhausted, his hands soaked in blood. "That's the best I could do, breds." Hospedales, his pupils just as swollen as Grecia's, nodded. He held his cane tightly.

We sat silently for a few more moments, shivering with our own thoughts, until static crackled the air, the sound of Peter-Called-Peter switching on his transistor radio. At first, with only the static's scratch coming through, we wondered whether the Mighty-Penguin-Mighty-Shadow-Bob-Marley-24-7 radio station had been lost, or was too far away for us to pull its signal, but then finally the static settled and we heard music. But it wasn't any of those three bards that we were used to hearing, but a new voice added to the pantheon, a fourth voice. It was a Venezuelan station that we heard, and although we didn't know what they were singing, we imagined that there was something in there that sounded to us like some kind of mercy.

18

A Cluster of Butterflies, and a Fury of Hummingbirds

MILAGROS AND HER grief and her tender ribs were lying low with Bunny and her husband Yoshi at Bunny's reconstructed house in New Felicity Village. It was Yoshi and his rudimentary first aid skills that patched her up even though he urged her to go to the hospital. "A scratch," she said.

"More than a scratch."

"Two scratches then."

"Tough woman, eh?"

Yoshi was a serene replacement for the chipped men from the village's past—a missing tooth here, a floating eye there, a bulleted leg—all of them gone, and now, with this new house supplanting the village's sagging forebears, including Catherine the Great Disembow-eler's notorious house of ill repute, and a smooth beach replacing the rickety jetty and the splintery boats and the missing sand, this New Felicity was a cosmetic reflection of the village's past.

Except.

Venezuelans still unsteadily boated their way to the island. With the village all but gone, including its jetty, newcomers were forced to disembark in the water, causing them to suck in their breaths as they jumped from the boats, the water surprising them, splashing some-times to their ears, sometimes to their chests, or sometimes to their chins, the adult newcomers holding smaller children above the water as if offering them to the sky.

They kept coming, kept risking, because Bunny and Yoshi had done something remarkable—they'd appropriated the old plantation house and repurposed it as a place for the newcomers. What had previously been trepidation after the new arrivals' journey now felt something adjacent to welcome. Bunny and Yoshi now taught kindergarten at Abercromby House for about a dozen Venezuelan children. They held basic English language classes for their parents. One or two families also temporarily stayed at Abercromby House until they found more permanent accommodations. Others found themselves in Bon Bois a village away. The refugees were startled to have enough food to eat, sometimes more in a week than they'd had for a month. It was too much for some. Many broke down in gratitude.

Milagros, when she arrived where the village used to be, exhausted, dust-covered, and aching, was overwhelmed by her return and any last drips of adrenaline abandoned her. Her torn side screamed, and she all but collapsed in Bunny's arms. Bunny put her to bed at once. It took Milagros a day to recover, with Yoshi cooking ground provision soup for her dinner, Bunny reflexively ferrying in tea for Milagros throughout the day, and Milagros downing more analgesics than recommended on the bottle. What sat outside the windows brought memories, so she avoided them. Her side still screamed, her wrist still ached, and against Bunny's recommendation she continued scrolling fruitlessly through her phone for information about Mauricio or Faisal, for sources on the island who might be able to help her locate her mother. For her mother herself, as though she'd find her on the internet after all this time. Her mind was still a frenzy. So when Milagros finally took to her feet toward the end of that first day, and wandered unevenly down to the beach, the waves' sighs calmed her in a way that she hadn't anticipated. The beach rendered the landscape more picturesque than she recalled. True, there were a couple of abandoned derricks about a quarter of a mile from the village entrance that applied for eyesore status, but only one of them had been switched on before nature had its way, the tsunami sweeping through, shutting down the derricks as if saying: enough.

Milagros was standing on the beach with a glass of sea moss and looking out toward a hazy South American mainland when Bunny joined her. Gray threaded through Bunny's hair now, and crow's feet had claimed the corners of her eyes. Milagros estimated that Bunny must have been around Milagros's current age when she took her in, but now she had gracefully shifted into her fifties. Looking at her, Milagros was struck, for a moment, with profound admiration: the woman who had stunned a shark in her youth, who had helped Milagros to find her feet and find direction, had finally traveled to Japan and found, fell in love with, married, and returned with, one of the few Caribbean Japanese men there. She'd mapped a plan for her life and stuck to it.

They kept their eyes on the horizon. "Tell me a bit more about what happened here," Milagros said. "Where have all the local characters gone off to?"

"I'd tell you if I knew. The men all disappeared after the tsunami, not long after we left for Grenada. But no one thinks they're dead."

"And no contact from any of them?"

"None."

"Do you think they're alive?"

Bunny shook her head. "Who knows? It happened over fifteen years ago. They've always been resilient, although their judgment was often questionable. They were mostly good men even though they were always bad boys. I wouldn't be surprised if they've founded a men's-only commune for over-the-hill high-functioning alcoholics."

"And what about the women? The wives, mothers, sisters? Stacy? Miss Titus?"

"Scattered around the island. I've reached out to a few of them, but they're just as confused about what happened after the tsunami. They weren't here when it occurred." What she didn't have to add: *Neither was I.*

"And they're okay with their men missing?" Milagros was gazing toward Venezuela and thinking about her continued pursuit. Her permanent pursuit. *How could the women stop looking for their families?*

"They've all experienced some sort of trauma. Unfortunately, it's just another strike on most of their ledgers."

Milagros stood in silence for a moment, weighing her words. Then she said, "Do you remember Imogen?"

She expected Bunny to stiffen, but her eyebrows merely raised.

"That crazy woman from the beach?"

They had not spoken of her in fifteen years.

"I was surprised she was real, you know," Bunny added.

"She said I would see my mother again," Milagros said. "Do you think she could be on the island?"

Now Bunny looked surprised. "Your mother?" Milagros held her breath. "Is that why you returned?"

"I've had some information that suggests she's on the island."

Bunny shook her head. Milagros.

"Would anyone possibly have information? Maybe someone from the police who shut down that club?" Milagros saw something that she hadn't expected from Bunny. Not bewilderment, but something close to disappointment. She momentarily recalibrated. "Let's forget the ghosts for a bit. Tell me about the present. Tell me about Yoshi. About your project here."

Mild smile lines creased Bunny's face. She took one of Milagros's hands, so gently that there was no memory of the pain that previously troubled her wrist. "Mila," she said. We can discuss all of that later. If not a sabbatical from being a journalist, then at least take a breath while you're here. For now, more rest." Still, as they returned to her house, Bunny explained aspects of the halfway house's operation. Explained that she and Yoshi worked with a local charity that outfitted the new arrivals with clothing, food, and medicine.

"What about government assistance?"

Bunny's smile faded. "Their allowing us to do this is assistance enough."

Milagros shook her head. "I never thought you'd end up running a halfway house for Venezuelan refugees."

Bunny shrugged. "No one knows the future."

"And at that house no less." Milagros recalled strobe light snatches of her experiences at the old plantation house underscored by brief mentions in her mother's letters, both of them kept there against their wills, and Milagros kept separated from her mother. She had repressed most memories of her time there. The house had been sinister then, and Milagros wondered if she could even enter it now, whether she could cross its threshold. Had Bunny known about Milagros's time there? To what extent? Milagros couldn't remember. She knew Bunny wouldn't bring it up, so she wouldn't either. She remembered Miki rescuing her; he always owned a special place in her heart. Now a tsunami victim.

"Abercromby House's history will always remain problematic," Bunny said. "The government considered razing it after the tsunami. But when the structure wasn't even damaged, much less washed away, they reneged." She wrinkled her nose. "Then reconsidered wanting to be associated with a plantation house, even as a museum. Then, like various other government initiatives, they just forgot about it. If I were to guess I would say that the contractors felt some kind of evil force and wanted nothing to do with it. I'm hoping that repurposing it will help reverse some of that."

Milagros snorted. "You don't believe in any of that, do you?" She drained her drink. "Did you have someone bless it?"

Bunny smiled mischievously. "Yoshi performed a secular sutra."

Milagros laughed, then grew quiet thinking about the house's history, its dark secrets, her mother's own relationship with it, her temporary stay in it. Despite all her research, all the work on her article, she hadn't thought about what it was like to be there for so long. What it was like to be *here* for so long. She remembered New Felicity in bites and crumbs, half a dream here, a flash of a vision there. The beach. The Clearing. Her mind drifted to her mother's words about it, her letter.

"Did you avoid the Clearing," she asked Bunny, "because of what it could do? What it is capable of?"

"And what is it capable of?" Bunny asked innocently. "Should Yoshi perform a sutra there too?"

"Bunny."

Bunny waved her away. "Jumbie stories," she said.

"Does anyone ever go there?" Milagros asked.

Bunny shook her head. "The bigger children go now when they want to scare themselves."

"The men used to drink there," Milagros said.

Bunny shrugged. "They used to drink everywhere."

Milagros knew she couldn't continue with the subject much longer. That just discussing the space unsettled Bunny too much regardless of her dismissing it. "How many times have you been?"

"Just once." She paused. "Twice." She shrugged. "Maybe three times."

Although she hadn't seen Bunny in so many years, she could still read the look she gave her: *Please stop*. But Milagros needed a few more answers. The journalist in her pushed. She measured her words. "Is Abercromby House connected to the Clearing in some way?"

"That would be a question for those men," she said. "Nello liked to bring up the distant past." She paused, and her eyes unfocused. "Royston did some research, if I remember. Used to spend a lot of time dredging up the terrible past of the plantation."

Milagros pulled a thumb drive from her hip pocket. Handed it over. Bunny pulled on eyeglasses and inspected it. "I don't follow."

"A gift from Royston Burns a long time ago."

Bunny searched her memory. “You-We?”

“He started writing it. A history of the village.”

“When did he give this to you?”

“Just before we left for Grenada. A sort of peace offering. He was contrite about offending me one time. Offending us.”

“He’d said something to you one time,” Bunny remembered. “We had just come back from a boat ride with Miki.”

“I remember,” Milagros said, “the trip but not the details.” Small memories returned. “Anyway, he’d researched and documented a lot of the history of the village. History of the family that owned the sugarcane estate here. At one point the Clearing was one of the sugarcane fields.”

“I don’t doubt it.” Bunny held up the thumb drive to the light as if inspecting a diamond’s color and clarity. “I don’t doubt it at all.” She handed it back.

“Mostly harmless academic stuff. But he annotates the history of the Clearing. The Scottish Cruickshank. A spirit of the Clearing named Mama Binti.”

“Oh lord,” Bunny said. “That jumbie story.”

“Is that all it is?”

Bunny saw where Milagros was leading her. “You think that place holds some kind of magical connection to your past. To your mother. Your parents.”

“Am I being silly?”

Bunny sighed. Stood. Retrieved a piece of paper from her purse. Scribbled on it. “This,” she said, “is an address. Don’t say it out loud or you won’t ever be able to find it.” She gave Milagros an amused look over her glasses’ frames. “Supposedly. But when you get there, someone may be able to help you with this folklore that you’re so insistent on validating.”

Milagros studied the address. Wanted to set out right away, but Bunny wouldn’t let her go alone. She didn’t want the night to catch her there. "You don't know that part of the island," Bunny said. "I'll send someone along with you in the morning." She gauged Milagros's eagerness. "Tomorrow," she repeated.

That night, nervous and excited, Milagros texted Juanita. *Just wanted you to know that I'm on the island*, she texted, *and that I'm fine. How are you?* She didn't expect a response. Nothing on Faisal or Mauricio either. She reread her mother's letters. Her journal. She fell asleep with Grecia's words spread out around her.

The next morning, Milagros was ready to leave at 8:00 a.m. Bunny and Yoshi had already left for the refugee house, and when Milagros saw that whomever Bunny had promised to assist her on the trip wasn't coming, she sank her breakfast plates into the sink and tried to figure out how to get herself there. She was about to leave when a knock sounded at the front door. She opened it to find someone who occupied the shadows of her memory, but each time she tried to shine a light on it, he stepped farther into the dark. Then his name caught her off guard: Clem. Lorraine's ex-husband. He was sheepish, this last man from New Felicity Village. He now lived one village over at a rooming house in Bon Bois, his house in New Felicity long sold, then washed away. He beamed at Milagros. "Good to see you one zero," he said. She remembered him as thin, but now he was gray as well. A harmless sheep too old for slaughter. She spied the slight tremor in his hands.

"So you're my guide," she said.

His grin was genuine. "Haven't seen you in donkey years zero zero one." He scratched his nose. "The last time was when all the ibises showed up zero one zero." She tried to think if they'd ever spoken to each other before this moment. Probably, but she still regarded him as an insect in her memory's amber.

It was as they walked toward the main road for a taxi to take them into town that he began to apologize. He said that he'd spent time with her mother in the estate house. "Nothing indecent one zero one," he said, but he hung his head. He'd only talked to her, he insisted, but he didn't do anything to help her either. He realized this was wrong, and it had troubled him for a long time.

Milagros squeezed his shoulder. Here was someone who had known Grecia. With each moment she felt like her mother was a whisper away. As if recalling the right memory would produce her.

It took a few taxis. They drove to a part of the island with which, as Bunny noted, Milagros was unfamiliar, and she was grateful for Clem's company. They ended up in the main county within the capital in a town where the houses were knitted closely together, as tight as hands joined in prayer. It was a working-class neighborhood that had been settled by emancipated Africans. The taxi driver wouldn't drive her to the exact address; he said he didn't know it. But Milagros could tell it was because he was fearful. "I know it, man, zero one zero," Clem said as he hopped out. "Only about five minutes' walk." The walk helped stretch her back. As they strode ahead it was clear that this wasn't a neighborhood that easily suffered strangers, but Clem knew people. He lifted a hand to hail a man here, said righto to a woman there. "This way," he said, leading them up a slight incline.

They cut across a field that held a large square of grass, discolored from having been covered for a stretch of time, Milagros suspected, with a tent of some kind. "Faith revival business zero zero," Clem said. "This way one one zero." Their destination was the upper unit of a two-family abode. They needed to go through a large red door to gain the yard.

On the ground floor that surrounded the building there were weeds mixed with flowers, with butterflies darting above them. But what first seemed like ten or twenty monarchs grew exponentially each time Milagros blinked, so that by the time they arrived at the foot of the staircase, there were over three hundred butterflies. The effect of them stopped her in mid-breath. Clem snapped her back to reality and, toward the rear of the building, they climbed an external staircase to the upper unit. The butterflies didn't follow. At the top was a blue door split through the middle like a belt. Binary Clem knocked hard. Then he took Milagros's hand and pulled her back a step, just in time to avoid the top half of the door swinging out and clouting her in the face.

A young boy, no older than ten, stuck his head out. He was so short that he must have been standing on a stool. He wore a T-shirt that said BOOTS, BOOTS, BOOTS. His eyes were gold. The boy eyed Milagros for a few moments. "What you need?" he asked.

"I want to . . . I'm here about . . . the Clearing." The little boy just watched her, his gold eyes unblinking.

Clem spoke up. "We need to buy a calabash one one one," he said. The boy's eyes moved to Clem, studied him too, then he slammed the door.

Milagros was confused. "Should we leave?"

"Wait zero zero," Clem said. Five minutes later the top half of the door swung open again, and this time an aged woman stood there, taller than Clem, her face a nest of wrinkles, and whose gold eyes had no reason to still be that clear at her age. That sharp. She wore a green headwrap tied tightly to her scalp. She wore the same T-shirt that the boy who was just there had worn, and when she spoke, she spoke with the boy's voice as well.

"So you here for a calabash?" the woman asked Clem.

"Yes, miss, zero one zero."

"Is for you or for her?" The woman assessed Milagros.

"Me, miss," said Milagros.

"So why he talking?" She turned to Milagros. "What the calabash for?"

Milagros turned to Clem, who remained silent. "I'm looking for my mother Grecia," Milagros said. "In New Felicity Village."

The woman remained still for a moment then bent down out of sight. When she reappeared she held a large gourd. She laid it on the door's sill. Just as Milagros reached for it, the woman gripped Milagros's hand with a claw's strength, and Milagros's wrist buzzed with recounted pain. The woman's gold eyes were terrible. "You sure you know what you're doing?" she asked.

"I only know that I'm looking for mi mami," Milagros said. "And I was told that you could help."

The woman released Milagros's hand. "Plant this in a large open space with rich soil," the woman said, handing the calabash over the door's equator to Milagros. From the way that the woman had held the gourd with one hand, Milagros thought that the calabash would be manageable, but when she took it into her hands, the weight of it almost made her drop it crashing to the ground.

As Milagros struggled under the weight, the woman quoted a price. Clem pulled out his wallet before Milagros could blink. The woman kept her gold eyes on Milagros as she folded the money into her bosom. She watched them walk down the staircase and into the field of butterflies.

The butterflies clustered around Milagros's face as she walked, and Binary Clem produced a racing pool betting form to fan them away. The butterflies didn't just gravitate toward Milagros, but to the burden that she carried, the calabash making her seem pregnant, and she barely made it out of the yard. Most of the butterflies remained behind in the field and were gone by the time Milagros and Clem reached the road. No eyes from the neighborhood followed them on the way out. Based on the diminishing trail of butterflies, everyone knew who it was that Milagros had been to see, and they wanted nothing to do with her.

Due to the calabash's weight, Milagros had to stop a few times to rest as she and Clem walked to the city's taxi stand. Clem didn't offer to help; they somehow both knew she had to carry it on her own.

It was early afternoon by the time they returned to New Felicity. She thanked Clem for his help. She tried to reimburse him, but he wouldn't hear of it. "Happy to help one one one," he said. With a wave of his hand, he made his way back to his own village, his step featherlight.

Milagros planted the calabash in the Clearing that same evening. Bunny refused to accompany her, but Yoshi went along. They arrived at dusk. Yoshi carried a spade while Milagros struggled with the calabash. She knew that she had to dig the hole herself. It took her a long time to spade the earth deep enough to deposit the gourd. "Now what?" she asked herself once she filled in the hole, breathing heavily.

"Say the magic words and there should be a beanstalk in the morning," Yoshi joked. They stood for a moment inspecting the fresh earth, which looked uncomfortably like a grave, and Milagros grew aware of how little she knew about Yoshi. He'd been mentioned in an email. She'd seen pictures of him and Bunny online, Bunny saying he owned a mischievous sense of humor, a boy's humor really. So when his voice came again, deeper this time, a statesman's voice as they stood there, she startled. "She really missed you, you know. When I met her in Japan, and I asked her to talk about the island, to help fill in the stories that my parents had given me, instead she talked about you."

"That's kind of her," Milagros said, not knowing how else to sidestep her sudden discomfort. She didn't think she was with Bunny long enough for Bunny to unfurl several pleasant memories. She wondered what she'd said but didn't ask. If Bunny wanted to give Yoshi a full picture, she would have needed to tell him how much she'd ached for her mother, how she threw tantrums to want to be with her again. Now the same ache sharpened, and she briefly felt the need to stamp her feet and demand her mother's return. She was glad to have sent the article to Saskia.

Ricardo Maldonado had been to this dusty little village behind God's back so many times that he knew it like parts of his body. Even with the falling-down jetty gone, and the sand that he'd helped excavate somewhat replenished, the village felt too familiar. He knew where everything fit. He paused at the derrick that had been turned on and then off. Stopped to feel the sun on his face. The village had always been good to him.

He inspected the replenished sand. He'd been told there was only so much on the planet. A limited resource. It was why this sand had to be stolen. But look how it had been filled back in. Almost as good as before.

The village had become a ghost of itself when the oil derricks had arrived, forced down on its knees and awaiting a final blow to dispatch it. That he'd helped make it so didn't trouble him. The villagers had been doing it to themselves, and the place had been dying bit by bit. Day by day. What was a fishing village without fish? Maldonado knew that the ridiculous gentleman's club that the minister had secretly bankrolled had been a silly idea, but his job was not to poke holes in silly ideas, only to execute Fortunato's assignments. He did his part and he was paid. This was the axis on which his world spun. The Minister of National Security was not as surgically precise as Ebrahim Fortunato, but he didn't have the assistance of prophesying parrots.

Maldonado stooped and lifted a handful of the golden sand, let it spill through his fingers. There had been only so much the village could give—first the sand, and then the oil—before it collapsed upon itself. No body could donate all of its organs and survive. And the final collapse, via tsunami he'd heard, had been spectacular. But the water had receded, and the land remained. Now the villagers were gone, but the little girl, Milagros, now a woman, was back. It wasn't long before he'd gone to prison that she'd disappeared from the island, along with that steadfast woman who looked after her. He'd liked that woman. The fight in her. Maldonado had thought about her while he'd been in prison. Thought about all the characters who he had encountered here, the men with their fake machismo. They'd protected their women. He would give them that. The men threw themselves in front of the women as far as they could without taking the bullets that he'd threatened them with. It seemed like on the island he was always under obligation to shoot, either by direct order or at Fortunato's discretion.

Fortunato had wanted the minister shot, had said that the country's government was cleaning up corruption and would eventually nail the minister, that sooner or later he would give Fortunato's name. Under orders, Maldonado had shot D'Souza, but he must have either been wearing a vest or had lived a charmed life, because he was still walking around. When Fortunato'd had Maldonado broken out of prison in just over a month, he had heard that the minister calmed the resulting uproar by saying that Maldonado had been extradited to Venezuela, where he was also a wanted man. Fortunato said this was according to plan. Maldonado never questioned the old man's decision. There was a method. A grand blueprint. The parrots knew.

And now Fortunato wanted the woman silenced. Liquidated. Maldonado hadn't asked. He never did. Who knew how Fortunato's mind operated once his silly perriquitos whispered in his ear. They had probably advised him that the woman was now bad news, that she'd become tainted in some immeasurable manner. Most likely she'd written an article that shone a light on Fortunato's activities. That's what Andres had thought. But Andres wasn't called on to do this dirty work. Whatever the transgression, it meant that her wings, so to speak, needed to be clipped. *Why hadn't Fortunato just had her taken care of in Venezuela?* When a fly grew to be annoying and wouldn't exit an open window, then you rolled up a magazine. Maldonado dusted the rest of the sand from his hands, stood, and stretched.

There were no village houses left, them all having been washed away by the great wave. But there was one house that had been rebuilt, and it was that house to which Maldonado now went. He entered Bunny's home, knowing at once that it was empty. It was a knack he had—to know immediately if a building was occupied. But in return he was never certain if people who would return to an empty house would also sense his presence. To some extent everyone owned this knack. It frustrated him not knowing to what extent others shared his ability.

He removed his boots at the front door. Glided through the house. He found Milagros's room, flipped through the diary on the bedside table. If she wasn't here, then she had to be at the house that was once a brothel. It was the only other structure remaining. Maldonado stood. It would have been easier if she'd been here at the house, but it didn't much matter. Time was his friend, a never-ending resource throughout his life.

Every so often Maldonado examined his feelings when he was dispatched as an angel of death. He didn't curate any particular feelings for Milagros Alzola, a person who seemed to take a turn through his life as regularly as a comet, a person who he had seen live longer than any other person who was pulled at some point into Fortunato's orbit. He'd actually saved her life once, sighted her through his scope as she'd crossed into Colombia. He didn't understand why he was made to do that, but he served at Ebrahim Fortunato's pleasure. For Maldonado, he experienced neither gratification nor disgust in carrying out orders. He felt an odd kind of impotence standing in his socks which was counterbalanced by the weight of weaponry on his body: a butterfly knife on his hip, a .22 in his boot, and even a length of fishing line if he needed it; all kept him safe. Invincible. Still, the rifle strapped to his back was his true safeguard.

He examined the picture of a boy, clearly Venezuelan, on the desk. The boy's smiling face reminded him of his brother Pedro. Maldonado liked to think of himself, in pursuit of his victims, as a diving hawk. He's never told this to anyone. When he and his younger brother Pedro were growing up in Petare, there had been a hawk that used to sit atop a tall tree and inspect everything. It rarely moved. Once Pedro had wanted to pelt it with rocks to watch it fly off, but Maldonado had stopped him. Once—only once—Maldonado had seen the hawk drop into a dive, and when it swooped back into view it clutched a large rat. Later, when he was in the company of Fortunato and his perriquitos, Maldonado would half-close his eyes and imagine how, as a hawk, he could easily tear apart Fortunato's silly birds as if they were rodents. It was a pleasurable revenge that he mentally visited upon Fortunato again and again, and he didn't care if the brujo could see into his heart and know his feelings.

He replaced the photograph of the boy and instinctively touched the scar through his eyebrow. He'd caught the scar when he and Pedro, aged six or seven, were jumping on their mother's bed when she was out at the store. Her return startled them. Surprised, Maldonado slipped on the edge of the mattress and sliced his brow open on the bedhead. Blood sprouted everywhere, but his mother still belted him. The wound needed a few stitches that he'd never received, and the concussion needed a dark place and a few hours of quiet, which were also denied him.

Fortunato had taught Maldonado a valuable lesson the day that he took Pedro away from him: always be as alert as a hawk, and if you weren't, and were attacked, well that was your own fault. Outmaneuvered by Fortunato in Pedro's death, Maldonado could only see the option of joining the old man. Yielding. Bending a knee. His life was no longer his own.

He picked up the photograph again. It wasn't often that Maldonado thought of his brother. He'd just about forgotten how he looked.

But now Pedro's face came to him today in the resemblance of the boy in the fotografía that was on Milagros's desk.

What a strange place this world was.

The next morning, when Milagros returned to where she had buried the calabash, her breath dissipated. What was once the Clearing was now a cane field, verdant and fertile, the stalks over six feet tall, growing right throughout the Clearing's space, all the way back to where the silk cotton tree stood. Hesitant at first, slightly spooked by the cane's sudden appearance, Milagros held her breath. When she inhaled again a smell of oranges floated through the cane. She looked back toward Bunny's house, fearful that if she stepped among the stalks, that she would be forever trapped. She felt her phone vibrate and read a text from Juanita: *Glad you're safe, Mila. Call me?* Milagros smiled, then slipped the phone into her back pocket. She worked on controlling her breathing, and it was when her breath was most still that she felt herself step into the cane. When she checked her phone, the signal was gone.

An immediate external hum ran among the cane that corresponded to a hum within her. Like a call and response, the hum was gentle, welcoming. On a different register to motorcycle engines. More like waves on the shore. The smell of oranges deepened. Through her shoes, Milagros knew the earth was cool. She was tempted to slip off her flats. Her walk through the cane felt familiar. In some places the cane was so thick that she could barely pass between the stalks. In other places she could walk three people abreast. She ran her hand along the stalks. Smelled the syrup within them, in concert with the oranges, and she snapped off a stalk, fought off the bark, and sucked the cane juice within.

The cane's color changed as she wandered in deeper, more purple than green. Ripening. The cane called to her, beckoning, welcoming.

The pain in her wrist, and her sides, faded the further in she strode. She would recognize her destination when she got there.

And then she was at the center of the cane, and the humming stopped. Wind flowed from all directions. The coolest that she'd ever felt. Milagros caught movement in the corner of her eye—hummingbirds above her head, half a dozen of them, hovering. When she moved forward so did they. They stopped when she stopped. When she suspected that she was precisely at the Clearing's center she knew the voice would appear before it sounded, before it settled in her ears. Layered, again, with other voices, but one audible most of all.

Grecia.

[You've been gone a long time] her mother said. [Now you've come a long way]

"A very long way," Milagros responded. "A very long way."

The thatch of sugarcane startled Maldonado as he moved toward the old estate house. He paused. Knew not to enter. This was clearly something that existed in the realm of Fortunato and his perriquitos. But he knew with certainty that someone was within the cane and knew even more assuredly that this someone was Milagros. His head stuck between two cane stalks felt like a prisoner's head stuck between a cell's bars. The temperature was at least five degrees cooler than outside of the cane's perimeter. He slipped in.

Milagros had shucked her shoes and marveled at the soil beneath her feet. She bunched her toes. It was as cool as she'd anticipated, but there was something else. She felt a rare connection to the earth. Yet something still troubled her.

[This is a difficult decision] the voice said.

"It's you," Milagros said. The hair on her forearms lifted. "Finally."

[This is a decision that, once made, cannot be undone] the voice said.

The wind picked up. Milagros gripped a cane stalk. "Tu eres mi mami," she said.

[You need to say it] the voice said. [You need to say the words so that there is no confusion]

"You are a part of me, and I am a part of you."

[There is no reneging]

"We will be together?"

[We will be one]

Milagros needed to know nothing else. This was her mother. The wind lifted her, turned her, lifted her, turned her, twisted her, enveloped her.

The cane dissipated Maldonado's sense of direction. Incensed him. It took him twenty minutes to struggle back out, and he wanted to spit blood. Two reasons: he prided himself on his sense of direction, and for it to fail him so completely deeply unsettled him. The second reason was that he'd marked his way in, notching lengths of cane with his butterfly knife, but the notches kept vanishing; he could not make his way out or determine where he'd been. Fury boiled within him. This was Fortunato-level sorcery. When the cane finally spat him out he was only about fifteen feet from where he'd started. The fury in his mouth tasted bitter.

He spied a tree at the edge of the sugarcane patch, one both imposing and terrifying, and he knew that he first had to conquer the tree and, in climbing it, and using his rifle's scope, that he would find his target. He knew that the tree was old, and that the tree would resist at first, that if the tree had to choose a side, it would choose Milagros's. What he needed was to tamp down any rage that he'd felt toward the sugarcane field, not to allow that rage to linger or for the embers to reignite. His thoughts congealed. It wasn't just that his intuition had dulled, but, it felt like the cane had replaced it with a deeper perception of the village and the land and the people within him. Like this tree, which probably knew everything that the sugarcane was trying to tell him. The tree was odd, with huge roots aboveground that led to its trunk and then a short trunk that quickly thickened to branches. The climb would be smooth, but with his equipment, a challenge. Other than his rifle, which he'd keep slung over one shoulder, he shucked off the rest of his weapons.

Maldonado climbed the tree and, perched on a thick branch, he swung his rifle's scope through a few cardinal points, a ninety-degree sweep. At first he saw nothing. The cane was an ocean. But then, movement. Tiny birds that floated from a small bald spot in the middle of the cane.

There.

Her.

Milagros.

The wind, gentle at first, grew in intensity and threatened to boost Milagros free from the earth. She grasped a canestalk, felt the ground barely retain her feet. But then the wind grew to a terrible strength. She fought to keep her grip on the cane. It felt like the wind was passing right through her, into her mouth and out the back of her head. The wind didn't unsettle her because her mother was part of it, not just her voice, but her entire being. *Mila*, the voice said. *Mi corazón*. Milagros needed nothing more. She released the cane. Opened her arms. Felt herself rising, disconnecting from the earth. Embracing Grecia.

Maldonado watched the wind part the stalks, but he kept his breathing shallow. The sudden appearance of the cane, the tornado that now swirled at the center of the clearing, the odd look of ecstasy on the girl's face. He sighted her through the scope. He steadied his breathing.

Everything was wrong about what he was about to do, the mechanics of it. He didn't have a spotter, or even a snatch of cloth to help him gauge the rebellious wind. It was not a long shot, but it was a miserable one. And he couldn't see the target clearly. He would probably have to take a second shot, since the spiteful cane would probably botch the first.

He placed his finger on the trigger. Held his breath. For a moment he was again out in the forest picking off smudges of glass bottles. He recalled the moment when he had been training with the viejo, and he had felt Pedro's breath on his ear, and he had known before he pulled the trigger that the shot would be true. Now, the cane, the tree, seemed to portend another breath from his brother. He exhaled. Inhaled. Then he exhaled again and squeezed. He felt breath on his neck and, as the wind tossed him into the air, he knew that it was Pedro's, but it wasn't the breath of devotion, but of betrayal.

He swore as he flew, unsure if he'd hit his target. But he'd been tossed so high that he knew what the landing would bring. He released the rifle, and off toward the direction of the ocean, far beneath him, he saw Pedro as a boy, one hand shielding his eyes, the other held up in greeting.

Author's Note

UPON THE DEATH of Hugo Chavez in 2013 and the ascension of his successor to office, mismanagement of Venezuela's resources led to runaway inflation and poverty. International asset blocking sanctions, particularly on Venezuela's oil, of which it holds the world's richest deposits, had a deleterious effect on the population. The fallout was dire. The cost of groceries and medication skyrocketed.

In the years that followed, Venezuelans fled their homeland, seeking safe harbor in various locations throughout the Americas. Colombia, an immediate neighbor, became a favored destination. So did Trinidad and Tobago, the island nation which lay between five and seven miles across the sea at its closest points. This proximity didn't lessen the journey's treachery. Stories of refugees lost to the ocean surfaced. Those who made it to land faced severe hardships, including the island's lack of a codified refugee policy, the legal status of such refugees, and the refugees' inability to hold certain jobs. These hardships often evolved into tragedies.

The trafficking of Venezuelan women in T&T mushroomed. The number of reported heartbreaking stories exploded. Two cases haunted me. In 2019, four Venezuelan women were rescued from a house painted to look like a police station. The corruption of an institution of justice astonished me. In a 2022 case, 27 women were rescued in what was described as a multi-billion-dollar human trafficking ring. I wanted to provide exposure and light to these tragedies and, knowing the island's history of transatlantic slavery, I decided to additionally explore the historical parallel with this contemporary catastrophe.

While writing from my various characters' points of views proved challenging, Hany's turned out to be particularly so. Her voice was difficult to pin down. She refused to speak the estate owner's language. The expansive history of transatlantic slavery on various West Indian islands pushed me to attempt to represent as many enslaved regional voices as possible. I finally settled on a mélange of West Indian nation languages in the hopes of representing not just one but many Caribbean voices of resistance.

Acknowledgments

THANKS TO MY parents, sisters, and the Haynes and Richardson families. Thanks to the Blues Brothers for a lifetime of kindness, generosity, and guidance. Gratitude to N. Anthony Richardson for his largesse and his kindness. Grand merci to Vera Kutzinski for continued guidance and boundless optimism even in the face of defeat. Many thanks to Tiphanie Yannique, Jericho Brown, Nora Lewis and Tayari Jones. Emory is lucky to have each of you. Thanks to Jenny Offill for getting me hooked on Pocky when I needed it most. Thanks to those who kept me sane in Richmond, Virginia, especially Mimi Carter, Christopher Brooks, Angelo Robinson, and Therese May. Thanks to various Trinbagonians for their kindness, including Elizabeth Nunez and Mr. Minsh. Love and thanks to Father Bob Brownell and the Venerable Edward Wesley, OSF, for wisdom.

I owe a debt of gratitude to Trinidad and Tobago's daily newspapers for excellent reporting on the full scope of the country's migration situation. Vital research for *Ibis* was conducted at the University of Michigan's William L. Clements Library and the University of London's Institute of Commonwealth Studies.

Thank you to Ismita Hussain and Liz Nealon at Great Dog Literary. Thanks to my tireless and intrepid editors, Abby Muller, Zack Knoll, and Ruby Pucillo. Many thanks to the amazing Katie Freeman.

Thank you to Reanna Ursin for the art conversations and all the support through the crazy times and to Kelly Baker Josephs for deadpan humor and always having the right answers.

Many hands helped to lift me before this project was viable. Boundless thanks to Marita Golden for early encouragement and to the writing workshops at the Hurston/Wright Foundation. Many thanks to Charles Rowell and the Callaloo creative writing workshop and especially to Ravi Howard. Foundational thanks to the MFA program at the University of Notre Dame, especially Valerie Sayers, William O'Rourke, and Steve Tomasula. Gratitude to the late Joseph Skerrett and R. D. Skillings for their guidance. Love to K2 for continuous joy.

Salute to friends in the trenches, especially Kevin A. González, John Dethloff, and Chirag Menon, and thanks to friends who helped lift me out of it, including Neron Ferguson. Thanks to Sarah Terry and my colleagues at Oglethorpe University and to my many students over the years.

Much of this work was written and revised due to fellowships awarded at various residencies including the Fine Arts Work Center in Provincetown, the Wisconsin Institute for Creative Writing as a Carl Djerassi fellow, the Vermont Studio Center, Art Omi, the Nicholas Jenkins Barnett Fellowship in fiction at Emory University, the Tin House Summer Workshop, and the Kimmel Harding Nelson Center for the Arts. I am grateful for their support.